The Long-Awaited Prequel
to *The Days of Peleg*

D1282123

The Days of
Laméch

Chris!
God Bless!

JON SABOE

Outskirts Press, Inc.
Denver, Colorado

The Days of Lamech
The Long-Awaited Prequel to The Days of Peleg
All Rights Reserved.
Copyright © 2011 Jon Saboe
v2.0

Cover Photo © 2011 JupiterImages Corporation. All rights reserved - used with permission.

Outskirts Press, Inc.
http://www.outskirtspress.com

ISBN: 978-1-4327-4643-8

Outskirts Press and the "OP" logo are trademarks belonging to Outskirts Press, Inc.

PRINTED IN THE UNITED STATES OF AMERICA

HIGH PRAISE FOR
THE DAYS OF PELEG

"….an adventure comparable to Homer's Odyssey. This fictional-
ized account of early civilization…gives timeless questions new
scope and accessibility…. The author… delve[s] into myster-
ies and events that have puzzled humanity for millennia. Here
he reinvents Sumerian mythology, stitching in themes from the
Torah and adding his own flourishes of philosophy, theology and
geography….A gripping, first-rate epic that challenges current
dogma."
—*Molly Simms, Kirkus Reviews*

"…. Sometime in every man's life, his beliefs and values are
challenged, but Peleg experiences more than a mere awaken-
ing. To say he finds himself is an understatement. He is shaken
to his very core of reality, or reality as he knows it…. *The Days
of Peleg* is an adventure, a voyage into self and a mind-opening
experience…. Well written with excellent research and vivid
descriptions."
—*Shirley Roe, Allbooks Review*

"…. Regardless of how you approach the book, you will leave it realizing that it is a profound and thought-provoking work…. It will haunt you long after you finish reading it…. Saboe is a master storyteller with a forward-moving storyline, descriptive language, smooth segues, detailed kinetics during fights, vivid action scenes and landscapes that will be as clear in your mind as if they were in front of your eyes…. I cannot praise this book strongly enough."
—*Alicia Karen Elkins, Rambles.net*

"Few writers have done much with such early times, but this massive 600-page fiction can delight novel lovers on several levels. The first level to enjoy is pure adventure…. Science is another level. Peleg—and Saboe—know a lot about astronomy, math and music, metallurgy, navigation, and other sciences…. With all these levels there is something for almost everyone. After reading this, you will never again view early history the same old way."
—*Dr. Ruth Beechick, expert on ancient Sumer, author of <u>Genesis: Finding Our Roots</u>*

"blends ancient history and fiction in a way that is enjoyable to follow….well-researched historical events and legends…. will be appreciated by anyone seeking a different perspective on man's early history."
—*Suzanne J. Sprague, Historical Novel Society*

"It is a rare work that can combine truth with a good read. Saboe does just that with this work that is rightly called an epic. With lively imagery, fluid characters, and an engaging story line, *The Days of Peleg* captures the imagination while touching the spirit…. If you have a bent toward *Lord of the Rings*, you will like this book."
—*Roddy Bullock, Author of <u>The Cave Painting</u>*

"…a fantastic book…that describes a plausible history of culture, science, linguistics, geography, and more from this time period…. Saboe has obviously spent countless months researching…ancient history, ancient religions, and the sources of many old myths as he weaves a tale of adventure…. I promise, when you run out of pages to read, you'll wish it were longer."

—*Matt Mitchell, Modern Historicus*

DEDICATION

To that select vanguard of Peleg readers whom I would have
never known had they not reached out in enthusiastic and encouraging response—and who have since become dear friends.

Special love and eternal gratitude to Atom tha Immortal, Rabbi
Akiva, Gary "Zvi" Selikow, and the Grand Negus of the Osmosian
Order.

My heart and mind have been immeasurably enriched and expanded because of you.

ACKNOWLEDGEMENTS

I first wish to thank my amazing and wonderful wife, Valory, for her encouragement, understanding, and patience as she witnessed another four years of unconventional priorities and scheduling while *The Days of Laméch* took form. I am also forever indebted to her for her wisdom, comments, and insights while I read the final manuscript to her.

Secondly, I want to thank my chief editor, Vivian Smith, for her chapter by chapter corrections and her vigilant determination to rescue me from misspellings, split infinitives, misplaced modifiers, continuity errors, and rambling ambiguous sentences.

The penultimate manuscript was also proofed by Phil Norman, Rob Smith, Della Rembert, Leslie Nord, and Bruce Lynn—all of whom made critical catches and invaluable observations—and for whom I am immensely grateful.

I also wish to thank Jerry Breen for his wonderful map found at the opening of the book.

Lastly—and most importantly—I owe an incredible dept of gratitude to the thousands of amazing Peleg fans who insisted that this book be written. It would not have happened without you. I am humbled by your continued support and appreciate each and every one more than you can know.

INTRODUCTION

In the late 1800s, an eccentric genius by the name of Nikola Tesla performed many experiments in the fields of high and low frequency telegraphy, resonance transformation, and electromagnetic power transmission.

In his labs on Knob Hill, near Colorado Springs, he had many successes, the most impressive of which was, in 1899, when he utilized his "magnifying transmitter" to broadcast more than 10,000 watts a distance of twenty-six miles, powering more than two hundred light bulbs and several small engines!

Although various political and commercial reasons prevented many of his breakthroughs from becoming commonplace, the lesson to learn is that there are many directions and paths that technological advancement can take.

In writing a novel of antediluvian times, great consideration was given to assess the potential technologies that may have been feasible to those who lived then. In so doing, many attributes of the early earth—many much different than today—had to be taken into account.

One of the attributes that would have been different from today is the Earth's magnetic field. John Tarduno, a professor of geophysics and chair of the Department of Earth and Environmental Sciences at the University of Rochester has suggested that our magnetosphere at that time was at least three times stronger than it is today.[1] Using his university's "SQUID" (Superconducting Quantum Interference Device), he and his team were able to measure individual crystals known to be free from contamination. He also used this to match paleointensity readings from modern lava flows and compare them with known levels, confirming his technique had a high degree of accuracy.

Dr. Humphreys, a physicist at Sandia National Laboratories in Albuquerque, New Mexico, has developed a revolutionary new model for the formation and development of planetary magnetic fields.[2] He successfully used this model to predict the magnetic strengths and attributes of the outer planets and several moons long before probes arrived and confirmed them.

His research (using his model, in addition to projections of measurable *decreases* in recent field strength history) has suggested that, as recently as six to eight thousand years ago, the Earth's magnetic field was as much as eight to ten times its current intensity.

A second trait of the antediluvian world was a denser atmosphere that contained more than fifty percent more oxygen.[3] Analysis of microscopic air bubbles trapped in fossilized tree resin, along with the crushing of ancient amber released into a vacuum chamber of a quadrupole mass spectrometer, shows that this early air contained upwards of 35% oxygen, as compared to the 21% we enjoy today.

Denser air may have enabled large pterosaurs to remain airborne, and, perhaps, even contributed to their size.[4] In fact, the subsequent reduction in oxygen to its present levels may have assisted in their demise.[5]

On a planet with increased oxygen, life in general would grow much larger, allowing for the possibility of giant lady bugs and dragonflies with two-and-a-half-foot wingspans![6]

An additional side effect of high oxygen content may be found

---

[1] < http://www.unisci.com/stories/20011/0302011.htm >
[2] Humphreys, D. Russell, *The Creation of Cosmic Magnetic Fields*, 1984.
[3] Anderson, Ian, *Dinosaurs Breathed Air Rich in Oxygen*, New Scientist, vol. 116, p. 25.
[4] Ibid.
[5] Discover, February, 1988, p. 12.
[6] Kaiser, Alexander, *Giant Insects Might Reign If Only There Was More Oxygen In The Air*, Science Daily, Oct 2006.

in modern hyperbaric medicine. Patients in high pressure/high oxygen environments heal much faster as wounds repair themselves and often even neuro-rehabilitation occurs among many who undergo such therapy.

This would imply that life in the antediluvian world would be one of rapid healing, increased health, and unexpected longevity.

These two major differences (in addition to numerous others) from the world that we now inhabit bring us to this question:

What is the possibility that technologies or abilities *might* have existed in antediluvian times, but remain forever lost, unable to be replicated, since the environmental requirements upon which they relied no longer exist? Could the numerous ancient tales of extreme longevity, flying crafts, dragons, and pyramid energy sources have a modicum of truth to them?

Finally, two quick notes about the narrative:

Throughout *The Days of Lamech*, cubits are used as the primary unit of measurement. However, in the ancient world, a cubit could be anywhere from eighteen to twenty-seven inches, since it was generally accepted to be the average length of a man's forearm. Interestingly, the further back in time one goes, the longer the cubit becomes. For the purposes of this narrative, the "six-palm" cubit of just over twenty-four inches is used.

Secondly, the map presented in the frontispiece is based, loosely, on generally accepted outlines of Rodinia, the antediluvian landmass. This is in conjunction with the theory of Catastrophic Plate Tectonics, postulated in a paper of the same name by Dr. John Baumgartner. A more detailed coverage of this theory can be found in Appendix C.

I hope you enjoy this prequel to *The Days of Peleg*.

As always, chapter one occurs, chronologically, much later in the book.

Jon Saboe
June, 2011

The Days of Laméch

CONTENTS

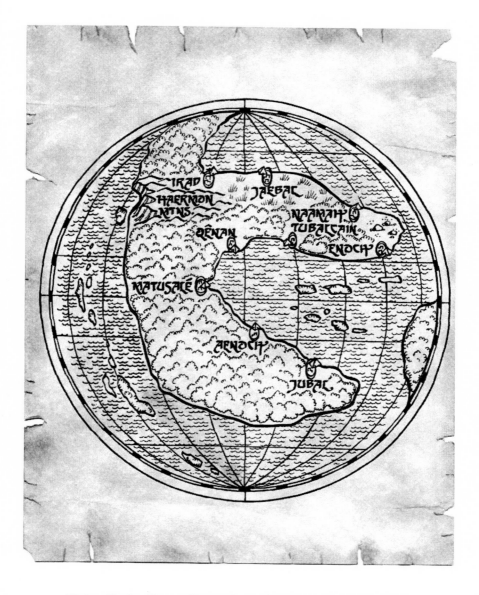

Cities Rebuilt or Founded after the Family Wars
Frontispiece from *The First Two Thousand Years, Volume II*
Amoela the Librarian

PART I
ESCAPE

What has been done will be done again.
There is nothing new under the sun.
It has been already,
in the old time which was before us.

King Solomon

Semjaza's ever-present rage reached a new fervor as he looked out over the expanse of Matusalé City from his Observation Platform.

He hated people!

The city stretched out before him; beautiful buildings made of carved marble, adorned with elaborate hanging gardens and ornate metalwork of silver and brass. The dome of the primary observatory pressed against the darkening western sky, while small lights could be seen from within the central library chambers where late-working attendants busily tidied the memory and meditation rooms for the next day's clientele.

From the east he could feel the energies of the coastal pyramid emanating, and beyond that, the endless ocean which was already dark enough to reflect some of the brighter stars overhead.

He hated people!

All of this should belong to him*! Belong to him and his kindred! Not just Matusalé City, but all of the cities throughout this world. And the world's resources! The minerals, the precious stones, the silver, the gold!*

Gold.

What a pure element! Somehow, it was symbolic of all that should have been theirs. It should have all been theirs*! The entire planet—in fact all of creation rightfully belonged to* them*! For* their *use! For* their *glory!*

He hated people!

It had been the greatest betrayal of all time. Only his kindred knew how to use and appreciate such amazing resources! Only his kindred had the knowledge and wisdom to properly understand the true opportunities that this universe offered. Yet, what should have been theirs was now in the hands of these ignorant, feeble fools who somehow felt they were gods in a world to which they had contributed nothing! Despicable fools!

He hated people!

Semjaza shook as a new wave of fury coursed through his entire being. His kindred would find a way to make these people pay! A way to somehow undo this eternal injustice. And if successful, a way to hurt, damage, or perhaps even overthrow the One who had betrayed them! The One whose promises were never to be trusted again! It was worth everything—even their own destruction—to accomplish this vengeance.

He hated people....

CHAPTER 1
ABDUCTION

*"The irony of what brought about the end of the
Family Wars was the realization that the abhorrent de-
humanization inherent in those wars would be replaced
by a surreptitious scheme to redefine humanity itself."*

—Amoela the Librarian,
The First Two Thousand Years, Vol. II

Gaw-Bolwuen looked down at her pretty green shoes with the platinum clasps, secretly delighted at how well they matched her sash.
Glancing back up at the mirror, she saw her dark emerald eyes (which
also matched her sash!) peer back at her briefly before she lowered the
silk-chiffon veil over them. She adjusted her dark auburn hair to make
sure that it flowed properly over her shoulders, peered down again at
her shoes through the veil, and finally looked away, satisfied.

She had just turned thirteen, and was among a select few who
would soon be attendants to Semyaz officers, nobles, and perhaps
even ambassadors. She and her classmates had been in training for
several years and she was preparing for the upcoming Passage Ceremony which was only minutes away.

THE DAYS OF LAMÉCH

To say she was excited would have been an understatement—she had dreamt of this day for as long as she could remember. Gaw had been brought here to the Haermon Mountains just before her second birthday, and she could remember very little of her life before then. This place had been her home, her family, and (as she had spent her short lifetime discovering) her destiny.

She knew very little of the Semyaz—only that they had been very instrumental in ending the Family Wars of the past century—and now offered peace-keeping, instruction, and stability throughout the world for those cities that desired their help. They had settled here in the Haermon Mountains more than a thousand years ago, and it was from here that their message of hope and tolerance had spread to the cities and brought an end to the senseless devastation that had been destroying untold thousands of lives.

She also knew that the Semyaz had wisdom and understanding far beyond that of the other peoples of the world. She had heard tales of vast research facilities in the mountain caverns beyond her school where their superior knowledge was being applied for the betterment of society and the improvement of humanity.

She had been told that the Haermon Mountains were the tallest in the world, some towering more than a four hundred cubits above sea-level. A few offered sheer cliffs that plunged directly into the adjacent ocean; and in fact, this structure, where she had lived and studied the last eleven years of her life, was a large school and dormitory complex carved from the inland directly into the back of such a cliff.

The passage chamber, which she would soon be entering, had a large window that peered from the face of this cliff out onto the ocean, and she couldn't wait to meet her sisters who would soon be joining her there. They had gazed out of that clear crystal window often, watching the surf crash on the boulders below, often straining to see the face of the cliff as it extended far above. On a few occasions they had seen rare glimpses of the floating forests which roamed the world's oceans—some as large as the biggest islands. It was fascinating to watch the crowns of the tree-tops mimic the gentle waves that traveled beneath them.

The door to her quarters opened and her counselor, Rin-Kendril, entered the room. She was a tall, strong woman with piercing blue eyes that bore down on anyone who misbehaved—or hadn't studied sufficiently. But Gaw had soon learned that those same eyes could soothe and support when needed.

Rin-Kendril smiled, causing her eyes to dance slightly.

"I'm so proud of you, Gaw," she said warmly, looking down at the shimmering white robe that her charge was wearing. The green sash rested across the girl's right shoulder and came to a point near her left thigh where it was fastened with a miniature dragon fashioned from platinum with wings made of gold crystal.

Gaw looked down respectfully as she shuffled slightly to mask her embarrassment. Praise came seldom, but when it did, it was sincere. Eventually she looked up with a question.

"Are my sisters ready?" she asked with more impatience than she had intended. "Will I be joining them soon?"

There was the slightest delay before Rin-Kendril answered.

"Absolutely," she said quickly, making up for the pause. "If you are ready, we can leave now."

Gaw's face broke into a huge smile.

"Oh, I'm ready," she announced, beaming. She made one final adjustment in the mirror, placed her spun-platinum bracelet (from which her colorful agate memory rings dangled) on her forearm, and headed towards Rin-Kendril's outstretched hand.

They exited her room as the thin stone door slid silently shut, and proceeded down the hallway towards the passage chamber.

These were the same dark polished granite hallways she had walked these past eleven years, but somehow they shone a little brighter as she drew near her Passage Ceremony. Reflected light from the glowing *tsohar* panels that ran along the edge of the ceiling caught her shoe buckles and sparkled back onto the walls, creating a constantly shifting mosaic of light-specks which resembled random constellations that accompanied her as she walked.

The corridor turned to the right several paces in front of them, but even before they reached the corner, Gaw could see the illumination

from the *Light of the Creator* emanating from around the bend. They
slowed slightly, and as they turned, they could now see the source
of the light, coming from a large alcove carved into the left side of
the hallway.

The *Light of the Creator* was actually a light sculpture—a mon-
ument to the Creator, in honor of the wisdom and care which he
bestowed upon humanity. The knowledge which the Semyaz utilized came from him, and all hopes of human improvement—and
perhaps someday immortality—depended upon how successfully
the Semyaz applied his imparted wisdom.

They slowed and stopped, bowing slightly before the light. At
first glance it appeared to be nothing more than a brilliantly lit column of swirling white fog which stretched from floor to ceiling,
covering a space about two cubits in diameter. But as they stared
into the luminescent interior, a vague form began to appear from
within.

Iridescent green and purple lines materialized near the top of the
column, forming symmetrical curves which slowly coalesced into
gleaming wings. Soon a large head emerged above the wings which
sparkled and radiated its own light from beautiful shining eyes that
were both inviting and intimidating. As the wings undulated ever so
slightly, a lean, tapering body appeared beneath them until (when
the mirage was complete) a fully formed tail could be seen descending from the torso, coiling slightly before arriving at a point just
above the floor.

Gaw was overwhelmed as always with a sense of both admiration and fear, and she glanced up sideways at her counselor—but
Rin-Kendril was oblivious, her eyes focused, unblinking, into the
light. When Gaw looked back at the column, there was only the
swirling cloud of brightness, and no amount of staring could cause
the apparition to re-emerge.

A few rows of petroglyphs were carved into the wall to the right
of the column of light, and Gaw read them reverently as she always
did.

ESCAPE: ABDUCTION

The Creator of Light
Emerged from on high
Restorer of Man
The Divine to draw nigh.

She looked down at her five memory rings, carefully matching the appropriate colors with the correct item of her catechism.

The first ring was a brilliant, shimmering white circle which symbolized eternal light. Light—which had always existed—was constant and unchanging, and it was *from* Light which the Creator himself had emerged. A pitch-black ring was next, followed by a shining blue-green agate. Together they represented the cosmos formed by the Creator and the beautiful world of water and life which he had placed in it. The fourth ring was a polished rich brown which represented the simple people who had first inhabited the earth, while the fifth ring was a mixture of the first and the fourth. A spiral of white and brown (Light *merging with Humanity*) was woven throughout this final stone. This reminded her (and all those who served the Light) of the time when the Creator had come upon those simple people and remade them in his own image. This fifth memory ring was simply named Transcendence.

Light. Cosmos. Earth. Humanity. Transcendence. These five principles outlined everything that humanity needed to realize its full sense of history, self, and destiny. Meditating on these provided purpose and actualized the deepest needs and desires of a servant—if done with urgency and sincerity.

Rin-Kendril blinked suddenly, shook her head, and looked down at her hand which was still clasping Gaw's. Gaw was surprised to see something that seemed to resemble sorrow in Rin-Kendril's face, but it vanished as their eyes met. Gaw pulled slightly to encourage her counselor to resume their walk, and they continued towards her Passage Ceremony.

Gaw had never seen an actual Semyaz. She *had* met those who served them directly: ambassadors, artisans, inventors, and others who supported the Semyaz and their mission. It was these to whom she would soon be privileged to be an Attendant.

They passed through the archway into the ceremony chamber, and Gaw looked around quickly for any sign of her sisters who would be graduating with her. She saw none, and turned quickly to Rin-Kendril.

"Are they coming?" she asked, concern creeping into her voice.

The look on her counselor's face startled her. It was a strange mixture of pride and regret. Had Gaw been more mature, she would have also discerned a carefully concealed panic.

Rin-Kendril spoke quickly and determinedly, her face bending down to soothe.

"Gaw-Bolwuen, you have been selected for a very special purpose," she said, striving desperately to appeal to Gaw's sense of duty, while at the same time begging forgiveness for having lied to her earlier.

"You and your sisters have all been groomed to attend those who serve the Semyaz. But," she paused to get her emotions under control, "*you* have been selected for a much higher calling." But were her emotions those of elation or trepidation?

"You are not to become an Attendant of those who serve the Semyaz," she said quickly with finality, as if hurrying through a rehearsed statement. She closed her eyes and spoke with forced excitement.

"*You* have been specially chosen to be the consort of an actual Semyaz!"

Her eyes opened and then she said the strangest thing that Gaw had ever heard.

"Always remember that I have loved you."

With that, Rin-Kendril suddenly spun around and exited the chamber, closing the heavy wooden door behind her and leaving Gaw standing alone—stunned and wondering what was going to happen next.

Gaw did not know whether to be excited or alarmed. She was also taken aback by her counselor's declaration of love. Rin-Kendril had never spoken like that before. Gaw moved towards the door and tugged on it, only to find it fastened securely. Then, with no other plan, she moved towards the center of the chamber fighting back tears—and the fear of the unknown—to await whatever was in store for her.

Suddenly a movement in the domed ceiling caught her eye, and she watched as a section began to slide away, revealing a large space behind it. A cloud of dark-green smoke began to unfurl from the opening, descending slowly into the chamber.

Panic gripped Gaw as fears about her counselor's behavior began to clash in her mind. Why had she seemed so confused?

Why had she lied?

The thick smoke uncoiled and began to move directly towards her.

A thunderous explosion at the far end of the chamber forced Gaw to drop to the ground, grasping her ears in pain. A huge crack had suddenly appeared under the crystal window from which smoke and the smell of burning metal emerged. The clearing smoke revealed a metal spike which blossomed into multiple barbs that gripped the wall below the window.

Another huge explosion—as the window buckled outward slowly until it collapsed into shards that (mostly) flew out into the open air and the ocean below. But some of the pieces were pulverized into tiny crystals that hovered for a few seconds in the air before blowing back into the room and cascading down on Gaw, creating dozens of tiny cuts in her skin and clothing.

There was now a gaping hole that extended all the way to the floor where the beautiful crystal window had once been, and Gaw could feel the stiff breeze of the ocean winds blowing into the chamber.

She glanced up and saw the green cloud retreating in the face of the incoming gust of air. Filled with never-before-experienced confusion, she sat motionless on the chamber floor, petrified with indecision.

Suddenly a collection of ropes flew into the chamber through the opening, coalesced into a large net that covered the room and descended down around her. The net began to constrict across the floor, and as she struggled to get out from under it, she found it was covered with a sticky substance that only entangled her further.

Her beautiful gown! And her shoes! She shuddered at her irrational and vain concerns—mental screams which had come unbidden to her mind.

The edge of the net approached her, catching her feet and arms, and rolling her up into a sticky matted ball. The bottom of the net constricted underneath her, enveloping her completely, and then began to drag her slowly toward the edge of the opening—beyond which was the sheer cliff face that descended into the rocky waters far below.

All vain thoughts disappeared as she realized she was being pulled through the opening, and she scratched and clawed with all of her might, trying desperately to cling to anything she could reach through the netting. But there was only polished granite, and even the stickiness of her hands could not slow the relentless pull towards the cliff's edge.

A man's gruff voice shouted from beyond the opening.

"Tell Laméch we only got one!"

"What do you mean?" another voice responded. "We were told this would be an entire class! Where are the others?"

"Don't know," said the first voice. "We only take what we can get."

With that, the net containing Gaw slid over the edge and she screamed as she felt the gut-wrenching rush of free fall. The side of the cliff which she and her sisters had often tried to view from the window was now rushing past her as she descended swiftly towards the rocks below.

Her descent ended abruptly as the rope to which the net was connected grew taut. She looked up and saw two giant winged creatures facing away with what looked like a large box or container fastened between them. The other end of the rope from which she was swinging was attached to this container.

Two heads emerged from the container, and she realized these must have been the source of the voices she had just heard. They were holding the rope and slowly hauling her up towards them. One of them shouted a command—apparently to the two creatures—for they immediately began to fly away from the cliff, lurching at unbelievable speed out over the expanse of the ocean below, spinning and jerking Gaw in every direction as she was slowly reeled up and into the container.

Eventually she was hauled over the edge and rolled unceremoniously into the center of the compartment.

Through her netting, she could see the cliff get smaller and smaller as they flew out over the unknown ocean below. She watched as the only home she had ever known quickly disappeared over the horizon.

As she tore her eyes away, she looked around and saw a third man with a large dimpled jaw standing over her. He said something softly before turning away.

"Even one is still worth it all."

CHAPTER 2
DISCOVERY

"The savaged, broken masses who survived the Family Wars welcomed the civilizing philosophies of the Semyaz as a drowning man welcomes air. It required subsequent generations who had never known the horrors of war to realize that the Semyaz were patiently engineering their own pervasive and furtive agenda."

—Amoela the Librarian,
The First Two Thousand Years, Vol. II

Laméch pressed the edges of his feet into the divisions between the tiles and paused for a final breath as he neared his goal.

He clung to the side of Matusalé City's main pyramid, only a few cubits short of its summit. The pyramid towered more than forty stories above the other structures in the city below, which now appeared to Laméch to resemble an expanse of toy buildings made of clay and ceramic, with a mirror-like model of a shipyard directly below to the east.

The beginnings of sunrise could be seen over the ocean as some of the eastern-most stars began to fade. Behind him, far to the west, he thought he saw a glint of light reflected from a Semyaz observation platform.

He had evaded the night Enforcers and began his ascent shortly before midnight, creeping slowly but steadily up its smooth inclined face using nothing but his bare toes and his specially made gloves and thigh-leggings treated with resin. Early on he had maneuvered to a corner where two of the pyramid's faces met, and now he was in position to continue on to the next phase of his operation.

The pyramid was known simply as the Power House. Deep in its bowels were mechanisms that generated waves of ionized power which leapt from its apex in short jagged bursts of static lighting which glowed—incandescing the surrounding air with all the colors of cascading polar aouroras. Laméch knew very little of how energy was generated within, but had heard there were giant tidal-driven machines which twice daily generated vast power. This was somehow stored and then amplified and released upward, being focused into the tip of the pyramid before escaping into the sky to provide the power needed for the city's nearly twenty thousand inhabitants.

It was the standard power plant and city model designed by the great city planner, Aenoch, and was used by all nine of the world's cities which had populations similar to Matusalé.

Aenoch was famous throughout the world for his city architecture and energy systems, but he had not been heard from in over eighty years. According to some rumors, he had set out alone on a secret venture to infiltrate and examine the technologies of the Semyaz, but any attempts to confirm or deny this had failed. Those who had set out to investigate had also never been heard from again.

To Laméch, this account of Aenoch provided an excitement that his scholarly but uninspiring father never could. He could never understand how someone who knew so much could be so indifferent and apolitical.

Laméch's skin ached as the ionized air continued to charge his body hairs, tugging at them constantly—but not *too* painfully—as he prepared his next step.

Carefully lifting one hand from the surface, he reached over his head and freed the rope that had encircled one shoulder during his ascent and swung it lightly before tossing and uncoiling the free end up and over the pyramid's peak. The rope had a prepared lasso which formed a large circle that glowed with released energy and levitated for a moment in the ionized field before finally lowering down over the tip and coming to rest around the peak of the pyramid.

Laméch tugged to confirm it was secure and then removed his sticky gloves, casting them aside where they tumbled slowly down the face of the pyramid. He then released a catch on his backpack. With a click it unfolded, blossoming into a man-kite constructed mostly of dragon skin with a cast-aluminum skeleton. This would be his first time trying this from such a height—but this flight wasn't just for fun. This was for a special cause. *This* would be a protest that could *not* be ignored!

Laméch smiled as the first glimmers of sunlight began to appear above the seaport at the eastern edge of the Power House. The fishing boats were already on their way out of the port, and soon the city streets, docks, and shipyards would be teaming with people who would have no choice but to witness his demonstration this morning.

Laméch was part of the underground resistance opposed to the Semyaz and their hidden but intrusive control of his city and the lives of everyone in it. The rebellion was simply known as *The Path*, and throughout the city, people would often encounter the twin blue lines marked on buildings and bridges which represented a path or trail. The symbol proclaimed that citizens of Matusalé should be free to forge their own path, and no longer be subject to the philosophies and "proposals" of the Semyaz—no matter how beneficent and wise they *claimed* to be.

This city had been built by the hard work and ingenuity of his family and the families who lived here, but somehow the Semyaz had mastered the art of extracting profit from the city coffers when they had done nothing to contribute to them other than presenting "guidelines" for intra-city relations—and then following up with threats and sanctions when these guidelines were not followed.

ESCAPE: DISCOVERY

Laméch didn't care that the Semyaz seemed to have advanced knowledge in just about every area he could think of. It still didn't give them the right to meddle and act like patronizing tyrants; nor did it give them the right to demand so much gold in exchange for their "wisdom".

After today, everyone would be talking about *The Path*, and they would all see how important it was to overthrow the Semyaz and send their Emissaries packing back to the Haermon Mountains! Laméch's smile turned into a grin.

It was almost time. It would not be good to wait until it was too light. He could see the noble-globe street lamps stretching to the north and south. Modern cities were always designed in an oval shape, stretching from north to south because of the manner in which energy traveled. Noble-globes, which were also used in every home and business, were illuminated by the Power House's energies that radiated along the lines of the world's powerful magnetic field. As a result, a Power House's range extended much further along longitudinal lines, so naturally, Aenoch's cities were designed to take advantage of this.

Laméch's man-kite had two thin brass rods extending outward from each side, and they were now encased in dazzling blue fire as the air around them ionized. The rods narrowed to sharp points where gleaming sparks shot out in random directions. He was ready.

Hanging from his rope, he swung around with his man-kite extending behind him and landed firmly on his feet facing down, overlooking the eastern seaport. He waited for a gust of incoming morning breeze, and when the right moment came, he released the rope and leaped out into open space.

The first few moments of dizzying free-fall brought forth a yell and a laugh from Laméch. Such death-defying activities were the only way to know that one was truly alive! Then the wind filled the wings, shaping them into the proper curvature, and he was flying out, away from the Power House, high above the shipyards from where he would eventually head out over the open sea.

The tips of the brass rods flamed into brilliant blue torches, releasing their energies as Laméch cut through the early morning sky, leaving two brilliant streaks of blue. The mark of *The Path*! His control bar pressed against his chest as he concentrated on keeping his inevitable descent as slow as possible. He reached for a small trigger next to his thumbs which released a small stream of tiny phosphorus fragments from pouches just in front of the rods. They mixed with the early morning humidity, exploding in fiery blue-white light, and Laméch was pleased to see that some dock-workers had already noticed, looking up and pointing—no doubt encouraged by Ruallz and other clandestine Path members mixed in among the local traffic.

This was going to be even better than expected!

It was normal to see colorful light displays emanating from atop the Power House, but no one had ever seen two blue-white jets of fire traveling away from the pyramid, perfectly aligned and leaving a lingering trail.

Soon he could see hundreds of people shouting and pointing up into the sky as he slowly made his way over the shipyard. He couldn't have asked for a better response!

A green flash covered the area for a split second as the sun emerged from the ocean, and now everyone was looking up and shouting. Laméch imagined (or hoped) they were cheering. Nothing like a good stunt to raise awareness. They would all be talking about *The Path* now!

The twin blue arcs traveled over the larger cargo vessels and soon Laméch was flying out over the open sea. Just for fun, he wanted to see how long he could stay aloft. No matter how far out he traveled, he would have no trouble swimming back to the northern shore. Of course, he would have to return far from the city to avoid the Enforcers who would certainly be looking to arrest the scofflaw who had dared to present such dissension so publicly—and so outlandishly. Such flagrant demonstrations could *not* be allowed!

He had another reason for not allowing himself to be caught. Unlike most twenty-one-year-olds, Laméch actively led a double life.

To his collaborators in *The Path*, he was the enthusiastic thrill-seeker who allowed no one to best him, and who could always be counted upon to provide new and exciting ideas in the furtherance of their cause—fighting fearlessly for freedom and the overthrow of the Semyaz.

What none of his Path collaborators knew (with the exception of his close friend, Ruallz) was that Laméch was the wealthy, pampered son of the city's founder, Matusalé, and that he lived in the mansions of the central administration district where attendants waited on him constantly and no need ever went unmet. No need, that is, except the need for excitement.

His Path companions never questioned his inexplicable ability to provide funds for their exploits, and they also kept secret their constant curiosity concerning his place of residence—which he never revealed.

Conversely, no one in his family or anyone that worked or lived in his household suspected his activities on the streets of his father's city. They observed him coming and going at random, eating regularly, and dutifully listening (although paying little attention) to his father's laborious lectures on history, art, science, and other fineries of higher culture.

In certain circles, his father, Matusalé, was famous for his knowledge of history and anthropology, but Laméch had little care for the past. He fancied himself a visionary of the future. However, those who knew Laméch (in either life) recognized that he actually only lived for the present—and for himself.

The present came crashing in on him as he spotted twin dark-blue sails in the distance.

Enforcer ships!

He had descended to an altitude of approximately twenty stories and his brass rods were still discharging their blue-flame lightening. But in the twilight of the rising sun, the silhouette of these dark sails created a panic that he was *not* accustomed to.

There was no way the Enforcers could have moved their ships so quickly in an attempt to arrest him at sea! And they would never be out this far so early in the morning unless…

Someone had talked. The demonstration had been planned with the utmost secrecy, and no one (except Ruallz, who had staged the necessary diversion) had been with him when he evaded the guards. However, distrusting Ruallz was unthinkable.

No time for speculation now. Laméch had to make sure he never reached the waiting vessels.

He wrenched his control bar to the left, twisting his man-kite into an uncomfortable dive aiming for a distant place on the bay's shoreline far to the north. He then reached up and released the twin rods which fell blazing into the sea below, reducing his weight. Laméch smiled as the final violent discharges of lightning leapt towards the sea just before the rods plunged into its depths.

Laméch could hear angry shouts from the Enforcer ships as they saw him twist away, and he grinned as he imagined the frustration on their faces as they watched their ambush begin to fail. A few arrows narrowly missed him before he soon pulled out of range.

Oarsmen slapped at the waters as the ships took pursuit. There was no realistic way they could catch up to him while he flew; but if Laméch did not make it to shore and crashed into the water instead, they could certainly pursue and outpace a swimming fugitive.

Laméch eyed the northern shoreline, trying desperately to stay aloft as long as possible. His turn had cost him much altitude, and he no longer had the lift of the incoming morning breezes. Normally he would have avoided landing in the forests, but the prospect of being arrested (or worse, discovered) mentally propelled him into the thick foliage which was his only means of escape.

He arched his shoulders in a feeble gesture of lift, twisting in desperate attempts to stay aloft, and after several more minutes he realized with relief that he would make the shoreline—which turned out to be a small brush-covered outcropping with a small body of water behind it. The pool was obviously one of the scattered hot springs that appeared sporadically throughout the forests, and he could see the thick steam rising from it into the cool morning air. Such springs were heated by hot underground currents, and contributed additional steam and moisture for the thick foliage and trees of the forests. If he could just make it over this outcropping of brush and rocks, he might be able to land in the warm waters and avoid the dangers and discomfort of a ground landing! Usually the surface waters of a hot spring were not *too* scalding.

As he flew over the thick underbrush, he tucked his legs under him, aiming for the water on the far side. However, the heat and moisture from the hot spring created a bubble of warm air which lifted him up and over—and through the warm fog—to come crashing into the thick deciduous canopy of tree branches on the far shore.

Just before he hit, his body arched in pain from the most powerful static shock he had ever received as he discharged his remaining energies into the tree branches, which clawed at him, shredding his man-kite from his body, and ultimately depositing him in a shaken, bruised heap on the forest floor.

He shook his head to clear it, grinned happily that he had no broken bones, and began the painful lurch through the thick forest—slowed by his bare feet. The Enforcers would soon be there, and they would certainly search this area thoroughly.

He was quickly soaked as mists from the ground and dew from the trees saturated him more and more with each step. He could not see anything beyond the trees, but he kept the growing sunlight that filtered through the trees on his right guiding him in a northerly direction. The Enforcers would assume he was heading west, back to the city.

As he ran, he suddenly heard a loud *crunch*, and the ground gave way beneath his right foot—creating a hole which tripped him, flinging him forward. His knee twisted painfully as he spun violently to avoid breaking it, and he landed hard on his hip and side. The impact of his fall shook the surrounding ground, which also collapsed, sending him into a dark emptiness below. It was as if the sod had suddenly turned into boards of rotten wood which were now, after many decades, collapsing under his weight. In fact, Laméch observed splintering beams as he passed through the sudden opening to fall several cubits before striking his temple on a hard object, twisting his neck, and rendering him immediately unconscious.

THE DAYS OF LAMÉCH

* * *

He awoke with a bright beam of light streaming through the hole he had just created. The trees above were not so thick as to prevent the noon-day sun from shining down through them, and as Laméch groaned and picked himself up, he began to look around this place where his fall had deposited him.

It was damp, musty, and (he soon realized) filled with many crawling creatures. He shook off the ants and spiders which had welcomed him while he slept and tried to use the ambient sunlight to explore.

It was soon apparent that this was a man-made wooden structure that, for some reason, had been buried here in the distant past. As he groped around, he noticed shelves, two small tables (one of which he had struck with his head), a large bench, and a variety of round clay jars scattered around on the floor.

The jars were sure to hold folded parchments and other valuable documents and ledgers, customarily sealed in such containers. They would no doubt be of interest to historians like his father, but Laméch scarcely gave them a glance.

What caught his attention was a clay tablet resting on the far table which had some markings on it, and a stylus placed next to it as if someone had just finished inscribing.

He jumped suddenly at the unbidden thought that someone else might be down here. He dismissed this quickly, only to consider that he might find bodies here instead. A quick look around assured him that he was quite alone, and he bent over the tablet to study it further.

He was startled—and excited—to realize that his own name was inscribed among the larger characters that appeared in its heading. The rest of the writing was smaller and filled the tablet with many rows of script.

Unfortunately, Laméch did not read.

He knew enough to identify his name, but that was all. Reading, inscribing, accounting, and engineering were activities that servants and employees pursued, not wealthy rulers and their sons. Even his father hired Librarians to supply his research, and then archived his observations with the same Librarians.

Laméch took another quick look at the tablet and turned his attention to more important matters. How was he going to get out of here?

He froze at the sound of approaching voices. *Enforcers*! But he relaxed as he overheard one shout, "He's not anywhere around here either! He must have headed back to the city."

Another voice responded, "I'm sure you're right. At this moment he's probably trying to sneak into the city gates while we march around in this soggy forest."

Laméch heard other voices grunt their assent, and gradually they moved off to the west, talking and joking loudly.

The opening was about six cubits above the floor: the height of two grown men. Even if he stood on one of the tables he would never reach the surface; nor would he have anything to grab onto to pull himself out without bringing down more of the rotten ceiling— and himself with it.

He looked around for ideas. The southern wall was the furthest from the sunlight and completely shrouded in darkness. He walked over to it, searching for anything that could help. Everything was equally cold and damp, so he felt around, totally blind.

His hand brushed something metallic, and then jumped as something bit him! He pulled his hand away, quickly realizing that it was a cut rather than a bite. He felt a trickle of blood on his finger, and he reached forward again.

Gradually it dawned on him what this place was. It was an armory! Stored along this dark wall was an array of swords, daggers, spears, and shields. A few random words from his father's boring lectures slipped into his brain, and he realized that this place must have been an outpost during the Family Wars! This would have been a hidden underground base for sentries to be used either for defense or as a warning station. He shuddered at some of the grisly tales of atrocities he had heard about those wars. How could any people descend to such uncivilized savagery?

He checked his thoughts quickly. Fears of returning to that kind of age was what kept people in subservience to the Semyaz. His generation aspired to more elevated thinking, and they could certainly avoid the barbarism of those days without *their* help.

His hand followed the length of one of the spears and he suddenly realized that these were no ordinary spears or even lances. These were full length *pikes*—the kind that were placed at an angle in the sand along beaches or around cities to sink boats or ward off attacking cavalry. A landing craft that ran aground on one of these or the riders who found their mounts impaled on a phalanx of such instruments never fought again.

Laméch suddenly realized how he would escape this place.

Such pikes were seldom used by an individual warrior since they were about seven cubits long—more than twice the length of two grown men! Laméch was not going to climb out. He would pole-vault out!

He brought one of the pikes into the light and firmly placed one end into a dirt hole on the floor—off center from the opening above. He would not be able to run and pick up speed for this vault, but he would be able to stand on a table and kick up against the near wall, swing up and out, and then launch himself out into the world above. He just hoped he would travel far enough to not come crashing down and create another opening into this room.

He pushed the smaller table next to the close wall, climbed on top, and positioned the pike carefully. He bent it back, stepped out against the wall, and with a kick, pulled himself up.

The pike straightened up beautifully, and Laméch bent his legs up to lead him out of the opening. Just as he was about to clear it, his face slammed into the ceiling next to the hole, causing him to lose his grip and return with a yelp to the floor below, landing flat on his back and knocking all the air from his lungs.

Laméch swore as loudly as one could with no breath, glad that no one had witnessed his failure. But he also realized a better—if less dramatic way—to exit this ancient outpost.

He placed the pike directly up through the opening, where it extended about two cubits. He leaned it against the edge of the hole in the direction of the nearest wall and began climbing.

His weight caused the pike to rip through the ceiling, carving a jagged line which rained debris down on his face; but eventually it reached the far wall where it stopped, and Laméch was able to complete his climb and pull himself onto the ground above.

He hauled himself to firmer ground, and then stood and glanced back at the opening. He was surprised to see how well it blended in, and he realized that after a few days of falling leaves it would be invisible.

He climbed partway up a tree where he was able to spot the Power House poking out of the horizon in the southwest. Then he glanced up at the sun, noted the time, and dropped back down to the ground.

After making sure he wasn't too badly damaged, he shook off the debris he had collected during his ordeal, grinned, and headed back to the city.

CHAPTER 3
CURSE

"Until the advent of Aenoch's city design, establishing settlements was always fraught with the difficulties of holding the ever-encroaching growth of the thick forests that blanketed the planet at bay. By laying a marble foundation that rested upon the invariably soft soils and erecting surrounding walls which separated societies from the elements, large cities and centers of commerce were finally able to flourish."

—Amoela the Librarian,
The First Two Thousand Years, Vol. II

Ruallz was rudely awakened by a handful of small rocks landing painfully on his legs. He curled up instinctively to avoid any subsequent barrages—or being struck in more painful regions—and then leapt from his bed as he realized what was happening.

He rushed to the open-air window, his hands held in front of his face in the event more pebbles were forthcoming, and peered out over the trees below.

"*Laméch?*" he hissed, the sound dampened by the foliage below.

In response he heard nothing but two hoots from an owl.

It was Laméch.

Ruallz shook his head and reached for the rope ladder and flung it over the sill.

Ruallz's home was built into the city wall with a bedroom—and window—that faced out into the surrounding forest. It was positioned along the north-western section of the city's oval, and he often enjoyed spectacular sunsets and moonsets from this same window.

At the moment it was completely dark outside, and Ruallz knew that Laméch had waited until the moon had set before waking him. It was much easier to spy an intruder to the city when under the lunar spotlight!

Ruallz heard a rasping as the rope ladder scraped on the sill, and he knew that Laméch had almost completed the three-story climb to his home. Soon Laméch pulled himself over the sill, and collapsed in a heap on the floor of Ruallz's bedroom.

Ruallz was already rushing to remove the impedance cone from the noble-globe as he demanded an account from Laméch.

"Well, what happened? The last I saw of you, you were heading into the trees on the northern shore."

With the cone lifted, the energies from the Power House charged the gases within the lamp, filling the room with a radiant, white light.

Ruallz choked slightly when he saw Laméch's appearance.

Laméch had a large welt under his right eye which was surrounded by cuts and scratches smeared with mud and dried blood. His light brown hair was matted and filled with bits of leaves and small twigs.

As Laméch rose slowly from the floor, Ruallz saw that his tunic and leggings had numerous rips and tears, and he could see bloodstains surrounding many of them. There was a large cloth bandage (ripped from the tunic) wrapped tightly around his right knee, and his feet were covered with gashes and sores which were oozing mud and pus all over his polished granite bedroom floor.

Ruallz chose not to react, and looked back up at Laméch's face.

His friend was grinning from ear to ear, his scratched right arm and fist lifted into the air.

"I did it!" he exclaimed in a loud, hoarse whisper, followed by several more fist-punches into the air.

"I did it!" he said again, reaching forward to give Ruallz a big, self-congratulatory hug.

Ruallz pulled back, scowling with disgust. One did not hug that kind of filth—especially while wearing one's bed-clothes. It didn't matter *what* the occasion was.

He pointed to the doorway.

"Wash," was all he demanded. His expression added, *I'll hear all about it when you return.*

Laméch knew better than to argue. His grin faded slightly as he limped towards the archway and exited the room.

He returned a few minutes later with his face and arms scrubbed clean, and his feet wrapped in small towels he had found. Ruallz could now see Laméch's features clearly in the light. His large chin gleamed, darkened only by the shadow of its one deep dimple. A few of the newly washed scratches oozed slight traces of blood, but they would coagulate quickly. He had also found a blue robe which barely came down to his knees. Laméch was almost a head taller than Ruallz.

A bottle of Jaerad Wine dangled from Laméch's hand, and he sipped it casually, giving no indication that this single flask was worth more than Ruallz earned in three months. This was the finest and most expensive vintage from the vineyards in the grasslands between Jaebal and Irad, and Laméch always made sure that some was stored at his friend's apartment for occasions such as these. Ruallz never touched it.

Ruallz nodded for his friend to share his story, and Laméch launched into his tale excitedly.

"I know you saw me launch off of the Power House over the docks," Laméch began breathlessly, "but what you don't know is that somehow there were *Enforcer* vessels out in the bay waiting for me!"

He paused for drama and the implicit excitement of discovering there might be an informant somewhere. But Ruallz simply shifted his eyebrows to say, *I agree that is a concern, but it's nothing I could know anything about. Please continue.*

Laméch obliged.

"I had to shift violently to the north to avoid them, and all the while I was outrunning the ships, they were constantly firing volleys of arrows at me which I was somehow able to evade. Fortunately, I had enough skill with my man-kite to leave them far behind and arrive inland along the northern shoreline."

Laméch waited for the appropriate admiration from Ruallz and continued.

"I descended into the trees, but I continued north, since I was sure the Enforcers would expect a normal person to return to the city." He grinned to reinforce his brilliance, and Ruallz had to nod with acceptance. Most people didn't voluntarily spend time alone in the forests that surrounded the city—the thick forests that covered almost all of the land on the planet. Only the cities and other specifically designed structures could halt their constant growth.

Ruallz looked back up at Laméch whose eyes were glowing with an astonishment and excitement that he had never seen before.

Laméch continued with a conspiratorial hiss.

"You'll never guess what I discovered out there buried among the trees!" Without waiting for a response he continued, his voice rising. "I found an old war outpost buried in the forest filled with weapons, some canisters, and an old tablet with my name on it!"

This time he paused, took a swig of the expensive wine, and insisted upon a response before continuing.

Ruallz met his eyes calmly and eventually asked, "What did it say?"

Laméch glared at Ruallz to remind him that reading was a menial job for common workers.

"I just recognized my name next to some other large markings," he said eventually. "Beneath that, there were several rows of smaller markings."

Ruallz turned and reached for a clay tablet he kept next to his bed. He procured a stylus from a shelf and handed them to Laméch.

"Do you remember the larger markings?" he asked.

"Of course," Laméch said scowling, placing his bottle on the nightstand. He pulled the tablet and stylus from Ruallz's hands, smoothed the tablet's surface, and began carving the strokes from memory.

Eventually he handed the tablet back to Ruallz who studied it for several moments before looking back up at Laméch.

"This was everything in the tablet heading?" he asked.

Laméch nodded. "Of course it was dark, but that's what I saw. Is it missing something?"

"Not really," Ruallz stated. "It's just a little ambiguous. Quite simply, it says, 'The Curse of Laméch' or literally 'Laméch's Curse'. But I can't tell whether it means a curse that was proclaimed *by* Laméch, or one that was placed *on* Laméch. It's missing a qualifier. However, the word order implies the latter."

He stared directly into Laméch's eyes with a slight smile.

"It looks like someone has placed a curse on you."

Laméch twisted uncomfortably and retrieved his bottle. He was determined not to let something like this upset him.

"That was written years before I was even born," he protested. "That certainly concerns someone else named Laméch." He didn't like the fact that this was bothering him. And he had never heard of anyone else who shared his name.

Ruallz's smile widened.

"Unless, of course, it was inscribed by a seer who somehow both foreknew you, *and* knew you would someday find that outpost."

Laméch dismissed him with a wave. The sudden strange idea troubled him, but there was no way he could allow Ruallz to know this.

"We have to return immediately to this outpost so you can read the rest of the tablet," he demanded suddenly. This involved *him*, and therefore had acquired a much greater urgency.

Ruallz recoiled at the thought of venturing out into the forests.

"I don't think that is necessary," he said. "Why don't you simply ask your father about any stories or historical references that include characters who have the same name as you? He's a student of history."

It was Laméch's turn to recoil.

"No, that's not possible," he said. "My father would be concerned about my sudden interest, and that would only lead to risks of discovering my other activities."

This led to a moment of silence which Ruallz finally broke.

"I suppose we could find a Librarian who might know about such a story—or perhaps about others named Laméch."

Laméch hesitated. He had never visited the Library—or even used the services of a Librarian. He had met them occasionally in his home as they would sometimes actually make house calls for someone as important as his father. But to actually *go* there? It also might take a while to find the correct one.

Ruallz interrupted his thoughts.

"I'm going to get some sleep," he stated with finality. "Tomorrow morning we'll try and make an appointment. I've never been there either."

Laméch nodded; slightly miffed that Ruallz assumed he had never been to the Library—even though his friend was correct.

"Well that's the plan then. I should get some sleep, too." He grinned, placing his now empty bottle on Ruallz's nightstand.

"It's been quite a day."

Ruallz nodded towards the corner where an extra mat was stored. This was not the first time that Laméch had spent the night—or had to hide—at Ruallz's place. The mat was always there for him—and there was even an emergency change of clothing that Laméch would use the following morning.

Soon Laméch was stretched out along the wall, his head resting on a divan cushion. His muscles had been through quite an ordeal today, and he hoped that a few hours sleep would restore them.

As Ruallz lowered the impedance cone over the noble-globe, he couldn't help but make one final comment in the newly darkened room.

"Perhaps we'll discover that this curse applies to *anyone* named Laméch."

The divan cushion flew across the bedroom striking Ruallz squarely in the face.

CHAPTER 4
RESEARCH

"For centuries, the Librarian class provided the repository of all human knowledge and culture. However, as inscribing became more popular and necessary as an economic tool, the proponents of writing claimed that now mankind need never forget anything—to which the Librarian would reply, 'Not so. Rather mankind will remember nothing'."

—Amoela the Librarian,
The First Two Thousand Years, Vol. II

L améch and Ruallz paused before ascending the mica-laced granite staircase that led into the central Library courtyard. The Library itself rose seven stories above them, a shining, milky-white marble structure which gleamed in contrast to the surrounding city structures made mostly of carved granite. Alabaster carvings of abstract geometric designs adorned the different levels, and, at the base of the staircase, a large fountain surrounded by a mosaic of pink gypsum tiles shot water up into the air into arcs of varying sizes. A blazing noonday sunlight reflected off of the surrounding marble street, creating miniature mirages that danced and refocused onto the adjacent law offices, accounting stables, and architectural firms—industries that benefited from their close proximity to the Library.

They had arisen slightly before noon, and after a quick meal of rice, figs, and strawberries, they had started their trip to the center of the city. The observatory could be seen bulging up in the west, while the Power House dominated the south-eastern sky—its powerful energies all but invisible in the daylight.

On the way, Laméch had purchased a pair of polished teak sandals with hemp lacings, dark-green pleated leggings, and an off-white flaxen blouse—discarding the old clothes that had been stored in Ruallz's home. He now wore his new garments proudly, his blouse open at the chest; and although it was warm, he had a dark red cape (the only item from Ruallz's home that he had *not* discarded) flung over his right shoulder.

The cuts and scratches on Laméch's face and body were now almost completely healed, and only the slightest discoloration under his right eye indicated where his face had smashed into the ceiling of the underground bunker.

Ruallz was dressed as a simple city worker—for that is what he was. He always wore plain sandals, canvas leggings, and a simple cotton tunic. He spent his days (when needed) reviewing inventories for shops in the textile sector near his home. Laméch often counted on him to reveal the latest fashions and the dates when they would arrive from Jubal.

Laméch grew uncharacteristically nervous as they strode up the steps. He was certain this was not due to the fear of encountering and utilizing the services of a Librarian for the first time; and he was also quite sure he was not uneasy about the outcome of their search for more information about the curse which was so inexplicably associated with his name. He carefully hid his discomfort, deciding that its source would be revealed eventually.

A small group of Lawgivers—identified by ceremonial daggers of truth affixed to their belts—descended past them, closely followed by a variety of accountants, authors, and other researchers—

also identifiable by their various insignias, jewelry, headgear, and other accoutrements.

They reached the top landing, crossed the open courtyard, and entered the relative cool of the covered receiving area where several clerks (all with the right half of their heads shaved and wearing the short-sleeved white robes of apprentice Librarians) sat on a long raised bench awaiting clientele.

Laméch walked boldly towards the central clerk with Ruallz in his wake, but as he drew near, he suddenly could not think of a thing to say—prompting the clerk to scowl at him quizzically.

"Submissions and archiving are down that corridor," she announced, pointing to a hallway behind her and to the right. She had a bored, slightly contemptuous demeanor as she apparently made a quick judgment based upon Laméch's clothing and attitude.

Ruallz arrived and politely corrected her.

"We're not here to submit an oral or musical composition," he said with a slight bow of his head. "We're interested in research."

Surprise registered in her face as she assessed the strange pair in front of her.

"I'm so glad to hear that," she replied, her voice now somehow filled with respect and helpfulness. "Usually the youth only use our services for preserving their impulsive and undeveloped expressions. It is so annoying when our halls are overflowing with the knowledge and creations of the greatest minds of the centuries who…"

She suddenly ceased her rant—dismissing it with a wave—and focused on the two young men before her.

"Literature or music?" she asked.

"Literature," Laméch replied.

"Historical or fiction?"

Laméch paused, unsure of how to respond, until Ruallz answered.

"We're not sure," he said. "We're looking for a reference that may be historical or mythical, but it has to do with a possible decree or curse pertaining to a specific name or character that may have…"

The clerk raised her hand to stop Ruallz and pointed behind herself.

"Topical research is one flight up on the stairs behind me," she offered. "There will be other clerks there to refine your search."

She smiled warmly with a slight bow, somehow honoring and dismissing them simultaneously.

Laméch and Ruallz nodded their thanks and headed for the indicated staircase. Upon reaching the top they found a single clerk seated behind a desk to the right of the landing with an empty chair that apparently belonged to a second clerk who was nowhere to be seen.

The clerk raised an eyebrow to ask, *How may I assist you?*

Again Ruallz took the lead.

"We're looking for a reference to either Laméch's Curse or The Curse of Laméch. It may be historical, pertaining to the Family Wars, or perhaps a prose account—maybe even fiction."

The clerk closed his eyes slowly, then re-opened them.

"Music?"

Ruallz shook his head.

"I doubt this was anything musical or poetic." He looked at Laméch.

Laméch pictured the tablet in his head and could see nothing that might indicate verse or musical structure. He shook his head as well.

The clerk closed his eyes again, and upon reopening them, stood and gestured for them to follow. Without looking back, the clerk walked swiftly and smoothly as Laméch and Ruallz walked obediently behind.

They spotted the second clerk emerging from a meditation chamber, and the first one waved for her attention.

"She is more advanced in cataloging and indexing than I," the first clerk stated casually, "and will be able to point you to the correct Librarian."

He turned to her and in a softer voice quickly said, "Laméch… Curse…", then turned back to them and stated, as if explaining himself, "*I* specialize in music." He then headed back down the hallway in the direction they had come.

The second clerk scowled at her colleague with disgust (for no apparent reason) and then turned her attention to the two young men. After a brief nod, she closed her eyes, and after reopening them a few moments later, she (just as the previous clerk had done) indicated they should follow her.

She headed to a staircase at the far end of the corridor where she led them up two flights of stairs and along a long narrow hallway before stopping in front of a small archway that covered the short anteroom leading to a meditation chamber.

She pointed through the archway and said, "You may wait here." She then turned and left the two friends staring at each other.

After a few moments of silence, Laméch said, "I guess there must be a Librarian in there," pointing towards the door of the chamber.

"I wonder how we will be announced," said Ruallz.

"Should we knock?" Laméch asked tentatively.

Ruallz shook his head quickly.

"I don't think that would be a good idea. We should just wait like the clerk requested."

They moved slightly into the archway and found a small granite bench where they sat, eventually becoming lost in their own thoughts.

Librarians prided themselves on becoming devoid of all personal preferences and biases while performing their duties. Their training began early in life when it was determined that their natural aptitudes for memory and recall were significantly superior to the average child. All people had total recall for basic things like conversations, simple anecdotes, and instructions. However, when someone wanted to author a book, record a legal contract, submit a musical composition, or register a patent, a much more highly trained mind was required.

People brought their submissions to the Library where the assigned Librarian would carefully memorize the book or contract, and then archive and index it with the appropriate colleague. Librarians had specialized duties based upon their individual abilities. Some recorded large volumes of information, while others cataloged, others indexed, and others duplicated submissions from one Librarian to another.

Some with extraordinary skills in audiographic or pictographic memory were assigned to record musical performances, artwork, and patents. And certain Librarians, called Controllers, recorded all recent submissions (of any category) and traveled to other cities where the new information was replicated to be archived in their libraries.

Since the Librarian was often the final arbiter in a contract dispute or intellectual property case (as only the Librarians involved knew the exact wording of the document in question), they had to be above reproach or any semblance of partiality, impropriety, or bias. Also, since they collectively shared the combined knowledge of competing businesses and interests, clients must be absolutely certain that Librarians would never violate their confidence or use their knowledge for unauthorized or personal gain.

To that end, Librarians were prohibited from investing, making external business deals with clients, or participating in any endeavor that might infringe or damage the interests of their clients—hence, their training to suppress personal preferences, ambitions, or partiality. They must always be counted upon to be the impartial repositories of human knowledge and creativity. Trust in the Librarians was absolute.

And then there were those Librarians who simply stored the expressions of the endless supply of would-be authors, composers, and poets who felt the need to archive their masterpieces for the edification and posterity of all humanity. But since this service required a modest fee—and since there was no end of people who felt such needs for self-expression—a large percentage of the library's financial revenue came from such submissions.

The grinding scrape of a large marble panel sliding open brought the two men back from their thoughts. Light from the chamber grew, inviting the men inside where the silhouette of the Librarian could be seen against the open window through which the sun was shining brightly.

Laméch and Ruallz entered the room cautiously as their eyes began to re-adjust to the outside light they had left only minutes earlier. Their Librarian was standing with his or her arms folded in front. In recognition of their impartiality, Librarians were fully shaved and wore long white robes with full sleeves—resulting in an austere, androgynous look designed to reassure the client that they would receive the most objective, impartial service possible.

As they approached the Librarian, their eyes focused more accurately, and Laméch was finally able to discern that their Librarian was indeed female.

Ruallz began to speak, but the Librarian spoke first.

"There are more than two-thousand references to 'curse', but none with references for both the name 'Laméch' and 'curse'," she began.

Laméch looked sharply at Ruallz, wondering how the Librarian could have possibly known the topics of their request. Ruallz looked around the room quickly for signs of a secret door or signaling device.

"However," the Librarian continued, "there are only three source references to the name Laméch. One is included in one of the many origin stories categorized under mythology, while the second is a poetic reference from our historical indexing. The third is a simple birth registry of the child Laméch, son of Matusalé, this city's founder. From which of these would you require more information?"

She paused, waiting for a response.

Laméch looked at Ruallz who shrugged and said, "I don't think we need anything from a fictional source, and it's obvious what—or who—the third reference is."

Laméch nodded and addressed the Librarian.

"We'd like to hear the poetic reference," he said, a little too loudly.

The Librarian nodded.

"The reference is a quote attributed to an unknown Laméch."

With that, she closed her eyes and began to recite.

> *Laméch said to his wives,*
> *"Adah and Zillah, listen to me.*
> *Wives of Laméch, hear my words.*
> *I have killed a man for wounding me,*
> *a young man for injuring me.*
> *If Cain is avenged seven times,*
> *then Laméch seventy-seven times."*

With that, she re-opened her eyes.

Laméch looked up in astonishment. "Is that all?" He spun around to Ruallz.

"Is that all?" he asked again.

But Ruallz was speaking to the Librarian.

"If this Laméch is making a personal statement justifying his self-defense, then I suppose this could be construed as a 'curse' on anyone who would attack Laméch in vengeance or retribution, correct?"

"It is not my place to provide or offer interpretation or unspecified insight into the reference," she intoned, obviously having said this many times before.

"Never mind," Laméch said to Ruallz disgustedly. "This was a waste of time. And what ridiculous names for wives…"

Ruallz was taken aback by the rudeness demonstrated in front of the Librarian, but she did not seem to notice.

"The Librarian is simply doing her job," he said quickly.

He turned back towards the Librarian.

"My apologies, Librarian," he began. "Perhaps the mythological reference…"

"Never mind," said Laméch for the second time, pulling at Ruallz's arm. "I'm sure this is a dead end anyway."

He looked back towards the Librarian.

"Besides," he said, "who is this Cain anyway?"

"I'm sorry," said the Librarian, again sounding as if she repeated this sentence many times each day. "If you wish to begin another topological search, you may contact one of the clerks."

She lowered her arms while continuing to speak.

"Am I correct in assuming that you have completed this session?"

Laméch gave a grunt as Ruallz nodded.

"Then you may take your leave. Thank you for using the Library."

With that she turned and faced the window as her arms returned to their folded position.

Ruallz looked at Laméch with a shake of his head, and the two slowly backed out of the chamber. They made their way to the main corridor, down the stairs, and eventually out past the fountain into the open streets.

After a few minutes of wordless walking, Ruallz finally broke the silence.

"Why were you so curt with the Librarian?" he asked, wondering why Laméch wasn't already talking.

"After she gave her recitation," he began slowly, "I suddenly realized that there was only one place to find our answer."

He paused for dramatic effect until Ruallz glared at him to continue.

"Her reference was much shorter than the inscriptions on that tablet, so obviously," he paused again, "the only solution is to go back into the forest and find that underground room and read it for ourselves!"

Ruallz choked with a shake of his head.

"I don't think there is any reason to do something that crazy," he said. "I know you've got your mind made up, but there is really no reason for *us* to go."

"Well, you know me," Laméch grinned, "I'll try anything twice!"

He grabbed Ruallz's arm.

"You *have* to come with me," he said with sudden urgency. "There may be other writings there, or artifacts that would interest you. Besides, we may need to carry some things back."

He studied Ruallz's wavering countenance.

"We may find something of great archeological importance!" Laméch concluded.

Ruallz broke out laughing.

"Now I know you're desperate," he said. "When was the last time you cared about anything historical?"

Laméch knew he had won.

"If we leave right now, we will be back before the gates close," he said quickly. "We can head out from the ports and follow the coastline. I know exactly how to find it."

Ruallz shook his head in defeat.

"You must buy us some food before we leave," he said. "I expect to eat well for all of the troubles you put me through."

Laméch grinned.

"Of course! Only the best for my friend, Ruallz." He took off running, waving to Ruallz to follow.

"I know just the place!"

CHAPTER 5
AMBUSH

"Following the advent of Aenoch's walled cities, humanity became less and less concerned with the vast forests and jungles that surrounded them. Commerce was conducted by sea and the untamed and forgotten wilds were thought to be uninhabited—save for occasional malcontents and recluses."

—Amoela the Librarian,
The First Two Thousand Years, Vol. II

I t was becoming increasingly apparent that they would *not* make it back to the city before the gates closed.

Laméch had ordered a fine meal of spicy fish with leeks and wine for both of them from one of the kitchens at his father's home. He had insisted on returning there to get a fresh set of clothing to wear on their trip. The house attendants dutifully looked the other way as they were used to Laméch bringing strange people into the estate.

Finally, they had headed down past the ports and started the long journey through the coastal marshes and foliage of the northern shore. After three hours, Laméch had looked up at the sun, compared it to the looming silhouette of the Power House, and announced that it was time to march inland.

Ruallz did not enjoy the thought of trekking through the forest. In addition to the dangerous (and sometimes large) creatures that inhabited the woods, there were the rumors of strange people who lived in the wild: crazy savage people who waited for intruders to enslave or kill slowly for their unspeakable ceremonies. Of course, no one actually lived in the jungles that surrounded the cities. Ruallz was *quite* certain that these were simply stories designed to scare children.

Now, two hours into the towering foliage, Laméch was scrambling up a tree (as he had done numerous times before). After comparing the orientation of the sun and Power House (as he had done numerous times before), he dropped down to the ground and announced (as he had done numerous times before), "We're almost there!"

Ruallz groaned with fatigue—and a slightly growing fear. It would be dark soon and he did not look forward to hiking back to the city by moonlight and camping out in front of the city gates—although it certainly had happened on prior occasions due to his involvements with Laméch.

But Laméch was grinning and beckoning him on, so Ruallz obediently trudged forward, barely dodging a small branch that Laméch had thoughtlessly allowed to snap back on him.

Laméch suddenly stopped and inspected the ground before them. He walked carefully in a small sideways pattern until he spotted what he was looking for.

"There it is!" he exclaimed, pointing to a sharp stick protruding out of the ground. "This is where I climbed out!"

He motioned for Ruallz to come closer, and as he did, he could see a dark trench leading away from the stick that ended in a small black hole.

"I escaped from the room below by placing this large spear up into the hole and vaulting out. I ripped this line in the ground," Laméch concluded with a grin, pointing to the trench.

He bent over and grasped the end of the pike.

"All we have to do is climb back down." He looked up and grinned at Ruallz. "Come on, I'll show you the tablet!"

He twisted the pike in a circular motion, ripping out the ground from around it to make the hole bigger. Finally he got to his knees, straddled the pole, and began his descent. As his head disappeared below the ground, he waved and shouted "Come on!" one more time.

Ruallz looked around, wanting to do nothing but head back to the city as quickly as possible. But he was intrigued at whatever Laméch had discovered here—and he certainly wasn't going back home on his own—so he crouched down with a groan and slowly clambered onto the protruding pike.

He descended feet-first slowly into the darkness but was soon forced to abandon his balance by flipping over and hanging from the pole—lowering himself hand over hand until his feet finally touched the ground.

Before Ruallz's eyes adjusted to the dim light, Laméch was already talking.

"Here is the tablet I told you about," he said as he hefted the flat stone to Ruallz. Layers of dust fell from its side, clouding Ruallz's vision.

As it cleared, Ruallz began to silently scan the document, until Laméch's impatience was forced to interrupt.

"Well, what does it say?"

Ruallz glanced up excitedly.

"This *does* open with the reference the Librarian quoted," he said with a smile. "But it continues with some sort of basic genealogy."

He looked up with a shrug.

"I would doubt that this is of any real significance."

At Laméch's scowl, Ruallz continued.

"However, this room may be quite a find," he said. "You indicated it was some kind of weapons cache, correct?"

Laméch brightened.

"Over here," he pointed, dragging Ruallz towards the far wall, "are all forms of weapons: swords, spears, axes…"

They were suddenly interrupted by loud rustlings overhead that soon developed into the sounds of running feet stamping through the forest above them. Loud shouts accompanied the noise, and the pounding feet began to shake the ceiling violently. With a prolonged *crack*, they watched as the roof imploded, crashing to the floor where they had been standing moments before.

Naked bodies began dropping among the wreckage, but these people did not appear dazed from their fall. Instead, they appeared ready for battle, armed with wooden clubs and growling as they brushed themselves off and began looking around.

"Forest people!" Ruallz choked, as he spun around to Laméch.

Laméch was already grabbing blindly for whatever random weapon he could find, but soon the new inhabitants of this room saw the two men, and began to press towards them.

Neither man knew how to properly use any of the instruments, but they desperately grabbed handfuls of whatever they could and *threw* them at the invaders. Soon axes, bows, and spears were tumbling through the air, but they were easily dodged by the oncoming attackers.

As the two men stepped backwards, pressing against the wall, Laméch's right foot suddenly sank through a small hole in the flooring twisting his ankle, and the jagged edges cut a large gash into the side of his shin as he jerked it back out. He felt a sudden draft of hot damp air on his right cheek, and noticed that a small panel had slid aside, offering an escape! Some mechanism in that hole had opened it. He reached out and grasped the edge of a panel that was just beginning to re-close, but he could not keep it open.

"Ruallz!" he shouted, just as his friend was being dragged to the ground by two forest people. Laméch rushed to him, wildly swinging a bow in front of him. He kicked the two attackers in their faces, forcing them to let go and grabbed Ruallz's arm, dragging him in the direction of the panel.

He swung Ruallz around by the waist, striking the nearest attackers with his friend's flying feet, and pulled him back to where the panel was. He found the hole again and stomped into it, ignoring the excruciating pain in his ankle.

Again, there was the draft of hot air, and he pressed through the narrow opening, dragging Ruallz behind him. He tossed Ruallz to the other side, and reached for the panel which was actually a very thick mahogany board. He grasped it with both hands, and forced it back along its track until he heard it click back into place.

From the forest people's perspective, the two men had simply disappeared in a confusing flurry of feet and weapons, and they began to attack the wall with their clubs and newly found arsenal.

Laméch collided with the dazed Ruallz who was getting back on his feet. They could feel the pounding behind them, and realized they could not stand fully upright, since they seemed to be in a small wet cave.

They were standing in warm mud as wet tendrils of something dripped onto their heads. The air was thick with water vapors and other mineral smells, and was almost hot enough to feel like steam.

"Well, that was lucky," Laméch grinned in the dark as they caught their breath.

"You'd better not be grinning," snapped Ruallz angrily.

"Well, you know my formula for fun," Laméch retorted back.

"Yes, I know," Ruallz grunted. "Danger plus survival."

They moved cautiously for a few steps away from the wall, where the clamor was still continuing.

Eventually Ruallz broke the silence.

"That opening must be there for a purpose," he observed as he checked himself for any damage. "I'm guessing this little cave must go somewhere if we can figure out how to follow it."

The pounding from within the room grew louder.

"Well let's see where this goes," said Laméch cheerfully.

Ruallz glared at Laméch in the dark and they began to feel around their new space.

Soon they realized they were surrounded by a small muddy enclosure which quickly shrunk to a small muddy crawlspace—apparently the only way out.

They crouched, with Laméch leading the way, and began their crawl.

It was a hot, muddy, groping experience, and they had no way of knowing what direction they were traveling, what the final destination would be, or what the slimy things that kept falling on their heads and sliding off their backs were.

They traveled like this for several minutes when suddenly the tiny crawlspace angled down sharply. They were forced to move slowly to maintain their traction, and eventually had to switch to crawling backwards, just in case the angle of their descent suddenly increased. They did not want to plummet down into the black unknown face first.

Eventually their crawlspace leveled out and they heard the sound of running water. In the resulting echoes, they realized they were no longer in a crawlspace, but in a large underground cavern. They stood up, stretching, wondering how long they had been progressing needlessly on hands and knees.

The noise of the forest people, which had been quieting to almost nothing as they crawled, suddenly grew louder again, and they realized their attackers had discovered the door mechanism and would soon be upon them.

Following the sound of water, they came upon an underground stream which was flowing quickly to their "right"—whichever direction that might be.

"If our objective is to get away from them as quickly as possible," Laméch began, "then I say we take that stream in whatever direction it is going and get as much distance between them and us as possible."

Ruallz grunted in angry agreement.

"You promised we would be back at the city before nightfall," was all he could muster.

They could feel the heat from the stream before they reached it. Carefully they both stepped into the almost scalding flow and slowly began to allow the current to carry them along. Fortunately, their feet could maintain contact with the bottom, and soon they were bobbing along in the dark, trying to avoid the sharp rocks that lined the stream's edge.

The stream began to narrow, causing the current to grow stronger. Suddenly Laméch's head struck an overhanging rock, and as he reached up with his hand, he realized the roof of the cave was just above their heads.

"Watch out!" he called out to Ruallz. "The roof is closing in!"

Both men raised their hands and felt as the cave's ceiling grew closer and closer as the space above them—and its precious air—grew smaller and smaller.

The current tore at their feet, causing them to lose their footing, and soon they could no longer control their passage. As their hands felt the roof of the cave continue to close in on them, they were soon forced underwater. They tried to keep their hands above them to feel for openings, but soon the rare pockets of air were gone.

Totally disoriented, they tumbled along the small, underground river, running into outcroppings as their skin was slowly scorched by the hot muddy flow. Totally helpless, it was now only a matter of minutes before they drowned in this tube that no doubt fed the numerous hot springs like the one that Laméch had seen on his flight the day before.

A sharp strike on Laméch's cheek caused him to open his mouth. A large volume of hot sludge poured in, and in his desperation to avoid inhaling it, he choked and swallowed the grainy, muddy water.

His head felt as if it were going to burst, and the pounding of his heart grew louder and louder as it echoed from the surrounding hot waters into his skull.

As they coursed through the underground channel, it suddenly occurred to Laméch that during all his years of relying on his formula for fun, he had never seriously considered the possibility that the "survival" portion of his adage might be in question. A strange, unknown fear began to claw through his chest as he desperately imagined impossible ways to reverse his course, or to somehow undo the chain of events that had brought him to this point. Each panicked thought began with *If only…* as moments from his life appeared unbidden into his mind.

Suddenly he felt the surrounding temperature cool, and a quick glance through his burning eyes revealed a dim brown light filtering through the muddy water. The light from the setting evening sun was filtering down into the muddy hot spring, which he had just entered! As he stretched out his arms and legs in preparation for the trip to the surface, he felt something wrap tightly around his right ankle. He tried to shake it off as he headed upward for some desperately needed air, but whatever was attached would not let go.

He broke the surface with a loud gasp and began to pull himself to the edge of the pool. As he swam, he realized that it was Ruallz's hands which were clasped around his ankle in a death grip. With his one usable leg, he reached the shore, towing his friend in with him.

He crawled up onto the bank, and then reached back to haul Ruallz out. As he rolled his friend over, Laméch realized that he was not breathing. He turned Ruallz on his side, and gave him a quick punch in the stomach which ejected a large quantity of the muddy sludge. He then opened Ruallz's mouth, cleaned out more mud, and then waited with no idea what to do next.

Ruallz just lay there as Laméch wondered how to get someone to start breathing again. He finally decided that if Ruallz wouldn't take a breath on his own, that he would have to force the issue.

Glad that no one was around, Laméch pinched Ruallz's nose and blew a lungful of air into his friend's mouth, watching his ribcage rise. His friend exhaled with a gurgle as Laméch applied pressure, and then Laméch repeated the procedure. He could feel Ruallz's heart pounding swiftly, so he knew his friend was alive. He could only hope that this artificial breathing would eventually trick the body into doing it on its own. He continued the process several times, losing count.

Finally, Ruallz coughed violently, twisted on the ground, and rolled over, vomiting up more of the warm sludge.

Eventually he relaxed and turned around to face Laméch, who was grinning wildly.

"I hate you," was all Ruallz said, and then closed his eyes again.

"I just saved your life," Laméch protested.

"Yes," Ruallz admitted with a grunt, "after you tried to kill me." The eyebrows above his closed eyelids added, *and that doesn't count.*

He reopened his eyes to glare at Laméch who was still smiling.

"I suppose this qualifies as the most fun you've ever had," Ruallz said with a strange combination of disgust and disbelief.

Laméch's grin faded briefly.

"Well, I'm just glad we're alive," he said, and then, as his grin returned, added, "You *do* have to admit that was rather exciting, though, don't you?"

Ruallz gave him a final glare and rolled over away from him.

"Just figure out how we're going to get home," he demanded.

Laméch finally relaxed and looked around while his friend rested. The sun was about to retire, and he could see the warm vapors as the evening breeze mixed with the heat from the water's surface. The Power House was still visible in the distance against the setting sun, and he was sure they could follow the coastline back home.

The pool was actually fed from a small river that flowed from someplace inland, and he could see a wide outlet which most certainly continued on into the open sea. The underground flow they had just exited apparently kept the pool warm, but the river that flowed through it kept the pool fresh and clear.

Thoughts of the forest people suddenly entered his mind, and he twisted around to see if there was any sign of them.

He was startled to see a lone figure, standing slightly above them, watching silently. The man was draped in a gray cloak or robe with a dark hood covering his head. Laméch shook off his shock and waved at the person. The person did not wave back.

Laméch turned back to Ruallz.

"Ruallz!" he hissed. "There's someone here. Get up!"

Ruallz sat up on his elbow and turned to look where Laméch was pointing.

There was a soft *whoosh* in the air, and a tiny dart with small red and yellow feathers suddenly appeared in Ruallz's throat.

As his friend shuddered from the impact, Laméch turned quickly back to the figure. There was a short rod in the person's hands with one end placed against his lips.

Another *whoosh*—and Laméch jerked as he felt the impact of a similar dart in his own neck.

His eyes began to blur as the figure started to walk towards them, but nowhere in his imagination could he determine who this person might be or what he might want.

He reached out for Ruallz, but the drug had already rendered his friend unconscious for the second time that day.

He felt his consciousness going, and as it faded, a strange thought entered his mind—one that he had never considered before:

Perhaps there are *things in this world I don't understand.*

CHAPTER 6
DESTINATION?

*"Although the Semyaz believed in their right to con-
trol the world—and its ultimate outcome—they failed,
initially, because they simply did not appreciate the
vastness of the planet. Their focus on controlling people
politically eventually had to be replaced. Their new focus became the control of their minds."*

—Amoela the Librarian,
The First Two Thousand Years, Vol. II

Laméch gradually awoke, flat on his back, to a strange gentle motion accompanied by a cool breeze. As he opened his eyes, he was greeted by a thousand painful stars shining directly into his face from overhead. He closed them quickly and turned his head to the side.

Cautiously, he re-opened his eyes and began to assess his situation. His wrists were tied, but after a simple tug from his teeth, he easily removed the bonds. He raised himself on his right elbow, rolled slightly on his side, and began to look around.

He seemed to be on a large, flat skiff that was moving quickly, but silently, across the open sea. It was about eight cubits wide, but Laméch could not tell how long it was. Above was a clear, moonless sky lit with brilliant stars.

He turned to his left and saw Ruallz sleeping beside him, apparently waiting for the drug from the dart to wear off. Laméch rubbed his own neck in remembrance and found nothing but a tiny bump where he had been struck.

He rose slowly to his knees, moved to the right side of the craft, and looked along the horizon.

He could see nothing in any direction that resembled land, and it was actually quite difficult to determine where the sea ended and the sky began, since the smooth waters created a mirror image of the constellations above.

He could now see that the skiff was about twenty cubits long. It seemed to be totally empty, except for a strange ceramic-looking cone that protruded up out of the center, ending in a rounded point about two cubits above the deck. He looked down over the side and saw, just below the surface, a narrow flat panel that glowed through the water in a ghostly sliver of refracted starlight. It reminded him of a wing—somewhat like the wings on his man-kite—but more solid. He noticed another one closer to the front, and he assumed there was an identical pair of "wings" on the left side.

He looked behind and was surprised to see a complete absence of any wake. There were no waves to indicate any movement. Looking back down at the side, he noticed the slightest waves from the wings; but other than the swift movement of water beneath them— and the breeze on his face—there was nothing to indicate their movement across the sea.

Regardless of these strange observations, it was still a simple flat-bottomed skiff swiftly carrying him and the sleeping Ruallz to someplace unknown with no apparent means of propulsion. A skiff with wings.

He looked back up at the stars—and was astonished at what he saw.

His skies had always been filled with the luminous energies of the Power House, which washed out much of their radiance. But standing beneath them, removed from any artificial light, he was amazed at how numerous they were, and at how they seemed almost crystalline in their clarity. He had also never noticed their vast variety of colors before and he almost felt he could reach out with his hand and touch them.

He shook his head to focus on more practical matters. He had heard there were people who knew star names, and what certain constellations were called. Supposedly these people could actually use them to navigate and help when they were lost.

Naturally, Laméch knew none of this. That was the kind of studies his father pursued. Laméch vaguely recalled that there was a constellation called "The Virgin" and perhaps another called "The Goat". He scanned the sky uselessly to try and spot something that resembled one of these, but he quickly gave up since he had no idea what a stellar virgin should look like anyway.

He finally rose to his feet and began walking cautiously forward towards the ceramic cone. He touched it tentatively as he passed it, half expecting to feel the pulse of some kind of energy or mechanism, but there was nothing.

He neared the front of the skiff and watched as the skiff slid silently under the expanse, and considered, for one desperate moment, diving overboard. It was useless, of course. He had no idea where he was, what direction he was going, or how far they were from any land.

"I'm glad you're awake."

The pleasant female voice startled him like nothing ever had. He jumped—pulling a back muscle—and spun to identify the speaker.

Seated in front of the ceramic cone was the robed figure from the hot spring. *She* was still hooded, creating a black opening where her face should be.

"I must apologize for drugging and binding you," she continued. "It was necessary until we reached a point at which you would not try to escape."

Her head lifted just enough to allow some starlight on her mouth, which broke into a careful smile.

"You *won't* try to escape," she said in a strange combination of question and command.

"Where are you taking us?" Laméch demanded as he approached the woman, discovering a target for his long delayed rage. "I order you to return us immediately!"

The woman laughed slightly.

"That is quite impossible. I have no control of this vessel." Her head tipped down, obscuring her mouth again. "I am sorry, but you are quite helpless at this moment. Any attempt to harm or coerce me will accomplish nothing, as you will arrive at your destination regardless of any action you may take."

The head lifted again and Laméch saw the same careful smile.

"Unless, of course, you choose to throw yourself overboard."

Laméch glared at her.

"And what is this destination?" he demanded.

The figure shrugged under her robe.

"Who knows," she said calmly. "It keeps changing."

"And how long will this trip take?" he continued.

Again the shrug.

"I have no way of knowing that either."

Infuriated, Laméch moved toward the woman but continued past her to grasp the sides of the ceramic cone.

"Does this propel the ship?" he demanded.

"Initially," she responded with a simple nod. "It receives energy from a Power House, charging a simple engine which propels us. However," she continued, "we are far beyond the range of a Power House now. We used it to maneuver from your city out to the open sea. We utilize a much swifter and more efficient source of energy for the great distances between cities."

She rose to her feet and pointed far out in the direction they were traveling.

"Look there," she instructed.

Laméch found his anger abating as an unusual curiosity overtook him.

He strained his eyes to look forward, but could see nothing.

"No," she corrected, coming to stand close to him, "Look at the *surface* of the water."

He stared harder and was startled when he saw a tiny splash in the distance. He then noticed multiple tiny wakes that expanded and overlapped, apparently moving in the direction of the ship as it overtook them.

Finally he noticed a tiny object halfway between them and the splash. It appeared to be a shiny round ball.

A second tiny splash occurred in the distance.

Just as Laméch was about to attempt a guess, the woman explained.

"A trained dolphin team," she said. "They are harnessed and attached to that large ball you see in the distance. The ball is a thin metal sphere which is hollow, and no amount of force from the dolphins could ever submerge it."

Laméch nodded in partial understanding.

"This vessel is attached to that ball, which pulls us forward, regardless of whether our dolphins are near the surface or swimming far below. Otherwise, they would pull us down with them. They have very long leads for maximum freedom, but collectively they keep us moving in the right direction."

She turned, and again the starlight exposed her smiling mouth.

"Of course, when they rest, we rest also. But they *will* transport us to our destination eventually."

"And where is this destination again?" Laméch asked.

"As I stated," she replied calmly, "it is always moving. I honestly couldn't tell you."

Slightly less angry, Laméch thought of another question.

"What are those struts or wings attached to the sides of the boat?"

"They provide lift to the vessel, much the same as the wings of your man-kite provide lift." Her head turned to face him, and he could see her eyes shining out from under the hood—eyes that dared him to ask how she knew about his kite.

Laméch ignored them as she continued.

"They simply provide lift in water instead of air. Once this vessel reaches a certain speed, the wings cause the vessel to rise slightly from the water. Eventually the bottom no longer drags on the water's surface, and the vessel moves faster, requiring less effort. The dolphins soon realize this and are happy to swim faster since, to them, it greatly reduces their load."

Laméch nodded, impressed, and as his anger finally faded away, he began to think more clearly. He suddenly realized something that should have occurred to him much sooner.

"I recognize your voice!" he exclaimed. "You're the…"

She lifted her hands swiftly and violently, interrupting Laméch.

But she was simply raising them to throw back her hood.

In the starlight stood the Librarian they had met that morning (or the previous morning) her shaved head shining in the starlight.

"You're the Librarian!" Laméch finished.

She gave a full laugh, which completely destroyed Laméch's vision of a Librarian.

"Actually," she said, "my name is Lyn-Golnan."

This further shocked Laméch, who had never considered the obvious fact that Librarians might have personal names.

"We've been watching you for some time," she continued. "You're the rich, spoiled son of Matusalé who secretly funds *The Path* in a somewhat naïve attempt at protesting the Semyaz and their controls. You and your friends do little activist stunts, which accomplish nothing other than to make yourselves feel important."

Laméch was shocked and offended, but Lyn-Golnan kept going.

"We have been searching for that missing tablet for decades—the one that contains your name—and when you suddenly showed up asking about it, we were sure you would lead us to it. As you will soon see, you have become quite valuable to us."

Laméch was suddenly less offended, but still confused.

"I thought that Librarians were completely impartial and didn't partake in causes or choose sides."

"That's only when we're on duty," she answered with a laugh that clearly considered his observation to be silly. "I have been part of a *real* anti-Semyaz underground since long before you were born."

Her face suddenly became deadly serious and she spoke slowly.

"Where we are going, you will learn how to *truly* fight the Semyaz. No more juvenile stunts, no more symbolic signs and slogans. We take the fight to them. We care not who gets the credit, nor are we concerned with how long this battle will last. We are assured of victory, although no one knows how many years—or how many generations—this war will last."

Laméch was completely taken aback. This Librarian had suddenly transformed into a deadly serious partisan—using words like "battle" and "war". It both excited and scared Laméch, who had never truly considered taking his anti-Semyaz sentiments this seriously. He was also embarrassed that she was right. His motivation for activism was always the pride and bravado it brought him in front of his peers. He wasn't sure if he could truly join a cause if he wasn't guaranteed at least some credit. He was used to being the hero.

"I suppose I have no choice in this," he stated eventually.

"Not true," she said, the smile returning. "There are always choices."

She spread her arms indicating the surrounding ocean. Did she mean that he had the choice to jump?

Her smile faded.

"We simply happen to know what your choice will be."

Laméch turned and stared forward into the oncoming sea. He didn't like being controlled—or second-guessed. However, he felt a strange sense of destiny as if he would soon discover a place and purpose far greater than he had ever known. The metal buoy danced ahead of them.

Lyn-Golnan interrupted his thoughts.

"Your friend should be waking soon," she said quietly. "He was given a stronger dose to allow us this conversation."

Laméch stared at her, trying to form the obvious question.

Suddenly there was loud chirping and chattering from far in the distance.

"Hang on!" Lyn-Golnan shouted suddenly as she grabbed the edge of the skiff.

The boat tipped slightly and began to shake. Suddenly it pitched forward and dropped a full cubit, striking the water and splashing spray into their faces. They slowed immediately, which caused Laméch to lurch forward, almost flying over the bow. The craft shuddered again, eventually settling on the swells of the open sea.

Lyn-Golnan smiled.

"The dolphins have decided to rest."

They traveled in this manner for twelve days. Lyn revealed a storage panel at the stern of the skiff which contained rations of dried fruits and vegetables, and an awning which lifted to protect them from the sun during the day. Two large metal containers were used to collect water from the ocean for drinking and makeshift washing. Their swift rate of speed prohibited a leisurely swim or bathing alongside the skiff—except when the dolphins chose to rest.

The ocean water was not nearly as fresh as the cool streams from the springs which fed Matusalé. Those waters flowed into the sea, carrying dirt and other sediment which—Laméch reasoned—contributed to the stale taste of the water that currently kept them alive. He wondered if, because of this, the waters of the ocean would someday become undrinkable.

The sun would rise each day in front of them, burning away the morning mists and informing them that they were traveling east. The moon had risen in the sky during their third night of travel, shining its glowing, pinkish-blue beacon as it passed overhead.

Ruallz had been sullen at first, but gradually accepted his fate, becoming more concerned with survival and less concerned with the life he had left behind. He was certain he would find his way back—he had contacts with different shipping personnel in other cities.

During the dolphins' periods of rest they would swim up to the edge of the skiff, chattering and playing with them. When Laméch expressed concern that they would get their lines tangled, Lyn shook her head saying, "I think they're smart enough to avoid that."

She spoke little, but when she did, it was words of optimism and assurance mixed with vague statements about where they were going.

On the thirteenth day, the sun rose on their port side, indicating their trip had taken a sudden shift to the south.

Laméch simply pondered the direction his life had suddenly taken. He found himself more excited than worried—almost as if he were preparing for the biggest jump of his life. He didn't know what Lyn and those she represented had in store for him.

But he knew his dislike for the Semyaz *was* sincere—and it really didn't matter *how* he would eventually oppose them.

On the morning of their twenty-third day at sea, the clearing mists revealed a coastline in the distance. As they drew near, Laméch could see a thick forest of trees which were very tall, and at the same time, very thin. They swayed slightly, almost like tall grasses, but they clearly rose higher than any of the trees that surrounded Matusalé.

He then noticed something even stranger. As he watched the tops of the trees, it appeared that the tree-line was moving up and down, as if mimicking the waves of the surrounding ocean. It was almost as if the trees were performing a dance by becoming shorter, and then taller again—each tree closely following its neighbor. He laughed as the image of trees bending their knees flitted through his mind.

He scanned the base of the coastline and noticed something else. No beach. The edge of this land rose about twenty cubits directly from the sea and appeared to be a thick carpet of dirt, roots, and vines. It was as if someone had ripped a thick section of sod from the grounds of his home and placed it in one of the pools.

He turned to Lyn.

"Is this a floating forest?"

"Yes," she answered. "This is our primary base of operations."

Laméch had never seen a floating island, but he had certainly heard stories from mariners. And he also knew they never went near them.

"Sailors say these forests should be avoided. Aren't they dangerous?"

Lyn laughed.

"Not dangerous," she said. "Just useless."

She looked at Laméch's puzzled brow.

"One cannot do shipping or commerce with a land that is constantly moving, and for which there is no way to re-discover."

Loud chirping from the dolphins signaled their final drop in the water, and Lyn reached over the bow to release the tethers attached to the buoy. Laméch watched as the silver sphere suddenly darted away to the left, following the coastline.

"Their handlers will care for them," Lyn said.

Laméch stared as the wall of mud, dirt, and roots moved towards them. He could see nothing that looked like a dock or shipyard. Nothing to receive their ship. No place to disembark.

Lyn reached into her robe and withdrew a long tube. Laméch flinched, thinking she was going to fire another dart at him, but she simply smiled and placed it to her lips.

A loud, shrieking whistle came from what was obviously a flute, forcing Laméch to cover his ears. Several short bursts mixed with longer ones.

She lowered the flute and smiled.

"Now we wait," she said.

Laméch stared at the bobbing coastline, looking quizzically at Lyn. A thought suddenly occurred to him.

"How many times have you been here?" he asked. "Does the Library allow you…?"

Lyn raised two fingers.

"Twice," she said. "I was here once many years ago when I was recruited. Of course, *here* was on the other side of the world, far to the north. As I said, I truly had no idea where we were going, or how long we would travel. My contact simply activated me and gave me instructions, this vessel, and this flute."

She smiled.

"The dart tube was my own."

Laméch stared at her for a few moments, and then shook his head, turning away.

His thoughts turned to Ruallz.

His friend was sitting back by the cone, staring at nothing.

"I don't think I'll find any shipping contacts here," Ruallz mused, cocking an accusatory eye at Laméch as he approached. "I knew you were lying when you promised we would make it home before the gates closed, but I never could have imagined just how wrong you really were."

Laméch started, defensively, "I had no idea this was going to happen. I'm just as much a victim as…"

"There have been times that I thought you had ruined my life before," Ruallz interrupted, "but this time it is certain."

He looked directly into Laméch's eyes with anger and disgust.

"Thanks."

Laméch began to protest, but could think of nothing to say. He turned back to Lyn.

A loud whistle sounded from above their heads, and Laméch saw two large struts that had been hidden by large bushes emerge from overhead. Soon, four cables appeared and began to descend towards them. As they approached, Lyn instructed Laméch to reach for them, and soon they were each holding two.

"Attach yours to the stern," she instructed. Laméch took the cables which had clamping hooks spliced into them and went to the rear of the skiff. He looked over the edge, but could find no place to attach them.

"Where do I hook these?" he shouted back to Lyn.

"At the sides near the stern!" she shouted back.

He looked over the starboard side and found a heavy metal ring which was obviously designed for the hooks in his hand. He attached it securely, and then did the same for the port ring.

"We're attached," he called out.

Lyn raised her flute again and let loose another volley of piercing notes. Laméch watched as the cables became taught and then slowly lifted the skiff from the sea. Water drained from the wings as they rose towards the scaffolding above, barely clearing the edge of the coastline.

Soon they were suspended above the newly revealed landscape, and Laméch could see just how flat this land was. In the distance he thought he could see some simple tents and small buildings, but he couldn't be sure.

They were hanging from a winch that was attached to a wooden crane with wheels. Laméch watched as the crane began to roll inland, carrying them with it. Soon they were hanging over dry ground and were slowly lowered until the skiff came to rest on its wings. Surrounding their landing were about thirty men, some holding what could only be weapons of some sort, but he didn't recognize them. They were dressed in simple breechcloths and appeared very slovenly and unkempt, distressing Laméch greatly.

He turned to Lyn who was grinning excitedly, her eyes glowing with ecstatic fervor.

"We're here!" she exclaimed happily. "I never dreamed I would be able to return."

She looked into Laméch's eyes, forgetting for a moment that he was her captive.

"Isn't this wonderful!"

"For you, perhaps," Laméch retorted. "I have yet to understand why I was kidnapped."

Lyn's eyes softened, and she nodded slightly.

"You'll see…"

Laméch watched as the men approached them.

"Over here!" one of the men ordered, and the three passengers stepped out and walked obediently towards them.

The man who had spoken approached Lyn, apparently because

she was robed—and also seemed to be the only member who was happy to be here.

"*What guards the garden?*" he demanded.

"*A flaming sword,*" was Lyn's swift answer.

The man nodded and motioned for them to follow him and his companions.

Soon Laméch, Lyn, and Ruallz were walking across the spongy grounds of a floating forest somewhere in the southern part of the world, following ragged captors into an uncontrollable future. The slender trees bobbed alongside them.

Laméch tried to remind himself about his formula for fun, but he was unsure of how to factor in such a prolonged danger.

Or the variable for which he had no experience:

The *unknown*.

CHAPTER 7
REVELATION

*"The enigmas surrounding Aenoch are plentiful. His re-
nown as the world's greatest architect and city planner
has since been overshadowed by his two major disap-
pearances. The first was a period of more than eighty
years after his completion of Matusalé City. Upon his
return, he had transformed from a brilliant engineer
into a mad prophet of impending doom.
His dire warnings were, unfortunately, unheeded."*

—Amoela the Librarian,
<u>The First Two Thousand Years, Vol. II</u>

They marched through the strange, undulating forest for several
hours, following the men who certainly knew where they were
going, although Laméch could not discern any path or special landmarks. He noticed several small animals scurrying past that he had
never encountered before—and many he didn't recognize.

Lyn tried to start a few conversations with the men, but they
adamantly—although politely—refused.

Eventually they arrived at a large one-story house apparently built from nothing but leaves and branches, and the men escorted them gently inside.

Upon entering they saw a chair next to a simple table in the center of a room, lit by open slots in the thatched roof above. They could also see that the building's internal structure was much more solid than it appeared from the outside.

But it was the items that covered the table which brought out gasps of excitement and relief from the three travelers.

The table was covered with food!

Sliced leeks and melons of all different sizes and colors were laid out, surrounded by leafy salads of legumes mixed with berries and fruits—many of which Laméch had never seen before. A large wooden pitcher of some unknown beverage sat near the edge, next to three empty wooden flagons.

They glanced at their captors who simply nodded, pointing to the table.

That was all the encouragement they needed. After twenty-three days of dried rations and ocean water, this was indeed a welcome sight!

They surrounded the table and quickly ate their fill. The pitcher contained a strange but delightful tea which would have been even better had it not been room temperature.

The captors ate nothing but watched silently; causing Laméch to wonder, briefly, if something had been done to the food. He dismissed the thought quickly as he consumed another large grape.

As they finished, they looked for something with which to wipe their hands and faces, but it soon became apparent that a single large cloth draped over the lone chair was the only item available for this purpose.

One of the captors, a man with a small square face, deep furrowed brow, and a large golden band on his left arm, slid open a door at the far side of the room and motioned them towards it. Once they were through, their captors closed it firmly behind them, remaining in the first room.

This next room was darker, also with a large table that was

empty. Shelves hung from the walls containing clay tablets and some simple wooden carvings. Four chairs surrounded the table—with a man seated in one of them.

Laméch was shocked to recognize him!

He realized his error almost immediately. The man seated in the chair—if he were dressed properly and groomed with a decent shave and haircut—looked exactly like his father! He stared at the face rudely until the man stood slowly and responded.

"I have waited a very long time for this day," the man stated, staring long and hard at Laméch, as if he knew him but did not expect any recognition in return.

After a few moments of this, Lyn seemed slightly impatient—as if she were being overlooked—and introduced herself.

"Greetings, sir," she began. "My name is Lyn-Golnan and I have brought Laméch and his friend here as instructed."

"We are so grateful," said the man, never taking his eyes off Laméch. "Come closer, Laméch," he instructed.

Laméch approached and was surprised when the man swiftly embraced him, planting a kiss on both cheeks. He recoiled at the unkempt man's familiarity, but remained calm.

The man held Laméch by the arms and looked into his eyes.

"You *do* know who I am," he stated confidently, "or you at least have some intimation?"

Laméch nodded almost as confidently.

"Are you are my grandfather, Aenoch?" he offered cautiously.

"Yes!" Aenoch smiled warmly.

He grasped Laméch in another embrace.

"I heard of your birth some twenty years ago, but I have been engaged these past eighty years with a task so momentous—and so secret—that I have been unable to appear anywhere in society."

He released Laméch, then smiled briefly to all three visitors and said, "Please, sit with me."

They sat surrounding the table, Laméch across from his grandfather. For the first time, Aenoch looked at Ruallz, and then at Lyn-Golnan.

"I believe you have something for me," he said to her.

Lyn nodded and slowly reached into her robe to extract a large blue satchel which she rested on the table. The straps from the satchel remained around her neck as she reached inside and removed a clay tablet which she placed on the table and pushed towards Aenoch.

It was the tablet from the underground room! Laméch could still recognize his name in the carved markings. He watched as Ruallz strained to get a better look, but Aenoch lifted the tablet from the table, studied it reverently for almost two minutes, and then stood.

Finally, in a very quiet and calm voice, he said, "This is excellent." He then carried the tablet to one of the shelves and placed it next to the other tablets.

He returned to the table and sat, looking again at Laméch.

Laméch was aghast. After all they had been through—apparently because of that piece of clay—this man could only say "*excellent*"? He looked at Ruallz to express his disgust and impatience, but before he could say anything, Aenoch interrupted his frustration.

"So, I understand that you are opposed to the Semyaz?"

Laméch stared, puzzled for a second, but eventually nodded.

"That is good," said Aenoch. "Suppose you tell me what you know of them?"

Laméch was startled by the question. Everyone knew about them. He started to reply, but became suddenly aware that he actually did not know any great details.

"Well," he began, "they have advanced technologies which they promise to use for the betterment of humanity."

"And what is wrong with that?" Aenoch challenged.

Laméch stared, surprised by the question.

"Nothing, I guess," he said. "But it is the rules and guidelines they enforce on the cities, and the tribute they collect. I simply don't see any actual benefits. I know it costs my father a great deal."

"So it is the affront to your family's personal wealth which offends you?"

'No," Laméch answered quickly and defensively. "It is simply an offense for any one—or any group—to take possessions that they have not earned. Besides, it costs everyone in Matusalé City a great deal."

He looked into Aenoch's eyes and repeated one of the slogans from *The Path*.

"Taxation in exchange for services becomes extortion when services are withheld."

Aenoch nodded thoughtfully as Laméch continued.

"I just don't see why we should pay someone else to tell us how to run our cities and our lives."

"So," Aenoch said eventually, "you just don't like being told what to do."

Laméch nodded.

"That's probably right," he admitted with a slight smile. "I just feel that only conquered people pay tribute—and I don't like the idea of feeling conquered, no matter how beneficent my conqueror is."

Aenoch nodded again, followed by another "Excellent."

Laméch looked around the table. Ruallz seemed to be drifting off, fighting sleep, but Lyn's expression startled him. She was watching every word of Aenoch with excited, glowing eyes, as if every sound uttered by him carried unimaginable importance.

Laméch shook his head. His grandfather was not *that* exciting.

"And what," Aenoch continued, "do you know of the religious teachings of the Semyaz?"

Laméch was silent for a few moments. He had never considered the Semyaz beliefs in any detail, or as anything relevant. He knew of some people who treated their supposed advancements with reverence.

"I'm not quite sure," he began with a shrug. "I believe it has something to do with light, as in, light is the eternal force which created us all. Some people believe the Semyaz are superior to us in that they are more in tune with this creative light and have thus become more…enlightened?"

This last was more of an awkward question since Laméch wasn't sure of his details. He was also not sure just how seriously he was supposed to consider Aenoch's queries.

"Laméch," Aenoch continued, ignoring Laméch's response, "I believe you need to understand some history before you can fully understand who the Semyaz are and the actual dangers they represent. Are you familiar with the Family Wars?"

Laméch nodded.

"No, you are not," Aenoch said calmly. He sat back in his chair and began lecturing the insulted Laméch.

"The first cities developed quite naturally along the coasts, and were founded along family lines. They were not the walled, powered cities of today, but they each developed their own area of expertise and commerce.

"As the populations grew, they began to have growing pains as the cities could no longer support the populace. They developed stringent rules regarding what type of people could be allowed to live in the cities and soon specialized criteria were developed along the lines of intelligence, fitness, and strength. These bureaucratic policies began to be carried to extremes, and soon every person born, coming of age, or entering the city was measured with a large variety of tests designed to determine whether or not a person was optimum for use within that city. Those deemed unsuitable were considered 'non-optimums' and exiled from the city.

"As time progressed, committees were established to determine the viability of city residents, and the criteria for being 'fully optimum' became more and more stringent. External features like nose size, eye shape, skull curvature, and skin tone had to be within a very small margin; and tests of math and logic aptitude became more and more difficult to pass. Failure initially meant banishment, but, as populations continued to increase, it eventually meant execution—since inferior features and aptitudes could not be allowed to pass on to subsequent generations."

Laméch listened incredulously, not exactly sure what he was hearing, but intrigued all the while. This was nothing like the boring history lectures his father gave.

"As I stated," Aenoch continued, "the cities originally were founded along family lines, and the real tensions began because each city had developed its own unique criteria for determining who was a viable human and who was not. Some of these differences related to the family features of each city's original founders, but many differences were simply because the criteria that each city had developed were completely arbitrary.

"Commerce between cities became tense as travelers were not allowed to engage in business without passing certain tests. Also, those who were exiled sought refuge in other cities, who in turn, believed their populations were being deliberately defiled by the cities from which they had come. As vast numbers of people realized that no place would welcome them, they headed into the forests to somehow carve out their lives away from the cities.

"With each city now firmly convinced that its standards for defining humanity were the *true* ones; and also firmly convinced that every *other* city represented a threat to their own family bloodlines, the wars began."

Aenoch paused to scan the table. Lyn-Golnan's expression had not changed.

"Cities launched full assaults against each other to try and exterminate the 'non-optimums' located in their neighbor's boundaries. Chemical weapons, attempts to poison food and water supplies, firestorms, and explosives launched from great catapults were among the methods employed to rid the planet of 'inferior' humans. You must understand, it was the future of humanity that was at stake, and the degraded, mutated '*non-opts*' that lived in the *other* cities could not be allowed to poison the future bloodlines."

Aenoch paused again, drew a deep breath, and continued.

"It was three and a half years into these wars that the Semyaz arrived."

He stopped and looked at Laméch.

"I was part of a division fighting in Tubalcain when it happened. We were raiding an armaments depot, trying to confiscate some of their superior weapons. By this time more than half of humanity had died, and the cities were little more than smoking ruins. Libraries and observatories were razed; the marble streets, reduced to rubble.

The wars had degenerated into one-on-one combat, and we were simply determined that whatever few humans survived the wars, those humans must be from *our* city."

Aenoch leaned forward.

"Have you ever seen a Semyaz observation platform?"

Laméch nodded, shocked at the sudden change of topic. He was fairly certain he had seen one. Almost everyone thought they had witnessed one, but there were very few reports of large groups of people observing them. The Semyaz claimed to pilot these platforms over the cities to observe and "oversee", but such sightings were very rare. Laméch heard of such sightings, perhaps twice a year. Supposedly they were golden, disc-shaped crafts, and most reports stated they were blurry or "out of focus".

Aenoch continued.

"One of these platforms appeared suddenly in the skies over each city with brilliant flashes of light. All fighting stopped immediately, and we all heard a loud voice commanding us to lay down our arms. We were told that all people were of equal value, and that we were all 'Children of Light'. Soon emissaries claiming to be from the lands of the Semyaz arrived in the cities and began to instruct us in the peaceable rebuilding of our lives.

"The Semyaz claimed to be an unknown race of humanity living in the far western coastal regions, where there were no known cities. They had developed advanced technologies independently and had watched for many years as our cities had descended down the path of destruction. Finally, they were no longer able to stand idly by and were compelled to intervene on our behalf.

"I was able to return home and resume my engineering. Working side by side with Semyaz representatives, I developed the modern city model with its walls, the tidal power generators, and the energy coils which we now all take for granted."

He paused and leaned back in his chair.

"I helped build Matusalé for your father, but during those years I developed a mistrust of the Semyaz. I once was allowed to travel with one of their envoys to the Haermon Mountains and saw the places where they lived, carved from inside the granite cliffs. I have never been there since, and to my knowledge, no one else been allowed inside. But I made one unusual observation."

He leaned forward again.

"While there, I realized that I only saw emissaries and representatives. I never once met an actual Semyaz."

He paused as if sharing a deep secret.

"As a result, eighty years ago I disappeared on a mission to discover the truth about them. In all of my research, all of my questions, and in everything I observed, I could find no clues about their history, their origins, or their purpose. Eventually, I came to two final conclusions."

It was Laméch's turn to lean forward. History had *never* been like this with his father.

"*One*," Aenoch said slowly, "I believe it was the Semyaz that *started* the Family Wars." He paused until the stunned Laméch was forced to ask for the second conclusion.

"And two?" Laméch prompted.

Aenoch stared directly into Laméch's eyes demanding his full attention.

"The Semyaz are not human."

CHAPTER 8
MISSION

"The Haermon Mountains are a great geological oddity. Jutting directly from the northern oceans of the Western Sea, they rise higher than any other on the planet, and are covered with almost no vegetation. They merge with the planet's bedrock and are comprised of pure granite, but give the appearance of having been split apart by some cosmic catastrophe—as if half of the range had disappeared, falling away into the oceans below."

—Amoela the Librarian,
The First Two Thousand Years, Vol. II

A s Aenoch had been talking, Laméch's respect for the older civil engineer *had* been growing. He also was somewhat pleased at the honor of being one of the few people who now knew the whereabouts of the mysterious Aenoch who had vanished some eighty years ago.

But with Aenoch's last comment, the limits of Laméch's credulity were reached and all of his accumulated respect vanished.

His grandfather was obviously insane. With a mental snap, Laméch began laughing.

"I may be opposed to their policies and actions," he began, shaking his head, "but they have never indicated that they were any different from us. They claim *we* are 'Children of Light' just as *they* are. I am not opposed to the Semyaz because I view them as evil or alien. I am opposed to them because they keep us down. They tax us, give us only what they deem important, and hide their technologies from us. I don't want to *destroy* the Semyaz. I *may* want to hurt them and damage them, but it is because I want the opportunity to have what they have and to be *like* them!"

It was now Aenoch's turn to be startled. He straightened in his chair as if he had been struck. Lyn-Golnan's eyes suddenly looked at Laméch as if he had said something treasonous. Ruallz, for the first time, seemed wide awake.

Eventually Aenoch's eyes calmed and he emitted a small laugh. He sat back in his chair and finally spoke.

"I understand that you enjoy danger," he said, suddenly changing the subject. It was not a question.

Laméch was taken aback, but eventually he nodded as a slight grin emerged.

"In fact," Aenoch continued, "I understand you are a great risk-taker, and love to challenge fear and even death."

Laméch wasn't sure how to respond, so he simply stated one of the lines he was famous for.

"Well, I'll try *anything* twice."

Aenoch smiled with a slight shake of his head and leaned forward.

"We have brought you here for a reason," he began. "We have a special mission for you. This will not be like your silly, useless stunts which accomplish nothing except personal vainglory and bragging rights. We have something for you that will actually do some damage to the Semyaz and bring you into full conflict with them. Are you interested?"

Laméch was actually stumped by this turn of events. He certainly knew, from his conversations with Lyn, that this was coming, but he had forgotten until now.

He started to answer, but Aenoch continued.

"This will be the most dangerous thing you have ever done. It may last for several years, and no one—except us—will ever know about it. There will be no praise for you, no chance for you to enjoy the title of hero. Your only reward will be in knowing you have done something worthwhile in the battle against the Semyaz."

Laméch started again to answer, but Aenoch interrupted.

"Before you answer, you should know something about us," he began. "Just as the Semyaz have a belief system, so do we. Both claim to worship a 'Creator', but *we* worship the *true* Creator."

Laméch thought, sarcastically, *Of course you do*. He shrugged as Aenoch pointed to the tablets along the shelves.

"These tablets contain recordings of the revealed words of the *true* Creator. They were inscribed during the Family Wars, and deposited in various places around the world to protect them. We have been collecting them to try and piece together what the First Ones told us. They tell us of the source of all human suffering and also of the coming *Seed* who will be the final resolution to that suffering."

He turned back to Laméch.

"With your discovery, the restoration of our collection is almost complete. Soon we can begin anew, telling humanity the truth of its origins and of that coming resolution."

Any remaining respect for his grandfather vanished. Laméch was completely disinterested in any mythologies, and certainly had no use for people who seemed to treat them as if they were true.

"I'm sorry," Laméch said eventually. "I have no use for such beliefs. I'm not interested in nonsense of any sort—yours or that of the Semyaz—and would certainly not fit into your little group. Only fools believe in such transcendent, unverifiable garbage."

Laméch had never been concerned about offending people before, and he certainly wasn't going to start now. He tensed for the expected defense from Aenoch.

Instead, Aenoch rose with a large smile on his face and began applauding. Lyn-Golnan looked confused, and Ruallz actually sat up and took notice.

Aenoch responded to the confused look on Laméch's face.

"That is why you are so qualified for this mission," he said, his smile remaining as large as ever. "The Semyaz are very sensitive to our beliefs, and can somehow instantly discern when one of us is in their midst. Many of us have embarked on this very mission, and all have disappeared. We believe they were discovered almost immediately."

Aenoch returned to his seat and leaned towards Laméch.

"But *you*," he continued, "can infiltrate unnoticed. With your death-defying stunts and a mind dedicated to simple facts, you will be perfect! All others traveled to the Haermon Mountains over land, but since you enjoy climbing things, you will enter from the cliffs."

Aenoch's eyebrows rose to indicate his shrewdness.

"No one guards an impossible access point."

However, Laméch had heard only one word.

"Others?" Laméch asked. "You have sent others?"

"Naturally," Aenoch responded. "We have been trying for years to discover what they are doing in those granite cliffs."

"And what have you learned so far?" Laméch asked.

"Nothing," answered Aenoch. "None have ever returned."

He smiled.

"Actually, we truly have no idea whether or not any ever reached their complex. That is why you are so important to us. You are able to access their complex in an unprecedented manner—and we will at least be able to confirm that you arrived."

Laméch's mind reeled as he realized he had just been hired. He sought furiously for various excuses, but soon realized that this was something he was unable to decline. Finally he shrugged at the inevitable and said the next thing that came to his mind.

"When do I leave?"

Aenoch leaned back.

"Not immediately," he said. "First, you'll need some training and familiarization with our equipment and technology."

He smiled.

"The Semyaz aren't the *only* ones with advanced abilities."

* * *

Over the next several days, Laméch learned what Aenoch meant. They had agents in every city, and they all used their city's Power House for an amazing and unusual purpose.

Instead of using the energies to power a light or turn a small motor, the energies were focused on a quartz crystal embedded in a device designed by Aenoch. This device would then re-radiate energy with a specific pattern (determined by the crystal) that could somehow bounce across the skies and be received by a similar device. At certain times, weather permitting, it was possible for a person to speak into one of these devices, and for those words to emerge from another one of the devices—even if it was located halfway around the world! Laméch was informed that he would carry such a device with him and was quickly trained in its use.

Aenoch maintained a small Power House on his floating forest, but it was powered by wave motion, not tides, and generated only a fraction of the power that an average city did. Aenoch's device, kept in a separate structure, allowed him to communicate with his operatives from anywhere in the world. In fact, it was Lyn-Golnan's message concerning the Laméch tablets which had dispatched a nearby dolphin team and brought them to this floating island.

This small Power House also powered a sub-sonic transmitter that was thrust through the forest and down into the ocean below. It was this transmitter that allowed the dolphin teams to always know where to locate Aenoch's Island.

"Lyn-Golnan and Ruallz will return to Matusalé," Aenoch announced on the day of Laméch's departure. "We have a cover story for each of them. Ruallz is returning from a vacation in Jubal, and Lyn-Golnan is returning from a visit to the Library in Qênan. Both will be provided with the necessary verifying witnesses."

They were all standing near the crane which would lower their crafts into the waters.

Aenoch turned to Laméch.

"You will be provided with a dolphin team and a navigator, who will steer them to the base of the Haermon Mountains in the Western Sea."

Laméch nodded.

The skiff for Lyn and Ruallz was ready, so they said their farewells.

"I promised to get you home safely," Laméch said, half tauntingly to Ruallz.

His friend grinned slightly, but was not amused.

"If fun is danger plus survival, then I guess I've had the best time of my life."

Laméch shook his head, feeling sorry, but not knowing what to say.

"Give my best to *The Path*," he said. "Somehow assure them that I am abroad, working for the cause."

Ruallz nodded, and then suddenly grasped Laméch in an embrace.

"I'll see you when you return to Matusalé," he said. He then turned and climbed aboard the skiff with Lyn.

Laméch and Aenoch watched as the craft lifted up, moved towards the sea, and then lowered slowly, disappearing below the edge of the forest floor.

Soon Laméch's skiff was ready, and he was introduced to Iraed, his steersman. He was a quiet man who apparently made such trips often.

"Do you remember your mission?" Aenoch asked again, for the twelfth time that day.

"Yes," Laméch nodded impatiently.

"Remember," Aenoch insisted. "I believe that, even though the Semyaz saved humanity from the Family Wars, they are ultimately planning our destruction. Your job is to find out how they plan to do this, and what, if any, weaknesses they may have. This is information gathering *only*. No direct action."

Laméch nodded again. He understood. He also had no intention of obeying. He did not believe what Aenoch was saying, and he had his own reasons for gathering information. And for doing whatever else he might find necessary to do once he learned more.

"I must show you something very secret," Aenoch said suddenly, as if he had just lost a debate with himself.

Laméch looked at him with a raised eyebrow.

"Those of us who believe as we do," he began slowly, "share a symbol which allows us to identify ourselves to each other."

He looked cautiously into Laméch's eyes.

"I should not share this with you, but there may come a time when you will need it."

Aenoch's eyes commanded that Laméch never share this with anyone. He then stooped over and drew a shape on the ground with his finger. It was a simple oval that stretched vertically, but came to a sharp point at the bottom.

"This is a seed, which, of course, represents the coming *Seed*," he said, solemnly.

Laméch nodded, somewhat amused at the simplicity.

Aenoch bent further and wiped away the right half of the seed, leaving a slightly curved line.

"If you ever wish to discover whether or not someone is one of us, simply trace this mark. They will complete the other half revealing the seed—and who they are."

His finger returned to the ground where it restored the remaining half of the symbol. He looked up at Laméch who nodded.

"Obviously, if someone presents you with this partial marking, you must use your discretion as to how you may respond."

Laméch nodded, and then realized a verbal response was required.

"I understand," he said.

They shared a look that bound them together much more than Laméch would have liked. Aenoch kept the gaze as he carefully wiped out the marking with his foot.

Laméch finally nodded again. He was not all that excited about this new revelation, and also not thrilled that someday Aenoch might make him choose between the two differing creator myths.

Aenoch glanced down to make sure the marking was fully eradicated.

"Don't be surprised where you may discover one of us," he said, looking back up at Laméch. "We have many in every city, and also among those you call 'forest people'."

Aenoch's eyes suddenly flashed a warning.

"However, it is very unlikely to find one of us among those who serve the Semyaz in their mountains," he said, urgently. "They are the descendants of stolen children who were taken before they could be taught. They now serve the Semyaz with nothing but the beliefs that their captors have imposed upon them."

Laméch nodded, not really caring what the servants of the Semyaz thought. He was very anxious to begin his adventure and leave this island as soon as possible. As he turned towards the waiting skiff, Aenoch interrupted his thoughts once more.

"One more piece of advice," he said.

Laméch looked back at him wearily.

"The Semyaz may be more intelligent than we are," he said, "but they have one major limitation. I worked with their emissaries for many years designing cities. They have virtually no creativity. That is why they rely on us—even when they are planning our own destruction."

Laméch nodded one more time and clambered into his skiff, following Iraed.

Then they were lifted and eventually settled into the sea. Iraed quickly began attaching the eager dolphin team to the buoy, and connecting it to the skiff.

Soon they were heading northeast across the open sea on a journey that Aenoch had promised would take at least two months.

For the first time, Laméch wondered if his father had missed him yet.

PART II
ENGAGEMENT

Love and War are the same:
stratagems and polity are
as allowable in one as in the other.

Miguel de Cervantes

CHAPTER 9
INFILTRATION

"Centuries before the Family Wars, the Semyaz were abducting children, using the piracy that always proliferates alongside shipping and commerce. These children were conformed into the isolation and servitude of the Semyaz social structure; and the first Emissaries at the end of the Family Wars were their descendants. After the Family Wars, the descendants of refugees who escaped into the forests provided a new supply of abductees—and test subjects."

—Amoela the Librarian,
The First Two Thousand Years, Vol. II

Jameth was preparing another variation of his latest biological agent when he glanced up and saw his new intern watching him closely.

His latest assistant was most unusual. He did not have the dead eyes that most of the new slaves had, and his dimpled chin, sandy hair, and facial features indicated that he came from someplace far beyond the usual regions where new recruits were typically collected.

Somehow this intern managed to make his ragged uniform look tidy and stylish, although it was nothing more than a piece of dark blue tarp tied at the waist.

His intern was watching with great interest, prompting a momentary burst of personal pride. Naturally, there was no way a mere slave could understand the great work Jameth was doing, but it would be fun to try and share anyway.

"Laméch, come closer," Jameth instructed.

His intern moved in as Jameth continued.

"Do you know what we are doing here?" he asked.

"Improving humanity," was Laméch's dutiful answer.

"Of course," said Jameth, "but what is the process? How am I accomplishing this?"

Laméch paused for a moment, and then gave a careful answer.

"Before you can improve humanity, you must discover the means whereby hereditary traits are transferred from one generation to the next."

Jameth suppresses an amused laugh at this slave's obvious mimicry of an overheard statement, but then he scowled slightly, impressed that his intern seemed unusually observant. He obviously listened to everything, and apparently even formed his own conclusions.

"Very good," Jameth said, wondering if this intern was one of the very rare ones who *wanted* to work here.

He looked around his lab, pleased that it had been recently assigned to him. It was a simple cube, carved from granite, with two air vents at opposite corners of the ceiling—one that brought fresh air and one that extracted air. The intake vent was directly above his workbench and a noisy breeze could be heard at all times as the atmosphere was constantly being replaced. A small basin with a source of running water was opposite the doorway, and a shelf with several recording tablets was on the left.

A simple *tsohar* panel ran along the edge of the ceiling, illuminating his workbench, a small container of water, and the work at hand. A small black, metallic cylinder rose upright from the desktop where a chemical flame could be summoned with a simple twist of a small valve.

Every hour he received two or three sealed ceramic vials inscribed with a code, containing biological or chemical agents which he would combine for the experiments in other labs later that day. A special mechanism allowed him to combine various ratios of the vials (which were never opened!) into a single, larger canister. Once combined, this canister contained the mixture for that hour's testing.

He then labeled this canister with the code that indicated its contents and ratios and connected it to another mechanism which transferred a portion into two tubes—one blue and one red. These tubes would be detached and eventually connected to intravenous needles. However, before the needles were attached, one of the tubes was boiled in water.

Jameth glanced up at the red stone panel just above his workbench—a panel that he hoped he would never have to use. If one of these vials or canisters broke, he would immediately depress this panel, sealing the ceiling vents and doorframe. (The door was always closed.) Upon pressing the panel, a jet of chemical fire would instantly descend into the room, incinerating everything and everyone inside. This did not trouble Jameth in any way. It was a simple matter of duty.

"You see, Laméch," Jameth continued his impromptu lecture. "This is a process of elimination. The best way to track the manner in which hereditary information transfers from one person to another is with the use of diseases. The Semyaz have discovered an almost limitless supply of sicknesses and ailments of which most of humanity is unaware. They have even found such diseases within other organisms so as to provide us with the greatest possible variety."

Laméch looked quizzically at Jameth who continued.

"I'm sure you have heard of rare instances where someone became ill with a sickness that could not be traced to any kind of food disorder or poison. There are other poisons in the air and water, and, although the body usually protects itself, on rare occasions this does not happen, and a person can become sick or even die."

His young intern shuddered involuntarily at this last comment. It was not something that was discussed often, but Jameth enjoyed seeing the squeamishness that often resulted from explaining his clinical work to underlings.

"As you know," Jameth continued, "such sicknesses are rare, but the Semyaz are devoted to completely eliminating disease. Their objective is perfection. They know that mankind already lives long and relatively healthy lives, but they won't rest until all maladies are eliminated."

He looked into Laméch's eyes.

"They are abolishing death entirely," he said, almost conspiratorially with a barely disguised excitement. He had forgotten momentarily that he was speaking to an intern. "Their goal is immortality for everyone—and I believe they will succeed. It is such an exciting honor to participate."

"I see," answered Laméch in a voice that was clearly non-comprehending.

Jameth gave a look of disgust as he realized he had expected too much from his lowly assistant.

"Let's get to work," said Jameth, pointing Laméch to his workbench.

Jameth finished transferring his current combination into the canister and affixed the two tubes. Once they were filled, he disconnected them and handed the red tube to Laméch. This was the last sample of the day.

He pointed to the red panel.

"Do you remember when to use this?"

"Yes," answered Laméch, "if any of these containers break."

Jameth nodded. He had not told Laméch what would happen if the panel was depressed, but he doubted that his intern suspected.

"We will boil *your* tube," Jameth instructed.

Laméch filled the container with water and carefully placed his tube into it. He then activated the chemical flame on the workbench with a button that sparked like a flint and placed the container on a stand situated just above the fire.

Soon the water began to bubble, and after a few moments of a full rolling boil, Laméch extinguished the flame. They could hear the vent above them sucking out the flame residue and water vapors.

Jameth reached into the container and extracted the red tube with a pair of tongs. It was slightly larger as it had expanded from the heat. He placed it next to the blue tube on a tray, and then arranged the labeled canister and the now empty vials next to the tubes.

"These vials," Jameth continued, "contained samples from the Semyaz collection. They may or may not be lethal, but in the interest of objectivity, *we* don't know."

He pointed to the canister.

"This contains the current test sample which *also* may or may not be lethal. It is quite possible that combining non-lethal vials might still create a lethal sample."

He then pointed to the tubes.

"We boil the red one to kill any biological agents that are in the test sample. This allows those who administer the tests the opportunity to determine whether or not a sample that turns out to be lethal *is* so because of biological activity, or simply a chemical reaction."

Jameth's intern nodded, and then suddenly asked a question as if he could not help himself.

"Who administers these tests?"

Jameth glared at Laméch.

"That is none of your concern," he stated tersely. Jameth was all too aware of researchers who wore the yellow robes and worked in the levels below. He also knew that it was very unlikely that their privileged lifestyles would be his.

Jameth lifted the tray and pressed a wall panel to the side of the workbench. It slid aside, revealing an opening into which Jameth placed the tray. As soon as he withdrew his hands, the panel slid closed with a thump.

"We are finished for today," he announced.

Jameth walked towards the door.

"Clean up this place and return to your compound," he commanded. He released the door catch and pushed open the stone slab into the adjoining hallway. Without looking back, he exited, allowing the door to close tightly behind him.

Laméch had been very fortunate.

After eleven weeks of travel (during which his twenty-second birthday had occurred) he had arrived at the cliffs, scaled them in less than nine hours, and spent part of the night at the summit under the stars, overlooking the Semyaz complex and adjoining facilities. He was surprised at how cool the air was at this high altitude.

He knew that most of the Semyaz work was underground, carved into the mountains beneath him, but the workers and support slaves lived in large tents and other enclosures above ground. He could see right away that there was no escaping, since large fences surrounded the compounds and various attack animals patrolled the perimeter.

There was only one event that could be considered a disaster.

His crystal communication device had fallen during his ascent, crashing on the rocks below. It had been in a separate pack from the rest of his equipment, and had snagged on a rock before tearing away. However, he didn't consider this a major concern, since he had never relied on such a device before. Besides, increased danger simply meant the potential for increased enjoyment. He knew where he was and was confident he could find his way to one of the cities—even though they were all on the eastern coast.

He had used his fifty cubit rope to descend the approximately sixty cubits into the slave compound without incident. He certainly didn't *need* a rope, but descent was much easier and faster with one. He also might need to haul something back up to the summit and wanted to be prepared for any eventuality.

He had clambered down the final ten cubits, leaving the end of the rope sequestered in a crevice above his head. There were no guards to avoid or barriers to cross since he was already "inside" once he had crossed the cliffs above. Besides, no one ever guards a slave camp to prevent people from *entering*.

ENGAGEMENT: INFILTRATION

He had found appropriate slave attire and a place to sleep by rudely opening up random tents, apologizing to the startled occupants, and eventually finding an empty mat and someone's discarded uniform—a dark blue tunic worn by everyone. He had buried his traveling clothes and a few other items where he could find them later, and went to sleep in a tent with about twenty other inhabitants.

Sirens had awakened him before dawn and he arose with the others, applied some dirt to his face to fit in, and slowly trudged into the laboratories with his fellow slaves.

He had wandered around stupidly, allowing his new bosses to yell at him, berate him, and treat him like the ignorant idiot that he was. However, he soon learned what was expected and, after a few days of this, eventually found Jameth and claimed to be his new assistant.

Laméch's new boss had not questioned this, since he had just been assigned a new lab, and felt that he fully deserved a personal intern. Jameth wore his newly earned light-blue smock with pride, as it identified him as a full lab-tech. He was a dark-skinned man with light brown hair that curled slightly over his ears. There was also a calm, trusting look in his eyes that had initially attracted Laméch's attention.

Laméch soon discovered that there was a great difference between himself and his fellow slaves. Most had been abducted from the forests or other cities and had soon learned that there was no future for them other than their current situation. Others were children of slaves with no knowledge of another life. Laméch kept his countenance in a state of perpetual lethargy (and dirt), always keeping his eyes down and scuffing his feet as he walked.

But there were things that could not be hidden from Jameth, and soon his new boss was discussing more than just the menial tasks he was expected to perform.

Something about this whole experience excited Laméch. He had always enjoyed leading a double life, and now he was adding a third. Also, it was a new and interesting concept for him to play dumb. He enjoyed the dichotomy: The brilliance of appearing stupid!

In fact, he was about to add a new definition for fun: Deception!

At the moment, he was dutifully cleaning the basin in Jameth's lab, making sure everything was spotless for the next day. He studied the workbench, trying to determine what maintained the flame. He looked at the red panel, quite certain that pressing it meant instant death. He knew they were dealing with deadly substances, and also knew that they could not be allowed to escape beyond this room.

He looked at the panel where Jameth had placed the tray, and cautiously pressed it. It slid open to reveal an empty tray, which Jameth would probably retrieve the next time he was here.

Laméch looked into the opening to try and see where it led, but could not see anything. He tried to strain his eyes upward in case the opening was the bottom of a chute, but before he could focus, the panel snapped shut. Apparently it was on a spring or timer of some sort.

Satisfied that the room was properly scrubbed, he exited into the hallway. He tried to determine what was behind the room where the panel was, but the only thing next to Jameth's lab was another lab. He continued down the hallway until he came to a bridge which crossed a large chamber below. He tried to see the ceiling above, but the curving granite walls appeared to merge upward into a dome, and it was too dim and indistinct to determine how high it rose.

In the chamber below the bridge, Laméch counted eighty people, all wearing bright yellow robes. They were facing his direction, and were moving slowly into a room beneath him. He also noticed they were wearing protective face masks that matched their robes.

Laméch hurried to the far side of the bridge and watched them from the other side of the chamber as they entered the room one at a time. A guard was forcing each one to lower his or her mask, and also checking a small tattoo on the top of each person's left hand.

"That's not the way to your compound!"

Laméch looked and saw a guard coming towards him from the far side of the bridge. He submissively lowered his head and began to walk slowly towards him.

"My compound?" Laméch repeated dumbly.

"Get over here!" the guard yelled. "Yes, your compound!" He looked at Laméch's tunic. "You're supposed to go that way!" he shouted, pointing over his shoulder in the direction of Jameth's lab.

Laméch slowly nodded, heading the indicated way. As he passed the guard, the guard gave him a knee in his lower back, knocking him down.

"Get up," he demanded, "and *move* to where you are *supposed* to be."

Laméch got up—not too quickly—and nodded again, moving in the right direction.

"Don't ever let me see you over there again," the guard shouted after him, pointing to the far side of the bridge.

Laméch limped along until he was out of the guard's sight, and then moved quickly towards his quarters with a grin, rubbing his back.

There were many things he was unsure of in this new place, but there was one thing he was absolutely certain about.

He *had* to get one of those yellow robes for himself!

CHAPTER 10
ATROCITIES

"Two inescapable facts slowed and impeded the Semyaz in their research, adding untold decades to the realization of their objectives. First, they shared their acquired knowledge with few outsiders. This led to endless, regimented trial and error experiments which lacked understanding and intuition. Secondly, although the Semyaz had great mental prowess, they lacked a fundamental knowledge of the material world, which those they sought to subvert understood innately."

—Amoela the Librarian,
<u>The First Two Thousand Years, Vol. II</u>

Laméch spent his days working for Jameth and then sneaking away to discover as much as possible about everything that happened in the labyrinth under these mountains. He found where food was stored and prepared, where shipments of supplies entered the mountain complex, and various other factories where additional necessities like uniforms and equipment were manufactured.

Strangely, there did not seem to be a Power House or anything similar to one. The lighting along the corridors did not look like the light from any of the noble-globes at home, so Laméch assumed they were powered in a different manner. They were usually embedded along the edges of the ceiling, and he soon learned that they were called *tsohar* panels.

It also occurred to him that, with no Power House, his crystal communication device would have been useless anyway.

He did his exploring with surprisingly little difficulty. Fellow slaves he met averted their eyes, careful *not* to learn what another slave was engaged in. Those who worked for the Semyaz ignored him as one ignores any slave. He simply moved quietly, and not too quickly, blending in with the expected movements of any menial wearing a blue tunic.

He did make one interesting discovery. He had been peering over the edge of a balcony when a large doorway opened and eighty yellow-robed people emerged. He soon realized this occurred regularly, and as he studied the patterns—and compared them with the entrance timings of the first group of yellow-robed people he had encountered—he concluded that one group entered at the same time another group exited. And they seemed to make this exchange in four-hour shifts.

Laméch had to assume they were entering and exiting the same chamber. He also noticed that upon exiting, each person handed his robe and face mask to a slave who placed them in a large wheeled container—presumably for washing or for security collection. Beneath the robes, Laméch saw they each person wore a yellow smock, much like the blue smock that Jameth wore.

Out in the compound, Laméch did his best to study the layout—although most of his exploration was done at night. Overhead *tsohar* lamps—apparently powered by the same unknown source—lit the edges of their compound with their unique light, and he soon discovered a sequestered area to the north where he saw similarly dressed slaves—except that their tunics were dark yellow. In the mornings he saw them entering the mountains through a separate access, but realized that only a handful left each morning, leaving the remaining yellow-tunics behind. This was unlike his "blue" group who were *all* required to enter for work each day.

He also realized that at the end of each day, no one in the "yellow" group returned.

On the night beginning his third week, he returned to the cliff summit where he had spent his first night. He scaled the first ten cubits and found the end of his rope which he had hidden in the dark crevice along its descent. Just as he had descended in the shadow of the compound lights, so he was now able to climb back up the way he had first arrived. There was virtually no security there since the idea of escaping by scaling the vertical mountainside was unthinkable—and no one would ever consider fleeing to the impassable cliffs which were on the far side.

But Laméch had no intention of escaping—yet. However, he was fully aware that whatever plans he had made for retrieval had disappeared when his crystal device had been destroyed. He still had no plans—and no idea how he was going to leave this place—but he still felt the need to set up a staging area just in case an opportunity presented itself.

He began setting up a private camp on top of the Haermon Mountain Complex where, every few days, he brought dried foods, water, small pieces of equipment, and various items he impulsively thought might be useful. He had discovered a storage area with a collection of large clay jars, and on each climb he filled one with supplies, wrapped it in a canvas tarp, and carried it up on his back. He also retrieved his small pack of original traveling clothes, which he had buried, and returned them to the summit.

He spent many hours looking out over the cliffs and the waters below, wondering what was happening in the world he had left behind. He hoped Ruallz was safe, and also hoped that his grandfather was faring well—even though Aenoch had been annoying and somewhat crazy, and was responsible for placing him in this state of affairs.

ENGAGEMENT: ATROCITIES

On one such night, it suddenly occurred to him that, if he had scaled the cliffs a few hundred meters to the north when he first arrived, he would have found himself inside the "yellow" compound instead—and been among those who disappeared each day.

One evening, instead of scouting in the complex, he exited and went immediately to the compound barrier between himself and the "yellows". The barriers were thick mesh metal cables anchored in stones which were set at regular intervals, strung between granite pillars that supported the compound lights.

His fellow prisoners warned him that contact with the other compound was forbidden, but words like "warn" and "forbidden" had never elicited any recognition from Laméch, and they certainly weren't going to start now. He moved to the far north-eastern corner and began to study those imprisoned on the other side.

He watched as the different men and women in the yellow compound moved around, some very careful to avoid any eye-contact with him. A few angrily tried to wave him away, but he persisted.

At first, they did not appear any different from the prisoners with which he had spent the last few weeks, but slowly, as he observed, he saw marked differences in their demeanor and attitude.

His fellow slaves (in blue) were generally indifferent, but easily frustrated and often quarreled out of boredom. Also, they were usually exhausted at the end of their days. Most were engaged in actual slave labor, unlike Laméch who had somehow—amazingly—found himself tasked with lab work.

But the "yellows" exuded a sense of fear and despair—no doubt based on watching their numbers dwindle. Each day they watched as some of their own were taken, never to be seen again; and they spent their days idle, feeding on their worries and dread knowing that any day they could be next. He had heard anguished cries in the mornings as loved ones were removed from each other.

An attractive young girl with dark skin, wild unkempt hair, and piercing jade eyes caught his attention, and he instinctively smiled at her. Her eyes caught his for a split second, and then darted away in panic. But Laméch continued watching, and a few moments later her eyelids lifted and she stole a quick glance at this daring stranger from the blue compound.

At Laméch's wave, she turned and ran, but not before Laméch saw the corner of her mouth lift in the slightest beginnings of a smile.

Laméch's pulse jumped; excited for the first time since arriving here at something that could finally be considered normal. He realized with a suppressed anguish that it had been months since he had done anything as simple—or as natural—as flirting.

Every night, after leaving the complex, Laméch would return to the same section of the barrier; and every night—eventually—she would manage to walk within eyeshot of him. She never approached him or even came close enough to talk, but she always appeared, always allowed their eyes to meet briefly, and then (always) turned away—but not before that same slight smile began, indicating her appreciation of his attention.

Anytime Laméch tried to wave her closer, she would run.

Once while waiting for her to appear, Laméch was jumped from behind by guards who beat him, reminding him of the warnings his fellow prisoners had given him. This of course didn't deter him, since he was now unable to get her dark beauty out of his mind. Of course there were suitable—and even attractive—women in his own compound, but there was something irresistible about the wild, forbidden girl on the other side of the fence. He simply was more careful in the future, finding various routes to arrive at their special eastern corner.

He also continued making regular visits to his private mountain-top camp, collecting and storing anything that he could scavenge that might be of use someday. His stolen goods were organized in an ever-increasing number of clay jars which were arranged next to various tools and small pieces of equipment bundled in sheets of canvas and tarp to protect them from the morning dews. He still had no idea how—or when—he would ever escape this place, but if he *did* come up with a plan, he wanted to be ready.

Today was the day! He had been studying the yellow-robed people as they entered and exited the large chamber beneath his level, and had finally arrived at a plan.

Although the eighty people who entered had their faces and hand tattoos scrutinized, the (presumably) same eighty people who emerged did not. In fact, he had not seen *any* guards near the exit doors—only simple slaves who collected the robes after they were removed.

When Jameth left for the day, Laméch hurriedly washed his face thoroughly, used a charcoal marker to draw a close approximation of the tattoos he had seen on his hand, and then rushed from the lab, neglecting his cleaning duties.

He arrived at the balcony overlooking the exit doors below. He knew he had less than four minutes before the doors would swing open, and he still had not found a stairway down to the level below.

It didn't matter.

There was a sharp angle between the wall and the corner where the balcony protruded, and after checking to see that no one was watching, he quickly crawled over the balcony's edge and wedged himself in the tight space where the wall and balcony buttress met.

He was able to lower himself almost two-thirds of the way to the floor before the base of the balcony curved back under itself, widening his space. He extended his arms and legs, but soon began to lose his grip. However, he was now close enough to jump, so he pushed out with his right arm and leg and launched himself into the dark space beneath the balcony.

He landed in a heap, and was relieved there was nothing but an empty wall under the balcony and that no one had seen him. He moved quickly around to a more central part of the room where he met a slave pushing the empty cart on her way to collect the

robes. She had just emerged from an archway through which Laméch could see a long corridor—and guards. He had been unable to
see them from the balcony.

She looked at him with some surprise, but Laméch glared at her.

"Where have you been?" he asked gruffly.

The girl was startled—and scared—for a brief moment, but Laméch quickly softened.

"Don't worry about it," he said. "I'm supposed to help you.
What do we do first?"

She shrugged, slightly confused.

"We collect their robes," she said carefully.

Laméch nodded, giving her a wink. He grabbed the other side of
the cart, and they wheeled it towards the exit doors.

Immediately the doors opened, and the people filed out noisily,
placing their robes and masks into the container, ignoring the two
slaves as they headed towards the far corridor.

Laméch waited until the third robe was placed in the basket,
and quickly snatched it along with a mask. He stepped back quickly
behind the open doors, pulled the robe on over his head, and slapped
the mask over his face.

The slave girl, who had been trained by years of abuse to react
to nothing, quickly masked her surprise. Even before Laméch could
put his finger to his lips to silence her, she was dutifully collecting
the robes and fixedly staring into her basket—determined to know
nothing about the actions of this strange slave with the clean face.

Laméch emerged from behind the door, facing in the same direction as the people who were leaving. Only about ten had turned in
their robes, and a pool of yellow-robed people had formed, waiting
for access to the basket. Laméch could see the guards in the corridor
examining those who had exited, checking their tattoos and making
sure they were not removing anything from the room behind him.

He merged backwards into the crowd, still facing forward with
all of the other yellow-robes. He deliberately bumped someone
behind him who rudely bumped back and then pushed in front of
him.

Once he was in the thick of the crowd, Laméch began to slowly walk backwards, allowing others to collide with him, and then pass him.

Laméch knew that when a group of people leave a room, some walk faster than others, and there is always some bumping and passing. As he continued to walk backwards, against the crowd, each individual who encountered Laméch thought he was just another yellow robe who was walking slowly, and pushed past him.

Eventually, as Laméch continued to back up, he found himself inside with the forty or so yellow-robed people who had yet to exit the room, and he moved quickly to the side of the group and glanced around.

The chamber was much larger than he expected, and it appeared to be filled with rows and rows of tiny booths, each with a simple curtain for a doorway. The rows, which defined the walls, were about two cubits high, allowing an average person to peer over them into whatever was behind.

Laméch didn't have any more time to observe, however, since there were now only a few exiting people remaining. He nudged one of them.

"I forgot something," he said quickly before dashing off blindly into the chamber. He didn't wait for a response, or to see if any guards on the inside had witnessed his departure from the group. He hoped that it appeared *so* impulsive, that anyone who was startled by it would remain inactive for a few moments.

He moved quickly in the direction that seemed to lead towards the entrance doors, but it became difficult to maintain his sense of direction. There seemed to be an endless number of rows and cross-rows, and many of them ended abruptly without warning. He felt like he was in a maze, but eventually made his way to the opposite side.

He couldn't help but see what was behind the curtains of the various booths as he ran. In each booth there was a table and two small cots—with a slave wearing a yellow tunic strapped to each cot. He noticed red and blue tubes like the ones he and Jameth worked with on many of the tables. He also couldn't help but notice the looks of fear, pain, and anguish which filled the faces of those on the cots—and the groans and occasional screams which came from the booths.

He didn't dare stop, yet. He kept moving until he finally spotted the large group of yellow-robes who had just entered the chamber. He moved close enough to them until he was certain that any casual observer would conclude that he was one of them. Only then was he able to relax.

And grin beneath his mask.

He was in!

He began to move casually with the others as they split up and began their activities. Most of them paired off, and headed towards specific booths. Laméch followed several different couples from a distance, but never stayed with any one group of people for too long.

He noticed that this crowd of yellow-robes was only working in one section of this large chamber, leaving more than three-quarters of the booths unvisited. Presumably, other groups were assigned to other sections, allowing eight or even twelve hours to elapse between staggered rounds.

He watched carefully as a pair of techs went from booth to booth. During each visit, they would collect the red and blue tubes from the tables and attach a sharp needle to each of them. Then, without any hesitation or ceremony, they would inject the contents of the red tube into the thigh of the slave on the right, and then immediately inject the blue tube into the slave on the left.

Any protestations were completely ignored as the slaves groaned, recoiled, and even attempted to thrash against their restraints. It appeared to Laméch that they had been drugged slightly to subdue them, but not enough to affect whatever experiments were being done.

The techs then dutifully recorded their visit on a thin slate affixed to the wall, and moved quickly on to the next booth. Their actions were very meticulous and regimented, indicating a high degree of precision and dedication.

Laméch quickly stepped into one of the booths that had just been visited. He noticed a black tattoo on each slave's forehead, and saw that a corresponding mark was at the top of one of the columns on the slate.

He tried to look into the faces of the two slaves before him, but there was no recognition. The one on the left had his eyes closed, while the one on the right had her mouth open in an unmoving, silent scream. Her sunken eyes were unblinking through her clammy countenance, and Laméch was forced to leave the booth quickly in revulsion.

What were the Semyaz doing here? Could the quest for improving humanity justify all of this suffering and anguish? He could not imagine how—but he was sure of one thing.

He was certainly glad he had not ended up in the yellow compound.

He moved carefully towards an area of the chamber where the yellow-robes had not gone, but before he could glance inside any of these booths, he was interrupted by a group of techs wearing red smocks. They walked confidently, with an air of authority and purpose, and were obviously the superiors of those in the yellow robes.

There were twelve of them. Some were escorting a line of new subjects into the booths, while others were busily placing red and blue tubes on the tables inside. Laméch quickly ducked away, and resumed his casual sauntering with the other yellow-robes.

An alarm siren suddenly screamed from somewhere overhead, causing Laméch to jump. Had he been discovered?

The alarm was followed by a voice which echoed around the chamber.

"Everyone will assemble immediately at the platform."

Laméch had no idea where the "platform" was, but he quickly followed the other yellow-robes as they hurried to the far side of the chamber near where Laméch had entered.

Soon a sea of eighty-one yellow-robes was assembled before a small platform where an imposing woman with a long red robe was standing. She was tall and pale, and wore a simple headband of what appeared to be spun platinum. The techs in the red-tunics stood guard along the perimeter of the stage, and it suddenly occurred to Laméch that perhaps he should start figuring out how he was going to get out of here. He didn't have the right tattoo or the correct clothing under his yellow robe. He began looking around for other ways in and out of the chamber.

The woman began to speak.

"You are all to be commended," she began, "for the excellent and thorough work which you have accomplished." She nodded approvingly without smiling. "As a result of your tireless dedication, we find ourselves ready to proceed with the next phase of our research."

This time she forced a smile as the assembled yellow-robes looked up at her with eager eyes from behind their masks.

"You will complete your rounds for today," she continued, "but tomorrow you will follow a new procedure."

She paused to ensure total attention.

"Each booth will now only contain *one* patient, and you will find a single green tube on each table. You will simply administer this single tube and record it as you have been doing."

She smiled again, somewhat more sincerely.

"If there are any among you who have felt concern for our brave patients, you will be pleased to see that, as we progress, we require less and less subjects. Their sacrifices—and the imparted wisdom of the Creator—are bringing us closer to the day when all disease and death will be forever removed!"

She raised her arms as cheers (muted by their masks) erupted from those assembled around the platform. She then turned and exited through a panel which slid open upon her approach and closed quickly behind her. Laméch noticed that before reaching the panel, she had pressed a small, hidden indentation in the wall.

Laméch was relived that the announcement had not involved him, but as he returned to the booths with the rest of the yellow-robes, a series of thoughts came to his mind.

He had always heard how the Semyaz had amazing, advanced technologies. However, he had yet to witness anything that surpassed—or even equaled—the common tools and equipment he had used and witnessed during his life in Matusalé. The *tsohar* presented a slight mystery, but lighting was still lighting, whatever the source.

It also occurred to him that these techs—Jameth and those in the yellow robes—had absolutely no idea what they were doing. They had prescribed routines, designed and calculated by unknown others who certainly *did* have a master plan of research and experimentation.

These techs were no different than the other slaves. Sure they had nicer clothing, and (presumably) better living conditions, but they worked entirely by rote with no comprehension of the actual research they were supposedly engaged in. In a strange way, the techs were doing nothing but repeating simple platitudes and engaging in repetitive rituals.

Laméch concluded that the *real* technology—the actual wisdom and knowledge—was carefully hidden far behind the scenes. There were probably only a few—perhaps only the actual Semyaz—who had this knowledge. He imagined how an immense research program would require a great deal of extra time and people, if the actual knowledge and objectives were known by a select few. It would require tedious planning, and above all, amazing patience.

He remembered what Aenoch had said about the Semyaz lack of creativity. This system *suppressed* human creativity, so it was clear to Laméch that the true ingenuity behind what he had seen today was elsewhere. Probably behind the panel where the lady in the red robe had disappeared.

He discarded his partially formed escape plan—which had been to exit with the other yellow-robes and make a run for it—in favor of a new idea.

His realization that everyone who worked here was a slave caused him to recognize that he possessed a special advantage. As slaves, even the blue smocked techs like Jameth and the yellow-robed people who surrounded him were totally conditioned by the masters they served. Most had never known any other life, and never thought beyond the lines that their masters had created for them.

This also created a great complacency in their masters, who were completely confident in the control that their simple conditioning and crude reward systems created.

As a result, no one had ever considered following the lady in the red robe. And no one had ever noticed the concealed movement which had allowed her to exit the stage and enter the regions beyond the platform.

Grinning behind his mask, Laméch waited as the last remaining yellow-robes returned to their booths, and then he slowly returned to the platform area.

He estimated there were about forty minutes remaining before this group exited, so he hid behind a granite column and waited.

What were the Semyaz doing in this place? Trying to achieve immortality? Laméch thought this was probably a noble goal, but he certainly had never known anyone who considered it an urgent or critical issue. It simply wasn't something that anyone really thought or cared about. How had this concern become such a primary one? Or were the Semyaz working towards a completely different objective?

Another alarm sounded, and he watched as the yellow-robes rushed towards the exit, assembling in a small crowd waiting for the doors to open.

When all eyes were focused on the opening doors, and before the newly arriving techs could notice, Laméch rushed to the top of the platform and quickly depressed the same indentation that the lady in the red robe had pressed.

The panel slid silently open, and Laméch ducked into the darkness beyond as the door snapped immediately shut behind him with a loud click. He turned around and noticed the door mechanism just above his head. A large spring was now stretching, ready to re-open the door the next time the indentation on the other side was pressed. He also saw a powerful coiled spring in the recess which apparently propelled the panel shut again. It would not be wise to traverse that doorway slowly.

He was in a dark corridor which angled downward and slightly to the right. It was barely lit with a small *tsohar* light affixed to the edge of the left ceiling. Although it was weak, it looked just like all of the other illumination in this place. Another light could be seen dimly much further down the passageway.

He quickly discarded his robe and mask, leaving them in a heap behind a small support beam. He figured that if he was caught, it would be better to be found wearing his blue slave tunic than a stolen robe.

He moved quickly down the passageway until it emptied into a larger corridor which ran level and intersected the descending hallway at an oblique angle. Laméch could either continue on, traveling slightly to the left, or turn sharply to the right and explore in the opposite direction.

This new corridor was also dimly lit and stretched to the left as far as Laméch could see. There were closed doorways along both sides of the corridor, and they seemed to be spaced about thirty cubits apart.

He glanced around to the right and saw two large wooden doors, about forty cubits away, sealing off this end of the passage. Laméch stepped out cautiously into the corridor, feeling completely exposed, and turned right towards the doors. At any moment, someone could emerge from one of the many unknown doorways behind him.

As Laméch slowly approached the doors, he noticed a large winged serpent carved into each of them. Cradled gently in each serpent's wings was a small ball with markings which Laméch realized (upon closer scrutiny) outlined the coastlines of the world.

Just as he reached the doors he spotted a small archway cut into the wall to the left of the doors. He could see the beginnings of a small winding staircase just inside.

He pressed his ear against the wooded doors, and after listening carefully for a few moments, he was rewarded with the sounds of people talking. He couldn't make out any words, but it seemed like some kind of important meeting was taking place in the room beyond.

A large noise echoed loudly down the corridor from behind him, causing Laméch to jump. He looked back and saw that one of the doors had opened, and that a tech wearing a red smock had emerged. He was looking at a slate in his hand, muttering to himself as he headed in Laméch's direction.

Laméch froze momentarily in indecision, and then silently slipped into the archway beside the doors. He took a few steps up the staircase and held his breath as the man approached. Soon the tech passed by—still studying his slate and muttering—and casually pushed aside the large doors and entered into the room.

Laméch listened as the voices suddenly became intelligible when the doors opened, and then ceased as the doors swung shut. He then allowed himself to breath again and considered what to do next.

He decided to follow the winding steps upward, but soon realized they ascended into total darkness. The staircase was obviously for accessing different parts of the complex, but one definitely needed to carry a light source to use it. He climbed slowly and carefully, listening to the fading voices—and was surprised when they suddenly became louder.

They were the same voices from the meeting below! As he turned towards the sound, he felt around and discovered a ledge at about shoulder height. It was a small crawlspace, and by going up a few more steps he was able to pull himself up and in. Soon he was squirming along on his stomach, and moving closer to the voices. He grinned in the darkness as he was suddenly amused by his circumstances. He had no idea how far underground he was, yet he was deliberately entering into a tight dark space which was probably only used to clean out dirt and dead animals from the ventilation.

He suddenly noticed a tiny light in the distance and continued to move towards it. Soon he was looking through a bronze air grate directly down into a room where twelve men and women—all of whom were wearing red smocks—were seated on both sides of a large granite table. They were the same people who had been ushering the new subjects into the chamber above. One of the men was speaking, and Laméch recognized him as the man who had just passed him in the corridor. Standing at the head of the table was the lady in the red robe who had addressed the yellow-robes, bringing the total number of people in the room to thirteen.

"It simply does not make any sense," the man was saying. "We destroy the lethal biological agents with heat, making them totally harmless. But when we mix them with the non-lethal agents—also totally harmless—the resulting mixture terminates the subject every time."

The people around the table were nodding with him, as if he was summarizing something they had all experienced.

One of the women said, "I can't explain it. Somehow the dead, inactive agents are still mutating the non-lethal ones!"

"And inexplicably killing our subjects," said another.

There were more grunts and mutterings from the table as people concurred.

Finally a complete sentence emerged.

"I don't see any solution," said one of the men, resignedly. "We may be faced with an impenetrable anomaly of nature."

"*Enough!*"

The woman at the head of the table brought the discussion to a sudden halt. All eyes looked to her.

"Have you forgotten what our goals are?" she asked pointedly. "The subjects are irrelevant. What is important is learning how hereditary information is transferred from one organism to another. Remember, it is the contents of the vials that we are researching, not the subjects. The subjects are simply convenient processing labs."

She looked around at the seated men and women, her face softening slightly to introduce a new topic.

"You are viewing your results incorrectly," she announced accusingly. "You are too quick to admit defeat."

Her techs stared up at her, fearing what might come next.

"You have just made an important breakthrough," she declared as the surrounding eyes registered careful optimism. "The lethal nature of the first mixture is, itself, a hereditary trait, and the fact that it can be transferred—even though it is dead—and affect the non-lethal sample is proof that hereditary instructions can be transferred by purely chemical means."

Without smiling, she nodded with an intense excitement that was infectious.

"You have eliminated an avenue of research which we no longer will be required to pursue. You are to be commended!"

Sighs of relief and even elation emerged from around the table, and a few even slapped their hands on the table's granite surface in self applause.

Laméch understood very little of this, but there was one sentence which was etched in his mind.

The subjects are irrelevant.

If people were irrelevant, then how could the objective be to somehow create immortality for people?

The lady in the red robe continued speaking to her newly energized audience.

"In our next round of testing we will be drawing blood samples from the subjects to confirm these findings, and use them to determine the true source of life."

She paused, and then quickly added, "…as designed by our Creator, of course."

She waited for their nods, and then continued.

"I am confident we will soon be ready to move forward into the next round of our exploration," she said, her voice taking on a lecturing quality.

"For this next stage we will require a much larger supply of subjects. Partially, because the experiment cycles will be much shorter, but, more importantly, because the vast majority of the subjects will not survive."

Laméch was taken aback by this statement. Hadn't this same woman told the yellow-robes that they would soon be requiring *fewer* subjects? But he was more disturbed by her next statement.

"Our process is a slow, patient one," she continued. "We

anticipate fully completing this phase within the next forty years. At that time we will finally be able to utilize all that we have learned to initiate the final stage of our goal."

She looked around the room, her eyes gleaming.

"We will then be able to implement the improvements that we have worked so hard to discover. At that time, we will require a new and diverse supply of subjects to produce the fruits of our research. Naturally, these subjects will all be female."

She raised her arms and closed her eyes as Laméch watched in consternation.

"We are responding to the call of the mythical *Seed* with a literal one, created by our own hands!"

The seated men and women closed their eyes as well and rose in unison with their arms raised. They began chanting, "*All praise to the Creator*" over and over again, as they bowed repeatedly.

Laméch had never been more stunned in his life. How could a secret research meeting turn into a religious experience? He watched as the men and women became more frenzied in their wailing and bowing. Strangely, he noticed that the woman in the red robe had lowered her arms and opened her eyes. She was watching them with a strange dispassionate aloofness. For the first time, Laméch saw a *natural* smile play across her face.

Laméch wondered about the Seed that she had mentioned. Did it have anything to do with the one that Aenoch had spoken about? Someone who would bring an end to all human suffering? Aenoch had said that *his* version of the Creator was going to send this Seed, whereas *her* version of the Creator was apparently engaged in a centuries-long project to somehow manufacture one, requiring assistance from an endless supply of scientists, slaves, and test subjects. But why would an all-knowing, all powerful Creator need such help?

In all actuality, neither Creator made much sense to him.

As the worshippers below grew louder and more enraptured, Laméch had one final observation:

Even those wearing the red smocks are slaves!

CHAPTER 11
OBSESSION

"The location of each of the world's cities was not determined by random nautical commerce or logistical convenience, but rather by a multitude of geological and geographical requirements that were often contradictory. For example, a modern city had to be coastal for access to the tidal forces needed to energize its Power House, but it also required a solid landscape for its foundation, which was rare (particularly in coastal areas) due to the pervasive subterranean streams and hot springs that carved out constantly changing channels that weakened the ground.

Seldom were these two requirements met, and as a consequence, distances between cities were much greater than one would expect from colonization and expansion."

—Amoela the Librarian, *The First Two Thousand Years, Vol. II*

ENGAGEMENT: OBSESSION

L améch sat in silence behind the grate long after the insane meeting had ended and the people had exited. Eventually, they had collapsed on the table in front of them and the lady in the red robe had instructed them to return to their duties. They had wiped their eyes and shuffled out under her watchful gaze.

Then she had looked upward, directly towards Laméch where he was certain she would discover him, but she had eventually looked away and followed the others out of the chamber. The lighting had also winked out as she left.

In the darkness, Laméch tried to conjure up a plan, but could not. He could not go back the way he had come. Even if he collected his yellow robe, he could not re-enter the research chamber because he would still be faced with the same exit problem: A bad tattoo and his blue slave tunic. And he couldn't just wander the large hallway below only to be discovered by some red-smocked tech who would no doubt take him to *that* lady.

He squirmed his way backwards out of the crawlspace and eventually found his footing on the spiral staircase. Without actually making a conscious decision, he found himself slowly walking upward, just to see where it would take him.

He didn't climb far before he struck his head on a ceiling. He reached up and pushed against it, only to discover that it moved slightly. He took another step and bent forward, pressing against it with his neck and shoulders.

It lifted, revealing itself to be a floor panel, rather than a ceiling. As he raised it, he was able to look in one direction where he saw a dark, narrow hallway which curved around to the left. He slid the panel to the side and slowly pulled himself up into the hallway.

Seated on the floor, he slid the panel back into its space—where it dropped with a loud stony *clang*, reverberating up and down the corridor.

He heard loud shouts of alarm from the other end of the hallway, and as he looked up, he saw several guards running towards him. The hallway was quite long and the guards were still a great distance away. The lighting at their end of the hall was very bright, but in the section where Laméch sat, it was almost totally dark. As a result, the guards could not yet see him—they were simply running towards the sound.

Laméch jumped up and began running away from them, around the corner into the ever darkening hallway. Just in time, he saw the end of the corridor loom in front of him and stopped suddenly— barely avoiding a painful collision with the rough granite wall.

He looked around and could see no way out. Far above, he thought he saw some air vents, but couldn't be sure of anything.

He could hear the guards' feet pounding closer and closer, and heard one of them yell, "There's no way out!"

As they rounded the corner, Laméch thought desperately. Finally, he placed the left side of his face firmly against the jagged surface of the granite wall, then jerked backwards violently, creating several bloody lacerations on his cheek and temple. He suppressed a yelp of pain as he did the same thing along the side of his left leg and left arm, scratching them severely and also tearing a section of his left sleeve.

Finally, he grit his teeth and placed the back of his left hand against the wall, wrenching it backwards and allowing the rough granite to slice his skin—and obliterate the bogus tattoo which he had drawn earlier.

He quickly dropped to the floor and lay on his left side, feigning unconsciousness just as the guards arrived.

"So, another one tried to escape from below," one taunted, as he gave Laméch a kick in the side.

"Get up," another one commanded. "You can't fool us."

"Maybe he *is* sick," said a third. "Those poor bastards below are put through a lot. He probably expended his last bit of energy just getting up here."

Someone grabbed Laméch's feet and began dragging him over the rough floor, but eventually thought better of it and picked him up, throwing Laméch over his shoulder.

"This one stinks," he said as he walked with the guards back around the bend and returned to the lighted portion of the hallway.

"Hey!" shouted one from behind. "This one's from topside! He's wearing a blue tunic!"

The guards stopped and stared at Laméch's form in the new light.

"He must have fallen from one of the air vents!"

"I guess he's even dumber than most. I've never seen that happen before."

The man carrying him set him down on the floor.

"He's really messed up," he said. "Still bleeding pretty bad."

Someone dumped a cup of water on Laméch's face, who whimpered slightly, then stirred as if regaining consciousness.

"Get up!" someone ordered.

"Can you walk?" another demanded without the slightest hint of sympathy.

Laméch slowly began to move, groaning incessantly. Eventually he stood, demonstrating that his legs were fine. Then he suddenly collapsed again, and began weeping loudly.

"I'm so sorry," he wailed, "I didn't mean to fall!"

"Get him out of here!" a new voice ordered in disgust, and immediately a guard scooped Laméch up onto his shoulders and began to march away with him.

As they left, Laméch heard a voice comment after him.

"Not only are they idiots, they also cry like babies!"

Laméch opened his eyes and watched with a grin as the guard marched up two flights of stairs, walked along a long narrow hallway, and then arrived at a stone door.

The door slid open, and Laméch was tossed onto the ground beyond it—up on the surface. As the door slid shut, Laméch looked around and saw that he was in his "blue" slave compound, but at the far southern end. It was several hours after sunset, and the only light was from the compound towers. He looked back at the doorway and realized he had never noticed this access before, nor could he even discern it now. It blended flush into the rough granite mountainside. He also realized that it was in the darkened corner of the compound far from the tents—and near the place where his rope to the summit was hidden.

He wiped the blood from his face and began to get up, but before he did, something caught his eye.

Scratched into a portion of stone, just to the left of the hidden doorway, he saw a marking. It was faint, but unmistakable. It was the sign of the *Seed* that Aenoch had told him about. It was clearly a vertical, oblong oval which came down to a point, but this one was pointed slightly down and to the left—as if it were pointing *at* something.

He got up and looked in the direction indicated. Down and to the left he saw nothing but a patch of ground—but it looked like it may have been disturbed sometime in the past, as if something were buried there.

He began to walk towards it, but suddenly realized that he had a large audience which had gathered when he was thrown from the mountainside door. He quickly reversed his direction and smiled lamely at the group, waving them aside. He lurched towards his tent, ignoring their quizzical faces.

He cast one final look back, only to discover that the mark was invisible from his current angle—and in the compound lighting. Apparently, it could only be seen from ground level.

He staggered towards a bathing trough, stripped, and plunged in, removing the dried blood and carefully fingering his recently disfigured face. He grinned slightly (and painfully) thinking how he would have *never* considered damaging his face for *any* reason, just a few weeks earlier.

He entered his tent and collapsed on his mat with a smile. Just before he dozed off, he suddenly realized he hadn't eaten anything since the noon break, but before he could gather the energy and will-power to do something about it, he was fast asleep.

Jameth was enjoying Laméch's wounds too much.

"I *told* you," Laméch insisted, "that I was in a fight back at the compound. It was nothing."

Jameth peered in closer at Laméch's face. Laméch's arm and legs were severely scratched, as if he had been thrown against some rocks, but on his face were pronounced lacerations that were only just beginning to heal.

Jameth smiled wickedly.

"It appears," he said, "that *she* has some very large and nasty fingernails."

Laméch turned away towards the workbench, refusing to continue the conversation. Jameth laughed until he decided it was time to get to work.

"We have a new procedure today," he told Laméch, "so you must pay close attention."

Laméch nodded, and then patiently listened as Jameth explained how they were to combine the red and blue tubes into the green vial that was provided with each new delivery. Laméch was careful not to reveal that he was already aware of the additional task.

The day continued without incident, and, as soon as they were finished, Laméch rushed back to the compound.

He *had* to see the girl with the beautiful jade eyes.

She was there, waiting for him, standing about twenty paces from the fence—closer than she had ever stood in all of his previous visits. She was hiding in the shadow of one of the tents, and when Laméch saw her, she stared directly into Laméch's face, catching him completely by surprise. Her eyes snapped angrily at him and with her filthy yellow tunic and wild feral hair, Laméch was instinctively—but only temporarily—afraid.

Before he could recover or ask what was wrong, she whispered—just loud enough to be carried by the evening air.

"You did not visit last night," she accused. "I was worried."

With that simple statement, her eyes softened and she stepped back slightly, looking downward.

Laméch had no idea what to say, so he blurted out something—beginning with words that he almost never uttered.

"I'm sorry," he began, "I was detained in the complex until very late." He was amazed and somewhat angered at his sudden irrational feeling of guilt. He hadn't done anything wrong. He watched her face as her eyes lifted.

Now, surprisingly, she was crying ever so slightly.

"You have been so kind to notice me all these evenings and I have no right to presume upon you, but…"

She paused to sigh heavily, then continued.

"There is no life here."

Totally bewildered, Laméch stood there for a few moments, wondering what she meant. He was positioned behind a tree away from the guard lights. He heard some movement behind him, but it was just another slave who averted his eyes and walked past.

"You are different," she began in explanation. "Everyone here has surrendered to despair, not knowing what awaits us when we are called into the complex. I have no family or friends here."

She pointed with her chin towards the "blue" compound. Somehow it occurred to Laméch that it was a very pretty chin.

"Everyone in *your* compound ignores us as if we are already dead," she continued. "You are the only person who ever looked over here, and," she paused, "your eyes betray you."

She smiled as Laméch's heart misses a beat.

"I can see that you have been in the presence of hope, and that you somehow believe that there is a future for you somewhere beyond this place. I have never seen that in *this* place and for some reason, I am compelled to tell you that I share your belief."

Her eyes bore into his.

"There *is* a future, and I intend to see it. That is what I believe for myself, and you are the only person I have found here with whom I can share this."

She moved slightly closer.

"It is in your eyes."

Laméch was dumbfounded, but pleased with himself. However, he hoped that the wrong people had not noticed the same thing she had. He considered Aenoch's comments about those qualities that had made him uniquely qualified for this mission.

While he was still trying to determine how he should respond, she began backing away.

"I apologize for burdening you with my thoughts, but I was compelled to share them with you." She gave him a smile, which, although it was small, seemed to Laméch to be the most beautiful smile he had ever seen. The smile stopped abruptly.

"I also must tell you that if you ever miss another evening visit, I shall never forgive you."

She gave the startled Laméch one last look, and then dashed away, disappearing between the tents.

A sharp blow struck Laméch from behind as a guard's staff landed on one of his kidneys. He dropped in electrifying pain.

"Get away from the fence!" shouted the guard as he peered over Laméch's now crumpled form. As the guard threw a kick to his butt, Laméch pulled himself upward and lurched away from the fence, jumping slightly to avoid another foot that swung past his knees. He turned and ran, grinning as he made his way back to his tent.

He curled onto his mat, a cacophony of thoughts vying for attention in his mind. Who was this girl? Why did she seem so interested in him? Was there anything buried next to the stone with the mark of the Seed?

Should he start making plans for escape? How much more information should he gather about this place?

What was her name?

An alarm sounded for the evening meal, and as Laméch moved towards the trough, he made one definite decision.

Whenever Laméch eventually *did* leave this place, *she* was coming with him.

He spent the next several days dutifully assisting Jameth, exploring more of the complex, and bringing additional supplies and other items that might be useful to his camp atop the cliff. A pos-

sible idea for escape was beginning to form, and he began construction of various items that might be required.

Every evening he joyfully—*not* dutifully—went to the north-
eastern corner to see *her*. However, she never again approached the
fence as she had that night when she spoke to him, choosing instead
to resume the actions of their previous encounters. Eye contact and
a smile which promised a meeting for the next day was all she allowed. No matter how much Laméch waved or hissed through the
fence, she refused to do anything but look appreciatively into his
face and then disappear.

Laméch made a deliberate choice *not* to be upset by her actions,
but rather to appreciate and simply enjoy the uncomplicated, non-
verbal exchanges. He had to admit, reluctantly, that it was probably
best for their safety—something he normally had little regard for.

Finally, one night, he was able to make it to the south end where
the mysterious sign was marked into the mountainside. His previous attempts had been surrounded by too many onlookers, but this
time—under a moonless sky—he approached the stone alone.

On his hands and knees he eventually spotted the mark, and went
directly to the ground where it pointed. He carefully pulled at some
of the weeds and topsoil until he found loose dirt and began digging
with his hands.

Soon he had a large hole about a cubit wide and half a cubit deep.
He thrust his fingers into the dirt hoping to strike a container or box,
but felt nothing. He kept scooping dirt out with his hands until his
fingers caught on a thin root which cut into him as he jerked away.

He inspected the root and discovered it was not a root but a thin
cord. He pulled on it further, and found it was attached to a small
canvas bag which—after digging it out—he removed.

He opened the bag to discover some small stones, a tiny, rolled
up parchment, and a round glass-like object whose function he
couldn't determine in the dim light.

He reached back into the hole and dug beneath where the bag
had been. He struck something metallic, and when he had excavated
it, discovered a small metal box.

He pulled it out excitedly and found a hinged lid, which he opened.

Inside was a crystal communication device, just like the one that had been destroyed during his climb! Laméch quickly closed the lid and reburied the box, filling in all of the dirt he had removed.

He tossed the topsoil and weeds on top and tried to smooth them out to leave them looking as undisturbed as possible. He glanced around, confident that no one had seen him, and immediately climbed up to his summit camp, the bag tied securely to his leg.

Once there, he studied the contents under the clear starlight and was able to discover what the unknown object was.

Inside of the glass circle was a floating compass—with its needle pointing determinedly north.

The next morning, he watched with consternation as more "yellows" were collected and brought into the complex. He was even more dismayed when he spotted one that appeared to be *her*. In the distance—and at this twilight hour—he could not be certain, but he fretted over her throughout the day as he worked in Jameth's lab.

That evening, when he anxiously went to look for his evening smile, she was nowhere to be seen.

CHAPTER 12
RESCUE

"Despite the instability of wars, insurgencies, societal collapses, and even the occasional famine, one industry, somehow, managed to persevere through the centuries, surviving—not unscathed—but remaining viable. This was the wine industry, located by necessity in the grasslands between Irad and Jaebal.

The most famous—and costly—of these was Jaerad Wines, founded long before the Family Wars, and it continued—and even thrived—until the last days.

Since no one was willing to risk the disruption of its flow, these vineyards—and the surrounding grasslands—remained untouched, and their proprietors allowed to develop great wealth."

—Amoela the Librarian,
The First Two Thousand Years, Vol. II

ENGAGEMENT: RESCUE

The lady in the red robe knelt before the *Light of the Creator*, pondering the revelation she had just received.

This light sculpture was one of five in the complex, but she preferred to meditate at this particular one located in the lower levels, since, on occasion, *this* one spoke.

She had been deep in worship, pondering the Five Principles in her usual thoughtful manner (unlike the hysterical, emotional, and even childish outbursts of her red-smocked minions above) when the words had sounded just as she was about to contemplate the fifth principle, Transcendence.

"There is an intruder among you."

It had been unquestioningly audible, yet the sound had a strange, metallic timbre as if something not entirely human had initiated the vibrations in the air surrounding the sculpture.

She thought of the previous times that spies had trespassed into the complex. Somehow, she had always sensed their presence and informed the guards to increase their vigilance. And they had always captured the intruder, extracting information before insuring they would never see their homes again.

Such intruders fell into two categories: Those who deliberately infiltrated for purposes of sabotage or espionage and those who— through their own ignorance—were unwitting tools of the enemy. The latter usually arrived as slaves and insisted on retaining the tribal convictions of their former homes. This was becoming more common as recruits were increasingly collected from the forest peoples. They were usually harmless enough, and seldom took it upon themselves to initiate any action.

There was a tap on the stone archway of the chamber. She turned and saw her Chief of Security standing there, awaiting her response.

She rose and nodded to him.

"Please forgive the interruption," he began, "but we believe that we have been infiltrated."

She smiled slightly.

"Yes," she said. "I am aware of this."

The chief stared, slightly stunned, wondering how much she knew and if he should continue. He certainly did not wish to waste her time.

"Give me your details," she prodded to her relieved chief.

He glanced down and then back up.

"We are missing a yellow robe," he said. "The number…"

"When did this happen!?" she interrupted sharply. Any semblance of a smile had disappeared from her face.

"I'm sorry," her chief cowered, "but we are not sure. It may have been several weeks ago. We have always accurately counted the number of researchers entering and exiting the chamber above, and there have always been eighty for each shift." His voice tried to become more confident. "There have been no exceptions."

He paused, waiting for the torrent of wrath that was soon to come, but she simply nodded—with her teeth clenched—for him to continue.

"We thought," he stammered eventually, "that somehow the discrepancy happened in the washing area and that perhaps one of the slaves had destroyed a damaged robe, or somehow lost it. Certainly none left the complex," he added with forced confidence.

He paused, unsure of how to form his next words. Her imposing gaze urged him on.

"There is something else," he said slowly.

Her eyebrows lifted, daring him to continue.

"If you recall," he stammered, "the last spy we captured carried one of *their* crystal devices?"

She nodded.

"And that it was buried at the edge of the blue compound and marked to possibly trap future infiltrators?"

"*Yesss?*" she hissed slowly.

"And that we left their small bag of items to alleviate suspicions?"

"Tell me what has happened!" she ordered, losing all patience.

The guard shifted on his feet.

"The ground has been disturbed…"

"No one saw who disturbed it?" she demanded angrily, stepping towards him. "That space was to be under constant surveillance!"

"We are sorry," her chief said quickly, placing great emphasis on "we" to diffuse the blame. "The small bag of personal items was removed, but the box beneath was undisturbed." He said the last words as helpfully as possible.

She glared at him for a moment, and then made her decision.

"Determine who was in charge of watching that space and have him executed."

She glanced at him, daring him to respond. When he did not, she continued.

"And, if anyone comes near that spot again and I am not informed, then *you* will be executed. Do you understand?"

He nodded, eyes downcast.

"Yes, I understand."

Satisfied, she prepared her orders.

"Immediately search the blue compound for any signs of that bag removed from the ground, and also interrogate the slaves in that compound to see if any of them saw anything. Any slave that seems suspicious will be brought directly to me."

Her eyes glowered at him.

"It will be a shame to find that one of *them* did your job better than *you*."

He stepped back slightly, looking at the floor.

"Report back to me every hour," she commanded. "I will personally go to the research booths and see what I can determine about the missing yellow robe. If there is an infiltrator or imposter hiding there, I will discover him."

She dismissed her chief with an angry wave, and turned back to the *Light of the Creator*.

"I will find the intruder," she promised quietly.

She turned to the doorway on the far side of the chamber where the stairs led to the upper levels. She would sense out this infiltrator just as she had done before. She knew the missing robe was no accident, and it was also no accident that a spy had appeared at this critical juncture of their research.

With her heightened awareness scanning the areas before her, she headed towards the research chamber above as the illuminations from the *Light of the Creator* faded behind her.

Laméch finished backing into the research chamber wearing another stolen yellow robe, and, as before, he announced that he had forgotten something and then ran towards the booths. The same slave girl had studiously ignored him as he repeated his performance from the previous week.

She *had* to be here! Thoughts of those beautiful jade eyes and that dark, feral hair blotted out all other considerations. All day he had been sick with worry and had rushed down here as soon as he had finished his work for Jameth.

Without waiting for the entering yellow-robes to mingle with him, he began looking frantically for her. He rushed to the rows on the far right side of the chamber and began moving from one booth to the other, peering over some and flinging back the curtains on others.

In each booth he saw a single restrained subject wearing a yellow tunic, each in various levels of pain and consciousness. Occasionally, he would see a green tube resting on the small desk beside the cot, but has he searched from booth to booth, none of the subjects was her.

He passed by a large section of empty booths near the entrance doors, and began inspecting an area closer to the platform. He was now moving with the newly arrived yellow-robes as he rounded the end of a row—when he saw the lady in the red robe walking across the stage.

She moved to the front of the stage and began descending the steps down to the main floor. Judging from the reactions of the others, this was very unusual. Muted gasps were heard, and the moving mass of yellow-robes slowed as she approached.

ENGAGEMENT: RESCUE

* * *

The intruder was *definitely* in this chamber. The lady in the red robe momentarily chastised herself for not sensing it sooner, but there was no mistaking it now. The back of her mind tingled as she scanned the room, and then slowly descended towards a group of yellow-robes.

She would identify the imposter and expose him. All she had to do was point and declare the spy, and the surrounding yellow-robes would attack and slay him instantly.

She raised her left hand, palm facing towards the slowing crowd as they began to make a path for her.

Laméch watched as she passed next to one yellow-robe after the other, briefly pressing her left hand on each forehead before continuing on to the next one. As she drew near him, he saw that she also peered deeply into each set of eyes. There was no question that she was looking for someone—most certainly someone who did not belong.

He tensed as he realized he was next. He exhaled slowly and held his breath in an attempt to slow his pounding heartbeat. She turned to him as he reverently lowered his eyes. Her hand descended on his brow.

"Eyes up," she commanded so softly that Laméch wondered if anyone else had heard. He looked up into her eyes, hoping that whatever nervousness she saw would be attributed to the fact that everyone in this room was uneasy at her proximity. He tried to force a look of calm helplessness into his eyes, mixed with the assurance of someone who had the right to be in this room. She stared into his eyes for what seemed much longer than her previous encounters, and Laméch could not help but notice a deep, powerful presence in her mahogany brown eyes. For a brief moment he succumbed to them and squirmed slightly as his eyes began to lower, but he reasserted himself, forcing his eyes to return and obediently focus on hers.

Her hand lifted and she broke away from their shared gaze, and Laméch was surprised to see a tiny look of disgust flicker across her face. He quickly lowered his eyes to conceal them as his body constricted for whatever would come next.

But she simply continued on to the next person. Careful to not let his relief show in his movements, he began walking away, towards the booths near the exit door. He found his arms and stomach trembling and his knees weak. For the first time in his life, he didn't feel the "fun" that was supposed to accompany survival. And he wasn't grinning.

She was becoming increasingly perturbed as she made her way through this group of yellow-robes. She could still sense the intruder, but it was getting weaker, as if he was further away, perhaps on the other side of the room. She checked a few more, and then waved them aside. She would simply make her rounds of this chamber, moving until her sense grew stronger. She passed through two more groups of yellow-robes as she moved around the booths by the entrance doors, and then traveled to the far side, away from her platform, scanning furiously.

Laméch moved past the platform and around to the booths by the exit doors, and almost ran into a group of red-smocked techs who were just leaving the nearby booths. Laméch recognized some of them from the meeting room below.

One of them pushed Laméch rudely without saying anything, and Laméch refrained from pushing back. Then he rushed over to the booths in the direction they had just left.

He glanced over the tops of two booths, but they were empty. He pulled back the curtain on the third booth, and there, strapped to the cot, was his prize!

She was marked with a forehead tattoo and appeared sleepy or slightly drugged; but she was obviously going in and out of consciousness. He slipped in and closed the curtain behind him and immediately untied her restraints. She became fully awake and twisted in fear as she looked up at him, but he lowered his mask and peered into her eyes.

"You're coming with me," he whispered with a wink.

Her eyes widened in astonishment and she attempted to rise from the cot.

Laméch helped her up to her feet.

"Can you walk?" he asked.

She nodded confidently, and then gave him the slightest smile. His knees weakened again for a completely different reason, and he had to refocus his attention on the matter at hand.

He put her arm around his shoulder and began to exit the booth, when he saw a green tube sitting on the desk next to her cot. He quickly snatched the vial and tucked it into the waist-cord of his blue tunic, under the robe.

He glanced out past the curtain and saw the platform on his right. It was empty, and there were very few yellow-robes in sight.

The lady in the red robe was nowhere to be seen.

The lady in the red robe was passing the final booths at the far end of the chamber, still inspecting random techs, and trying desperately to get a bearing on her target.

Suddenly, the tingling in the back of her mind blossomed, and she turned sharply. The intruder was nearby! She walked swiftly towards the booths near the exit doors, inspecting each of the yellow-robes as she hurried past them.

As she rounded the row of booths, she suddenly heard yells from the direction of the platform. At the same time, her sense of the intruder diminished sharply, and she hurried past the exit doors, heading towards her stage.

With his arm around her, Laméch had dashed straight for the platform, carrying her with him at his side. She had tried to contribute to the running, but Laméch was moving too quickly, and when he arrived at the stairs, he simply lifted her with his arm and headed towards the panel.

There were shouts behind them as a few yellow-robes noticed their sprint. Laméch found the indentation and pressed it. Knowing that the panel would slam shut immediately, he pushed her through the opening as soon as the panel began to move, and then dove in after her, arriving on the other side just as it snapped closed behind them.

She was sitting in a heap on the floor, and he rushed towards her just as she was beginning to get up.

"Are you hurt?" he asked quickly as he helped her up.

She shook her head and straightened her legs beneath her.

Laméch rushed to the column where he had hidden his first stolen yellow robe and was relieved to see that it was still there. He retrieved it and handed it to her.

"Put this on," he commanded.

He turned back towards the panel. He could hear more voices yelling, and footsteps ascending the platform. He reached up for the spring that opened the door and pulled it from its mount. It came away with a loud *crack*, followed by a metallic *twang* as it compressed painfully around his fingers.

He pried his hand loose and looked for the mechanism that matched the indentation on the other side. He found it and, using the end of the spring as a hammer, he smashed the catch that would release the lock.

The panel was now locked in place with no tension available to pull it open.

He turned and saw that the object of his rescue was fully robed and masked. Her beautiful jade eyes sparkled in the dim light, fully awake.

"This way," he hissed as he led her down the ramp.

They arrived at the corridor and he immediately led her to the spiral stair beside the meeting room. They slipped into the archway unseen, and rested for a moment.

"Can you climb?" he asked, pointing to the stair.

Again she nodded confidently.

"I am perfectly well," she said, her eyes smiling. "They have done nothing to me that I know of. They have not allowed me food, and the pain from this," she pointed to her tattoo, "is great, but otherwise I am ready for whatever you have planned."

What a melodious voice! Laméch was again distracted, and had to repeat her words in his mind to recall what she had said.

He was also suddenly aware that he *had* nothing planned.

The lady in the red robe arrived at her platform to see a group of yellow-robes shouting and pointing toward the panel. She also saw one of her red-smocked techs stupidly pushing at the indentation repeatedly, trying to get the panel opened.

The yellow-robes quieted as she ascended her platform and approached her tech.

"What are you doing?" she demanded.

"Trying to get this open," he answered breathlessly. "One of the researchers took a patient and exited through this panel."

"Well *that* is obviously not working," she snapped as she pointed to the indentation. She had always been so conscious to hide this from the yellow-robes. She glared at the tech who was *still* pressing it frantically.

"Stop that!" she shouted at him as she struck him across the face. He fell backwards on the floor, looking up at her with fresh blood coming from his nose.

She continued venting her anger on him.

"Have you ever considered that there might be other ways to open a door besides pressing a button?"

She pressed her hands against the panel and attempted to slide it sideways, but it wouldn't budge. After several attempts, she determined that the catch was still engaged.

Angered—and embarrassed—she turned to the surrounding yellow-robes.

"Get this panel open!" she demanded, urging them to ascend the platform where they had always been forbidden to walk before. Soon there were several people pounding on the panel, trying to pry it loose from its track or release the catch in the back.

Eventually she heard a loud crack, and she saw the panel slowly slide back. However, after it opened partway, the closing spring—which was still intact—engaged and the door snapped shut on them.

"Stand back!" she shouted.

The assembled yellow-robes hurriedly moved away.

"Off of the platform!" she ordered, and they swiftly descended to the floor, the old prohibition firmly reinstated.

There were now three red-smocked techs on stage with her, and, at her direction, they slowly pressed the panel open with just enough space to squeeze through. One held it open from the back so that she could follow them, and as the panel snapped shut, the stunned yellow-robes surrounding the platform staring incredulously after her.

Behind the panel, the three techs descended the ramp in search of the escapees as she followed, fuming silently.

All awareness of the intruder had vanished from her mind.

"Follow me!"

Laméch led the way up the spiral stairway. He pressed up the floor panel, and slid it carefully to the side.

He stepped out and then turned back to help lift her up onto the floor. She stood in the dark hallway and attempted to straighten her crumpled yellow robe. She stared at Laméch expectantly with her wild hair sticking out from behind her facemask.

Laméch heard echoed shouts from below as the lady in the red robe ordered full inspections of each room in the corridor beneath them. He also heard stirrings from the guards at the far, lighted, end of the hallway.

Sneaking out of here was not an option.

Laméch quickly kicked the heavy stone floor panel back into place, deliberately making it resonate as loudly as possible. All sounds from below were stifled immediately. He then ran directly towards the guards, yelling at the top of his lungs.

"Help, help!" he shouted as the stunned guards saw two crazed yellow-robes bearing down upon them.

"What's wrong?" responded one guard, while another yelled, "What is happening?"

"It's a complete catastrophe!" Laméch answered, using his best panicked, out-of-breath voice. It was not a voice he normally used. He began to push past the guards, indicating that they should be running with them.

"Everything is destroyed. It's a big fire!" Laméch continued, stringing random sentences of devastation together. "I think just about everyone is dead!"

A large guard emerged from around the corner and was startled for a moment before sizing up the situation.

"You are not allowed to be on this level," he said, pointing to the two yellow-robes. He was not going to be fooled by their manufactured panic. The other guards watched, confused.

Laméch tried to push past the new arrival, but the large guard wrapped his arms around both of them.

"There's a big fire below," he tried again, choking past the guard's hold. "Something broke." This last sentence sounded lame even to his ears.

The other guards began to form around them, and Laméch

thought furiously for other ideas. The image of the red panel in Jameth's lab and what it meant came to mind.

"That's right," he said, more insistently this time. "One of those vials broke and everyone is dying!"

The guards backed away slightly, and Laméch twisted in the large one's grasp and stomped hard on the top of his foot, digging his heel in.

This softened the large guard just enough for the two to wriggle loose. They ran a few paces, and then Laméch whirled around to face them.

He was holding the green tube in his hand and waving it menacingly.

"One of these broke below, and the fires are now consuming everything!"

The guards took one look at the vial and Laméch was pleased to see small beads of sweat appear on their foreheads. Apparently they knew better than Laméch what it contained.

Laméch began to back away from the guards, moving in the direction of the surface.

"We have to get this to one of the labs," he said as the thought occurred to him. They backed away a few more steps, then turned to run.

"I don't care what they say," shouted the large guard. "They still don't belong on this level. Get them!" he ordered, pointing.

Laméch and his weakened companion began running and the guards began following—with reservations. However, their concerns began to fade, and soon they were chasing full speed after them.

Suddenly, Laméch turned to face them holding the green vial high above his head. The guards slowed, ignoring the urgings of the large one, until they finally stopped about thirty paces from them.

Laméch launched the vial from his hands, careful to make sure it landed directly at their feet. It smashed on the floor in front of them, allowing the liquid within to spray up into a thin cloud, splattering their clothing, hands, and eyes.

With yells, all of the guards (including the large one) placed their arms over their noses and mouths as they rushed away in the opposite direction—away from Laméch.

"Cover your mouth," Laméch ordered, even though they were both still wearing their yellow facemasks. He grabbed her arm and they continued as fast as possible along the corridor.

They rushed up the two stairways where Laméch had been carried a week earlier. This time, however, Laméch had to half-carry his feral-haired beauty who was obviously very hungry and on the brink of exhaustion. They headed down the long narrow hallway towards the stone doorway that led outside, but just before they exited, Laméch spotted a small room to the right.

"In here," he whispered.

They stepped through the archway and saw that it was nothing more than a maintenance closet. Laméch let her rest against the wall as he removed their facemasks.

"Let's get rid of these robes here," he said finally, removing his to reveal the blue slave tunic beneath. He then helped her out of her robe and was suddenly very conscious that they were closer together than they had ever been before. In the almost total darkness, her body heat created an outline which confirmed to Laméch that she was even more beautiful up close.

He resisted all of the obvious natural urges, telling himself there would be time for that later.

"Let's go," he said with a quick shake of his head.

They exited the closet and crossed over to the doorway, which opened as Laméch applied pressure. Obviously, the door was designed to only prevent access from the *outside*.

They emerged in the relative light of the blue compound, which was actually under a clear, starry sky.

But the place was in chaos.

Shouts from the distant tents carried in the night air as swarms of guards tore through the compound, apparently engaged in searches and interrogations.

However, this meant that no one was looking their way, so they stepped out into the dark edges of the camp unseen.

Laméch headed for the patch of ground where the communication device was buried, and when he arrived, he knelt down and began digging.

"What are you doing?" she asked, slightly confused.

"This is something we may need," he said quietly.

Suddenly, a large wooden staff descended through the air, plunging into the dirt, barley missing Laméch's fingers. He heard it crunch into the buried box as a deep voice spoke from overhead.

"I've been waiting for you!"

After inspecting the corridor below and ascending the spiral staircase, the Chief of Security came upon the dead guards. He pulled back quickly, covering his face with his right forearm.

What else could go wrong today?

He hurried back down the staircase, determined to find another route. He had spent his entire day looking for signs of the intruder.

Unfortunately, the only proof he had found was the subject that had been stolen, in spite of his best efforts.

And now, guards who appeared to have expired while writhing in painful convulsions.

What was he going to tell *her*?

The guard stood over Laméch grinning gleefully, his hand firmly grasping the staff which had just landed, destroying the box beneath them.

What Laméch did *not* know was that the guard's life had just been spared by his discovery, since he had been assigned to this piece of ground and was due for execution that night if the intruder was not found.

The guard's reprieve was only temporary as Laméch grabbed the staff with both hands, pulled himself upward with his arms, and then lifted his entire body from the ground—including his legs and feet. The guard began to fall as the staff suddenly acquired Laméch's weight, and Laméch swung his right leg up and planted his heel directly into the guard's chin, spinning his head.

The guard's neck snapped instantly and his head tipped over at an impossible angle, dangling to the side—the grin still in place.

The guard—and the staff—fell on Laméch, pinning him painfully on his back and right hip.

He pushed the dead guard off of himself and looked around without getting up. He saw that the bedlam in the compound was still running unabated, and that the extinguishing of the guard had gone without notice. Apparently, this spot was this guard's responsibility, and did not warrant anyone else's concern.

He ignored the jade eyes which were watching in widened disbelief and went back to the hole and retrieved the damaged box.

But the device was completely destroyed.

Four months ago he would have said that such devices were impossible. Now he had witnessed the destruction of two of them, and never once had enjoyed the opportunity to use one.

He shrugged and stood to his feet.

She was still staring at him, but now spoke impatiently.

"Whatever you intend to do, you had better do it quickly. We won't remain unnoticed for much longer."

He nodded, wincing at her sudden pragmatism. He also realized that, in a compound of slaves wearing blue tunics, she was wearing yellow with no chance of hiding or blending in.

He grabbed her arm with a slight tug.

"This way," he said with as much confidence as he could muster.

He led her to the southern end of the compound where his rope was hidden in the dark crevice leading to his summit camp. He heard shouts in the distance from one of the tents where another group of guards had entered to continue their search and interrogations.

"We must climb here," Laméch announced when they arrived.

She glanced at the mountainside and looked back with fear and disbelief.

"You must go first so I can help you," Laméch continued, deliberately ignoring her.

"You are truly insane," she stated simply, her eyes raised but tired. She began to look around as if desperately trying to discover a better plan of her own. Laméch saw a wave of exhaustion come over her face, and he suddenly remembered that she had not eaten and might still be fighting the effects of being drugged.

"Don't worry," Laméch said quickly, placing as much compassion as possible into his voice. "You only have to climb about ten cubits. There is a rope there which is fastened to my camp at the top."

Her eyes calmed, and she gave Laméch a look which he pretended was one of admiration.

"I will guide you to the rope, and when you've found it, I will fasten it securely to your waist."

He waited for her to nod, and then continued.

"I will climb to my camp while you rest, and then pull you up."

He smiled and pointed.

"The rope is hidden in the crevice, up to the right. I'll guide you as you get closer."

She looked into his eyes, shook her head, and turned towards the mountainside. She reached for a handhold, placed her foot on a rock outcropping and made her first move.

Laméch supported her, and began pushing her up for her next step. He began his own climb, partially lifting her until she was above him.

"Rest one foot on my shoulder if you need to," he offered. "As I climb, you'll be able to push yourself further."

They continued as she scrambled for new handholds. Laméch could hear her breathing become more and more labored.

"You're almost there," he encouraged. "It's just above your right hand."

He adjusted his footing as her weight shifted on his shoulder.

"You'll have to go slightly past the rope so we can wrap it around you."

He heard a scream from the compound as someone failed to give the desired answer.

"I've got it!" she declared with a whisper. After a few more upward shoves, he decided they could stop.

"Get your feet on a good ledge," he instructed. He felt her foot leave his shoulder, and he guided it to a large crevice.

"Just rest there," he said.

As she clung to the mountainside, he climbed over to the rope and carried it to her, but as he brought it close to her, he realized it was going to be too short to wrap around her waist.

"I'm sorry," he said. "We'll have to climb a few more steps."

She emitted a slight groan, but managed to joke, "Thanks for the rest," before pushing upward.

"That's good," said Laméch after they had traveled another two cubits. He made sure her handholds and footholds were secure, and then slipped the end of the rope around her waist. He fastened it with a special knot that didn't allow the loop to slip, and then climbed up along side of her.

"I'm sorry," he said. "There are more comfortable ways of tying a rope around you, but we can't do that in mid climb."

She smiled weakly at him.

Laméch pointed to the rope as it passed near her right hand.

"Go ahead and grab the rope," he said, as he supported her.

With a quick, desperate move she released her hand and clamped down on the rope.

"Just lean back," he continued, "and let the rope support you."

Laméch watched as she slowly obeyed, and then saw a look of relief fill her eyes as she no longer had to support her own weight.

She smiled again.

"Keep your foothold secure and rest here until I begin to pull the rope up. You'll still have to climb slightly to keep from striking the mountainside, but the hard part is over."

He flashed her a big grin, and then proceeded to scale the remaining fifty cubits to his camp, staying far to her right to make sure that any dislodged rocks would not strike her.

She watched him patiently travel upward as she clung to the rocks until her neck began to hurt. She tipped her head down and glanced out over the compound where she saw a group of blue tunics being lined up at the complex entrance.

"*Ready?*"

"*Yes,*" she whispered back.

The rope began to rise, and she let it carry her up as she pushed away from the mountainside to avoid the rough outcroppings.

As she approached the summit, the angle of the rope became too abrupt as it passed over the edge into Laméch's hands.

"You'll have to climb the last few steps," he said.

She grabbed hold with her feet and pushed upward to clear the summit. There was a final terrifying moment as she tipped forward with her unsupported legs dangling out over the edge, but Laméch pulled her in as she scrambled onto the narrow plateau of the summit, and soon she was resting securely on her hands and knees.

Laméch lifted her to her feet, released the rope from around her waist, and led her over to a blanket which he had prepared for her. She collapsed into it, closing her eyes and allowing the remaining air to escape from her lungs.

Laméch watched her for several moments until he wondered if she had fallen asleep. But she suddenly stirred and lifted herself up on her left elbow.

"I'm certain that you have something to eat up here," she said with her eyebrows raised. Although there was a smile in her eyes, it was not a question.

Laméch quickly went to his supplies and returned with dried fruits and a small bag of nuts along with a skin of water.

She ate the offered food slowly, and then took a long drink from the skin. When she had finished, she passed the skin back to him.

"How did you find me?" she asked, but before he could answer she followed with another question.

"What made you come and look for me?"

Her lovely jade eyes pierced through the darkness, lit by the sharp sparkles of the gleaming stars overhead.

ENGAGEMENT: RESCUE

He looked past her in the direction of the compound where the noise was finally abating. A glowing moon was rising, bathing the slave compounds and the surrounding mountains with its brilliant pinkish-blue light. It back-lit her feral hair creating a beautiful aura which served only to darken her eyes and enhance the glistening within them.

"Well," Laméch began awkwardly. "You weren't there when I came to visit so I had to find out why."

He looked into her eyes with increasing confidence.

"Your smiles are important to me," he continued, "and if I am to be deprived, I demand a good explanation."

She tipped her head upward and smiled broadly. Laméch's stomach lurched in absolute appreciation.

"Well," she said eventually, "I truly thank you. I don't know what they were planning for me—or for us—but I am forever grateful that you came for me."

She turned back to her blanket and began to lean back.

"I believe I will get some sleep now," she said calmly. "I'm certain that you have a great deal of work to do for the next stage of your plan."

She lay down and turned on her right side facing him.

"We can't live up here together forever."

She closed her eyes and soon collapsed into a deep sleep.

Laméch watched her silently in the moonlight as he contemplated his next step. He had hoped to use the device to contact someone—if he was ever close enough to a Power House—and then wait until help arrived. But that was based on stockpiling a great deal more supplies and the ability to move in and out of the complex.

And traveling alone.

This rescue had changed all of that and rushed his timetable. Now they had barely enough supplies for a day or two—and no option of returning to the complex below.

However, these concerns were surpassed in his mind by something much more important which overshadowed everything else regarding their current situation.

Her last sentence—uttered by that beautiful hushed voice—had been a pragmatic observation of concern, but the only thing his distracted emotions had heard was *"live...together forever."*

And he still did not know her name.

The Chief of Security did not enjoy giving the lady in the red robe bad news. He enjoyed, even less, her response.

"Destroyed?" she yelled at him. He had just explained how the crystal device had been found, destroyed and uncovered—and also how the guard responsible for securing that spot had been found dead, his neck broken.

"You fool!" she glared at her chief. "This is how you train your guards? That captured device was buried purposefully so that a future intruder might discover it and we could learn its function."

Her chief swallowed nervously, but was silently astonished at the admission that the Semyaz did not know the purpose of that strange device.

"You were ordered to capture anyone who disturbed that spot, but because of your guard's impulsive and brutish behavior, it is now destroyed."

Her eyes bore into the chief as he wondered what would happen next. He certainly would have given anything to be someplace else.

"I assume," she continued coldly, "that you have some good news about this intruder? Is he captured or dead?"

She stared at him from under her furrowed brow, daring him to respond with a third option.

His eyes dipped down as he slowly stammered a response.

"I am sorry," he began, "but we can find no sign of the intruder—or of the subject who left with him."

Before she could respond with more fury, he pushed forward, looking back up at her.

"We *did* find two yellow robes in a maintenance closet near the exit by the device," he said helpfully. "Apparently they surprised the guard when they exited..."

"...And destroyed their own device?" she completed his sentence with an exasperated question.

She pointed to the archway where he had entered.

"Get out of here," she said in a soft, terse voice which meant that his execution was stayed for the moment. "The intruder and that subject must be someplace, hiding in one of the compounds or cowering someplace here in the complex. There is no place for them to go, and they must find food or assistance eventually."

She rose and turned abruptly away from her chief, indicating that this audience was ended. However, in her rage, she forgot the order she had just given him and strode out of the room through the opposite archway and into the corridor beyond, leaving her chief both bewildered and relieved—relieved that he had not been forced to tell her (yet) of the dead guards found in convulsions in the hallway above the meeting room.

She knew it was hopeless, however. Somehow the intruder had vanished, taking with him one of their valuable subjects. She would have to inquire as to which subject it was, and what stage or status that subject represented in their research.

She arrived at the *Light of the Creator* in the lowest level and knelt carefully in front of the light sculpture.

After several moments of silence, she spoke slowly.

"We have lost the intruder," she said simply with no attempt to sound remorseful or apologetic. Any attempt to engender sympathy or forgiveness from the Semyaz was a fruitless endeavor.

"I *know* I sensed him in the research chamber," she continued quietly, now speaking mostly to herself. "Somehow he disappeared with one of our subjects. The guards are still searching for him, but I am quite certain that they will find no one."

Her final words tapered into a whisper. She knew better than to expect any response from the *Light of the Creator*, but one came anyway.

"*The intruder was female.*"

CHAPTER 13
SURVIVAL

*"The floating forests provide the world with several
important environmental benefits, including a traveling
source of transpiration across the large spans of otherwise arid oceans. Of greater interest, though, are the
strange and numerous life forms which exist on these
islands which are never found on the fixed continent.
In addition, the unusual hollow constructs of the plant
stems and roots are perfectly designed for a mobile ter-
rain that must be knit securely together, but which cannot bear great weight."*

—Amoela the Librarian,
<u>The First Two Thousand Years, Vol. II</u>

"I am called Keziah."

The sun was bathing the mountaintop with mid-morning light
and she had awakened to discover Laméch watching her sleep.

She smiled and continued her announcement.

"Since I have entrusted my life to you, I must now entrust my
name."

She spoke in a clear, relaxed voice that Laméch had never heard. In the compounds—and while on the run—she had only spoken in subdued tones, denying Laméch the full richness of her voice. She also spoke with a strange accent that struck Laméch as beautiful and exotic.

Laméch eventually found his own tongue.

"My name is Laméch," he said, "and I am from the city of Matusalé. I came here to learn more about the Semyaz."

She rose slightly from her blanket and pressed her hands together, her eyebrows raised in appreciation.

"I am honored to meet you, Laméch," she said politely, but her eyes registered the slightest surprise at the mention of his city's name.

She sat up and looked around.

"So," she said eventually, "what is your plan for today?"

During the night, Laméch had decided on their next course of action, but was still unsure of how he was going to convince her.

Instead of answering her question, he said, "I have some preparations to complete," as he pointed towards his collection of items that he had acquired from below. "When you are ready for the day, I will let you know what will happen next."

He nodded towards a large boulder where she could find some privacy, and she rose. Laméch watched with admiration as she disappeared behind the rock.

He turned towards his collection and shook his head. His plan *had* been to construct a rudimentary man-kite, fly out to the floating island which was still barely visible from his summit, and then somehow construct a craft which he could use to find a shipping lane and return to civilization. He hadn't worked out any details.

Now, because of her rescue, he had run out of time.

His man-kite was almost finished, but it would never carry two people the distance to the island. At best, it would support them long enough to prevent a deadly plunge into the rocky ocean below.

The mountaintop was barren with no plants and no wood that could be used for floatation. Even if they made it safely into the ocean, they would need a raft of some kind. Even *he* could not swim the distance to the island—so there was no way that Keziah could in her weakened condition.

And they had to leave now. After today, their only source of food would be on that island, unless they returned to the complex below—which was definitely *not* an option.

Keziah emerged from behind the boulder, her face—and even her hair—somehow clean and inexplicably tidy. Even her yellow tunic was straightened and she smiled as she walked confidently along the mountaintop towards Laméch.

"So, where are we going?" she asked casually when she reached him.

Laméch was fastening the last section of tent tarp to his kite frame with a piece of rope. He looked up and pointed to the floating island in the distance with a relaxed smile.

"We're going there," he said, cautiously watching her reaction.

She glanced out to the sea, following his finger, and then looked back at Laméch.

"I see," she said calmly. "And how do we get there?"

Laméch lifted the edge of the kite.

"With this," he answered, just as calmly. "This will support us in the air—just like a bird's wing—and lift us over the water. Of course, it won't take…"

"You are truly insane," she interrupted him with a nod, repeating her words from the previous night. Her voice was still calm, but it now carried the weight of conviction.

"Just as insane as last night?" Laméch countered with a cockiness that was hopefully not too forced.

She tipped her head, daring him to continue.

"As I was saying," Laméch said eventually, "this won't take us all the way to the island. It was built for one." He shrugged at the admission. "However, we have these."

He pointed to four clay jars from his collection. Lids were securely covering their openings and sealed with resin.

"We will attach these containers to ourselves—one will be

fastened to our chests with ropes, and the other will be secured to our abdomens. They will provide flotation when we reach the water."

Keziah's eyes widened in panicked disbelief, but Laméch ignored her and continued.

"This man-kite will be ready shortly. Let's eat as much of our supplies as we can and I'll complete the preparations."

She continued to stare at him with shock, but eventually managed a question.

"Will this succeed?"

Laméch smiled at her, trying to convey confidence.

"This is what I do," he said, grinning with badly concealed arrogance. "Let's eat."

He brought out jars which contained dried fruits and nuts and offered them to Keziah. Soon they were sitting on the ground, using as much of his reserves as they could hold. It was going to be a shame to leave all of his carefully collected plunder behind.

He left her to finish her meal as he made the final preparations on his kite. It was a simple triangle, and it had been difficult fashioning a frame. Eventually he had managed to use portions from the tent supports in the compound below and spliced them together. Using resin, pieces of rope, and sections of tarp he had hoped he could manufacture something that would take him to the island.

However, it was nowhere near ready to accomplish this. But the objective had changed. Now he only needed something that would lower the two of them safely into the water.

Keziah finished eating and approached him.

"I am ready," she said simply. Laméch was again distracted by her lovely jade eyes, especially now that there was a glimmer of trust in them.

Laméch blinked to regain his focus and led her to the kite. He tied one of the jars to her abdomen, running the cords around her hips and ribs. The second one was fastened to her chest with the ropes wrapped under her arms and over her shoulders, fastened in between her shoulder blades. He then held his containers in place as she fastened them (awkwardly—since her containers were in her way) to his torso.

Soon they were ready, standing side by side each with two clay jars fastened to them.

Laméch lifted the edge of the man-kite and allowed the gentle winds that blew from off of the ocean and up the cliffs to lift it and fill both sides with air.

"Hang on to this crossbeam" he instructed. "We must be next to each other as close to the center as possible."

Keziah reached for the beam, fastened her hands around it, and closed her eyes. Laméch repositioned her hands, and then clasped the beam placing his hands next to hers on her right. The incoming breeze tugged at the kite.

"Now we'll walk to the edge of the cliff and wait for the breeze to fill the kite. At the right moment, I'll say 'Now!', and we *must* lean forward and leap from the cliff together."

Her eyes snapped open and the reality of their endeavor set in.

Laméch smiled at her.

"We just want to move slowly towards the ocean. This is no different than a flower petal or a leaf from a tree floating gently to the ground."

Keziah rolled her eyes before closing them again.

"I'm ready," she said resignedly.

"Good," said Laméch. "As we travel, I may be kicking and swinging around to control the descent, but all you have to do is hang on." He knew he would have to maneuver the angle of the kite to make sure that it didn't pitch forward—or backward—and thereby lose the envelope of air. If that happened they would plummet directly into the water—and the jagged rocks below.

They stood facing the sea as the wind tugged at the kite. Laméch leaned into the wind and at the proper moment, said, "…and, *now!*"

Laméch pushed off with his toes and was pleased to discover that Keziah (with her eyes closed) had done the exact same thing. It was a perfect launch, and soon the wind traveling under his kite wing was propelling them forward and out over the ocean.

Keziah opened her eyes as she discovered they were not falling to their deaths. She laughed loudly, providing Laméch with a swell of confidence—and a great potential for distraction.

"So *this* is what you do," she shouted into his ear.

Laméch could only nod.

Suddenly he felt the front end of the kite drop slightly and he kicked his legs backwards to tip the front end up and collect more air.

The kite stabilized, but it was clear that they were falling rapidly. Any dream that it *might* reach the island was immediately extinguished, but their rate of descent would still land them safely in the water.

A flock of unknown birds that lived in the cliff rocks behind them flew out to the intruders, but kept their distance.

As they descended, Laméch watched as the floating island disappeared behind the horizon. He quickly glanced at the sun to make sure he wouldn't lose his bearings and the two continued to float towards the surface.

Suddenly Keziah began convulsing, and as Laméch turned to look at her, he saw that she was losing her entire morning meal into the water below.

As she twisted away from embarrassment, the kite twisted with her. Laméch watched in dismay as the wing on her side collapsed.

The kite tipped violently to the left, and Laméch moved to the right of the crossbeam, trying desperately to jerk the left wing upwards to regain its lift.

But the kite began turning to the left like a cart whose left wheel will not move. Soon it was spinning slowly as it dropped, faster and faster towards the water.

"Slide over to me!" Laméch shouted.

Keziah began to walk her hands along the crossbeam until she was next to Laméch. With the center of gravity now under the wing which still contained a full envelope, the kite began to stabilize.

Although their spinning didn't stop, their rate of descent slowed. Laméch watched as the water drew closer and closer. They lost all sense of direction as the kite—which was now no more than a

sheet—spun faster and faster until they eventually plunged forcefully—but harmlessly—into the water.

The kite settled around them and Laméch quickly tore it away,
leaving them bobbing facedown on their stomachs, clasping the
clay jars with their arms as they grasped their new situation.

The impact had caused the jars to bruise Laméch in the ribs
and smack him in the chin. He was sure that Keziah had fared
similarly, and he was relieved to look over at her and see her
smiling!

"We made it!" she shouted over to him.

Laméch's grin turned into a large laugh.

"That's what I do!" he boasted.

They adjusted to their new floats as Laméch looked up at the
sun and tried to determine which way they should swim.

"I'm sorry I became sick," Keziah said, "I was suddenly so
dizzy. I had never experienced anything like that before."

"Don't worry about it," said Laméch. "Let's just make it to
that island and hope we can find something to eat there."

He looked around to find the cliffs, then looked at the sun's
position in the sky.

"The island is in that direction," he said, pointing to the
southwest.

He looked over at Keziah whose hair had been straightened
by the water and was now dripping, fully lengthened, over her
lovely dark face.

"All you have to do is rest on those jars and kick your legs.
We'll get there eventually and we can rest whenever you need."

She nodded and turned in the direction indicated. Together
they began the long swim as they slowly kicked their way through
the water.

A thought suddenly occurred to him.

"These jars are designed to withstand water," he said, "but I
just realized that the resin which seals the lids might dissolve."

Keziah tipped her head towards him quizzically.

"You may need to hold down on those lids to make sure they

stay tight," he continued. "Otherwise, if water leaks in, those jars will help you sink rather than float."

She nodded with a smile—such a pretty smile—and they continued on their way.

Laméch's brief life at the Semyaz complex was over—and he knew nothing of Keziah's life before now. But together, the two of them propelled themselves across the open sea and away from their former lives. The cliffs of the Haermon Mountains could still be seen behind them, but somehow they were not nearly as daunting as when he had seen them for the first time, looming larger and larger at his approach several weeks earlier.

He now knew more about the Semyaz than ever before—but was less convinced of his own opinions about them. All he knew was that he had rescued a beautiful woman, and that he had a great deal of information to give Aenoch—if he ever saw him again.

After an hour and a half of slow kicking, the bobbing treetops of the floating island came into view.

Laméch was relieved, because, although he could never admit it, his legs were extremely tired and beginning to seize up. He was not used to such prolonged exertion. Amazingly, Keziah seemed to be slicing through the water effortlessly, her legs maintaining the same rhythm as when they first started.

Eventually the island coast became visible, and Laméch was not surprised to see the same wall of roots and dirt covered with vines that he had seen on Aenoch's Island rising up above the ocean's surface.

Upon seeing the island, Keziah suddenly increased her speed, and was soon resting in the shadow of the towering coastline, holding on to a large vine.

Laméch painfully increased his own speed, but his legs finally cramped just before reaching the island. He paddled furiously with his hands until he was able to reach for an overhanging root and pull himself in to rest. He pulled next to Keziah and grinned at her. She grinned back.

"I didn't think you were going to make it," she said with a cruel glint in her eyes.

Laméch ignored her.

"We can rest here for a while," he said, taking charge again. He looked up at the island's border which rose about twenty cubits. It would be an easy climb, but he wanted to have the full use of his legs before he began.

Keziah began removing her clay jars.

"Don't discard those," Laméch warned. "We'll shift them around and fasten them to our backs."

She gave him a look that said, *I think we should throw them into the sea.*

He gave her a look that said, *Trust me.*

Eventually they rearranged the jars to hang from their backs, and Laméch was ready to begin their ascent.

Slowly they tugged at the various roots and vines while sticking their toes into the soft sod-like material for footholds. Eventually they arrived at the top and pulled themselves over onto the spongy surface.

They moved away from the edge and looked across the undulating landscape. It was covered with the greenest grasses Laméch had ever seen. Tall narrow trees, which seemed to be scattered randomly, poked up into the sky, creating unusual shifting shadows on the ground in front of them.

They began walking carefully through the grasses, their feet constantly feeling as if they were going to break through the spongy surface and plunge into the waters beneath the island. Soon, as their confidence grew, they walked faster, and Laméch had the sudden thought that, if he were forced to spend the rest of his life on this beautiful island alone with Keziah, that would be fine with him.

He pointed to an area off to the right where there appeared to be a clearing with no trees. They turned and walked in that direction until they arrived at a large sloping depression which descended into a small lake. Laméch studied the angles of the depression and realized that the lake's surface matched the sea levels surrounding the island.

This was not a lake, but rather an opening that revealed the ocean beneath them.

"Let's not get too close," he advised. He did not want to fall through the thin turf which certainly surrounded that lake.

Keziah nodded and began removing the jars from her back, and Laméch followed her lead.

The grasses around the depression were much shorter, and soon they had trampled down an area which would suffice as a campsite.

Laméch reached for one of the jars.

"This is why we kept the jars," he said dramatically. He grabbed the lid and began to pry it off of the opening. Unfortunately, the resin held better than he expected and, no matter how hard he pulled, the lid would not budge. He tugged a few more times ignoring Keziah's suppressed laughter.

Finally, in desperation, he grabbed a second jar and smashed the two together, breaking both of them.

Amidst the shards which fell to the ground were dried fruits and berries, chopped roots, and assorted nuts.

Laméch looked up triumphantly.

"You didn't think I'd bring you here to starve, did you?"

Keziah laughed softly with a shake of her head. She reached forward and helped herself to some dried fruit, picking through the pieces of broken ceramic.

Laméch broke open the remaining two jars, revealing the traveling clothes that he had worn on his journey to the cliffs and the small bag that contained the compass.

He grinned as he displayed his resourcefulness, but as the glow of these revelations began to fade, Laméch slowly started to realize his actual predicament.

He had no other source for food, no idea where he was, and no way of leaving. As pleasant as the prospect of being alone on an island with Keziah sounded, he *did* want to return home someday, but for the moment, he had to grudgingly admit that they were stranded.

Keziah was watching his face, and when he turned to meet her eyes, they were full of concern.

"Have you ever lived *outside* of a city?" she asked carefully.

"Of course," Laméch exaggerated as he deliberately misunderstood her. "I used to leave the city often. Most of the people I know would never exit the gates, but I went out into the forests all of the time."

He grinned, hoping Keziah would be impressed.

But her look of concern never changed.

"Laméch," she said softly, "I have never lived *inside* of a city. In fact, I have never *been* inside of a city."

He looked at her in disbelief.

"No one lives outside the cities," he said, almost scornfully.

She shook her head.

"Actually," she said, "There are more people who live in the forest regions than in all of the cities in the world. My family lives among the refugees of Irad that fled during the Family Wars and settled far to the west of that city. There are thousands of us—and thousands of similar communities that were founded by refugees of those wars."

She nodded in confirmation and continued.

"I do not know much about the world of cities since those wars, but I am quite certain that their populations have not surpassed ours. In fact, I have never heard of your city, the one you called Matusalé, but I am sure there are not many more than those prior to the wars."

Laméch sat stunned as he listened to a description of the world which was unbelievably contrary to his own.

"Well," he countered eventually, "If you don't know about the latest cities, you may be wrong. There are nine major walled cities which are powered and two others which will be soon."

"You are certainly correct," she said quickly. "I can't know for sure. I only know of the seven walled cities from the time of the Family Wars."

Laméch nodded at her concession, but she continued.

"What I do know, is that you have no idea how to survive outside of the cities, which provide your food and shelter for you. I do not mean to be unkind, but if we are to survive in this place, we must establish some rules."

She looked at the incredulous Laméch before continuing.

"We will soon be eating the food that is available on this island, and you are not to eat a single fruit or berry before showing it to me. Some are very deadly."

She paused to allow her last words to sink in.

"If you hear anything moving in the brush or grasses, you will cease all movement immediately."

Laméch nodded dumbly.

"And finally," she said with confidence, "the only items that are *always* safe to eat are eggs. Any bird or reptile egg you find can be cooked or eaten raw."

She looked at him sternly.

"Just don't let any mother catch you stealing her eggs," she said with probably more fear-inducement than she intended.

She smiled suddenly and pointed to Laméch.

"You saved my life," she said thankfully, "and I only wish to return that favor."

The smile disappeared.

"But I can only do so if you follow my instructions and allow me to teach you."

Laméch nodded. He had never accepted instructions from anyone, and was not used to the concept. However, he had to submit to her expertise and he had to admit that he appreciated it, although he was slightly confused as his role of rescuer was quickly vanishing.

"Our first task is to collect materials for a fire," Keziah continued with her instructions. "We will go back into the forested area and find small twigs and underbrush. We will then bring them back here so they can dry. We will build the fire as the sun sets."

She headed back into the trees and high grasses, and Laméch rose to follow her.

He was falling in love.

They returned to their spot overlooking the lake carrying some small branches, twigs, and some underbrush.

Keziah had found some melons which she declared to be safe. She explained that they would probably be their only source of water for now, since they could not safely approach the lake, and the only other source of water was twenty cubits below off the sides of the island.

They finished enjoying the melons and then Keziah began the task of preparing a fire. Laméch watched for a while as she cleared a space and separated twigs from kindling, but soon his mind wandered as he stared out over the lake and the strange moving landscape behind it.

The Haermon Mountains were nowhere to be seen, and it was easy to pretend that the experiments and atrocities that were happening behind those cliffs were a distant fiction.

A movement in the lake brought him back to reality, and he watched as several small creatures leapt out of the water and dove back in. It seemed to be a small school of strange, orange-gray fish which were moving slowly towards the edge of the lake in front of them.

He watched as their leaps brought them closer to shore, but was shocked when their final jump carried them through the air to land in the damp grasses just beyond the water's edge. Soon a pile of forty or fifty fish were squirming and disentangling themselves from each other, sliding off each other's backs until there was a single layer of fish arranged at the shoreline.

Laméch hissed at Keziah and pointed. Her eyes opened in amazement, showing him that this was something new for her as well.

And then it happened. Something that Laméch would remember

the rest of his life. The fish began walking up the embankment, apparently supported on two sets of unexpectedly strong fins. They marched up the rise, flattening the short grasses as they traveled. Eventually, the school reached the two astonished observers, passing them on the right as they headed into the taller grasses and disappeared into the trees.

The two looked at each other wordlessly for a few moments until Laméch broke the silence.

"You have never seen anything like this?" he asked.

Keziah shook her head.

"No, I have not," she said. "But everything is different on this island."

"What do you mean?" Laméch asked.

"I have lived in the wild my entire life, but I have never seen the kinds of trees and plants which are on this island."

Laméch nodded for her to continue.

"The wood is very different," she said. "It is much lighter, and so many of the plant branches and stems are hollow."

She raised her eyebrows.

"And now we see walking fish." She paused before exhaling. "It appears that the life here has been specifically designed for the floating islands. It is lighter, and apparently even the fish are able to enjoy it."

Laméch thought carefully before responding.

"I was on a floating island once before and saw similar plants," he said, nodding in agreement—as if he too were an expert on wildlife. "However, I did not see any walking fish there."

He smiled at her with a wink.

However, she had returned to her fire preparation and appeared to be frustrated.

"How is the fire coming?" he asked. "Do you need anything else?"

She spread out some more twigs before answering.

"I think we will have to do without a fire," she said eventually. "Everything here is too damp, and the hollow and porous nature of these branches makes it impossible to dry."

She looked up at him.

"Also, I am used to using a flint or phosphorus minerals to start the flame, but there simply are no rocks on this island."

A look of irritated anger flashed over her face.

"Of course, there are many other ways to start a fire," she said, "but I can't do it when the kindling is this damp."

She smiled in defeat.

"We'll have to continue eating raw for a few days, until I can figure out how to dry this," she said, pointing to her work. "But if the morning dews are as heavy as they are on the continent—and I would guess that they are probably worse—I think we'll be living on fruits and roots for a while."

She shrugged.

Laméch moved to sit down next to her.

"Don't worry," he said, trying to sound as optimistic as possible. "We'll be fine."

But he failed as his tone betrayed his lack of confidence and sounded hollow and worried instead.

Her eyes snapped as she looked into his face with a strange combination of exasperation and confusion.

"Of course, we will!" she spoke sharply. "You certainly didn't come all of this way, infiltrate the Semyaz Compound, learn whatever you have learned, and then escape based solely on a whim or a slight chance that you might succeed."

Before Laméch could respond, she continued, although her voice had become caring and earnest.

"You obviously have a very important mission, and have been sent to accomplish a great task in the war to rid the world of these monsters. Never imply, whether in word or deed, that you might *not* be successful."

Laméch watched her, stunned, as he waited for her eyes to soften.

They did not.

Eventually, he found his voice.

"I promise," he began, and then stopped. "Yes, I was sent here, and I do believe that this is an important mission." He paused. "I'm not sure if that mission is to destroy the Semyaz, or to simply learn their secrets, but ... I promise *not* to imply that failure is a possibility again."

He grinned at her and was eventually rewarded with a returned smile.

She moved to sit closer to him on his left, and the two stared out over the lake for several minutes.

After a while, Keziah picked up a long stick, and began scratching casually in the ground in front of them. Laméch watched as she began carve out a line in the dirt beneath the short grass. She began as far as the stick would reach and slowly drew a large half-circle which curved to the left until it came towards her. Laméch's pulse jumped as he began to suspect what she was doing. His fear was confirmed as she suddenly angled her line, bringing it to a point in front of them.

It was the sign of the Seed!

Aenoch had shown him this sign in case of danger, but Laméch knew that it was reserved only for those who believed as Aenoch did.

She dropped her stick nonchalantly as she looked away into the distance, deliberately giving the impression that she had made the mark absentmindedly.

Feeling like there was a fist in his stomach, Laméch picked up the stick, deliberately forcing any reasons why he should *not* do this from his mind. He raised it in front of him, placed it on the spot where she had begun her line, slowly scratched out the right half of the half-circle, and then carefully angled it inward to complete the seed.

He dropped the stick next to him, also placing his gaze in the distance

Silently, Keziah moved next to him, resting her head on his shoulder.

"There is *always* a plan," she said softly. "We must wait to see how it unfolds."

A second fist struck his stomach as he reeled in his lie. For the first time in his life, instead of enjoying his deception, he felt a powerful wave of guilt.

However, he pushed it aside as he thrilled at her sudden nearness, and together they looked out over *their* lake as darkness spread across the night sky. It was important that she trust him, he reasoned, and at least now she knew that he was on her side. But deep within was the dread of how she would respond when she discovered his deceit.

Soon the constellations were blazing above them, and they watched as various small nocturnal creatures flew around overhead.

It was warm enough to not need any coverings, so Laméch collected his old traveling clothes and laid them out on the ground to hopefully protect against small creatures and the inevitable moisture from the coming dews.

Just before they reclined, Keziah pointed to the lake.

"Look!"

Laméch turned to the lake and saw small colonies of bioluminescent algae which were swirling and playing on the surface. Waves of bluish-white light danced around the pond illuminating the depths and casting flashes of radiance on the surrounding embankments, creating a mesmerizing light show.

Just then the moon rose over the treetops, bathing the entire scene with its own pinkish-blue brilliance. The colliding colors splashed around the forest, creating strange shadows and expressions in their faces.

Eventually they laid back and watched the heavenly presentation as Laméch wondered at the incongruity of his many conflicting thoughts and emotions, colliding much like the colors around him.

The delight of this beautiful display against the backdrop of being lost and stranded. The joy of her nearness against the reality of his subterfuge. The critical nature of his mission against the tranquility and isolation of this island.

As he drifted off to sleep, he was tormented by one thought:

From this moment, any future relationship will be based on a lie.

CHAPTER 14
ANTIQUITY

"In addition to seasonal and annual timekeeping, the earliest generations used the stars as fixed reference points for storytelling and maintaining cultural cohesiveness. Oral traditions and entire epics could be recalled with nothing but a simple finger pointed towards a constellation. The first of these recounted the story of the infant king who would someday come and restore creation to its original perfection."

—Amoela the Librarian,
<u>The First Two Thousand Years, Vol. I</u>

Laméch awoke, drenched from the island's morning dews. He rolled to his left into the cold puddles formed from the depressions in his soggy traveling clothes—and noticed that Keziah was nowhere to be seen.

He rose quickly and wrung out his blue slave tunic as best as he could, and then called out loudly for Keziah.

It was early morning, and the sun was beginning to clear the swaying treetops on the far side of the lake. Although the air was comfortably warm, he shivered from the dampness. No matter. His tunic would dry soon.

There was no answer, so Laméch looked around their campsite before venturing back into the trees to look for her.

He walked through the areas where they had collected food the day before, calling out her name. When there was no response, he headed further inland, trying to keep his bearings based on the rising sun and the direction of the lake.

The trees grew closer together as he traveled, repeatedly calling her name with increasing urgency. The strange, shifting silhouettes of the swaying trees were very disorienting, and he found himself startled at unexpected shadows which darted along the grassy surface.

Could there be other people here?

He brushed away the nervous—and silly—thought.

"Keziah!" he called again, beginning to feel uncharacteristically concerned.

A silent arm slid around his neck as an equally silent hand clamped down over his mouth. He fought instinctively by lurching forward, but a not-so-silent kick to the back of his knees brought him facedown into the grass with his unknown assailant landing on top of him.

"*Keep quiet!*"

It was an angry hiss—and it belonged to Keziah. She rolled from Laméch's back and turned him over, glaring into his stunned face.

"You don't wander in the forests yelling!" she chided furiously, still using her demanding whisper, "and definitely not alone!"

"What is the problem?" Laméch asked as they helped each other from the ground. He wasn't sure whether to be angry or relieved.

"First," she began, slightly calmer, "you have no idea what you're doing." She stared into his eyes, daring him to contradict her.

He did not.

"And second," she paused. "We are not alone on this island."

She stopped to allow her words to sink in.

Laméch stared dumbly for a moment before asking the obvious question.

"How do you know?"

Keziah grasped Laméch by the wrist.

"I'll show you," she said, as she pulled him in a new direction.

Soon they reached a clearing that was much smaller than the one surrounding the lake. In the center of this clearing was a large opening in the ground, about eight cubits in diameter. It descended rapidly into the depths of the island, and resembled a cone-shaped well more than anything else. As they drew close, they could look down into the darkness where small flickers of ambient light from the mid-morning sun reflected off the ocean waters at the bottom. They could see the column of water rise and fall in opposition to the rise and fall of the island.

But Keziah was pointing, not at the water, but rather at the neatly braided rope which was attached to a nearby tree and descended down into the opening.

"Only people make ropes," she stated confidently. "And here are the footprints of whoever tied this rope." She pointed with her right toe towards the ground, but Laméch could see nothing. He was, however, momentarily distracted by the curvature of the leg which resulted from that pointed toe.

But the rope was proof enough.

"We had better get out of here," he suggested. "Whoever placed this here might be nearby."

But Keziah placed her finger to her lips and reached for the rope. Suppressing his panic, Laméch watched as she slowly pulled the line up and out of the opening until (after about thirty cubits) she successfully reached the rope's end where a large object was attached. As the water and leaves rushed from the object, it revealed a strange collection of sticks which were tied together lengthwise in a somewhat oblong shape.

"What is it?" Laméch asked.

"A fish trap," Keziah answered.

She set it on the ground where it began to bounce around of its own accord.

Laméch knelt down to study it more closely and saw several fish thrashing about inside that had entered into the opening at one end, but had been unable to swim back out because of the arrangement of the interior sticks. He was impressed—and suddenly realized how hungry he was.

"Well, now we can have something substantial to eat," he mentioned casually to Keziah as he stood back up.

She looked at him angrily.

"This is someone else's trap," she snapped with a shake of her head as if she could not comprehend Laméch's suggestion.

Laméch pulled back, trying to repair his offence.

"I'm just hungry," he said, "and now we know how to get some fish."

Keziah shook her head again.

"We saw plenty of fish for the taking last night," she said.

Suddenly there was a loud *thwack* above their heads as the tree where the rope was attached abruptly began vibrating. They looked up frantically to see a large arrow with pale blue feathers sticking out of the trunk less than a cubit above them.

They turned to see where the arrow had come from and saw a man with a dirty breechcloth and long black hair emerge from the woods brandishing a large bow. He approached them slowly, and Laméch could see a quiver of arrows slung over his back—ready to be launched at a moment's notice.

Laméch and Keziah, who were still dressed in their slave tunics, watched as the man drew near. Laméch noticed that his thick hair fell around his shoulders in tight curls, and that his eyes were a very dark blue. A thick scar traveled from his left eyebrow to his ear.

The man spoke suddenly.

"You wouldn't be trying to steal my meal, would you?"

Before Laméch could say anything, Keziah responded.

"Absolutely not, sir," she said with a slight bow. "We thought there was no one else on this island, and when I discovered this rope, we wanted to see what it was." She nodded vigorously with a friendly, innocent smile. "We were just getting ready to throw it back in."

With that she picked up the fish trap by the rope, swung it up over her head, and flung it back into the opening.

"*Wait!*" the man shouted as the fish trap descended, followed by a muted splash a moment later.

They turned their startled eyes on the man as he suddenly broke into laughter. He began shaking his head and walked quickly towards them, placing his bow over his shoulder.

Laméch tensed as this strange and inexplicable man reached them, not sure how to respond or what to expect. Again, Keziah spoke as the man stopped a few paces from them.

"Why do you laugh?" she asked, again with total sweetness and innocence. Laméch shuddered as he considered how the owner of that voice had just attacked him moments earlier.

The man smiled.

"I laugh because the fish in that trap are actually for you." He stared at the stunned Laméch and extended his arm in greeting.

"You are Laméch, correct?" he asked with a smile, obviously knowing the answer.

Laméch nodded and extended his arm, unsure of how else to respond.

They shook arms, and then the man walked to the rope and began pulling it from the opening a second time.

"Aenoch told me to watch for you," he said casually as the fish trap emerged and was lifted from the ground.

"You have a communication device?" Laméch blurted out excitedly.

The man turned and smiled, nodding in affirmation. He stepped towards them, the trap dangling from his hand.

"I saw you two leap from the Haermon Cliffs," he continued, still smiling. "Very impressive."

His smile disappeared into a sudden scowl.

"And I see you decided to disobey," he said with a glance at Keziah. "You took action and interfered, even though Aenoch specifically instructed you to gather information only."

Laméch nodded again, defensively this time, trying to hide his ever-increasing bewilderment. He began to explain that Aenoch was not his commander and how no one had the right to criticize his brilliant rescue, but the man interrupted with another loud laugh.

"That's wonderful!" he announced excitedly, clasping Laméch's arm with his free hand. "Aenoch doesn't have to be in charge of everything. A little dissension is good for him!"

The startled Laméch carefully pulled away from the man's grasp with a thousand questions in his mind, but before he could voice them, Keziah spoke again.

"Excuse me," she began politely as Laméch shook his head. "Who are you?" Among all the questions in Laméch's mind, this simple one had not been among them.

The man turned to look at Keziah as if seeing her for the first time.

"I am called Kendrach," he said properly.

"I thank you for meeting us," Keziah said, equally formally, "My name is Keziah."

Kendrach smiled and lifted the fish trap high into the air.

"If you would care to accompany me, I would love to prepare a meal for you." He removed the trap from the line, and pointed towards the northwest.

Laméch and Keziah exchanged glances, and then nodded to accept Kendrach's invitation. As they began walking together in the direction he had indicated, Laméch finally was able to complete a question in his mind and voice it.

"Kendrach," he began carefully, "what do you do on this island? And how is it you were watching for us?"

Kendrach laughed as they walked, ducking branches. For a moment, Laméch thought Kendrach was going to ignore his question, but eventually he responded.

"I am completely alone on this island," he began, "and on this island I have but one duty. My only job, as it has been for many years, is to watch the Haermon Cliffs."

He glanced down at Laméch.

"I watch as ships enter and leave the port to the north, and a few years ago I watched as new rooms—or windows—were built into the backside of the cliffs."

He shrugged.

"I could tell you about some of the mating patterns of the birds that live atop the cliffs, but other than that, I watch nothing."

He indicated that they should turn left through the trees.

"I am simply a lookout," he continued. "I am here to report to Aenoch if anything should ever change here—if a large armada is suddenly launched, or if one of their observation platforms suddenly takes off into the skies."

"Platforms?" asked Laméch, suddenly intrigued. "Have you ever seen one here?"

"No," answered Kendrach with a shrug. "Strangely, I have never seen any over their own mountains." He focused his eyes on Laméch. "But I did witness the one over the city where I was at the end of the Family Wars."

Laméch nodded, and then waited for Kendrach to answer his original question.

"I watched you scale the cliffs," Kendrach continued, "but when Aenoch told me he had not heard from you, I was told you might try to make it to this island. All I could do was wait and see—and fortunately, here you are!"

Laméch felt an anger growing inside.

"Why didn't Aenoch tell me about you?" he asked, harsher than he intended. "I would have felt a lot better knowing someone was on this island."

"Because my presence on this island is a secret," Kendrach said, scolding. "Had you been captured, you would have been tortured into revealing this, so it was best you did not know. Either way, there were only two possibilities: You would be captured—or you would not. Besides, none of our plans are built around the concerns of what makes you feel better."

Laméch nodded, subdued. A new thought occurred to him.

"If this island is an outpost to observe the cliffs, how do you keep it in one place? Surely the current would move it away from here."

Kendrach laughed again.

"I keep it anchored," he said. "A cable was placed through the center to hold its position."

"But wouldn't the Semyaz become suspicious of a floating island that never moved?"

"Oh, I move it all the time," Kendrach responded with another laugh. "I raise the anchor often. I track the currents to make sure it stays within sight of the cliffs. Sometimes, I can move northward to observe the shipping docks where supplies—and human cargo—come in."

Laméch thought of the new faces that regularly arrived at the yellow compound. He glanced at Keziah who was studiously quiet.

"We have arrived," Kendrach announced as they entered a small clearing. Situated to the right was a small wooden structure with a thatched roof. It was slightly smaller than the building where Laméch had first met Aenoch, but it was similar in construction.

They entered through an open doorway to find a small table and what appeared to be a shallow fireplace situated at the right end of the room. Another open doorway to the left led into an adjoining room.

"I'm afraid I have no place to sit other than these mats by the door," Kendrach said, pointing. "I am not prepared for company, but if you will rest there, I will prepare our meal."

"Thank you," said Keziah, the first words she had uttered since thanking him previously.

Kendrach nodded as he carried the fish trap towards the other doorway.

Laméch interrupted him.

"Will you be informing Aenoch of our arrival?"

"Not yet," Kendrach turned and answered. "That won't be possible until the sun goes down. There is too much interference and my power source is not sufficient. Only the energies of a city's Power House can penetrate the noise." He smiled. "We will try to contact him when it is dark. Hopefully, it will still be night over *his* island."

He turned back to the other doorway and exited, leaving Laméch and Keziah to seat themselves on the indicated mats and wait—staring at each other. Through the flooring, they could feel the slight rise and fall of the ocean beneath them.

"That is strange," Keziah said suddenly, pointing to the fireplace. Laméch raised his eyebrows.

"Why would Kendrach keep his fire within his dwelling?" she continued. "It would be safer and more convenient to have one's fire away from the house where it could be as large as one wished and not endanger the building."

Spoken like a true forest person, Laméch thought. A fireplace belonged inside of one's house so that it could be enjoyed.

"The fireplace is inside to keep it hidden," Kendrach answered from the other room. He entered carrying a small armload of dried twigs and grasses for kindling.

"There are vents which disperse the smoke above the fireplace," he said as he approached. "I cannot allow any signs of habitation here."

He placed the kindling into the fireplace beneath some larger logs which were charred from previous fires.

"I must block any smoke during the day, and prevent any floating embers from showing at night," Kendrach continued as he began to attack a nearby flint with his knife. Sparks flew, eventually igniting the loosely packed dried grasses. "If any sentries—or anyone at the cliffs—saw signs of life here, my island would be overrun immediately."

He blew into the fire to expand the flame. Eventually, the kindling began to burn freely, and he rose, satisfied.

"I will return," he said as he exited the room for the second time.

Eventually he returned carrying three wooden sticks which were still green. At the end of each stick was a wide fork; and suspended between each fork was a fish from the trap. They were held in place by a simple latticework of green twigs that wrapped above and below each fish.

He handed a stick to each of them, and then handed a second one to Laméch.

"Hold these over the flames," he instructed as he turned and headed back to the other room. Laméch stared at the fish, which were covered in some unknown oil mixed with herbs he did not recognize.

Keziah immediately rose and offered her fish to the flames, and Laméch followed, roasting his fish and the one (presumably) for Kendrach.

Kendrach returned carrying three small wooden plates which were filled with fruits, nuts, and a small pool of reddish-brown paste. He placed them in front of their mats and then collected the second fish from Laméch's hand.

"I cook very seldom," he said. "I don't often start a fire here, but this seemed an important occasion." He looked at Laméch. "I'm hoping you have some good intelligence to offer."

Laméch nodded in silence.

"Don't forget to turn it over," Kendrach instructed as Laméch's fish threatened to burn on one side.

Laméch hastily turned his fish, and they watched the fire in silence as their meal cooked over the open flames.

Eventually, Kendrach removed his fish from the fire and returned to the mats. He carefully tugged at one of the green twigs allowing the fish to slide out onto his wooden plate—next to the paste.

Laméch and Keziah did the same, and soon they were enjoying their meal. They also followed Kendrach's lead and dipped pieces of their fish into the paste which had a deep spicy flavor. Laméch was amazed at how wonderful the fish tasted and told their host.

"You have been enjoying Semyaz rations," Kendrach said wryly. "However, what you are discovering is that fish taste best immediately after they are caught. Living in the city, you would not know this."

Laméch thought he saw Keziah smile at this.

After a few moments of eating quietly, Laméch decided to find out more about their host.

"I notice you use words like 'overrun', 'sentries', 'intelligence', and 'rations'. Did you fight in the Family Wars?"

The question seemed to stun Kendrach momentarily.

"*Everyone* fought in those wars," he said eventually with a weary sigh. "But if you must know, I was originally assigned to a clandestine unit that infiltrated Jaebal City. We had a simple mission: to eradicate any who did not meet the hereditary standards of my home city."

It was Laméch's turn to be stunned, and he made a face to indicate his disgust.

"They were very contemptible times," Kendrach continued. "We were all conditioned to weed out those who exhibited mutations. Naturally, each city had its *own* criteria for determining what constituted a mutation."

He looked solemnly into Laméch's eyes.

"In our case, we were taught that blond hair was an unacceptable mutation—and also people above a certain stature." Kendrach took a deep breath. "A large percentage of the residents of Jaebal exhibited these 'aberrant' traits." He looked away with a shudder.

"The message of the Semyaz brought an end to those wars," he said after a few moments, "but it was the message of Aenoch that has allowed me to live with myself—alone on this island."

He looked back up and Laméch was shocked to find moisture in Kendrach's eyes, but the warrior had nothing more to say.

There was a long pause as the three returned to their meal. It was Keziah who finished first and broke the silence.

"What do you hunt with *this*?" she asked, pointing to Kendrach's bow and arrows.

Kendrach managed a smile.

"Actually, nothing," he answered. "Occasionally, I may shoot a fish, but I keep these for practice—and in case I need to defend myself or my island."

"There are no animals on this island for hunting?" asked Laméch.

Kendrach spun on Laméch with an angry glare.

"Animals are *not* for hunting or food," he snapped, startling Laméch. "We don't consume innocent blood. All air breathers share the gift of life with us."

Laméch turned to Keziah, stunned, but she too had a shocked look as if offended that Laméch didn't know this.

"Aenoch teaches that only their skins may only be used for clothing," Kendrach stated in explanation.

Confused, Laméch nodded carefully, wondering how Aenoch had suddenly become a Lawgiver. He also noticed that Keziah was watching him with a confused look on her face. Had he said something that contradicted the values of *The Seed*? Perhaps he should explain the truth to her about his knowledge—and ignorance—of that symbol.

Later, he decided.

They finished their meal and watched in silence as the fire slowly began to die down. Laméch watched as Keziah, exhausted from the past two days, eventually lay down on her mat and was soon fast asleep. With the light from the fire gone, the room darkened and the shadows from the evening began to set in.

"We need to charge our power," Kendrach said suddenly.

Laméch shook himself from his reverie.

"What do you mean?" he asked.

Kendrach smiled as he rose.

"We have no Power House here," he said, "so I must generate our source manually." He held out his hand. "Come. It is in a separate clearing."

Laméch rose and followed Kendrach as he exited the cabin. He glanced behind at the sleeping Keziah, once again impressed.

They made their way heading south through the trees and brush until they came upon another structure, slightly smaller than the place where they had just eaten. They entered a room that was almost pitch black. Laméch could see no windows.

Kendrach steered him towards a large black box resting on the floor that appeared to have a large hand-crank on its side—the kind used for raising sails or lifting a large building block. However, nothing seemed to be attached to it.

"Turn this," Kendrach instructed, "and don't stop."

Laméch paused for a moment, and then reached for the crank. He began turning it, surprised at how easily it moved. However, he soon discovered that the faster he cranked it, the more resistance it gave.

Nothing happened. Laméch saw Kendrach moving at the far side of the room, and, for a moment, Laméch thought he might be the victim of some kind of prank.

Suddenly he saw a faint light to the right of the box. It seemed to be in the shape of a tree, and gradually the glow became more and more intense—along with a loud humming noise. He saw pulses of light filling what appeared to be a large crystal column with an inverted bowl or globe resting on top, and he let out a shout of surprise when several large bolts of miniature lightening shot out from the bowl.

He stopped cranking—which elicited a shout from Kendrach.

"Don't stop now!"

Laméch redoubled his efforts, eventually enjoying a blazing light show.

Kendrach returned to his side.

"What is this?" asked Laméch over the hum and static that accompanied the tiny bolts.

"This," answered Kendrach, "is a miniature, rudimentary version of what you would find inside of a Power House. This top portion is called a coil. An actual city plant uses daily tides to 'turn the handle', and also has systems which store energy."

He reached down and lifted Laméch's hands from the crank.

"That should be good for now," he said. "Look over here."

He led Laméch to the far side of the room which was now lit by the glow and flashes from behind. He pointed to a narrow desk where five crystal flasks were glowing brightly with different colors.

They were glowing from within, much like a standard nobleglobe, but he had never seen such colors. The first was a dark pink, followed by a deep orange, a bright sky-blue, a light pink, and finally, a dark purple.

"These show us when the coil is charged," Kendrach explained. "A noble-globe uses gasses from these first two, but these five were prepared by Aenoch in his labs to show the other known gasses which will glow when charged."

Laméch stared, amazed and impressed. He pointed to the third flask with its blue glow.

"This color reminds me of something," he said.

"It should," Kendrach responded.

He lifted his hands as if preparing for a lecture.

"The *phases* of the moon are based on its angle to the sun," he began.

Laméch nodded, not sure where Kendrach was leading.

"However, the moon still shines with its pinkish-blue light even from the regions *not* reflected by the sun. Even during a new moon, it still casts its *own* glow upon the earth."

The connection finally dawned on Laméch, and he nodded excitedly.

Kendrach pointed to the first and third flask.

"From this we know that the atmosphere of the moon is composed of a combination of these two gasses—and that it glows in the same manner as a noble-globe—but powered by the energies of the cosmos itself. This is why the moon is sometimes referred to as 'the lesser light to rule the night'."

Laméch grinned, actually excited at having learned something.

The glowing flasks suddenly began to fade, and Laméch looked over to see the coil was no longer shooting sparks.

"We waited too long," said Kendrach. "Please charge that again," he told Laméch, pointing to the crank. "Keep turning until all five lights are glowing brightly."

Laméch returned to the crank and began recharging the coil. Soon the miniature lightening was shooting out from all sides again, and he watched as the five flasks at the far side of the room began to glow brightly again.

While Laméch was turning, Kendrach was removing the cover of a box resting on a table between the coil and the flasks. Laméch looked over and saw a bright white crystal glowing in the middle of the box. The communication device! He left the crank and went to stand next to Kendrach.

A loud shrieking sound filled the room suddenly, accompanied by jagged hisses and sounds like rushing waters. Laméch grasped his ears frantically as Kendrach reached into the communication device and adjusted something. The volume decreased, but the noises remained.

"Someone is always listening on Aenoch's Island," said Kendrach as Laméch lowered his hands. Laméch nodded as he recalled being in Aenoch's communication center. He had been shown how to use the devices and remembered the annoying sounds. While he had been there, though, he had never heard an incoming message.

The noise suddenly stopped, leaving the room silent except for the hum and sparks from the coil. Kendrach began to speak into the box.

"This is Kendrach," he said loudly and clearly. "I have a report."

The noise suddenly reappeared, mixed with squealing lines of piercing pitches that rose and fell indiscriminately. Slowly the thick hisses coalesced and Laméch suddenly realized he could discern words emerging from the chaos. He thought he heard a man's voice say the word "garden".

Again the noise stopped suddenly, and Laméch heard Kendrach speak into the box.

"A flaming sword," was all he said.

The noise resumed and Kendrach turned to Laméch.

"We can not talk and listen at the same time," he said over the din. "We must listen to the sounds of the cosmos as they carry our messages."

He glanced at the colored lights on the left, which were going dim, and pointed to the crank. Laméch immediately rushed to the box beneath the coil and began turning.

A voice emerged through the noise.

"What do you have to report, Kendrach?"

Again the relieving silence as Kendrach responded.

"Please find Aenoch at once," he instructed. "I have Laméch with me, and he has a complete intelligence report of the Semyaz complex. Inform me when Aenoch has arrived."

Kendrach stepped back as the noise resumed, while Laméch rose from his re-charging and joined him.

"When Aenoch arrives," Kendrach said, "you must give him a complete account of your experiences within the complex. Tell him everything—no detail is insignificant."

Laméch nodded as he moved closer to the box. He now saw a small handle, and the vents from which the horrible sounds were coming. Suddenly a new voice emerged from the box.

"This is Aenoch." The distorted sounds made his voice barely recognizable. "I am glad that Laméch escaped from the Semyaz. He is there with you?"

Kendrach grasped Laméch's right hand and placed it in the box, directing him to a small panel. He pressed the panel with Laméch's finger and the noise stopped.

"Yes, he is standing here and will tell you everything about his mission."

Kendrach turned to Laméch.

"As long as you press this panel, Aenoch can hear everything you say. You may start now."

He stepped back and pointed for Laméch to proceed.

Laméch stared into the silent box, inexplicably nervous. How could he talk to a *thing*?

"Go ahead," urged Kendrach. "Just talk loudly and clearly."

Eventually Laméch took a deep breath and began. He started with his scaling of the cliff—including the fall and destruction of his own device. He then continued with his experiences, the layout of the complex, details of the slave camps, and his initial work for Jameth. While he spoke, Kendrach monitored the coil, turning the crank when needed.

Each sentence was a great effort, since Laméch was speaking to an unresponsive container. It took great resolve to continue, since there was no indication that anyone was listening, and there were no nods or sounds of comprehension that normally accompany conversations. He repeatedly looked over at Kendrach, who had to keep waving him on.

Laméch reported the details of his explorations, and also the places where he found supplies and how he had stored them in his base camp atop the cliffs. He then described the activities and experiments of the yellow-robes in their large research chamber, and the lady in the red robe who seemed to be in charge of all that transpired within that chamber.

He then told of his incursion into the lower levels, the strange meeting with its crazy emotional ending, and his escape back to the camps.

He saw Kendrach wince when he told of the rescue of Keziah, but Laméch was determined to leave nothing out. When he was finished, he looked over at Kendrach, who motioned for him to lift his finger.

The squealing hiss resumed as Aenoch's voice filled the room.

"…when I specifically told you not to! You were supposed to observe only."

They could hear Aenoch take a breath before he continued.

"What's done is done," he said. "We only have about three minutes before sunrise, and I have some questions. First, I need to confirm that the communication device that you discovered was destroyed."

Kendrach nodded to Laméch who pressed the panel down.

"Yes, the guard totally destroyed the device. It had apparently been buried by one of your people who made it into the complex, but never made it out."

He released the panel.

"My next question is this," said Aenoch over the noise, which was growing louder, making his voice more difficult to understand. "Were you able to retrieve any of the blue, red, or green vials?"

"No I was not," answered Laméch. "I only had one, and it was destroyed during my escape. Whatever was in it was very toxic, however, because the guards were very afraid. I don't know what effect it had on them when it broke, however, because I was too busy running." He grinned over at Kendrach as he lifted his finger.

Aenoch's warped voice was barely discernable beneath the wall of noise.

"… do you have any speculations or conclusions that you can tell us?"

Laméch quickly pressed the panel and answered.

"There were two things that I noticed most of all," he stated. "First, there did not seem to be anything like a Power House anywhere near the complex. The Semyaz apparently have a totally different source for their energy. There were lighting panels they called *tsohars* throughout the complex, and suspended spotlights over the camps, but they …"

Laméch stopped as he saw Kendrach waving at him.

"Hurry," he said, "they are running out of time."

Laméch nodded and continued.

"The second observation was that I did not see any technologies that seemed superior to those I am familiar with. In fact, everything seemed quite crude—including the systematic research. I looked around, but I could not..."

Kendrach reached over and lifted his hand from the console. Immediately the room filled with screeching noises, and they could barely hear Aenoch's voice as it faded beneath the whines and hisses.

"...so we should be able to get a team to you within two weeks. Excellent work, Kendrach, and be sure and tell Laméch..."

The noise suddenly erupted into a cacophonous explosion—drowning Aenoch's voice—and Kendrach quickly reached in and pressed the panel, ending it abruptly.

"They can't hear anything anymore," he said over the soothing silence. The hums and sparks from the coil continued quietly in the corner.

"How do we shut down the device?" asked Laméch.

Kendrach shrugged.

"We just have to wait for the coil to die," he said calmly.

A thought occurred to Laméch.

"Is it possible that anyone in the world who possessed such a device would be able to hear the conversation we just had?"

Kendrach nodded.

"As long as it was powered, and there was not too much interference, yes, these communications are open to anyone who has such a device." He paused to watch as the indicator lights began to dim. "That is why Aenoch had to confirm that the device you found was destroyed." He nodded. "We can only hope that the Semyaz still have no idea what their purpose is. Fortunately, since you say they have no Power House, our crystal devices are completely useless to them—even if they did discern their function."

The hum and glow from the coil finally ceased, and soon they were standing in a dark and silent room.

"We encode messages meant for higher level operations," Kendrach continued as he steered Laméch across the room, "but all of us are very aware of you and your mission. We have been excited about it ever since you left Aenoch's Island."

They stepped out into the night, which was brilliantly lit by the stars and a glowing pink-blue moon slowly rising above the treetops. Laméch stared at it with new interest, imagining it to be a giant colored noble-globe suspended above the earth.

They walked silently under the stars, and Laméch was once again amazed at their brilliance and apparent closeness. Surrounded by the cool serenity—and confronted suddenly with his isolation from the rest of the world—Laméch suddenly recalled a statement that Kendrach had made, and asked about it.

"You said," Laméch began, breaking their silence more violently than he had intended, "that it was the message of Aenoch that allowed you to live with yourself. Were you simply referring to living *by* yourself, or was it something deeper? What is it about Aenoch's message that is so special anyway?"

Kendrach stopped and turned to Laméch.

"It *is* difficult to live alone," he began. "Most men cannot, because most men are unable to withstand the company of their own thoughts. It is in our nature to provide friendships and diversions to distract us from our inner selves—and avoid the confrontation that exists in all of us."

He paused and looked slightly upward before continuing.

"The most difficult issue in life is *regret*. There is a point in life when there are simply too many acts and deeds for which one can not repair or atone, and something within rises up in ugly accusations—demanding that history be repaired or that consequences be undone. Our own thoughts *command* us to do that which can not be accomplished."

He looked back into Laméch's face. Shadows from the starlight added intensity to Kendrach's eyes, and somehow Laméch was suddenly aware that he was standing before a warrior who had committed unbelievable atrocities.

"You see," Kendrach continued, "we live in a world that is divided. There is something about our makeup that tells us the world *ought* to be a certain way, yet we are confronted with the reality of the world that *is*. We constantly fight and maneuver ourselves to try and repair the world and make it what it *ought* to be, all the time realizing that none of us are as *we* ought to be. We fight a war, build a building, join a cause, or engage in exhausting, distracting endeavors, only to realize that we will still never escape from being trapped within ourselves."

Kendrach's eyes pierced into Laméch.

"And do you know what the real dilemma is? It is the question of where this dire feeling came from in the first place. How is it we do *not* accept things as they are, but insist that things are not as they should be? All *other* creatures simply accept reality, but what kind of insanity exists in *us* that compels us to change it—or reject it?"

Kendrach raised his eyebrows to emphasize the futility of his question. Laméch's interest had initially been high, but it was slowly waning. His mind actually began to wander into thoughts of Keziah. He was startled suddenly as Kendrach grabbed his shoulders with a shake.

"And to compound the difficulty," Kendrach's voice rose in intensity, "each one of us has a *different* idea of what *'ought'* ought to be!"

Laméch glanced down at Kendrach's hands and pulled away slightly. He stifled a small laugh at Kendrach's last statement.

"I think you are making yourself disturbed over nothing," Laméch said, not really caring how tactful he was. He had never really enjoyed the deep talk of adults—and he also couldn't think of anything he actually regretted. "I'm sure you have always done whatever you needed to do."

He turned, prompting the older soldier to resume walking.

"You've never regretted anything you have done?" Kendrach asked after a few steps.

"Not really," Laméch answered quickly. "I've always made it a practice to decide *not* to regret anything *before* I do it." He grinned. "It saves me the trouble later."

He expected this to silence Kendrach temporarily, but the warrior's question was followed quickly by a second.

"And you have never had any internal conflict between the life that others witness and the life that is only known by you?"

Laméch thought of his double life back in Matusalé, and also of his recently discovered joy in subterfuge. But these choices were firmly sanctioned by his resolve in the causes he supported, and he reasoned they did not represent any internal conflict.

"No," Laméch said confidently. "I am very sure of who I am, and of my choices and actions which are true to that person." He laughed again. "I suppose that even includes when I am under cover—and deliberately pretending to be someone who I am not."

He stopped walking, bringing Kendrach to a halt.

"You see," he added. "I'm pretty much the same person no matter who I am with. Different people *may* know different things about me, but I am straightforward and forthright with everyone."

"I see," said Kendrach with a nod. There was a long pause before Kendrach spoke again. When he did, it was in a slow, quiet tone.

"Does this include the fact that, although you are not a believer in the *Seed*, you have allowed the lovely Keziah to believe that you are?"

Laméch was stunned into silence, wondering how Kendrach might have discerned this. He tried to find something to say, but all he could think of was the realization that perhaps he *did* have a few regrets.

Kendrach abruptly—and kindly—changed the subject.

"You *did* ask me how Aenoch's message applied to this," Kendrach reminded him a few steps after resuming their walk. "But I will need to show you something first."

He took Laméch's arm again.

"Follow me."

He pulled Laméch abruptly to the right, and they began walking quickly through the dark foliage, their way lit by the moon which was now almost overhead.

Soon they reached an open clearing along the southern edge of the island that afforded a view of the open sea. Directly in front of them was the brilliant expanse filled with stars—and their reflections on the water beneath. Laméch could see the glowing milky band stretching across the sky, almost as if they were a sparkling cloud of luminescent smoke. Far to the left was the jagged silhouette of the Haermon Mountains, rising from the ocean and blocking the heavens.

Kendrach stopped and turned to Laméch.

"Aenoch's message deals with the nature and abilities of the Creator—and His power," he began immediately. "As you know, there are many views on the Creator, including that which the Semyaz teach."

He turned to face the starry ocean in front of them, and waved his hand above his head to indicate the amazing spectacle in front of them.

"*If*," Kendrach continued, "this is the handiwork of the Creator, we have to concede that His abilities are amazing. He must be the source of all that exists, and this must include earth, space, life, time, and consciousness—everything and anything that *is*."

He turned to Laméch.

"Aenoch's message teaches that, in the world as it was originally created, there *was* no conflict between what *is* and what *ought* to be. And that the First Ones who lived here enjoyed a world in which everything occurred in complete harmony with itself as it was supposed to be. This is where *our* desire for such a world comes from."

He paused, allowing Laméch to consider his words. In a simple way, it *did* make sense to Laméch. People *did* feel the need to try and improve or *right* things, and some kind of ancestral motivation could explain it.

"If that's true," Laméch stated, more sarcastically than he intended, "what happened to cause this supposedly *perfect* creation to develop your conflict between *is* and *ought*?"

"Exactly!" announced Kendrach in a triumphant voice that stunned Laméch more than any other response could have.

"What do you mean?" Laméch asked, confused.

Kendrach was suddenly silent.

"*We* did it," he answered eventually. "*We* caused the perfect creation to fail. We asked for it!"

Laméch shook his head, confused.

"How?"

"The perfect creation included perfect people with perfect freewill. This allowed the First Ones to choose something other than what ought to be."

"How could they choose something that they didn't know existed?" Laméch was instantly proud of his insightful and deductive question. "If what *is* and what *ought* to be were the same, they couldn't know anything different."

Kendrach nodded.

"They were given a test, a simple prohibition, and the ability to *disobey* suddenly emerged. They were told that if they failed, there would be a separation—a fall from reality. The cosmos would no longer be as it ought—but rather it would veer away from perfection and descend into an alternate reality—one that could never regain its original perfection. Death, decay, and encroaching chaos intruded— profaning the original plan. From that moment on, *all* humanity has become aware of the difference between *is* and *ought*."

Kendrach shook his head, overcome. He then turned to Laméch and shrugged slightly.

"You *are* correct, Laméch," he said in a strange voice that was a combination of kindness and anguish. "They did *not* know the agony of what existed on the other side of that decision, but their failure was a statement to the Creator that *His* guidance and wisdom were no longer needed or wanted."

He paused and looked silently over the water. The moon was now almost directly over head—slightly to the south—filling the waters with its pinkish-blue radiance.

Eventually Laméch spoke.

"That is certainly an engaging myth," he said, simply. "It is fun to try and explain problems with stories." He wasn't deliberately trying to belittle Kendrach's tale, he simply thought it needed some perspective.

Fortunately, Kendrach was not the slightest bit offended.

"You haven't heard the good news," he said calmly. "The fact that the Creator cares enough for us—His creation—that He will somehow restore this damage. There will be a time, soon, when the world will again experience the peace and sanity where what *is* will also be what *ought*."

Laméch looked at Kendrach, genuinely interested. *This should be good*, he thought.

"This is why I brought you here," said Kendrach, pointing out at the stars. "Although the answer is written in the tablets that Aenoch is collecting, we will use the stars to tell the story."

Kendrach pointed to a group of stars, almost overhead, but slightly to the south.

"Do you see that bright star?" he asked, pointing to the brightest one in the region.

"Yes," answered Laméch, nodding in the dark.

"Now follow that one upward and form a line to the left with these next two stars."

Laméch grunted the completion of the line.

"Now, just above the first star is another star and you can use it to create a similar line that is somewhat parallel with the first."

"I see," said Laméch.

"Now continue both lines upward to the right to connect to those next two stars, and you have just outlined the legs and body of The Virgin."

Laméch stared for a moment before responding.

"I see," he nodded without too much enthusiasm. "I was trying to find that one when I left Matusalé," he added helpfully.

"Moving to the west," Kendrach continued either ignoring or not noticing Laméch's comment, "we see this rough circle of stars that outlines her shoulders and head, and that single star to the north is her extended right arm."

Kendrach lowered his hand.

"Do you see her?" he asked.

Laméch nodded, not really seeing anything.

"How does this answer the question of regret?" he asked.

Kendrach's hand returned to the bright star.

"That star is the Seed, near the Virgin's left hand, shining from her womb." His arm lowered. "Aenoch's message tells of the coming Seed who will be the Creator in human form. When He comes, His mastery of time and space will enable Him to right all wrong, and somehow repair all transgression and error—reversing their damage and restoring creation to its proper form."

He turned to face Laméch, his eyes gleaming in the starlight.

"There is no room for regret when the Creator has promised to use His foreknowledge and power over time to work all things for good." He paused, lowered his eyes, and then refastened them on Laméch.

"Since He knew my wrongs before I committed them, He has already devised a plan to rectify them. And when He comes, He will reveal that plan!" Kendrach's eyes were shining with passion.

"*This* is the message that has given me peace."

Laméch thought for a moment before responding. He had never

heard anything like this, but was intrigued. He had never before considered such mastery of time. He suddenly realized a major problem in Kendrach's story.

"If I understand you correctly, this Seed is coming from a virgin. How do you explain that?"

Surprisingly, Kendrach simply shrugged.

"I didn't create the message—or the manner in which the Seed will come; but consider this: I believe the Creator has the right to choose *how* He wishes to manifest Himself—and if anyone can create a life using only the seed of a woman, the One who created the woman can." Kendrach grinned. "Besides, you have to admit that such a birth would be one amazing sign."

It was Laméch's turn to shrug in agreement. He couldn't argue with the warrior's logic.

Kendrach raised his hand towards the stars again.

"Allow me to continue the story of the Seed in the skies. There are hundreds of such stories using the other constellations—many of them diverse and speculative—but I want you to understand the very basic prophecy as revealed to Aenoch."

Laméch nodded for Kendrach to continue.

"The right hand of The Virgin is pointing northward to that small group of stars called The Infant King. The *Seed* will be a great king at birth but he will work as a humble herdsman or guardian—which is the constellation to the right of the Infant King. You can see that dark red star in the center of The Herdsman."

Laméch scanned the stars, trying desperately to form the suggested images around them. But Kendrach was totally caught up in his excitement and oblivious to Laméch.

"And next, to the east, is the Great Hunter who is battling the serpent that is attacking His heel as He crushes the Scorpion's head! And as we move northward..." He paused to catch his breath as his eyes scanned the heavens wildly, searching for which story to reveal next.

Laméch was still trying to find a scorpion in the skies over the Haermon Cliffs when he suddenly noticed some low stars shining impossibly *through* the cliffs and reflecting on the water's surface. He grabbed Kendrach's arm.

"What are those?" he asked, pointing.

Kendrach's face changed immediately.

"Those are Semyaz attack skiffs," he said, his voice acquiring a military tone. "They must have discovered your encampment atop the complex."

Kendrach grabbed Laméch's arm painfully, turning him with an unspoken command to follow. They began running back into the woods.

"We have about twenty minutes before they surround the island," Kendrach said through clenched teeth as they sped through the trees.

"Why would they do that?" asked Laméch, trying to avoid missteps as he desperately followed Kendrach's silhouette.

"That is their strategy," he answered, suddenly turning right. "They will surround the island and try to force you from it."

"They're going to *attack* the island?" Laméch asked, incredulously.

"No," said Kendrach as he pushed aside a tree branch.

"They are going to destroy it."

CHAPTER 15
SACRIFICE

*"It was commonly assumed that the Semyaz possessed
an advanced technology and, perhaps even, a heightened intellect. The truth, however, was quite different.
They possessed, only, an advanced evil, which manifest-
ed itself with the unprecedented ability to swiftly expand
the defining boundaries of human malevolence—all the
while maintaining the façade of benefactor. Ultimately,
this resulted in an ever-increasing capacity for allowing
the unthinkable to become palatable."*

—Amoela the Librarian,
The First Two Thousand Years, Vol. II

They arrived at the communication hut still running and Laméch's
side was beginning to hurt. Kendrach, however, seemed like he
wasn't even breathing hard as he stopped suddenly at the doorway.

"Do you remember the way to my cabin?" he asked.

Laméch nodded, slightly bent over with his hands on his knees.

"Retrieve Keziah and return with her immediately," he ordered.
It was now more obvious than ever that Kendrach was a military

man. Without waiting for Laméch's response, Kendrach opened the door and dashed into the dark hut.

Laméch took a deep breath and then headed into the darkness towards the cabin. He couldn't run as quickly as he did with Kendrach, because he was unsure of the ground and, without Kendrach's lead, he had to watch for unknown obstacles.

Eventually he arrived and entered the cabin to find the room filled with the dark orange light of the few remaining embers in the fire. Keziah was still sleeping soundly on the floor. He approached her quickly and knelt beside her.

"Keziah!" he called out, not too loudly. He bent over and grasped her by her shoulder and rocked her gently.

Keziah's eyes opened partway.

"What is happening?" she said slowly. "What's wrong?" She rolled on her back.

Laméch stammered, suddenly realizing that he hadn't planned what to say.

"The Semyaz are coming for us!" he answered finally. "You must leave with me now."

Instantly, Keziah was fully awake. She arose quickly and shook her head, her wild hair shooting in all directions.

"Follow me," Laméch instructed.

They exited the cabin and Keziah followed Laméch as he headed back to the communication hut. As they ran, Laméch suddenly remembered that their supplies from the complex—along with his wet traveling clothes—were still resting beside the lake where Kendrach had first shot at them. He wondered if they would be able to retrieve them later or if they would now be abandoned. He also wondered what plan, if any, Kendrach had prepared. Were they going to fight—or simply hide from the coming onslaught? Somehow the fun of *unknown* danger was greatly diminishing.

They ran through the darkness as Laméch watched for obstacles. Upon reaching the hut, they saw Kendrach seated calmly on a small wooden platform next to the doorway.

"What is our plan?" Laméch asked, sounding more anxious than he intended. He was confused and concerned at Kendrach's apparent ease.

Kendrach produced two small hunting bows, and offered one to Laméch.

"Are you familiar with how to use one of these?" he asked.

While Laméch hesitated to admit his ignorance, Keziah answered.

"I am," she said confidently.

Kendrach tossed the bow to her, which she caught deftly in her left hand. He rose and handed her a quiver of arrows.

"Place these over your shoulders," he instructed. "You may need them later."

"What is our plan?" Laméch repeated, now becoming slightly frantic. "You said we only have a few minutes before the island is surrounded."

Kendrach smiled broadly.

"Our plan is to watch the sky," he said. "We must wait, and it will tell us when to act."

Kendrach looked at Laméch, obviously enjoying the young man's discomfort. He walked to stand next to him.

"Watch with me, and you will see."

They stared upward into the sky, looking at the same stars they had been enjoying earlier. The same silence surrounded the island, but Laméch could not help but envision the attack skiffs as they moved into position.

Suddenly a dark red light arched through the sky traveling from the northwest and brushed into a distant treetop. It erupted into a blinding white flame that spread, igniting the adjacent branches, and creating a sheet of fire that traveled quickly from treetop to treetop.

Laméch turned swiftly to Kendrach.

"Is that what we're waiting for? Is it time to act now?"

Kendrach scowled slightly.

"No. It is still too far away."

Another red orb rose from the east—and another treetop exploded, sending a second sheet of fire rolling along the treetops.

Laméch looked at Kendrach again, but didn't dare to repeat his questions.

"What are those?" he asked.

"They are phosphorus orbs launched from catapults aboard the skiffs," he answered. "It is difficult for anything to burn well on this island," he continued, "but these devices can start a firestorm which will cover the island quickly."

He grinned like only a war veteran can.

"They won't burn the trees to the ground," he said, "but if we are trapped under one of those traveling sheets of flame, it will roast us alive. It's a technique called 'crowning'. This is one of their tactics for rounding up slaves from the forest people enclaves."

His grin faded.

"The Semyaz do not know for sure if you are here, but their plan is to use crowning to terrify you and force you to the edge of the island—where they will then be able to see you against the backdrop of the flames and capture you. Or, watch as you are forced to dive into the sea to escape the fire."

The grin returned.

"As long as you don't wait too long, you should be able to out-run the overhead furnace."

Laméch shook his head—unable to restrain his next question.

"Then what are we waiting for?"

Another orb rose from the southeast, striking nearby. It was so close they could actually hear the strike and the roaring crackle of the treetops being consumed—and watch as the sheet of fire spread quickly in their direction.

"That!" answered Kendrach, pointing to the oncoming fire.

He pulled something from his garment and bent over. A spark appeared in his hand which ignited a small cord on the ground that Laméch had not noticed.

The flame traveled in a direct line towards the hut, and when it had almost reached the structure, it burst into a white-hot ribbon of sparkling fire that spread and wrapped around the perimeter of the hut. A two-cubit high wall of incandescent flame rose up to surround the building, and also began to burn *down* into the sod and vines of the ground that made up the floating island.

Soon there was a fiery trench growing ever wider under the building, until it slowly began to consume the hut. It tipped slightly as its foundation shifted, and they watched as the fire began to carve out a hole *under* the communication hut.

Suddenly, the ground shook, and they watched as the entire hut dropped more than half a cubit directly into the burning ground.

They turned instinctively from the heat, only to be met by the scorching of the oncoming inferno from overhead.

"*Now* we run!" shouted Kendrach.

He led them as they ran directly west. Laméch hoped that the Semyaz would not launch another orb in their path, but Kendrach had said their objective was to force him *to* the coast—so they probably wouldn't deliberately launch one next to the edge of the island.

They could feel the tremendous heat on their backs as they ran—but soon Laméch was able to see a few stars through the trees in front of him. They were nearing the coastline!

He could also see the lights from the attack skiffs arrayed along the horizon.

He heard a scream beside him, and saw that some of the hairs on the back of Keziah's head had burst into flame. He pulled her towards him and quickly smothered the scorched hair with his arms.

Kendrach stopped suddenly and shouted.

"Here!" he ordered, pointing downward.

Kendrach grabbed a large shrub and pulled with all of his strength. The shrub tipped over on its side, revealing a large opening in the sod.

"Jump in here!" he demanded, forcing Laméch in first. "Hold your bow and quiver securely," he instructed Keziah before pushing her in after Laméch.

Laméch jumped in feet first, expecting to find a hole that had been prepared for hiding. Perhaps, a hole that would allow the flames to pass overhead without harming them.

However, his feet struck nothing, and he was astonished to find himself falling freely. It seemed like he dropped for a full two seconds before he struck the side of the hole as it curved slightly under him. The inside was smooth and slippery, and he soon realized he was hurtling blindly down a muddy chute.

He was ejected from the side of the island a few seconds later and dropped the remaining few cubits into the ocean. As Laméch surfaced, Keziah landed in the water next to him, followed by Kendrach. Both were clutching their weapons to their chests, and soon all three were bobbing silently in the water.

Flickers of light came from overhead as the fires grew and covered more of the island. They could see four attack skiffs spread out in front of them, and they watched as one launched another phosphorus orb into the sky.

They quietly treaded water, invisible beneath the relative shade of the island's edge, and checked to make sure that no one was hurt. The back of Keziah's scalp was sore from the scorching, but otherwise, everyone was intact.

Keziah and Laméch looked to Kendrach to see what their next move was going to be, but Kendrach had turned and was digging through the roots and vines alongside the island's edge.

He eventually extracted two long black tubes and slid them side-by-side into the water. They were about three cubits long, and when Kendrach followed them into the water, he pulled them apart, revealing a lattice-work that connected them together.

The two tubes formed the pontoons of a raft, and when Laméch reached for it, it felt cold and metallic. He started to pull himself up, but Kendrach stopped him.

"We stay in the water," he whispered quietly—but it was still an order. "We hang on the sides and make our way to the coast."

He positioned the raft to face outward and grabbed hold of the left pontoon. He moved Laméch and Keziah to the right one, placing Laméch in front.

"How do we get past all of those skiffs?" asked Laméch, also whispering.

"We don't have to," answered Kendrach. "We only have to get past one."

He turned to Keziah.

"We will move as closely as possible to that first skiff on the left," he said, pointing. "Attack skiffs only have a two-man crew, so we must remove them before they can alert the other vessels."

"Why can't we simply sneak between them?" asked Laméch.

"Moving between two skiffs means that we increase the chance of both of them seeing us. The closer we are to one, the further we are from the others."

Laméch nodded, not quite comprehending.

"Only our heads will be above water," Kendrach continued. "When we are close enough to the target, I will take out the two men. We then board the boat and scuttle it."

"We're not going to take it?" asked Laméch. If they were going to board it, at least they should be able to use it.

"The boat must disappear without a trace," answered Kendrach. Even though he was whispering, his growing irritation with Laméch was becoming discernable. He was not used to being questioned.

"Keziah, you are my backup." Kendrach looked carefully at her as she nodded. "We must remove both men before they can call out."

She nodded again.

"You have a reverse two-braid hemp bowstring, so you need to retighten it. Can you do this while we move? Laméch will be propelling your side."

She nodded again.

"Good." Kendrach nodded back. "Because they have been damaged by the water, the strings will be worthless by the time we get to the shore, but they should be good for now. Remember to raise your entire bow out of the water when the time comes. It will be best if you hold it horizontally."

Another nod from Keziah, followed by a slight smile.

The light from the fires above was growing brighter by the minute, and they could now hear some of the crackling and rushing winds as they spread.

"Their eyes will be scanning the coastline above us for you,"

Kendrach said. "So we will keep as low in the water as possible. Also, once we launch, there will be *no* talking at all, not even whispering. Once we are away from the shoreline and the noise above, they will be able to hear any sound on the water's surface."

He turned to glare at Laméch.

"That means, no splashing when you are kicking. Your feet must remain under water."

Laméch nodded.

"We are not in a hurry," Kendrach stated as his last admonition. "We have all night to complete our mission."

With one last look around, Kendrach grasped the left pontoon, and they headed out across the water. Laméch could feel Keziah resting on their pontoon while working with her bow, and he watched as Kendrach masterfully retightened his while propelling his side.

As they drew near the skiff, Laméch realized that the light he had seen from each skiff was in reality a small fire that was raised up in the center of the craft. Behind the fire was a small trebuchet array that was no doubt responsible for launching the phosphorus orbs. He also noticed that the skiff seemed to be riding very high in the water.

Behind them, the island's treetops burned, and it seemed to Laméch that more than half of the island was now "crowning". He looked back to the skiff and allowed a moment for his eyes to readjust to the darkness.

They could see one man at the bow, the pilot, looking intently at the island, obviously watching for signs of anyone trying to escape the firestorm. To the stern, another man was holding a metal chain with a hook. He fastened a metallic orb to the hook and slowly lowered it into the fire. The orb was less than a cubit in diameter, and soon it began to glow dark red from the heat.

"We go after this next launch," Laméch heard the man at the bow say.

"I'll be ready," the man at the stern growled back.

Another orb rose from the sea into the southern sky before arching gracefully and igniting a patch of untouched foliage.

Kendrach turned to look at Keziah. Signing, he assigned the pilot to her, indicating that he would take care of the man at the stern. They also silently agreed to wait until this skiff had launched its orb so that it would not miss whatever scheduled launch rotation existed.

The man at the stern lifted the glowing orb from the fire by the chain and lowered it into the chain metal sling at the base of the trebuchet, releasing it from the hook.

"You may launch when ready!" shouted the man at the bow.

The man grunted and moved to the base of the trebuchet where he pulled aggressively on a large wooden lever.

Immediately the sling flipped through the air, launching the orb silently out over the water. At the same moment, Keziah and Kendrach released their arrows.

The force of the trebuchet caused the skiff to pitch violently. The bow lifted almost a cubit, but the stern plunged at least two. Laméch could see why it was important that the skiff ride so high—otherwise the rear of the craft would have gone underwater.

As a result, Keziah's arrow missed her intended target, striking the man in his left arm. Kendrach's arrow missed completely, striking the wooden frame of the trebuchet just above the man's head.

Both men yelped. One in pain—and the other in surprise at the sound of the arrow's close impact.

Keziah and Kendrach were completely prepared for a second shot—in case the *other* person missed. Keziah watched as the stern rose, followed her new target—and successfully planted an arrow directly into his throat just as he was looking up at Kendrach's first arrow.

However, the pilot dropped to the deck before Kendrach could launch his second shot. As long as the man lay flat, he provided an impossible target. At that moment, the wave from the rocking skiff struck them, knocking Kendrach from his pontoon.

"They're over here!" shouted the pilot. Fortunately, from his prone position, his words were muffled, and could just as easily have been a shout celebrating a successful launch.

Fully committed, Kendrach tossed his bow away, dove into the water, and headed for the skiff. Keziah kept him covered by firing an arrow every time the pilot raised his head above the edge of the vessel.

Kendrach arrived at the skiff and pulled himself over the side. The man was laying in the front, but was now turned over on his back—and waiting for him.

Somehow, the pilot had procured a small hand-held crossbow of his own and aimed it at Kendrach. Kendrach dropped down behind the platform that held the fire just as a small dart whizzed past his left ear.

The man turned over and began crawling towards him, reloading his crossbow. He didn't dare stand, because of Keziah's cover fire, but he quickly closed the distance to Kendrach, and prepared to fire again.

Kendrach was on his back with his feet facing the oncoming man. He pulled his legs towards him as the man raised his arm.

With a powerful kick, Kendrach struck the platform, shaking the flaming bowl and causing sparks to fly. The man glanced up with renewed fear as the bowl threatened to collapse to the deck, but his fears abated as the platform held firm.

A second dart flew, striking Kendrach in his left arm. He continued to kick at the platform repeatedly as the man approached on his stomach. All fear had strangely vanished from the pilot as he watched the wounded Kendrach kick in vain.

Kendrach's throat and chest began to seize up, but he continued kicking—willing the platform to give. Eventually he was rewarded as the platform's metal frame twisted slightly and began to slowly collapse.

The man looked in shock as the basin of fire—and some tubing and other attachments—broke free and began to tumble on top of him.

Flames, hot coals, and jets of unknown ignited chemicals rained down upon the pilot as he curled and cowered, covering his face with his arms—muffling any attempted screams.

Kendrach hauled himself slowly to his feet and made his way to the far side of the boat—away from the spreading flames—and carefully lowered himself into the water.

He made his way around the stern of the skiff—which was now burning fiercely. Although the skiff shell was mostly metal, there were many wooden components, and soon they were blazing away in the midnight sky.

Kendrach finally reached the raft and grasped his pontoon wearily. His vision was going, and he could barely breathe. Obviously there had been some form of toxin on the dart that had struck him.

"Must move," he hissed. "Get away from here."

Keziah slipped her bow back over her shoulders and moved to the left pontoon. Soon she and Laméch were propelling the raft as quickly as possible away from the skiff. Laméch could tell that Kendrach was unable to provide any assistance.

"Are you injured?" he asked Kendrach.

He received a small groan in response, followed by the words, "poison dart".

Suddenly a giant column of white-hot flame erupted from the center of the skiff as the fires reached and consumed the remaining cache of phosphorus orbs. The stern collapsed from the resulting hole, and soon the skiff was floating nose-up in the sea, with glowing embers and bits of twisted hot metal slowly cooling around it.

As they pushed out to sea, Keziah whispered.

"I don't think he's conscious," she said.

"We need to help get him to shore," Laméch answered.

"We need to carry him," she said. "But he's too heavy to place on the raft."

Laméch thought for a moment.

"Give me your bow," he said.

She removed it from her shoulder and handed it to him.

Laméch took the bow and slowly worked it through the lattice work between the two pontoons.

"Help me bring him to the back," he instructed.

They brought Kendrach to the back of the raft and rested his head on the joining lattice work. Laméch then took his hands and wedged them into the ends of the bow which was resting between the tubes.

"This is not very dignified," Laméch said, "but we can now tow him as we move."

He checked Kendrach's face.

"He's still breathing," he said, "but there's no way to tell whether he's going to survive."

Keziah looked over at Kendrach's still face and closed her eyes briefly. Then she looked up at Laméch before heading back to her position on the left pontoon.

"Ready?" she asked.

"Yes," answered Laméch as he grasped his tube. "The shore is that way," he said, pointing right, directly east.

They moved slowly toward the coast, covered by darkness. The island blazed behind them to their left, and Laméch couldn't help but realize that he had spent more time floating in the water with Keziah than doing anything else.

He also had many questions for Kendrach, and desperately hoped he would be able to ask them.

The men operating the two crafts on either side watched as the blazing skiff flamed and pitched. They offered a variety of comments ranging from, "Someone forgot to watch his fire control," to "The idiots blew themselves up." They knew from experience that maintaining the central fire on an attack skiff was a tricky process.

They could not break formation to investigate, but it was obvious that nothing could be done to help.

If anyone *had* survived, they would have to make it to the next skiff on their own.

Laméch and Keziah arrived at the coastline shortly before sunrise, severely hypothermic, their teeth chattering and their muscles cramped.

They were far enough south to be clear of the Haermon Cliffs, and were able to drag themselves ashore onto a gravely beach. They carried the now unconscious Kendrach to the grasses on a hill beyond the beach and placed him on the ground. Keziah made Laméch lie beside Kendrach to keep him warm, and then she headed into the woods. She returned with several deciduous branches filled with leaves and then lay down on Kendrach's other side, placing the branches on top of them for covering.

"We must pull together tightly," she said. Kendrach lay on his side with Laméch facing his back, and Keziah facing his front. "We must conserve whatever warmth we have left and hope we can survive until the sun rises. We can't risk a fire, and we have no other source of heat. I don't know if we can generate enough warmth to save Kendrach or not, but we will live longer holding each other."

Laméch nodded and locked arms with Keziah, holding Kendrach between them. He would have preferred a different arrangement, but trusted that Keziah knew what she was doing—and that this was the only chance to save Kendrach.

"If the sun doesn't arrive in time we will all die," Keziah added calmly as if offering needed clarification.

Laméch winced at the mention of death, and Keziah saw it in his face and smiled slightly

Suddenly she reached across Kendrach's shoulder and stroked Laméch's cheek gently.

"Thank you," she said simply, her smile widening.

"These have been the best two days of my life."

CHAPTER 16
BEGINNINGS

"There is no end to speculations and theories concerning the structure and system of the thousands of hot water springs that are found everywhere on the planet. Despite attempts to plumb their depths, the source of their heat, water, and reliability remains a mystery. The occasional underground channel of near boiling water has been found, but this only contributes to the question of their origins."

—Amoela the Librarian,
The First Two Thousand Years, Vol. II

It was a large empty cistern buried deep in the base of the Matusalé Power House—one of many reservoirs that filled at high tide to provide the pressure gradient needed to power the turbines located even deeper in the giant pyramid. It was currently low tide, and the cistern sat dark and empty with a shallow floor of water and a narrow floating walkway along the perimeter.

Two heads silently broke the water's surface followed by loud gasping that echoed loudly around the chamber as the two men sucked in much needed air. After hyperventilating, they had spent almost five minutes underwater—blindly negotiating the gates, ducts, and limestone shafts of the Power House's intake systems—before surfacing in this chamber.

After their breathing had stabilized—and the pounding in their heads subsided—they swam in the darkness until they located the walkway and pulled themselves out of the water. They walked carefully around the chamber, feeling the surfaces of the stone walls until the lead man felt the depression they were looking for and stopped.

Reaching inside, he pulled at the iron release handle attached to the wedge stone—designed to withstand the internal pressures of a full chamber—and a section of the wall swung out towards them. Stepping aside, they moved silently through the new opening into the dark access shaft beyond.

They pulled the stone panel back into place and walked silently up the narrow incline until they found the wall with protruding bricks, spaced for use as a ladder.

Each man had the internal architecture fully memorized, and, in the darkness, they climbed—heading confidently for their objective. They each checked their belt-packs to confirm that the needed tools were still intact.

The next two hours would be ones of extreme heat, blinding light, painful energy discharges, and nauseous disorientation. But, their mission would instigate the next phase of a centuries-old plan, devised long before either of them was born, and destined to be continued long after they died—which would be two hours from now.

It was a one-way mission—but the joy and excitement that each man felt grew with each step as they meditated upon the pleasures and rewards that awaited them after sacrificing their lives.

For the Creator!

Laméch awoke screaming in pain as different regions of his body alternated between blistering heat and stinging, piercing cold. His entire left side felt as if it were on fire, and he tried to force his unresponsive limbs to move.

Eventually he managed to twist onto his back—only to discover the fierce heat seemed to be coming from the ground and had traveled to his shoulders.

Through sheer will power he eventually sat up, pushing aside some of the branches Keziah had placed over them. It was still dark and the early morning breeze felt extremely cold. He tried to make sense of his situation and slowly realized that somehow the grasses he was sitting in were saturated with swirling hot water.

He felt a tug on the other branches and realized that Keziah was pulling the rest of them away.

"Help me move Kendrach," she said with a voice that sounded as agonized as Laméch felt.

"What is happening?" Laméch groaned dizzily as he pitched sideways and eventually got to his knees—transferring the heat from the damp ground to his legs. He realized that the temperature wasn't actually as scalding as it had initially felt. It was definitely very warm, but the shock to his cold, hypothermic system had made it seem like liquid fire.

Keziah was moving as painfully and as slowly as he was.

"There must be a hot spring further up this hill," she said. "It probably spills down the hill at this time every morning."

They were now both on their feet and tossing away the remaining branches. They could now feel the warm water swirl around their feet and flow slowly past them as it made its way down to the beach.

"I want to get Kendrach up to the hot springs," she said. "If the water is not *too* warm, we can rest there to regain our body heat until the sun rises."

They reached down for Kendrach, whose face appeared blue in the starlight. Fortunately, he was still breathing, although in very quick, shallow gasps.

They managed to hoist Kendrach on their shoulders, and then force their legs to move them uphill, slogging through the warm, soggy grasses. The depth and temperature of the water rose, warming their legs but slowing their progress, and, as they ascended, the warm waters became a small stream flowing against their progress. As they walked, the current grew stronger, forcing them up onto the bank of relatively dry grasses formed by the stream.

Eventually they spotted a large cloud of steam in the early morning air, which soon led them to the pool of heated water below it—and the breach which had created the stream and sent the warm waters flowing down the hillside.

Keziah carefully entered a bare toe into the hot water (and despite everything else, Laméch could not help but notice the lovely leg to which that toe was attached) and eventually announced that the water would not scald them.

They positioned Kendrach feet-first into the pool, and then slid in next to him, carving out footholds in the pool's muddy sides. The heat was excruciating to Laméch, as his increased circulation carried stinging pinpricks of pain swiftly throughout his body; but eventually he relaxed and allowed the numbing warmth to take over.

They held Kendrach's head above water and took a moment to look around. Some stars were visible through the fog, and Laméch suddenly realized that Keziah was smiling at him.

"We have to stay awake until sunrise," she said. "We can't risk drowning—or allowing Kendrach to drown."

These were not the words that Laméch had expected to correspond with her smile, but he nodded and smiled back. He then uttered something that he very seldom said.

"Thank you." He nodded, suddenly realizing that, if it weren't for these insane conditions, he could not have envisioned anything more wonderful than being with Keziah in some remote hot springs.

"Thank you," he repeated, "for saving us. We would be in much worse shape without your skills and wisdom of the forests."

She stared into his eyes lit by the foggy starlight.

"If it weren't for you," she said, "I would be undergoing medical experiments right now. You must believe me—that I would rather be here with you."

She reached out and, for the second time that night, gently stroked his cheek. Her warm fingers contrasted with the cold breezes that still moved past his head. He was suddenly conscious of his unshaven face and clammy, disheveled hair—soaked in cold sweat caused by the surrounding heat.

He raised his right hand from the warmth of the pond and carefully grasped hers. He pulled it towards his face and kissed her fingers. He then recklessly uttered something that he had *never* said.

"I love you," he said quickly, and then rushed to cover his brazen words with an accompanying nod. He waited, not daring to look away, for a confirming response.

"I know," she replied quietly, with her own accompanying nod and raised eyebrows. Laméch waited for more, but nothing was forthcoming.

Slowly they disengaged their hands and lowered them into the warm water. However, they reached behind Kendrach and reconnected them, placing them in support of his head. His breathing was still a series of short, shallow gasps, but even in the dim starlight, it was clear that his complexion had greatly improved.

In silence, they kept this warrior from a bygone war, a warrior who had risked everything to save them, alive—as they waited for the sun.

In less than an hour, the sky began to lighten, and soon the steamy fog began to burn away, exposing tall trees which blocked the sky to the east.

Kendrach's breathing was more relaxed, and it seemed as if he were simply sleeping—not fighting a deadly toxin.

"Let's get him back down to the beach," Keziah suggested. "It will be dry there, and the sun will shine more directly on us when it rises over the mountains."

Laméch nodded. They pulled their flushed and wrinkled bodies from the hot spring—lifting Kendrach between them—and started down the hill. The water level in the pond had lowered, and the flow from the breach had ceased.

A warm morning breeze blew up from the ocean, and as the sun emerged, Laméch began to feel almost normal again. He was tired from a sleepless night, but he imagined that there would be nothing to prevent him from enjoying a nap on the beach later in the day.

Kendrach suddenly shifted in their arms and awakened enough to complain about being cold before dropping his head in exhaustion and resuming his sleep.

The beach was warm and dry when they arrived, and they placed Kendrach on his back with some branches to cover him and protect him from the sun, which was now floating above the eastern hills.

"Watch him," Keziah instructed, "while I go and find something to eat."

With that, she dashed back up the hill while Laméch watched her appreciatively.

Laméch sat next to Kendrach and looked out over the ocean. He could see the island smoldering in the distance, but it was too far away to see if any Semyaz—or their skiffs—were still there. He reasoned that this was probably a good thing, since that meant they could not see him either.

He heard a commotion behind him and turned to see Kendrach slowly lifting himself up from the gravel beach. Laméch rushed over to support him, and Kendrach flashed him a weak grin.

"I guess we made it," was all he said before coughing loudly. A violent shudder went through him and he closed his eyes in apparent pain.

"What happened?" he asked as Laméch helped him sit up.

"We connected you to the pontoons and made it to the shore," he began. "We were numb and cold, but couldn't risk a fire, so we huddled around you and tried to keep warm. We woke up before dawn, soaked in warm water overflowing from a nearby hot spring, so we spent the rest of the night regaining our body heat in it."

He pointed to his still-wrinkly skin as Kendrach's laugh turned into another cough.

"We brought you back to the beach this morning to let the sun dry and warm you," Laméch continued.

"Treating me like an article of laundry," Kendrach said with another laugh—this time avoiding the cough. He looked around.

"Where is your friend?" he asked.

"Keziah left to find food," Laméch answered.

Kendrach nodded and the two sat in silence, looking at the smoke from the distant island.

"That was my home for many years," Kendrach said eventually, but Laméch was surprised that there was no tone of sadness to his voice. Kendrach smiled and nodded at Laméch, but said nothing else. The two returned their gaze to the sea.

Laméch began to think about what would happen next. They were alone, cut off, and had no transportation. The only "civilization" was back at the Semyaz complex, far up the shore to the north past the cliffs. And he definitely could not return there. He tried to imagine exactly what might be happening there this very moment: the subjects with the yellow tunics undergoing painful experiments, Jameth and the other techs mixing and comparing toxins—and the woman in the red robe watching over it all.

"They'll be coming for you," Kendrach said suddenly, interrupting Laméch's thoughts.

"The Semyaz?" Laméch asked as a jolt of fear went through him.

Kendrach looked at him with a reassuring smile.

"Oh, no," he said. "*They* believe you perished on the island."

Laméch breathed a quick sigh. He had thought he escaped them once before—only to be wrong.

"You seem quite confident," he said.

"That is because the Semyaz are confident. They are confident that no one could have escaped their siege, therefore you and Keziah are certainly smoldering, charred bodies that will never be recognized or found."

Kendrach flashed a cheery smile.

"What I meant," he continued, "was that Aenoch's people will be coming for you. They said a team would be here in two weeks, and since they won't be able to contact us again, they are certain to get here as quickly as possible."

Laméch nodded, relieved.

"But we're not on the island, now. How will they find us?"

"You'll have to watch for them," he said. "And it may be difficult since they will be avoiding detection—and the island may have moved."

"I thought it was anchored," Laméch said, confused.

"Not any more," said Kendrach. "Once I lit that fire around the communication hut, it burned straight down through the island, cutting a hole through which the hut and everything in it dropped into the ocean below. The energy coil and communication device are now sitting, inaccessible, at the bottom of the sea. We could not allow them to fall into enemy hands."

He stopped as another fit of coughing wracked his frame, and was forced to lie back down on the ground. He managed to mumble the word "dizzy" as he wiped his eyes and continued in a much weaker voice.

"I had to wait until one of their orbs landed nearby, so that when they saw our fire, they would think *they* had caused it. Otherwise, they would have seen it and made our position."

He paused for a breath, until Laméch had to remind him of the original question.

"So it's not anchored?"

"No," Kendrach answered with a slightly embarrassed smile. "The anchor was affixed in the foundation of the hut, so it also is at the bottom of the sea. You will need to wait a few days, and then make your way back to the island to meet …"

"Why do you keep saying '*you*'?" Laméch interrupted. "You said 'They'll be coming for *you*', and '*you* will need to wait'. Not 'us' or 'we'. Do you have different plans for yourself?"

Kendrach looked down and then back up.

"Yes, I do," he said slowly. "Within a few hours, I will be dead."

There was a moment of stunned silence until Laméch finally responded.

"How can you be sure of that?" he blurted with more severity than he had intended. He was uncomfortable with anyone discussing death, and even more distraught at hearing someone claim it for one's self.

But Kendrach calmly nodded, closing his eyes.

"I recognize the poison that is in me," he said. "It initially seizes the nerves and locks the muscles, but after *that* wears off, it slowly attacks the internal organs."

He reopened his eyes and spoke quietly, and Laméch was suddenly aware of the quiet but pounding surf as it rolled against the beach. The sun was now high in the sky and shining directly down on them.

"I appreciate the kindness and care you both showed me last night, but, although spending the night in the hot spring saved our lives, it also, ironically, speeded the poison throughout my system and has accelerated my demise."

Laméch began to react, but Kendrach stopped him.

"I was dead the moment that dart struck me," he said. "But it was most important that you escape and make it back to Aenoch."

He closed his eyes again and twisted around in apparent pain, but he was only reaching into his garment. Eventually he pulled out a small canvas bag.

"Make sure that Aenoch receives these," he said, handing the bag to Laméch.

"What is this?" he asked.

"Open it," Kendrach replied.

Laméch stretched out the opening and saw the crystal flasks from the communication hut. The brilliant colors from two nights ago were gone, however, and now, even in the sunlight, they appeared as nothing more than opaque vials of nondescript glass.

He looked back and met Kendrach's eyes.

"I'll be certain that Aenoch receives these," he said with conviction.

"I thank you," Kendrach replied, closing his eyes again. He suddenly erupted into a bout of coughing which gradually diminished in intensity and eventually ended in one final long wheeze. Laméch also saw that he was now shivering uncontrollably.

Kendrach's eyes snapped open, and he began to speak, but no words came out. Laméch watched as he painfully tried to mouth something, but it seemed as if Kendrach had run out of air.

Laméch bent over until his face was directly over Kendrach's. The dying warrior tried to speak again, and Laméch was now able to understand his silent words as he watched his lips and felt his breath on his face.

"I seem to have miscalculated," he said as he managed a slight grin. His eyes grew deadly serious as he continued.

"You have a great mission ahead of you," he said firmly, "but you can not accomplish it alone. You will need Keziah. Love her as you have, in the past, loved yourself."

He stopped to draw air slowly into his lungs, but his eyes glared into Laméch's, demanding confirmation.

Laméch quickly nodded.

Kendrach closed his eyes as a slight smile spread on his face.

"Since the transgression of the First Ones, this planet is cursed. It is no longer a fit place for immortality."

Laméch watched in bewilderment as Kendrach's smile grew, crinkling his temple scar. The muscles surrounding his mouth twitched and he managed to form his next silent sentence.

"I have been made for a better place."

His smile blossomed as his right eyebrow rose and his right eyelid flickered open once and then quickly closed in what could only be described as a reverse wink. Laméch leaned forward and placed his ear directly over Kendrach's nose, but could hear nothing. He saw Kendrach's chest lower—and not rise again—as the faintest gurgling sound emerged. A strange panic came over him as he considered the possibility that he had just witnessed his first natural death—and then remembered the poison dart.

He was also unnerved by the warm smile which remained on Kendrach's face—challenging his personal formula. Somehow it seemed that Kendrach had experienced fun even when he *hadn't* survived.

"How is he doing?"

Laméch looked up to see Keziah bounding down the hill onto the beach. She carried a large, hastily woven frond-basket filled with mangoes and pears. As she drew near, Laméch could also see she had fastened a bunch of bananas to her tunic's waist cord and had found a dark violet flower blossom to place in her hair—which somehow was miraculously tidy. Her yellow tunic shone brightly in the sun—as if she had washed it—and Laméch found himself wondering if even the sun was darker and more oppressive back at the Semyaz complex.

She stopped suddenly as she saw Laméch's expression. She slowly resumed her walk and eventually came to stand next to him.

Laméch looked up into her face and tried to formulate some words, but as he finally opened his mouth, she spoke.

"He's dead, isn't he?"

Taken aback at her bluntness, Laméch shrugged.

"I'm not sure. I guess so, but…"

Keziah dropped to her knees and reached for Kendrach's neck, pushing aside his long black hair. She placed her fingers alongside his throat and let them rest there for a few seconds.

Eventually, she raised her hand.

"He's gone," she declared through closed teeth. She looked up and met Laméch's eyes, and he was startled to see a flash of pure rage pass across her face. It was replaced almost immediately with a look of deep sorrow as moisture began to build around her eyes.

"I am sorry," she said to Laméch. "You and he were becoming friends."

Laméch was startled that her concern had shifted directly to him. He also realized that, other than the ocean crossing, she had spent no time with Kendrach.

"He did regain consciousness for a few moments," Laméch said eventually. "We need to make our way back to the island, once we are certain the Semyaz patrols have left. Aenoch's people will be looking for us there in less than two weeks."

Keziah nodded, wiping her eyes.

"We will return his body to the island which was his home for so many years," she said, rising.

Laméch rose with her and grasped her hand. His arm went around her waist as he looked down into Kendrach's still smiling visage.

"He died well," she said with a sigh. "He died to save us."

Her words caused a sudden jolt to Laméch's mind as he unexpectedly considered what it would be like for someone, someday, to say the same words about him.

He had always known that there were many things worth living for.

Were there things worth dying for?

Beneath the charred treetops that defined the island's skyline, Laméch and Keziah could see that the undulating landscape was already rebuilding its lush green foliage. They had concealed their pontoon raft on the far west side of the island—away from the cliffs—and were now standing over the grave of a warrior who, as swiftly as he had become an unexpected friend, had left them.

Keziah closed her eyes and spoke silently in a private incantation. Laméch wrapped his arms around her waist and pulled her close. Her eyes flickered open and she looked into Laméch's face with a glowing smile.

"I've had more adventure in the last few days with you, than I have experienced my entire life," she said as she pulled herself closer within his arms. "Until that day when the Semyaz captured me after I strayed too far from the village, I had enjoyed a simple, quiet life in the forest."

Her arms went around his back as she faced him.

"I can't imagine the adventures I'll have during a life with you."

Her eyes pierced into Laméch as he drew her up and kissed her—tentatively at first, and then with full passion.

Suddenly she pulled back—a clear indication that, for the moment, the kiss would lead to nothing more.

Laméch calmed himself, and smiled at her. He knew what he had to ask, and he did it quickly, before he lost his courage.

"Will you marry me?"

She released him completely and stepped back with a laugh. Laméch had not known what to expect—but certainly not this.

"And just where do you expect to find an Officiator here?" she asked, swinging her arm to indicate the island. Her eyes were sparkling with mischief, and Laméch realized that he had a lot to learn about Keziah. So much, that it would probably take *more* than a lifetime.

"I'm not sure," he stammered, getting his thoughts together. "Perhaps we can ask Aenoch if he can officiate. He was Founder of his own city. When his people arrive, they will take us to his island, and I'm sure he will be able to do it. If a city founder can't officiate, who can?"

She approached him, still grinning, and drew her finger down his cheek until it rested in the dimple on his chin.

"I still haven't answered you yet," she teased. "And you're already making plans."

Laméch shuddered slightly, and tried to smile.

"Well?" was all he could manage.

Her arms swiftly wrapped around him again.

"Absolutely," she declared. "I've known that I was going to marry you from the first time we met at the compound." She smiled broadly at him.

He returned her embrace with another kiss—which grew and ended in the same manner as the first.

She stepped back and looked at him—suddenly serious.

"The ways of the 'forest people', as you call us, may seem quaint to you 'city dwellers', but I assure you we have our reasons." She smiled slightly as if reminding him of something. "And the Way of the Seed goes far beyond mere customs of either forest people *or* city dwellers."

She took a deep breath.

"We will wait until we meet this Founder, Aenoch, and ask him to officiate our marriage."

Suddenly she broke into a wicked smile and rushed to him, placing her mouth over his ear and whispered.

"And I assure you it will be worth the wait!"

Laméch's knees buckled, as he instinctively stepped back from her rush. He grabbed her arms and looked deep into her eyes, suddenly recognizing the strong, intelligent *woman* that resided behind them. That *person* was now more appealing than ever, and he was overwhelmed with a love for her that he could never have imagined a few minutes earlier.

She pulled away again with a smile.

"We'd better make camp," she said. "We have a few more days before they arrive." Her smile grew. "If they come at all…"

Laméch glared at her.

"They'll be here," he said through clenched teeth—followed by a wink.

She laughed and together they made their way to the western edge where they could watch for their rescuers.

Together they set about creating their first, temporary, home.

On the morning of the eleventh day since Kendrach's communication, Laméch spotted the silver sphere which indicated an incoming dolphin team. It was arriving directly from the west, allowing the island to cover them from the cliffs to the east. As far as Laméch could tell, the island had drifted to the northwest, but not enough to prevent it from being found.

They had marked a large sign of the Seed on the western side of the island using large green leaves which contrasted with the brown of the island's edge.

Laméch called for Keziah, and they made their way down the vines and roots into the sea. Once they were sure they had been spotted, they obliterated the leaf pattern above them, removed their pontoon raft from hiding, and headed out to meet Aenoch's people.

The morning silence was suddenly broken by a chorus of dolphin chirps and clicks, and as they paddled their way past the sphere and towards the skiff, they watched as the dolphins jumped and played, celebrating the end of their long journey—and their recent release from their harnesses.

As they neared the skiff, with its familiar central ceramic cone, Laméch was startled to see Aenoch himself standing at the bow!

"It's Aenoch!" Laméch yelled to Keziah.

"Laméch, it is good to see you!" Aenoch shouted, waving. Laméch tried to wave back as he held on to his pontoon.

Soon they arrived and were pulled aboard the skiff by Aenoch and another man. Aenoch looked around as if confused, and then finally spoke.

"Where's Kendrach? What happened? We heard nothing from you, so we came as quickly as possible."

"The Semyaz attacked the island that night," Laméch answered. "Kendrach saved us, but he died from a poison dart in the process. He destroyed the communication equipment," he added helpfully.

Aenoch's eyes closed, and then reopened.

"We had feared the worst. Kendrach was a great friend and warrior."

His eyes closed again for several seconds until Laméch wondered if he were meditating.

They snapped open again and Aenoch smiled.

"This must be the young woman that you rescued," he said, excitedly. Laméch didn't have to be reminded that the rescue had been against Aenoch's orders.

"Yes," Laméch answered, "This is Keziah."

Keziah nodded and bowed as properly as she could in her wet slave tunic.

"I am very happy to finally meet you," she said to Aenoch, "and also very thankful that you sent this man," she pointed to Laméch, "to rescue me. And now here you are rescuing both of us!"

She beamed a smile at Aenoch, who could only smile in return.

"And now," she continued, "I believe Laméch has a question he would like to ask you."

Before Aenoch could respond, the man next to him muttered something in his ear and his smile immediately disappeared. Aenoch nodded.

The man rushed to the bow and gave a loud whistle. The dolphins' chirping ended abruptly as he stood there and waited for them to bring their harnesses to him.

Aenoch turned back to Laméch, his face suddenly grave.

"We must continue our journey without delay," he said.

"What is wrong?" Laméch asked, responding to the urgency in Aenoch's voice.

"The Semyaz have initiated the next phase in their war against humanity," Aenoch declared. "Clandestine agents have attacked your father's city."

Laméch was stunned. He hadn't thought about Matusalé City in weeks.

"What has happened?" he asked. "Did they hurt my father?"

"No," Aenoch answered with a shake of his head.

"They sabotaged the Power House."

PART III
ELUCIDATION

This—and no other—is the root
from which a tyrant springs:
when he first appears as protector.

Plato

CHAPTER 17
BREAKTHROUGH

"In the decades preceding Aenoch's final disappearance, the escalation of clandestine resistance against the Semyaz evolved into a most unusual conflict. Although the Semyaz increased their own covert incursions with proselytizing and subterfuge, they allowed no public acknowledgment of any resistance, preferring instead to present a unified, hopeful, and optimistic future to the cities of the world.

Later centuries would refer to these skirmishes as the Perception Battles—the precursors of the final Replacement War."

—Amoela the Librarian,
The First Two Thousand Years, Vol. II

Tûrell stepped back to study the large clay slates which were mounted on the walls of his study. They were covered with small markings, interspersed with numerous lines, arrows, and circles that delineated different sections and helped clarify his research.

As predicted, a pattern was emerging.

He leaned forward to the second slate and extracted a medium tipped stylus from his sleeve. He rubbed out a short string of characters with its blunt end, and then he reversed it and carefully incised another string in its place—marking the replacement with a small star to indicate its new function.

He stepped back again, sitting slightly against the edge of his stone desk which was cluttered with scattered scrolls and several stacks of clay tablets. He glanced around his granite study, looking up at the *tsohar* panels that encircled the room along the ceiling's edge. He stared at the glow, using it to distract him slightly as he calculated—mentally plotting a graph from his occurrence algorithm.

He looked back at the slates, his excitement growing.

It *was* a language—or at least a *very* sophisticated code.

Tûrell worked deep beneath the Haermon Mountain Complex and was one of very few people to work directly with the Semyaz. Not that he had ever seen one face to face—he knew few who enjoyed *that* privilege. However, he reported to them regularly as they gave instructions from behind the translucent windows that led to the corridors of their quarters even deeper beneath the complex. As a result, he saw only indistinct faces, but they all wore bright white robes—and his own white smock indicated his ranking directly beneath them.

It was difficult for someone who knew of only one language to grasp the *concept* of language. One needed multiple languages to compare and determine which attributes constituted a language—as opposed to other forms of encoded communication.

Fortunately, he had seen samples of Semyaz script—and even analyzed some of their phonetics from listening to them speak. It was a strange, singing language that seemed to be based somewhat on differences between tonal intervals.

He had also studied—and composed—some very complex cryptography during the Family Wars, and had learned two very important principles.

ELUCIDATION: BREAKTHROUGH

First: An unknown language or code appears random before it is translated or decoded.

Second: Apparent randomness can be exposed by analyzing character or word frequency, because each word or unit of information was placed deliberately by the sender.

What had eluded him until very recently was a process or simple formula to discern between deliberate nonsense and a communication that contained actual, instructional information.

Until now.

And these final tests were proof!

His amazing discovery applied to *any* communication that contained *real* instructional information. Even with an unknown or encoded language, it was now possible for him to determine whether a large portion of script was, indeed, an actual communication, or a deliberate, misleading string of random characters. Unfortunately, it did not in any way help in *translating* a specific communication—but he could now determine that it *was* a communication.

Once any unknown message was broken into words, syllables, or even character strings, one could assign a frequency of usage. There are always strings that occurred more frequently than others—and when the frequency of these strings was compared with their rankings, the results were *always* inversely proportional! The most frequent string occurred *twice* as often as the second most frequent string, which occurred twice as often as the *fourth*, which occurred twice as often as the *eighth*—continuing until the communication source was exhausted.

This phenomenon created a perfectly straight line when graphed. However, this phenomenon *never* emerged from random characters, bogus codes, or any naturally generated patterns—only from communications that contained *actual* meaningful information!

From the beginning, Tûrell had been studying the results from the experiments in the labs and chambers above him, and passing his analysis on to the Semyaz. They would, in turn, give him instructions—and the occasional inexplicable project.

He studied his clay slates intently, his excitement mounting. He felt that he was closing in on his primary directive—the one he had received from the Semyaz when he was first given this position almost a century earlier!

Their primary command was twofold—and it had never changed:

Determine how hereditary information is transferred from parent to child, and with this knowledge, find ways to improve the human species.

In front of him, was the accumulation of decades of study, research, and blind speculation—a seemingly chaotic clutter of chemistry and probability.

And now, somehow from this chaos, *this* phenomenon of language had emerged!

His excitement bordered on euphoria.

Just as humanity—and the Semyaz—had a language, so did life itself! And this language *had* to be the medium that transferred instructions from one generation to the next!

A smile broke across his face—a smile that was slowly diminished by the daunting realization that the subsequent and resultant requirements of the next phase would be even more demanding. After all, this was, still, a means to an end, and the Semyaz never let him forget that the *improvement* of humanity was paramount.

They were *not* interested in using simple techniques to highlight or emphasize specific human characteristics in the manner of a plant or animal breeder. Such techniques could only accentuate (or diminish) *existing* characteristics.

Rather, they were very adamant about discovering *anything* that would increase the strength, improve the senses, or extend the lifespan. They demanded a physical or mental alteration that went *beyond* humanity's current abilities and would provide clear and irrefutable evidence that *they* had contributed something to humankind's improvement.

It had always struck Tûrell as strange that, on the one hand, the Semyaz seemed devoted to creating a better human; while, on the other hand, they seemed to despise the very people they were helping. Sometimes, when they spoke to him, it almost seemed as if they regarded humanity as a scourge or plague—and that the planet would be better off without them.

A voice startled him from his thoughts.

"She's here."

The lady in the red robe waited in the antechamber outside of Tûrell's primary study with only the slightest apprehension. During her decades of service, she had been down to these levels only three times—and each time it was in response to Tûrell's summons.

She knew that he had several labs, and she had actually seen one of them on her last visit. It had been a wonderful experience to witness the amazing magnification and other optical equipment within. Often she wished she had access to similar tools, but the Semyaz knew best—and only the white-smocked technicians who worked directly with them were allowed to use them.

That last visit had been only seventeen years ago, when she had received instructions on implementing the new mating program for subjects—and the subsequent forced embryo removals and re-implantation procedures. It was the important "selective breeding" phase of the human improvement project, and it had the added benefit of reducing the need for male subjects—and the potential for ultimately providing their own source of research material.

Her visit *prior* to that one had been almost sixty years ago—when Tûrell had presented the discovery that hereditary instructions were transferred by purely chemical means. This had initiated the combining of the heated and non-heated biological agents into a single green vial to be administered to the subjects.

That was also the time that an intruder had abducted one of her subjects and escaped from the complex. Fortunately, they had both been killed on a nearby island where they had attempted to find refuge. It still angered her that she had not been able to detect the interloper.

"You may come."

The voice came from an aide who was beckoning to her. She walked towards him, turned right through the indicated archway, and entered Tûrell's study.

Tûrell was staring at the clay slates on his walls and did not turn to her when she approached. As in her previous encounters, he was wearing the bright white smock of those who report directly to the Semyaz. He also had the same thin brown beard and wide eyes which somehow gave the appearance that he never slept.

She stopped a few paces from him and he lifted his hand to point to the slates. He still did not turn to face her.

"This is the breakthrough we have been seeking all these years!"

He stared at his slates for a few more seconds before suddenly turning to her. He broke into a big grin which seemed highly undignified to her and was quite unsettling. She raised her eyebrows for him to continue.

His grin subsided.

"Since the beginning of this undertaking we have searched for the means to improve human life, but we have always been limited by how life's instructions travel from parent to child."

She nodded at this obvious foundational statement.

"And we have succeeded in many amazing ways to change or alter human life by using basic breeding practices, but—until now—we could only utilize actual traits as they exist in the parent."

She nodded again, her mind going to the hundreds of deformed and mutated offspring she and her team had cataloged over the decades.

She spoke for the first time.

"Until now?"

His grin partially returned and he faced his slates again.

"I have just discovered," he said, pointing, "that there is an actual chemical *language* that instructs the offspring's growth. Normally, this is a merging of the parent's instructions—which is why children demonstrate *both* parents' distinctive traits."

He turned back to face her.

"However, since this *is* a language, this means it can be translated—and *this* means we are no longer limited to a given parent's reservoir of features or attributes!"

He reached out and grabbed her by the shoulders—something he had never done before. His voice lowered.

"This is somewhat speculative, and I will have to work more with the Semyaz, but—," he sucked in a large breath of air and let it out slowly. "Someday soon we should be able to *design* whatever feature or attribute we want! If we want the offspring to grow to be four cubits tall, we simply change the instructions! If we want the offspring to have red hair, long legs, or even a large nose, we simply find the original commands for these attributes and replace them with new code. Of course, more complex changes will require more translating and understanding, but, in theory—and with enough time—we could create or design any form of life we desire!"

She pulled back slightly at the onslaught of his enthusiasm, amazed that Tûrell would be sharing this so casually—and shocked that he was admitting "speculation". But she also realized the incredible implications if his discovery was true—and she had no reason to doubt him.

He released her and stepped back, regaining his composure.

She knew that Tûrell had not summoned her solely to share advances or insights, and she waited patiently for the inevitable new instructions that accompanied her visits below.

He turned away abruptly, selected a scroll from his desk, and walked quickly to the left slate. He quietly compared the two, with an occasional mutter, almost giving the impression that he had forgotten his guest.

But she had not been forgotten. He spoke abruptly.

"How are you progressing with your Candidate Program?"

She nodded quickly—suddenly eager to please.

"Very well," she said. "I have five classes now, ages nine through thirteen. Each class has twelve girls, all being prepared for service—and each class believes it is uniquely groomed and knows nothing of the others. Also, each class has a mentor who is training the Candidates in the proscribed catechism so they have a full understanding of the Creator—and their special calling."

Tûrell turned to look at her.

"They *must* be ready," he said with sudden anxiety. "We are having great success in many areas and may have viable implants any day…"

He paused to begin a fresh sentence.

"We *must* have pubescent hosts."

She reacted visibly to his concern, but he responded with a smile.

"I am certain this will not present a problem," he said with a gentle wave of his hand. "You are doing well and seem to be on schedule."

The smile disappeared.

"Your mission from this point on," he continued, "is simply to insure that, at any given time, you will have a pool of Candidates aged thirteen through fifteen who are properly trained for implantation and full service to the Semyaz."

His smile returned.

"I am pleased to hear that your first class will soon be ready."

She smiled back and nodded.

"I will be ready no matter how long it takes," she said—and suddenly regretted her words. She hadn't meant to imply that his research might take longer than he hoped.

But Tûrell simply nodded his approval with a slight shrug.

"You are correct," he said with a tip of his head. "Such things often take longer than we wish."

He turned and walked back towards her.

"Of course, if our research *does* take longer, remember that we have no use for Candidates who are over fifteen. No class may be aware of the existence of the other classes, and each class must be isolated and believe it is unique and special in its mission and training."

She nodded, suddenly concerned.

ELUCIDATION: BREAKTHROUGH

"No use for those over fifteen? What am I supposed to do with a class once they are beyond fifteen?"

Tûrell gave her a confused look.

"They are to be discarded. You *are* making plans to initiate more?"

She quickly tried to mask her disapproval, but was unsuccessful.

"We cannot," Tûrell continued with urgency, his eyes hardening, "have educated, strong-minded young women who will begin to ask questions and become potential security risks. You *do* understand." It was *not* a question.

She nodded, realizing that the Semyaz—and the Creator—had superior perspective. Hers was a life of sacrifice and devotion—and the manifestation of the *Seed* was paramount.

Tûrell interrupted her thoughts.

"We have many years of work ahead of us," he said, "and my team—and the Semyaz—have the enormous task of learning and utilizing this new language."

He smiled.

"However, with enough tests—and enough time—we will soon be on our way to designing a *new* human. One with all of the improvements and abilities that the Semyaz require."

He grabbed her arms again—and again it startled her. Tûrell's eyes gleamed with elation.

"Just as the Creator re-made man in *his* image, so we have been privileged with the task of improving man in *ours*!"

He released her and glanced back at his desk. She couldn't help becoming caught up in his enthusiasm. She could truly see, more clearly than ever, the promise of success at the end of their endeavors.

She smiled back and nodded in obedience.

Tûrell waved for her to leave.

"You may return to your duties," he said with a nod. His eyes became serious.

"Be sure that I will have my Candidates when I require them."

She nodded quickly.

"You will have them. Everything is being prepared for your success."

His smile returned.

"All praise to the Creator," he said.

She nodded again.

"All praise to the Creator," she responded dutifully.

She turned and exited the archway, passing the attendant as she turned into the corridor. She thought furiously about Tûrell's discovery of a hidden language, impressed at the implications, but also somewhat perplexed.

If Tûrell was only now discovering this language, then the Semyaz obviously were as ignorant of its existence as he was. And if the Semyaz, who were intimately knowledgeable of the Creator's handiwork, were not aware of this language, then what was its origin?

If the Creator had not devised this language, then who?

Tûrell watched her leave—and immediately dismissed her from his mind. He turned back to his desk and absentmindedly picked up three small scrolls which he tossed casually from hand to hand.

These scrolls came directly from the Semyaz in response to the reports he submitted on inscribed tablets. The scrolls were usually accompanied by brief verbal instructions, but the majority of his time was spent reading the scrolls, adopting their instructions into his research, and meeting with his colleagues in sessions of speculation and conjecture.

His colleagues wore the white smocks because they were deemed the most creative and the most likely to arrive at solutions that were not readily apparent. Intuition was highly encouraged, and Tûrell thought it interesting that among all of the techs, he was the only male.

He had shared his statistical discovery with his colleagues at their last meeting, and he was certain that they would be engaged in further testing. He smiled as he looked forward to their inevitable confirmation.

His hands fumbled, and the scrolls tumbled onto the floor at his feet and began to unroll. He quickly stooped to retrieve them, and as he began to collect them, he detected something that he had not noticed in all of his decades of service.

As his fingers brushed over the script on one of the unfurled scrolls, he felt nothing! There was no impression or indentation from a stylus that normally accompanied such documents—the surface was totally smooth.

He examined the reverse side of the scroll and confirmed that there were no ridges to indicate the passage of any instrument.

He turned back to the front and closely examined a specific character. He rubbed it slightly to try and smudge the marking, but it remained clear, refusing to release any carboniferous residue. It had not been inscribed with a charcoal marker.

He looked around the room frantically to try and find another method of analyzing this enigma, but could think of nothing.

Just as he was deciding to take the scroll to one of his labs, he remembered the magnification lens that was still in the pocket of his smock from earlier in the day. He had been in one of his labs analyzing spectrums from the prism mounted on one of the combustion chambers. The chambers ignited small test samples and projected the refracted results onto a chemical sheet which preserved the results. He had been using the magnification glass to examine absorption lines.

He removed the glass from his pocket and rushed over to the desk. Pushing aside the clutter, he placed the scroll on the newly cleared portion. He peered through the glass at the same character he had tried to smudge earlier, and noticed that the magnified edges were amazingly clear. There was no graininess or extraneous ink that would normally surround the markings, and even when expanded, they exhibited clear straight lines.

He pulled the glass back to increase the magnification, and studied the curved edges of an adjacent character. He noticed that alongside the clear black edges, there appeared some brownish spots on the convex side of some of the curves. They reminded him of the edges of a fire—the browning that travels before a consuming flame and usually grows in an expanding circle surrounding the growing fire.

He placed the scroll and lens on the desktop and looked upward, his thoughts churning.

Were the Semyaz somehow able to *burn* their writings into the scroll? How could they possibly focus heat in such a controlled manner?

What other amazing abilities and technologies were hidden in their habitation levels deep beneath the complex? What knowledge had they not yet shared?

And why had they not shared it?

Again, Tûrell's mind fought the confusion that accompanied the apparent inconsistencies of the Semyaz. If they possessed such advanced wonders, why did they need him and his team? Despite their reclusiveness and apparent superiority, did they have weaknesses and shortcomings just as all other men?

Where had *their* knowledge come from?

If the Semyaz were, as they claimed, simply a human community that had arisen separately from the rest of humanity, how had they accumulated such vast science and understanding? And why did they need to operate in relative secrecy and rely on other people to advance their causes?

Did they have fears?

Tûrell suppressed all of his confusion and doubts by reminding himself that he should simply be thankful that he was allowed to serve.

He shook his head and returned his gaze to the inscriptions on his wall panels. As he resumed his ponderings, his mind took him, amazingly, to the same question that had entered the mind of the lady in the red robe moments earlier.

Why did the Semyaz appear to know nothing of this hidden language?

CHAPTER 18
EXTRACTION

"The news of the attack on the Matusalé Power House traveled swiftly from city to city and reawakened the horrors of the Family Wars in the minds of those old enough to remember. It provoked an almost panicked determination that the chaos and carnage of those wars should never be repeated, and demands were made to fortify and increase defenses. However, such demands went beyond the resources of local enforcer units—and city treasuries—and it initially appeared that sufficient protection would be impracticable.

However, Semyaz emissaries soon arrived with their solution."

—Amoela the Librarian,
The First Two Thousand Years, Vol. II

L améch grasped the control cables tightly, pulling hard to the left. They were coming in low along the coastline, and as they neared the Haermon Cliffs, he thought he spotted the section of gravel beach where the warrior Kendrach had perished so many years earlier.

This was the farthest he had ever driven this two-dragon team, but they were performing well—instinctively flying low and maintaining an ideal synchronized wing-beat.

There was a fixed harness between the two reptiles, and suspended beneath it was the enclosed gondola that contained Laméch and his two companions. Endrath was an astronomer and navigator, while Klaven was an expert at anything explosive.

Laméch watched as a floating island came into view on his left and remembered the scorched island where Aenoch had rescued him and Keziah. There was no way of telling whether or not this was the same island, but Laméch couldn't help but wonder—and be amazed at how green and thick the foliage had become, if, in fact, this *was* that island.

After that rescue—so many years ago—they had traveled to Aenoch's Island, where Aenoch, somewhat reluctantly, had agreed to officiate their wedding. After they were married, they accepted his invitation to stay, and soon began to work and live with the rest of Aenoch's people.

Laméch and Keziah built a small hut of their own with the intention of raising a family. However, although it had been many years, they remained childless, and Laméch wondered if the experiments that the Semyaz had performed on Keziah were responsible.

Although he shared Aenoch's purpose of subverting the Semyaz and their goals, Laméch found that as the years passed, he avoided Aenoch as much as possible. It was practically impossible to maintain a conversation with his grandfather, since every exchange soon led to dissertations that were far too metaphysical or ethereal for Laméch's taste. Aenoch always wanted to expound on how the Semyaz were destroying humanity's spiritual destiny, while Laméch was only focused on one thing. He had witnessed their atrocities and exploitations first-hand—and was only interested in stopping them.

Laméch almost never thought of his old life back in Matusalé, and only occasionally thought of his father—and of his old friend,

Ruallz. Their new home and new life was Aenoch's Island—but they soon realized they shared an addiction for adventure and were quickly involved in missions away from the island.

They traveled as couriers, visiting every city except Matusalé (where Laméch risked recognition) and sharing the latest intelligence with the underground, using (and trusting) Librarians as a network for both storing and disseminating information.

Laméch and Keziah spent many years traveling throughout the northern plains of Irad and Jaebal where rolling hills of thick tall grasses spread far inland from the shoreline. This was a contrast from the forests which covered the rest of the planet, and Jaebal was known for livestock and other range animals. The far-western Irad was famous for its fruits and wines, and large orchards and vineyards surrounded the city walls for as far as the eye could see. Keziah's ancestors had been refugees from Irad and had fled westward towards the Haermon Mountains prior to the peak of the Family Wars.

They visited the former weapons factories of Tubalcain where bronze and iron smiths now produced ship hulls, mechanical equipment, and various tools of industry. In fact, it had been a Tubalcain weapons cache that Laméch had stumbled into that morning of his man-kite stunt. Laméch and his wife also spent a somewhat fearful time in the city of Naamah, founded by Tubalcain's sister, which had also been a weapons garrison. Originally it had been an expansion of Tubalcain's business empire, but now mostly supported itself with kidnapping and piracy.

Laméch, who had only known the modern city of Matusalé, was always amazed at how old—and small—the other cities of the world were. It looked strange to see modern, sleek Power House pyramids that were less than two hundred years old, incorporated into the city walls that were often easily three or four times their age.

However, the oldest city they visited was the dismal and depressing city of Enoch—not to be confused with his grandfather's namesake, Aenoch. Other than the northern grasslands, the only place in the known world that was not covered with thick forests was the harsh and rocky landscape that surrounded Enoch. Its only industry was fishing; and the exporting of dried seafood was a very difficult and tedious business, which contributed more burdens to the already wearisome populace. Laméch could not understand how anyone had chosen this barren region to establish a city—and no one he asked could provide a satisfactory answer. However, there were some local traditions that held that the region had not always been so bleak.

A more pleasant city was Qênan, which was known mostly for its scholarly institutions and the fact that it boasted *two* libraries. It was just to the north of Matusalé, and Laméch knew his father often visited there. Also, Laméch knew that his grandfather's family had originally come from there. Qênan had attempted to remain un-involved in the Family Wars by simply screening and banning people with any undesirable traits from entering, but it soon became a target of refugee warfare and—with no real defenses—was soon overrun.

Laméch's favorite city was, of course, Jubal, where art, the latest music, high fashion, and the best wines could be found. It was strange to Laméch that the finest Jaerad wines were actually *difficult* to find in Jaebal or Irad, the cities nearest the vineyards, but was easily obtained in Jubal, the southern city farthest from Irad. It was explained to him that it was an economic principle regarding shipping and cargo. Since it cost the same to ship a keg of poor wine as it did to ship a keg of fine wine, it only made sense to strike deals for the most expensive vintages with those who lived the farthest away. Other shipping costs were incurred by any vessel that traveled too close to the disputed waters of Naamah—where ships risked being boarded by extortion patrols.

In all their travels and time spent visiting cities, Laméch was discouraged—and sometimes enraged—at the sight of Semyaz Security Forces that were now installed in every city. They supplemented the local Enforcers, and provided guards for the cities' ports, infrastructure, utilities, and, of course, Power House. This had been the ultimate response to the attack on the Matusalé Power House so many years earlier, but to Laméch they seemed like an invading army in their dark green uniforms and black helmets rather than security augmentation—which was their stated role. Every time he went through a check point or watched one question a visitor, Laméch always felt as if, in spite of all their efforts, they were moving backwards in their resistance. He wanted *less* Semyaz intrusion, not more. However, there had been no known incidents of abuse and the troops seemed to be very well trained and very civil.

No one had ever claimed responsibility for that act of sabotage, but within months of the attack, Aenoch had suddenly reappeared, traveling from city to city proclaiming that the Semyaz were the ones behind the attack on the Matusalé Power House and accusing them of being complicit in most of the evils of humanity, including the Family Wars. It was difficult to hear such things from this legend who was so highly revered for his engineering and scientific achievements. After all, it was he who had designed the modern cities that they all enjoyed. However, his indictments were received as nonsense by the people, who had only known the benefits of the Semyaz and could only surmise that Aenoch had lost his mind during his long absence. Besides, they reasoned, it was the Semyaz who had freely offered their own services to assist in additional future protection.

One area that *was* of great encouragement to Laméch was the inroads that they had made with the forest communities, hidden throughout the vast, wild areas far from the coasts. With Keziah's help, they had established great relationships and alliances with these peoples, and had provided them with help and defenses against the constant Semyaz attacks and culling of their population.

These trips had been long, arduous expeditions on foot, usually lasting many months or even years, but on one of these contact missions in the regions between Irad and the Haermon Mountains, Keziah had been reunited with the community from which she had been stolen. Unfortunately, her family had all perished during subsequent raids, but there were some people whom she recognized and knew from before, and it had been a wonderful time—both for Keziah and also for Laméch who enjoyed nothing more than to see her happy.

It was during this visit that the forest people had revealed their amazing abilities to tame and domesticate many of the great reptilian beasts that shared the forests with them. Soon after this, Laméch and Keziah put together their first "Dragon Team" patterned after the dolphin teams that the resistance currently used for world travel.

Laméch never ceased to be amazed at how these huge winged beasts launched themselves into the air. Although they only had two legs like other flying animals, the leading edge of their enormous wings, when folded, provided a large semi-flexible strut at the knuckle. The creatures would run several paces with their powerful legs to build up speed, and then bend *downward*, jamming their wing-struts into the ground. With a powerful heave, they would wrench themselves against the strut and *pole-vault* into the sky, often reaching heights of twenty cubits before unfurling their wings and commencing the concussive, hammering downdrafts that threatened to knock over anyone standing beneath them. Large cables had to be attached before this, and then riders—or cabins like the one they now rode in—were reeled in as the dragons hovered patiently.

Laméch was famous for having completed the first successful infiltration of the Haermon Complex, and he soon found himself training others. Many of these trainees were among the forest peoples, and soon many of them were *deliberately* allowing themselves to be captured. Most were not heard from again. There were some who escaped with information, but a few managed to gain positions among the Semyaz and work undercover, finding diverse and inventive means of communicating their findings to the outside. Strangely, only those who did *not* share Aenoch's beliefs were able to remain undiscovered.

Notes attached to trained birds, blinking lights from cliff windows, and even encoded communications sent through the regular shipping and courier systems were among the means that agents used to report. The Semyaz had long since learned to listen in on the crystal communication devices, and, as such, they were only used for short, coded messages, and were no longer carried by agents.

Laméch still held the honor of being the only person who had infiltrated, escaped, and re-entered repeatedly with his cliff-top campsite. Increased surveillance now rendered such campsites impossible.

The latest intelligence from the Semyaz Complex indicated that there had been a major shift in their research. In addition to the hereditary experimentation and unnatural selection procedures that they had been performing on subjects for decades, the most recent reports told of a new program to deliberately breed young girls as incubators to test their latest attempts at "human improvement". Apparently this breeding of young girls included training and indoctrination in Semyaz religion and culture, and Aenoch feared that this meant the Semyaz felt they were close to success. If they were concerned about the mothers' training, that meant they had moved on to environmental and psychological aspects in the growth and development of their offspring—and *this* implied that they might be close to actually creating and custom-designing nascent embryos—or as Aenoch contemptuously called them, "*man*-made Seed abominations".

The problem with any undercover work is that one often must accept and participate in activities that one would normally find detestable so as to remain concealed. The operative who had provided this latest information was a woman whom Laméch knew only as "Rin". Apparently, she had managed to become a trainer for such a class of young girls, and it was Aenoch's hope that the capture—or at least removal—of such a class would set the Semyaz research back many years.

"We're here."

Endrath's voice brought him back to the present.

Laméch felt the cabin slow and drop slightly. He glanced out of the window and looked at the sun's position.

"Perfect timing," he said, glancing at Klaven.

Klaven smiled and began preparing his equipment.

Laméch guided his dragons into a hover at the base of the cliffs, watching with appreciation as their wings scooped the air vertically to maintain a constant altitude. Any sentries atop the mountains would simply see a pair of winged reptiles—a not uncommon sight.

If Rin's information was accurate, her class of girls should be arriving in a chamber directly above them in a few minutes. Laméch waited patiently during those minutes, and then, with a nod to Klaven, ordered his team to rise.

The team turned to face away from the cliffs and lifted the cabin slowly, keeping the large open port in the rear facing the cliff wall. Klaven prepared his weapon, which had been humming for the past several minutes.

It was similar to a large spear-gun, but it was powered by a series of magnetic coils that were building up a powerful opposition charge. The spear, when released, would be repelled by that charge and be shot from the tubing at a speed and force far greater than any normal cross-bow or pneumatic system. It had been designed by Aenoch who was still the foremost authority of any system that dealt with electromagnetic energies.

The spear, however, was no ordinary spear, and *it* was the personal creation of Klaven.

Within the spear was an explosive chamber that contained a strong but thin grappling spike. At the tip of the spear was a spring sensor that triggered the explosion upon impact, and directly behind this chamber was a hardened concave ceramic dish which directed the force of the explosion forward. The spike was connected to a metal cable that would remain connected to the cabin after the explosion.

The cabin continued to lift along the cliff face until it arrived at the target window where Rin said the class would be. Laméch halted the rise, and nodded to Klaven.

Klaven's smile disappeared as he turned his weapon towards the cliff, aiming directly beneath the crystal window. He took a slight breath, and as he slowly exhaled, he released the restraining catch on the spear.

The spear flew from the cabin trailing its connecting cable and struck the cliff with a loud roar and blinding explosion. The internal spike pounded the weakened stone and punched a small hole through the remainder of the wall, where the empty space beyond allowed the spring-loaded grappling mechanism to release.

ELUCIDATION: EXTRACTION

As the smoke cleared, Klaven was pleased to see the fracture lines in the wall beneath the window. He had been counting on the fact that the cliff rock would have hidden stress fractures from the time of the window's installation, and that it would already be weakened.

"Pull away!" he shouted to Laméch as he prepared his second shot—a more typical field explosive.

But there was no need for Laméch to command the creatures, as they had been spooked by the explosion and were already attempting to flee. Instead, Laméch had to shout from the front opening to try and calm his team.

Klaven watched as the connecting cable swiftly drew taut and timed his second missile to strike at the moment the cable became a straight line.

It struck with a much more powerful—but less directed—explosion, filling the entire wall with blinding white light. As the team continued to pull away, the entire cliff face beneath the window buckled outward, being pulled from behind by the grappling spike. The crystal window began to sag into the space vacated by the collapsing stone and soon tipped out and exploded into pieces, creating a cloud of glass shards that began to descend into the ocean below. Large chunks of rock began to follow—including a large piece that was still connected to the cabin. Klaven quickly pulled on the cable and detached it, allowing the remaining rocks to fall with the cable trailing behind them.

Laméch was at the bow of the cabin, shouting at his dragon team to calm them. He tried to bring them back to a stable hovering position outside of the now gaping hole in the cliff face.

Endrath moved to the rear with Klaven and prepared the launching mechanisms.

"We're too far away!" Klaven shouted to Laméch.

Laméch was fighting with his team, trying to get them to back up into a blind spot where there had already been two frightening explosions. He shouted through his window at them, while desperately pulling on their control cables. Eventually he managed to pull them back into position.

Klaven nodded to Endrath, and they released the springs, launching a small ball into the opening which quickly blossomed into a large net with weights along its edges. It quickly spread over the entire chamber and began to descend, covering anyone who was inside.

They had been assured that this chamber was completely empty of fixtures, and that there would be no benches or podiums to snag the net. The only items to be captured by the net would certainly be the extraction targets.

Two cables were connected to the net. The first was the primary cable which would support the netting in addition to any people trapped within. The second was stitched around the edge of the netting and, when pulled, became a drawstring that quickly pulled the net closed. When targets fought against the net, this second cable would pull the weighted edges underneath, tripping and confusing them, and eventually close the only opening.

Klaven leaned from the cabin, pulling on this line to secure the targets within the net, while Endrath remained inside, hauling in the main cable that was attached to a large pulley system.

Klaven watched the now collapsed net as it was slowly pulled along the floor towards the opening, but he was surprised and disappointed at what he saw. Inside the net was only a single, small girl!

Klaven turned to Endrath.

"Tell Laméch we only got one!"

"What do you mean?" Endrath shouted back, cranking furiously. "We were told this would be an entire class! Where are the others?"

"Don't know!" Klaven yelled. He shrugged. "We only take what we can get!"

The entire cabin lurched as the net containing the girl slipped out of the chamber and began to drop. The force of the unexpected weight caused Endrath to lose his grip on the winch handle, and it began to spin as the net started to free-fall to the ocean below.

The girl's scream caught Klaven's attention, and with a growl and a shake of his head, Klaven rushed to the edge where he grabbed the cable and began to slow the descent, burning his hands in the process. He turned back to glare at Endrath who quickly joined him, and the two began pulling the net upward. The girl looked up, and when she saw the two men she stopped screaming—probably from shock.

Klaven looked up and shouted to Laméch who released his team, finally allowing them to flee as their instincts had been commanding all along. Soon they were flying full speed away from the Haermon Mountains.

"It's a good thing there was only one person," Klaven said, looking at his chafed hands. He glared up at Endrath who cowered under his gaze. "If it had been the whole class, you would have lost them."

Endrath muttered an apology as they kept hoisting the net, which was now spinning and jerking in response to their accelerating speed. Eventually they managed to pull the girl up into the cabin, and position her in the middle of the floor.

Laméch allowed his team to fly freely as they vented their panic and tied down his control cables. He moved from his station and walked to the rear where the young girl lay scared and confused, watching the cliffs disappear behind them.

Laméch had heard Klaven shout earlier, and was also disappointed that they had rescued only one. He knew that Aenoch's primary concern was the mission, and the desire to thwart the Semyaz program and their long-term goals. Although Laméch agreed with this, he was moved at the sight of this frail individual who had just been rescued from any number of unknown horrors which most certainly went beyond his imagination. And he had seen and could imagine a great deal.

She turned from watching the cliffs and looked up, directly into his eyes. He was surprised to see that she was wearing a beautiful green gown, and his eyes left hers for a brief moment as they fastened onto a shiny platinum dragon brooch—the same symbol he had seen on numerous occasions during his time in the complex.

His eyes returned to hers, and suddenly he could think only of his dear childless Keziah—and how *she* had been just one person. This young girl in the green dress was *also* just one person, and (if Aenoch's speculations were correct) possibly *had* no mother. He spoke softly, overcome with an uncharacteristic compassion.

"Even one is still worth it all."

After several rest stops on various floating islands, they arrived at Aenoch's Island three days later. They had flown due east for almost an hour before Laméch had steered them around to the south where they had landed on their staging island and allowed the dragons to rest. Any attempts at communicating with the girl had failed, but Laméch and his friends had removed her from the netting and had tried to make her as comfortable as possible, constantly reassuring her that she was safe.

Keziah rushed out to greet Laméch, but after a brief kiss, she immediately turned her attention to the girl.

Keziah took her by the hand and gently led her away. She turned briefly to Laméch with a smile and said, "I have some wonderful news for you," and then turned quickly away before Laméch could respond. He watched with a mixture of frustration and amazement, thinking that if anyone could comfort this little girl, it would be Keziah. As he watched her beautiful form walk away, he wondered how someone could consistently become more and more lovely— and how someone could be so cruel as to make him wait for wonderful news. He shook his head at her sense of humor.

"I have some bad news."

Laméch turned towards this new voice to find Mendos approaching him. Mendos was Aenoch's chief of security as well as a communications officer. He was a stout man with a small square face and dark heavy brows. He kept his hair very short and wore a large gold band around his left arm. He was also the man who had opened the door to Aenoch's study at Laméch's first meeting of his grandfather.

"What has happened?" Laméch asked.

"Aenoch was speaking at a city forum," Mendos answered, "and during his talk, Enforcers arrested him and took him away."

"Which city was this?" Laméch asked angrily.

"It was Matusalé," Mendos replied. "Your father's city."

Laméch was astonished—and outraged.

"People are always allowed to speak freely in the forums," he reacted angrily. "My father always demanded free and open discourse." He thought of his father who had the tedious habit of always insisting that every point of view be examined.

"Not this time," Mendos said. "It was your father who demanded his arrest." He looked carefully at Laméch. "He called for his silence, and when Aenoch refused, your father charged him with sedition."

Laméch recoiled at the word. There was no way that Aenoch would be seeking the overthrow of the city administration. He was probably the least political person Laméch had ever known. Aenoch only spoke about the hidden agenda of the Semyaz, calling for the end of their interference. Of course, Laméch had heard his speeches and knew that Aenoch could often sound quite crazy as he denounced the Semyaz and their religious teachings, claiming that the *true* creator would someday punish all humanity if they did not cease collaborating with the Semyaz. But Laméch's father had *never* outlawed 'crazy'.

Laméch appreciated Aenoch's zeal, but often considered his motivations to be excessive. It was enough to despise the Semyaz—it was not necessary to invoke a religious fervor in the call for their demise. He suppressed a flush of anger towards Aenoch. Laméch had always feared that someday, Aenoch's excessive speeches would undermine their efforts and do more harm than good.

He turned to Mendos.

"We must go and get him," he said with a mixture of weariness and disgust.

Mendos smiled.

"I knew you would say that," he said. "But, you will be going alone."

Laméch looked at Mendos, startled.

Mendos continued.

"I have a dolphin team and navigator who can get you to Matusalé City in two weeks," he said. "They can drop you along the coast near the city, but you'll have to continue from there on your own."

Laméch nodded, realizing that this would be his first visit to his home city since he and Ruallz had been captured and brought to Aenoch's Island. *That* trip had lasted twenty-three days. The island must be much closer now.

"We are counting on the fact that you probably know Matusalé better than anyone else, and will be able to get in without too much trouble."

Laméch nodded again.

"I assume that you have some plan or mission objective," he said, raising his eyebrows.

Mendos smiled again.

"Yes, actually it is quite simple. You are to discover where they are holding Aenoch, break him out, and take him outside of the city heading southwest into the forests."

Mendos stopped and nodded confidently until Laméch's glare forced him to continue.

"I will have a small guide team waiting for you in the woods, and they will lead you to a community of forest people about a two-day walk from there. Once there, we will provide a dragon-team to airlift you back here."

Laméch nodded again, thinking furiously.

"I can do it," he said in his usual casual and confident manner. "However, is there any way that I can get a message to Ruallz or someone in the underground?"

Mendos shook his head.

"Remember, it has been many years since the Semyaz learned of our devices and began monitoring our communications. We can use only short coded messages—like the one that informed us of Aenoch's situation. Besides, your friend Ruallz has never been a member of the underground. He was simply exposed to us during your recruitment, and has since returned to his normal life."

"I understand," Laméch said quickly as his mind moved on to further planning.

"There is just one thing that I will need," he said eventually.

"What is that?"

"I will need a fine, expensive suit of dress clothes in the latest style—preferably tailored in Jubal."

Laméch entered his home to find Keziah seated at the table with the young girl, who was busily eating a bowl of bark and watercress soup. Keziah looked up and smiled at Laméch.

"Her name is Gaw-Bolwuen, and she is in training to be a consort." She nodded to the girl, smiling warmly.

Laméch approached and also smiled at the girl who looked at him with eyes that were mistrustful, but not completely accusatory. He held her gaze for a brief additional moment, hoping for a different response, but none came.

Placing his arm around Keziah, he pulled her to him and looked into her eyes.

"Well?" he asked, trying to coax her into telling him the wonderful news she had mentioned earlier.

She smiled warmly at him.

"Gaw will be staying with some of the other women eventually, but I ..."

"No!" Laméch interrupted, his impatience exploding with a smile. "What is your wonderful news?"

She pulled away, laughing loudly. Then she rushed to him, wrapped her arms around him tightly, and whispered excitedly in his ear.

"I carry our child!"

CHAPTER 19
HOMECOMING

"Cities were always built with future population growth in mind. Even years after Aenoch's final disappearance, there were still many uninhabited apartments and places for businesses. In Matusalé, this was because it was the only city to be built after the Family Wars. For the remaining cities, their unused living space was due to the incredible reduction of their populations during those wars."

—Amoela the Librarian,
<u>The First Two Thousand Years, Vol. II</u>

I t was a strange and surreal experience for Laméch as he walked the streets of his home city for the first time in many years. He listened contentedly as his black dragon-skin boots tapped along the marble. He was dressed as a wealthy clothing manufacturer from Jubal, wearing a brilliant striped blue and black flaxen robe with spun gold and platinum embroidery, a large dark-blue silk scarf that hung to the side almost like a sash, and a black hat woven from zebra tail hair—their white hairs carefully extracted during the manufacturing process. The hat came to a small cone in the center, but (fortunately for his clandestine purposes) had a brim which extended over his forehead, casting a large shadow of mystery over his face.

The major landmarks were unchanged, but it was the unexpected subtle differences which struck him. Businesses had changed; clothing had changed; and small things like garden arrangements, street sculptures, and shop advertising were all different.

His mind continually threatened to wander back to Keziah and their coming child, but he forced himself to focus on the current situation. If he were not careful, he would be overcome with happiness and excitement—and start daydreaming about his future family and Keziah's joy at being barren no longer.

He shook his head.

There were two major transformations to the skyline that he had noticed as he approached the city. First, was a large, cubic, black-marble structure close to the administration center, which was the new Semyaz Embassy. Second, was a smaller, similar structure near the docks where the Semyaz Security Forces were housed. He also noticed smaller one-story buildings—also in a cubic, black-marble design—just as he had seen in other cities. These were for the ever-increasing number of worshipers who followed the Semyaz teachings of the Creator.

People stared at his audacious, foreign attire—and therefore did not stare at him. Laméch had allowed a full but trim beard (as befitted a fashion magnate) to grow during his journey, and although he had always been clean-shaven (he had never ceased being proud of his strong, dimpled chin) he could not risk anyone recognizing him. He headed purposefully towards the textile sector, nodding at everyone—and no one—as he walked.

Just before he had been deposited along the northern coastline, he had put on these ridiculous clothes and then climbed into a large coverall. He had walked along the coastline to the dockyards and, just before sunrise, removed the coverall, fluffed his robe, and proceeded to the city gate where he loudly and conspicuously announced his arrival. He had considered—and dismissed—all other covert access methods and chose, instead, to be flamboyant.

After announcing the prestigious slip where his fictitious private boat was moored, he was nodded through the city gate where everyone wished him a wonderful visit in Matusalé City.

He had observed the Semyaz Security with their green and black uniforms stop and question others, and he was intrigued with how proper and courteous they were, seeming to go out of their way to convey a sense of service and caring—and always deferring to the local Enforcers. For a brief moment, Laméch was tempted to think that perhaps the Semyaz weren't so bad after all—until he reminded himself of what was currently happening in their Haermon Mountain Complex—and his revulsion grew even greater.

As he crossed into the textile sector, the stares that people gave him began to change from incredulity to appreciation. He headed directly to a specific area and began to study the faces of everyone who passed by or who entered and exited buildings.

After a few hours—and the increasing discomfort of those he was watching—he finally spotted who he was looking for, just as the sun was reaching its zenith.

Ruallz had obviously become a supervisor or manager, based on his apparel, and he was emerging onto the street, apparently heading out for something to eat.

Laméch approached him quickly, giving his old friend little chance to look up and scrutinize his face.

"I have an urgent business matter which I must discuss with you personally," Laméch said as he approached Ruallz, placed his arm around his shoulders, and turned him to face the structure he had just exited.

Ruallz pulled away briefly, and then nodded at this apparently wealthy stranger who might mean increased business for his superiors.

They entered the establishment and Laméch followed Ruallz up two flights of stairs and into a small meeting chamber. Ruallz pointed to a chair.

"May I bring you a drink?" he asked.

"No thank you," Laméch responded. "Please sit."

Ruallz obeyed immediately, and then looked across the table into this insistent stranger's face.

Laméch removed his hat and waited. Almost immediately, he was enjoying the most complex facial contortions he had ever witnessed.

Ruallz's look of initial intrigue was swiftly replaced by one of bewilderment, followed quickly by shock, then disbelief, amazement, and finally, utter astonishment.

His mouth opened, then closed, and then opened again as he rose quickly and rushed to where Laméch was seated.

"Laméch?!" he blurted out, followed by a cough. Laméch grinned and rose to meet him, and the two embraced.

When they separated, Laméch spoke first.

"I see that you've had some promotions since we last spoke."

Ruallz nodded, his mouth still open.

"Where did you come from?" he asked finally.

Laméch indicated that they should sit again.

"I've been doing a lot of traveling," he answered. "I see you made it safely home—just like I promised."

Ruallz glared at him.

"That was so long ago," he responded tersely. "I have simply pushed that entire affair from my memory. It is simply two months that were stolen from my life." He left unspoken *who* had been responsible for the theft.

Ruallz's eyes softened.

"And I have only seen that Librarian once since then. I assume you two are still part of some great anti-Semyaz resistance?"

Laméch nodded.

"What ever became of *The Path*?" Laméch asked.

Ruallz shrugged.

"I'm too busy making a living now," he said. "I imagine there are some young people who still protest, but I haven't heard of anything lately."

He peered into Laméch's eyes.

"Besides, the Semyaz are simply too popular now. They are well-liked, well-received, and most people are very thankful for their help. They've been protecting our city—all cities—for many years, now, and there hasn't been one attack or any disturbance since our Power House was sabotaged." He paused briefly. "You *did* hear about *that*?"

"Of course," Laméch said hastily. "I haven't been *that* far out of circulation."

"I'm not saying I am a big fan of the Semyaz," Ruallz continued, "but their presence is something that is simply inevitable. And until they do something harmful or damaging, I simply accept them."

He gave a look of resignation, and Laméch shrugged back, unsure of how to proceed.

Ruallz decided for him.

"I am married now," he said, his eyes brightening. "Her name is Cam-Gindrel and she also works in textiles. She sews and designs—but also does some modeling." He smiled, bragging slightly. "We have seven children, and recently moved into a larger residence."

Laméch smiled back.

"That is wonderful," he said. "I am married also, to a beautiful woman named Keziah."

Ruallz scowled.

"That's a bizarre name," he said—and immediately grimaced in apology for his lack of tact.

"She's an unusual woman," Laméch responded with some pride. "She grew up among the forest people in a region on the far side of the continent, directly west of Jubal."

Laméch watched with satisfaction as his friend's face transformed into a look of incredulity. Ruallz gave a low whistle.

"I see that you have certainly been getting around," he said, nodding.

"And," Laméch continued with even more pride, "She is currently at home, pregnant with our latest child!" Once again, Laméch's ecstatic thoughts of Keziah and their child threatened to overtake him. He dismissed any concern over his misleading statement.

Ruallz smiled and reached across the table to grasp Laméch's arm.

"Allow me to congratulate you," he said, his eyes narrowing with sincerity.

"I thank you," Laméch responded, blinking quickly. "And I also am pleased to hear that you, too, are raising a family."

Ruallz nodded his acceptance and released Laméch's arm. They sat in silence for a few moments, until Ruallz suddenly broke into a large smile.

"Where did you get such outlandish clothing? You always were an eccentric dresser, but I never would have imagined this. Is that how all of you now dress on that island?"

Laméch laughed.

"No, this was simply a disguise to get into the city without anyone noticing…"

"If you wanted to be inconspicuous," Ruallz interrupted with a grin, "I think you failed miserably."

"You didn't let me finish," said Laméch, impatiently. "I meant, without anyone noticing that it was *me*." He grinned in self-approval. "You'll see that I was successful."

"I see," said Ruallz with a nod.

After another brief silence, Ruallz spoke again.

"I can't imagine that, after all these years, you have come to Matusalé simply to find me."

Laméch shook his head defensively.

"You were the first person I looked up," he said sincerely.

Ruallz nodded slowly, his eyes becoming more thoughtful—and somewhat contradictory. Laméch waited.

"You are here because of Aenoch," Ruallz concluded finally. "He was arrested during his last visit here while addressing the crowds. As I'm sure you are aware, he first reappeared shortly after the attack following our excursion, and has been traveling from city to city, speaking out against the Semyaz."

He gave Laméch an apologetic look.

"He hasn't had much effect, I'm afraid," he said. "As I said, their involvement grows, and any animosity towards them is all but gone."

"Did you see him when he was last here?" Laméch asked, hopefully without too much interest.

"Of course," Ruallz answered. "*That* is why you must have returned to Matusalé after all these years." His eyes became accusatory, indicating that Aenoch was the true reason for his visit, not simply to look up an old friend.

"What happened?" Laméch asked, acquiescing to his friend's indictment.

Ruallz shook his head, raising his eyebrows with some regret.

"This time he went too far," he stated with a nod. "His speeches *usually* concern the hidden agendas of the Semyaz: their secret experiments, their subversion of humanity, their ultimate plan for world domination." He shrugged and gave a slight grin. "The usual conspiracy topics."

He reached for Laméch's arm again.

"But people only know what they see. And they see the Semyaz as benefactors and as peaceful protectors. For many years now, since the Power House sabotage, there have been no incidents, and they helped rebuild the Power House and surrounding areas in no time."

Laméch pulled free of Ruallz's hand.

"You said he went too far?"

"Yes," Ruallz sat back and continued.

"This time he attacked your father, saying that he was in collusion with the Semyaz agenda, and that anyone who did not seek the overthrow of his administration was also complicit."

His eyes widened in intensity.

"Aenoch explicitly called for people to *remove* your father and he *then* claimed that the *true* Creator would soon judge all of humanity for its collaboration with the Semyaz and demanded the immediate expulsion of all Semyaz forces."

Laméch was stunned and leaned forward. Ruallz raised his hands, palms upward, and continued.

"Enforcers had to remove him just as he was calling for the cities of the world to unite with military force against the Semyaz home in the Haermon Mountains—and any city Founders who colluded with them."

His hands lowered and he shrugged.

Conflicting thoughts went through Laméch's mind as he pondered such a thing occurring in his city. He wished (as always) that Aenoch were not so incendiary—and wondered what Ruallz's true feelings and loyalties were.

"Where is Aenoch now?" Laméch asked.

"He is in prison, I guess." Another shrug. "I've never dealt with prisons and I'm not even sure where they are. I've never known anyone to go there. Most crimes are punished by restitution, not incarceration."

Laméch nodded.

"I need to find him."

Ruallz leaned forward.

"So you have been working with Aenoch all of these years? Why is he so excessive in his talk?"

Laméch took a deep breath.

"Because," he said eventually, "I have witnessed all that he speaks about." He nodded, raising his eyebrows in confirmation. "I may not subscribe to his more esoteric views, but I have personally seen the labs where the Semyaz are, even now, performing experiments on live humans in their quest to improve humanity."

Ruallz's expression became one of concern as if preparing for the worst. He nodded for Laméch to continue.

Laméch debated about how much to tell his old friend, but eventually determined that if Ruallz *was* undecided, only the entire truth of all he had seen would convince him.

Laméch told of his infiltration into the Semyaz complex, his discovery of the research that was occurring there, the kidnapped subjects culled from forest peoples from all over the world. He also boasted of how he had escaped along with Keziah—who later became his wife.

He told of the warrior Kendrach, of his battle with the Semyaz attack skiffs, and their eventual rescue and return to Aenoch's Island—and how he had married Keziah and joined the people there.

Ruallz listened with increasing attention and amazement as Laméch informed him of their excursions into the numerous populations of forest peoples, and the development of information networks as they continued to gather intelligence about the Semyaz and their activities.

However, Ruallz became dumbfounded when he began to realize that his friend was engaged in an actual clandestine war with the Semyaz—attacking their shipping, sabotaging their research, offering defense to the communities of forest people, and infiltrating the Semyaz complex. None of this news—even as rumors—had even remotely entered the world of Cities, which were calmly growing in peace and prosperity.

"What no one is aware of," Laméch said, in conclusion, "is that those whom we consider Semyaz: the emissaries, the advisors, the engineers, the shipping mariners—and now the defense forces—are *not* actual Semyaz. They are the descendants of other people who were stolen and kidnapped from cities and forests around the world centuries ago, and are now raised and bred to serve the Semyaz. The actual, *original* Semyaz are few in number and seldom leave their home. No one knows where they came from or when they established their territory in the Haermon Mountains."

"This is incredible," Ruallz said, after Laméch had paused for a moment. "It is difficult to imagine such large events occurring, and no one knowing."

He leaned forward.

"Why would the Semyaz be so malevolent?" he asked. "What could their long-term purpose be?"

Laméch shrugged.

"I'm not sure," he said. "I know that Aenoch has his own theories."

Ruallz nodded.

"So you are here to retrieve Aenoch." It was not a question.

Laméch nodded.

"Yes, I am here to somehow extract Aenoch and get him out of the city. There is a small team of Aenoch's men who will be waiting for us southwest of the city, and they will take us to a forest people community beyond."

Ruallz nodded in appreciation.

"I see you have the *completion* of your mission well planned, but your first phase seems rather vague." He grinned. "That's a little backwards for you, isn't it?"

Laméch scowled back at Ruallz.

"I just need to find where they are holding Aenoch," he said.

"Well, I know you didn't come to me for *that* information," Ruallz said, still smiling.

"Of course not," said Laméch, seeing an opportunity to redeem himself. "I came to you because I wished to visit an old friend."

"And," Ruallz added, "because no one is going to follow a crazily dressed man into the textile district." His smile faded to a slight grin. "Same old Laméch." Ruallz grasped his friend's arm again.

Laméch matched Ruallz's grin with a sheepish one of his own and grasped Ruallz's hand in his.

"I had to appear as if I had a specific destination," Laméch said, "and I knew my best friend worked in textiles."

Ruallz grimaced.

"It is good to see you again." He smiled sincerely. "So how *do* you plan to find Aenoch?"

"Now that I'm *in* the city, I know who to talk to," Laméch answered. "However, I believe you were on your way to find something to eat, correct?"

Ruallz released his grasp and leaned back.

"I was," he answered, raising his eyebrows. "However, I need to return to my work." He grinned. "Were you offering to purchase a meal for me?"

"I'm sorry," Laméch answered, shaking his head. "I only *appear* rich. Actually, I have no money."

Ruallz gave a look of complete shock.

"I see that some things *have* definitely changed for you," he said with a shake of his head.

Laméch stood slowly.

"Well, I must go and find out where Aenoch is being held," he said. "If I have time, I will find you and we can meet for drinks and discuss old times."

Ruallz stood with him, extending his hand in farewell, but shaking his head.

"No, you won't," he responded, smiling.

Laméch was silenced for a second.

"Well, I will try," he replied lamely, accepting the offered hand.

Ruallz nodded slightly.

"My eldest daughter is performing and singing the lead in an Ascension Play this evening at the Garden Amphitheater. That is where I will be this evening, if you are interested."

"*Ascension* Play?" Laméch blurted. "What is that?"

Ruallz grinned.

"You *have* been gone for a long time." He released Laméch's hand. "Ascension Plays *used* to be small street theater productions that the Semyaz Security men put on for children. They teach simple values like trust, unity, and a positive outlook. They are designed to promote higher, more enlightened thinking. Of course, today they are major productions—and my daughter, who has just turned twenty-one, is very excited to participate."

"I see," Laméch responded. "Perhaps you'll see me there tonight."

Ruallz extended his hand for a final farewell, leaving his previous *No, you won't* unspoken. Instead, he said, "Perhaps I will."

Laméch accepted Ruallz's hand firmly this time and pulled him close. The two friends embraced awkwardly, until Ruallz spoke.

"I wish you the best, my old friend," he said. "I hope you will finally discover what you truly need to provide contentment in your life."

Laméch almost responded, *I hope so, too*, but instead pulled away.

"You have always been a good friend," he said finally, locking eyes. Ruallz nodded, unable to reciprocate.

"Before I leave," Laméch said, raising his eyebrows, "I do have something for you."

He removed his fine zebra-hair hat, silk scarf, and black dragon-skin boots, and then carefully stepped out of his flaxen robe, placing everything in a gentle pile on the table. He now stood before Ruallz revealed as a low-level courier: barefoot in a simple brown burlap tunic and skullcap. Laméch slumped into character, and somehow his beard transformed from distinguished to disheveled.

He grinned.

"These are yours," he said, pointing to the valuable heap on the table. "I'm sure you can sell them for a fine price."

Ruallz stared at the attire, easily worth more than two years of his current wages. His mouth worked silently, trying to formulate words.

"This is incredible," he stammered eventually. "I don't know what to say!" He continued to stare for a few more moments until he blurted, "How am I going to convince anyone that I didn't steal these?"

Laméch shrugged, his eyes happy.

"That is your problem," he said, pointing to the pile of expensive fashion wear. "They are simply tools. If there is anything that both Aenoch and Keziah have taught me, it is this: One *cares* for people and *uses* things—not the other way around."

Suddenly Laméch shoved his right hand into the pile of clothing, digging with his fingers. Eventually, he extracted a simple pair of sandals which had been in one of the robe's many pockets.

"I *do* need these," he said, smiling with a nod. He bent and placed them on his feet.

He turned and exited the meeting chamber, feeling Ruallz's incredulous eyes on his back. He slowly descended the stairway, shuffling like a servant, and soon exited onto the street, grinning slightly at the consternation he was most certainly creating in Ruallz.

As he plodded along with downcast eyes, he was amused that

the same people who had admired him earlier were now avoiding him with grimaces on their faces.

People always base reality upon what they see, he thought, an uncharacteristic wave of despondency sweeping through him.

But what else *do they have to base it upon?*

Now that he was in Matusalé, there was only one person who could tell him where Aenoch was being held. He shuffled along the streets in the general direction of the administration sector as a second uncharacteristic emotion slowly emerged.

Apprehension.

It was difficult enough to meet someone whom he hadn't seen for many years, but even more difficult when that person is your own father.

Laméch tried to shrug off his concerns. It may have been years since he last spoke with his father, but, growing up, they had never really talked even when they lived in the same home. He had been raised by servants and stewards whose only job was to ensure that Laméch was contented and cared for—and presentable for public functions and dinners.

He tried to conjure up a childhood memory with his father, and the first image that came to mind was of his father angrily berating a nursemaid when he discovered her holding a sobbing Laméch. *If you are unable to keep my son happy, I can certainly find someone who will!* He had stormed away, his words still echoing, without inquiring about the source of the tears or attempting to see if there was anything he could do to help. The arch of his father's back, as if to say, *I have done my duty in protecting my son*, was a image etched permanently in Laméch's brain.

That was the only time he had ever heard his father raise his voice.

Laméch neared the stepped granite walls of his home (could he still call this *his* home?) and walked towards a servants' entrance which was never used—when he lived here—and was pleased to discover that it was totally overgrown with ivy and other weeds. This was the same entrance he had always used to sneak in and out of his father's house, and he began to pull away at the tough vines, cutting himself in the process and bringing large amounts of dust and dirt down onto his face.

Eventually the doorway was cleared, and with a great deal of effort, the small arched stone door began to move aside. He stepped into the dark corridor beyond and was greeted by cobwebs and the sound of tiny scurrying feet accompanied by panicked squeaks. It was amazing how small animals could take up residence in sealed chambers.

He pushed through the dark, cool passages from memory, just as confidently as he had as a youth returning from a *Path* activity. He made a final right turn—and placed his hands against the final flat stone panel that blocked his way.

He listened intently for any voices or sounds from the other side, and when he was satisfied, he pressed against the stone, pushing it sideways. Slowly, the panel began to move, exposing a small, walk-in linen closet lit by noble-globes from the adjacent laundry room.

He entered the closet, sliding the stone panel closed behind him, where it slid back flush against the granite wall—leaving no indication that a doorway existed. He brushed himself off (dirtying several nearby sheets) and moved into the main laundry chamber.

He adjusted his skullcap, tidied his beard, dusted himself off again more thoroughly, and grinned. Laméch was now an important courier with a special mission.

He strode confidently from the laundry and walked up two flights of stairs. He strode through the familiar hallways, nodding purposefully to the occasional servant, and headed towards his father's quarters, three more flights up.

His father was always in his study. He was either immortalizing his contemplations and conjectures with a scribe, or researching with one or more Librarians—who only made house calls for the city's founder.

The final difficulty was access to the fifth floor, where two security guards questioned anyone who approached his father's living area. As he reached the final landing, one of the guards challenged him.

"State your purpose!"

Laméch moved close enough to the guard to make him reach for his spear.

"I must see the Founder immediately," Laméch said with a nod.

"He is not scheduled for any additional guests," the guard replied.

"This is an unscheduled visit, and it is most urgent that you let me pass," Laméch insisted. "The Founder must hear what I have to say, and will be most displeased if you prevent me from delivering my message."

The second guard moved in closer.

"And who are you, who can demand an unannounced audience?" There was a slight sneer.

Laméch smiled slightly.

"I am Laméch, long-lost son of Matusalé, who wishes to visit his father without any news of his return reaching the public." Laméch removed his courier cap and placed a hand over his beard, allowing the stunned guards to study his face.

Eventually, the second guard stammered, "It's been so many years…"

"Welcome home," the first guard said, still studying Laméch's face. "I *thought* you looked familiar…"

"I have *not* returned home, and you never saw me," Laméch insisted. "Simply inform my father that I am here."

The first guard nodded to the second who disappeared in the direction of the study. Soon he reappeared.

"You may go," he said, pointing unnecessarily towards the study.

"Remember," said Laméch as he passed, "You never saw me." He turned back with a look to remind them of what happened to those who disobeyed, and then headed down the corridor.

ELUCIDATION: HOMECOMING

The large teak doors to the study were partially opened, and La-méch paused briefly before entering. Eventually he passed through them into the enormous room where his father spent most of his time. Scribes were busy filing and cataloging scrolls and tablets, and giant paintings were spaced evenly between the large, arched windows carved from the massive marble blocks from which the mansion was constructed.

At the far end of the room he saw his father stand up from a large oak table and begin walking towards him. A Librarian, who remained seated, was also with him.

Laméch was surprised to see that his father had also grown a beard during his absence, covering the distinctive chin that they both shared. The only differences in their appearance (other than attire) were his father's meatier face and slightly larger frame.

Father and son walked slowly to each other. Just before they met, Matusalé spoke.

"I always knew you would return home," he said with a quiet confidence. Instead of smiling, he lifted his eyebrows.

They met and clasped forearms.

"It is good to see you again," said Laméch, not knowing what else to say. "It has been a long time," he added tentatively.

His father nodded. There was a long pause, and suddenly his father scowled.

"We sent out search teams for you," Matusalé said angrily. "We scoured the forests and the docks, and even dispatched divers. We finally gave you up for dead until your friend Ruallz came forward—many months later—and told us you had run away."

He stopped abruptly, waiting for a response.

"I am sorry, father…" Laméch began.

"We had people looking for you in every city," Matusalé continued, "but no one ever reported seeing you."

He stopped again, raising his eyebrows in suspicious inquiry while he waited as Laméch's discomfort increased. Just before La-méch started to respond, Matusalé's face softened and he gave La-méch a slight smile.

"This," he said, waving his arms to encompass his entire study, "is what makes *me* happy. I love knowledge and conjecture—anything that exercises the mind."

He looked directly into Laméch's eyes—the first time that Laméch ever remembered him doing so.

"I must assume," his father continued, "that you have found something to make *you* happy."

Laméch realized this was actually a question, so he responded.

"Yes, I have," he stated, although he was not entirely convinced. He had never really considered his *need* for happiness.

His father nodded.

"For this, I am glad—and for this I demand no explanations. Nothing else matters."

He motioned to the desk.

"Please, sit with us."

As they walked towards the table, Laméch noticed with surprise that, although the Librarian wore the traditional long white robe, *this* one's head was unshaven. Instead, *this* one had a thick head of curly blond hair. The Librarian looked up at him with a pleasant, indistinct face and smiled kindly as he approached.

As they sat, his father spoke again.

"What has caused you to return home?" he asked.

Laméch took a deep breath.

"I am here to see my grandfather," he said carefully.

His father looked up sharply.

"You have had dealings with Aenoch?" His scowl had returned. "Have you been working with him? Do you support his radical beliefs?"

Laméch laughed awkwardly.

"No," he answered in a half lie, "I don't believe as he does, but I have followed some of his activities, and would like to be able to talk with him."

His father nodded.

"I am glad to hear that," he said. "Aenoch suddenly reappeared in his home city soon after the attack on our Power House." He looked down, closing his eyes. "That was an awful time, living in darkness with no engines or productivity." He reopened his eyes. "Soon after, he came here and began making his anti-Semyaz speeches—after they had offered to help make repairs."

Laméch nodded.

"Yes, I did find Aenoch just before then, and I know of some of his work." Laméch was unsure of how much to divulge. "But, you have to admit, that there are some serious issues with the Semyaz, and a great deal we don't know. For example, where did they come from originally? Do they have a larger, less benevolent agenda, and what knowledge do they have that they keep hidden from us? In fact, Aenoch claims that they aren't even human."

He stopped suddenly, realizing he may have said too much. His father's scowl had returned again and the strange Librarian (with the thick blond hair) had taken a sudden interest in his words.

"Of course," Laméch said quickly, "I certainly don't believe that. That is one of Aenoch's many absurd beliefs."

Matusalé and the Librarian exchanged glances, and then looked back to Laméch.

Eventually his father spoke.

"Laméch," he said, indicating the Librarian, "I would like for you to meet Danel."

Danel gave Laméch a second kindly smile from across the table. Laméch nodded back.

"Danel," his father continued, "is one of the original Semyaz. He was among the first settlers of the Haermon Mountains and is here in my city to oversee the latest deployment of their Security Forces."

CHAPTER 20
VARIANCE

"The First Power Houses were simple tidal generators, only providing direct energy at specific times during the day. However, with Aenoch's creation of energy coils and development of storage methods, continuous power was now able to be broadcast throughout a city. Subsequent improvements in efficiency permitted construction in equatorial regions where tidal changes were less pronounced, allowing the founding of his own city and that of his son's."

—Amoela the Librarian,
The First Two Thousand Years, Vol. II

Aenoch watched as the direct morning sunlight began to fade from his cell window and was replaced by the ambient light of the afternoon sky. This solitary window faced the sea, but it was about twenty cubits above his head—and four brass bars embedded in the surrounding granite prevented any egress.

The cell was a small square, about four cubits on each side, and the only access was a stone panel which had not been opened since his arrival sixteen days earlier. It was quite clear that he had been severed from any outside communication, and Aenoch began to suspect that his own son was planning to keep him hidden away in this cell indefinitely—forever prevented from spreading his "seditious" message.

There was a mat and stool in the cell, and a small panel beneath the door where a simple but substantial meal and a pitcher of fresh water appeared twice a day. A small hole in the corner completed all of the necessities of life, and Aenoch was quite satisfied to consider his situation "impossible".

Fortunately, he had witnessed many "impossible" events during his life, and could not bring himself to despair—or even worry. He knew that all situations had their purpose, and even if he remained here for years, this second "disappearance" might motivate hundreds of those who believed as he did and followed his message to emerge and take his place.

He actually smiled at the thought of accomplishing more while sequestered away than he had accomplished when speaking as a lone voice from city to city.

The ways of the Creator are far above the ways of men.

The closest thing to panic that Laméch had ever known shot through his entire body. Only an equally powerful act of will kept his face calm and his upper body muscles relaxed.

Danel (who was definitely *not* a Librarian) rose and began to walk around the table towards Laméch. His kindly smile remained, but somehow it now had a different effect on Laméch.

His thoughts churned as he wondered how he should respond. How much did this Danel know about him? What would he be willing to do in front of his father? How much did his father truly know about the activities of the Semyaz?

How complicit might he be?

As Danel neared him, he stretched out his arm in greeting. Laméch rose carefully, extended his arm, and the two grasped forearms.

Danel's arm was cool and soft to the touch, and when Laméch glanced down, he was surprised to see that it was completely hairless.

Matusalé rose quickly.

"I must apologize," he said, "for not properly introducing you." He looked at Danel. "I was distracted by the arrival of my son."

Danel nodded in response, but did not look away from Laméch.

"So you have spent time with Aenoch?" he asked, still smiling, as they released forearms. His voice was calm, yet strong, with a ringing quality that made Laméch think he might burst into song at any moment.

Laméch nodded quickly.

"Yes, I encountered him some time back," he said carefully as his father motioned for all of them to retake their seats. "I've heard some of his speeches but I don't know anything about his activities or his followers." Laméch moved smoothly into his lie, hoping that Danel would not notice—or would not know otherwise.

As he sat, he looked at his father.

"I came home when I heard he had been imprisoned for giving a speech," he said, trying to look accusatory. "I was surprised, since you have always supported diverse viewpoints and the free exchange of ideas. I had heard of such things in other cities, but never in my father's city." He raised his eyebrows to demand an explanation.

"Well naturally," his father said eventually, "we welcome all forms of discourse and expression, but we can not..."

"Young Laméch," Danel interrupted. Laméch spun to face him without trying to disguise his look of utter shock. *No one* interrupted the founder.

"Young Laméch," Danel repeated, "If you have heard Aenoch speak, then you have heard him make outrageous claims concerning me and my people." His kindly smile was gone. "However, are you aware that he has gone so far as to claim that *we* are not even human?"

Danel delivered this as if it would stun Laméch, so Laméch played along. He dropped his jaw as his eyes widened.

"I have never heard that," Laméch replied.

"As you can see," Danel continued, "this feeds into the ugliest passions of our tragic past, implying that if one's enemies are not fully human, they can therefore be discarded or even brutalized without regard for normal sensibilities."

Laméch decided to feign some slight defense.

"I can't imagine that Aenoch would believe something that absurd."

Danel leaned towards him.

"Perhaps not," he said, "but surely you have heard his accusations that we perform perverse experiments on people in our homeland, that we kidnap and enslave people from other lands to accommodate these experiments, and that we have some large encompassing goal to subjugate the cities of the world for our own nefarious purposes."

Laméch nodded.

"As with most lies, they are based on modicums of truth," Danel continued. His kindly smile returned. "Yes, we have large hospital facilities, and yes we do have a large influx of refugees—and their descendants—of the Family Wars. The severity of those wars still carries a lasting impact, and even to this day we find survivors who are scratching out a subsistence living in the wilds—and we rescue them. We care for them, integrate them into our society, and give them the benefits of our knowledge and ways."

He nodded briefly towards Matusalé.

"We do nothing to enrich ourselves. The small amounts of gold and other tribute that the cities present to us are used to fund these missions and others of our endeavors designed to uplift and ennoble all of humanity."

Laméch slowly allowed a feeling of relief to spread over him. This Semyaz had no idea that he was talking to someone who had actually toured their facilities—and who had actually witnessed their atrocities firsthand. He nodded politely, absorbing everything.

"What Aenoch fails to realize," Danel continued, "is the true history of the Semyaz. Aenoch's knowledge is limited to the last thousand years or so, and he has no knowledge of Deep Time—before the time of cities and before his 'First Ones'. This was the time that a small band of explorers and truth-seekers first settled in the Haermon Mountains."

Danel leaned back, but maintained his eye contact with Laméch.

"We were always few in number," he said, "but because of our beneficence and willingness to rescue those in need, we are a growing, thriving people who only want to share the blessings of our advantages with the world."

Danel paused and leaned forward again.

"I'm sure this is something with which you would agree," he stated as if requesting confirmation.

Laméch nodded dumbly, and suddenly thought of his time with *The Path* and also his first conversations with Aenoch. Wanting what the Semyaz had to offer *was* his primary objective.

"You are too young," Danel said, peering at Laméch intently, "to remember the savagery and atrocities of the Family Wars, but it was our message and our way of thinking that stopped those wars and brought healing to the world."

He nodded, prompting Laméch to nod with him.

"We are all children of light," he continued, "and this knowledge has ushered in a period of peace that the world has never known. With only minor exceptions, the cities have prospered and thrived in ways never heard of before. We share our wisdom and knowledge to unite the cities and insure that such violence never again occurs—and in our humble way, we provide the defenses that are needed to allow the cities their resources to grow and prosper in their understanding of our benefits."

Danel's face hardened.

"However, we must be careful how we share our knowledge," he said, leaning back. "Throughout the centuries we have been working on the proper ways to improve humanity, and also the proper ways to implement these improvements. There are those who disagree with how quickly we distribute these benefits, but—if you are willing to trust us with the assistance, you must also trust us in our delivery."

Danel's kindly smile had returned.

For a brief moment, Lamech found himself nodding and agreeing with the charming blond man. Perhaps Aenoch *was* somewhat extreme and was only fighting their inevitable progress. But it was only for a moment. The visions of what was truly happening in the Semyaz complex rushed through his head, and although he didn't fully agree with or comprehend all of Aenoch's beliefs, he could not be dissuaded from the cruelty and evil that he had witnessed—and that the Semyaz ultimately represented.

Still nodding, he leaned forward.

"Have you had the chance to explain all of this to Aenoch?"

It was a simple question, but for the briefest moment, Lamech thought he saw a flicker of anger in Danel's eyes.

"Yes, he was brought to me when he was detained," Danel replied. "However, sadly I fear that he is quite insane. There was no amount of reason or explaining that would change his mind. Even after seeing that I am but a fellow man, he still regards me as an alien presence."

Lamech remembered why he had come here in the first place and turned to his father.

"I would like to visit him," he asked. He was pleased to see Danel tense from the corner of his eye.

"That is not possible," Danel said quickly before Matusalé could respond. Again, Lamech was surprised at the interruption. "His very ideas must be quarantined to prevent further spreading."

Danel looked directly at Matusalé.

"We agreed," he said, urgency sounding for the first time in his voice.

"Father," Lamech said quietly, looking at his father with pleading eyes. "All I am asking is a chance to see my grandfather. I don't know how long you intend to hold him, but I only want a short visit."

"That is not possible," Danel repeated.

"This is *still* your city," Lamech continued looking at his father, emphasizing 'still' to imply that it might not always be so.

"May I see grandfather?" he asked quietly.

Matusalé looked over at Danel.

"It can't do any harm," he said.

Danel shook his head.

"That is not possible!" he reiterated for the third time.

Matusalé rose slightly.

"In this city *I* determine what is or is not possible," he declared, looking pointedly at Danel.

He turned to Laméch.

"Please dine with us," Matusalé announced, "and I will then provide an escort for you to visit Aenoch."

He looked back at Danel.

"It will only be a quick visit," he said quickly to the Semyaz. "After that, my son will be on his way."

What disturbed Laméch more than his father's dismissive comment was the subservient look he gave to Danel. It was a look that begged Danel's indulgence, yet was also filled with admiration—and a glow that bordered on adulation.

It was almost dark before Laméch was sent out with an escort towards the city's prison. It was a tall, narrow structure near the north docks, just inside the city wall, and was one of the few places in Matusalé City that Laméch had never visited. It only had twelve cells—also tall and narrow—within its double outer granite walls (highly polished, Laméch noted—he could never scale them). These cells were usually empty.

Matusalé promoted a criminal system that advocated restitution over incarceration, and as a result, only those guilty of dangerous or egregious offenses were usually detained. To be found guilty of a second, similar crime constituted a capital offense, so inmates never returned to the city prison a second time—unless they were being held for their execution in the immersion chamber.

The immersion chamber was just outside the city wall along the north dock, and was nothing more that a small cage of brass bars firmly embedded in a granite platform. It rose vertically from the dock and was situated to be visible from across the expanse of the ship yards and the eastern wall of the city. It was just large enough to contain a standing man of average height.

Executions were rare—but very public—and when they occurred, large crowds would form around the chamber. The prisoner was brought out of the city gate, and then secured inside the cage.

The actual execution was accomplished by the fact that when the prisoner first entered the cage, this particular lower portion of the dock was *above* sea level. What the public soon witnessed, throughout the day, was the rising tide as the prisoner clambered frantically, his screams eventually silenced as the expanding waters filled the chamber. Usually a twitching hand straining through the top bars was the last remaining sight.

A back panel was then released and the corpse was washed out as the tide receded. The cage was then prepared for the next usage—usually far into the future—but it remained visible at all times and served to deter potential lawbreakers as its empty bars submerged and re-emerged throughout the tidal cycles.

Laméch's escort presented an order to the guard and they were ushered through the doorways of the outer wall and into the corridor that surrounded the inner wall and the cells within. There were four cells on each floor, and each cell had a ceiling about three stories above the floor with a small barred window just beneath it. Two more sets of four cells were above the first floor, and a small spiral staircase along the inner wall provided the passage between floors.

Currently the prison held only one person, and the guard led Laméch and his escort around to the eastern cell door, released its latch, and slowly began to slide the granite panel aside.

The daylight from the small window above Aenoch's head had faded, but the glowing blues and greens from the Power House prevented complete darkness—or a star-filled sky—from entering into his cell. As he had often done before, he wondered at the wisdom of housing humanity in large, encasing cities that prevented people from properly appreciating the plants, animals, and stars of creation—cities which had received their modern iterations and design from him.

Suddenly Aenoch heard a grinding sound and he turned to watch the stone panel slowly slide open. He was startled because it had not moved since he had been placed in here sixteen days earlier, but he was more shocked when Laméch walked through the open doorway!

The guard and escort remained outside, and as the doorway slid shut, the guard said, "You may only visit for a few minutes. Founder's orders."

Laméch stared at his grandfather who was sitting on his stool and wearing nothing but the same leather breechcloth that he had always worn. The only light came from the ambient discharges of the Power House that flashed through the lone window far above them, creating strange shadows on the floor and flickering auras above their heads.

Aenoch met his gaze and the two men looked awkwardly at each other for several seconds. Eventually, Aenoch broke the silence.

"I imagine this is not one of your more enjoyable missions," he said with a slight smile.

Laméch shrugged.

"I was able to see father," he responded. He paused a moment and then added, "There was no other way to discover where you were being held."

"You have a plan?" Aenoch asked.

Laméch nodded and looked away at the interplay of light that cascaded around the cell walls. His anger—suppressed since the inception of this mission—began to materialize in response to this situation which seemed so unnecessary.

"You have something you wish to say?" Aenoch asked as he watched Laméch's face.

Laméch leaned back against the cell wall and tried to collect his thoughts—desiring to be respectful—while at the same time, deciding that now was the correct time to divulge all of his concerns and frustrations.

"I have been with you all of these years," he began carefully, looking up and away from his seated grandfather, "dedicated to resisting and thwarting the Semyaz and their endeavors, and joining with you in our efforts to inform humanity of their evils—and I have gone on your missions, submitted to your leadership, and followed your methods even though I have yet to see any real accomplishments or successes. We impede them; we disrupt them, but..."

He stopped abruptly and quickly looked down at Aenoch, hoping he hadn't gone too far.

Aenoch looked up into his eyes.

"And?" he asked. "Please speak freely."

Something snapped in Laméch.

"And then you have to go and say something stupid." Laméch tensed as his true feelings escaped. "We need to give people a practical message—explain what the Semyaz are all about, but you insist on adding all of your esoteric and religious nonsense, which only confuses the message and alienates your listeners."

He took a deep breath and continued, his voice rising.

"Now you have embarrassed our cause, brought public ridicule upon yourself, and now no one will care to hear what we have to say."

He stopped again, but this time it was because he had said everything. He exhaled quickly and looked away, waiting for Aenoch's response.

Eventually he looked back at Aenoch who was smiling slightly. There were several seconds of silence until Aenoch spoke.

"Are you the most intelligent person in the world?" Aenoch asked in a very relaxed and calm voice.

Taken aback by the strange question, Laméch answered quickly.

"No," he said, and then snapped back, "Are *you*?" He suddenly felt very childish and clenched his jaw in a futile attempt to keep Aenoch from noticing. He knew he should be respectful and impressed as he stood in front of one the most brilliant engineers and architects who had ever lived, but years of bitterness and familiarity had dampened his ability to appreciate.

Aenoch broke into a friendly smile and laughed slightly.

"Of course not," he answered. "But I think we can agree that some people are more intelligent than others, correct?"

Laméch nodded, wondering where Aenoch was going this time.

"And since," Aenoch continued, "varying degrees of intelligence *do* exist, it would stand to reason that somewhere, someone *must* be the most intelligent person in the world."

He looked up with a confident nod, but before Laméch could respond he added, "Naturally we understand that there are different forms of intelligence and also no proper method of quantifying it. However, as a question in logic, I believe my premise stands."

Laméch nodded again, becoming slightly confused. He had never doubted—or even seriously considered—his own intelligence.

"What is your point?" he asked, sounding more annoyed than he intended.

Aenoch seemed not to notice.

"Since we have this great range of intelligence, can we not at least theorize that there might exist—at least hypothetically—an intelligence that far exceeds that of our mythical genius?"

He paused for a response from Laméch.

But Laméch was becoming increasingly impatient.

"Why are you saying this?" he demanded, clearly irritated. "It certainly doesn't prove the existence of any creator or higher *anything*."

Aenoch scowled.

"Of course it doesn't," he snapped back, startling Laméch. "I'm simply pointing out the arrogance of assuming that an intelligence higher than us can *not* exist."

"Fine," Laméch responded. "But why are you saying this to *me*?"

Aenoch held his gaze.

"Because you are so self-satisfied."

"What does *that* mean?" Laméch asked, wishing that the conversation was over—and now angry with himself for continuing it.

Aenoch's tone softened.

"You are a very confident, secure young man who knows who he is, and has a very solid and established world-view."

Laméch listened, slightly confused at what seemed to be a compliment. He waited for the "however".

"This is all very good," Aenoch continued, "however, you have no room for change—no room for growth. It is as if you are encased in granite, and no new idea or observation can ever change your outlook on life. You have a prepared response for everything and have confidently pre-categorized any future experience. You, *personally*, refuse to acknowledge that there might, someday, be a better *you*. Just as a man refuses to accept…"

"What do you want from me," Laméch interrupted him angrily. "What would you have me do?"

He glared at his grandfather, waiting for the response.

"Well," Aenoch answered eventually, "You could bother to learn how to read."

An icy silence descended on them as both men knew they had crossed a line. Laméch's illiteracy had always been an issue between them, and Laméch felt as if Aenoch held this over him with an air of superiority. In their last argument, Aenoch had accused him of being *proud* of his refusal to learn.

Laméch looked away.

"I'm only here to rescue you," he said, dismissing the topic.

"And I'm trying to rescue you," Aenoch responded, his voice sounding almost tearful.

Laméch looked back down at his grandfather with eyes that somehow combined anger and boredom. He waited for Aenoch to speak next.

Eventually, Aenoch took a deep breath.

"You have a plan?" he asked, repeating his question from the start of their conversation.

Laméch nodded.

"Yes. I simply have a few questions regarding chemistry."

Aenoch nodded.

Laméch explained his rescue plan, asking Aenoch's help for a few science questions. When he had finished, he glared down at Aenoch.

"Make sure you're ready," he said, less kindly than he had intended.

Aenoch smiled up at him.

"I'll be ready," he said with warmth in his voice.

But Laméch was not in the mood to be mollified. He turned to the cell door.

"Guard!" he shouted. "I'm ready to leave."

As the stone panel ground open, he did not look back at Aenoch.

"I'm sorry that I irritate you so," Aenoch said to Laméch's retreating back—further irritating him.

Even as the doorway slid shut, Laméch did not turn back to look at his grandfather, who remained seated on the stool.

I'm sorry, also, he thought as he and his escort followed the guard around the hallway. Then he grimaced as a different thought crossed his mind.

Maybe an improved me would not be so easily irritated.

Laméch excused his escort and began walking the now darkened streets of his home city, randomly turning corners and following streets. His rescue plans would not commence until after midnight, and he had plenty of time to prepare.

The limestone and marble flickered with bursts of purple and green from the Power House overhead, but he saw nothing; he was oblivious to his surroundings—including the occasional passerby.

ELUCIDATION: VARIANCE

His thoughts churned furiously, as they competed for his attentions. Thoughts that questioned his devotion to Aenoch and their cause. Concerns about his father's possible collusion with the Semyaz. Resentment at being told he was "encased in granite". The idea that confident and secure was somehow a defect.

The thought of returning home in time to see his child come into the world took preeminence, and he smiled suddenly. Reflections of Keziah triggered warm feelings of love and longing that spread through his imagination.

His smile disappeared at the sudden realization that he considered Aenoch's Island "home".

The quiet murmur of a distant crowd brought him back to the present, and he realized that he had wandered into the arena district—and that he was nearing the Garden Amphitheater where Ruallz had invited him to the Ascension Play.

The arena district had several venues for sporting events, theater productions, and concerts, but the Garden Amphitheater was the largest—and open to the sky. It was encompassed by large hanging gardens (hence the name) that rose almost four stories into the air, and provided the audience with a feeling that the forests surrounding the city had somehow encroached upon them as they enjoyed performances that transported them beyond the city walls. The seating capacity was slightly less than the entire population of Matusalé City.

The noise from the assembling crowd grew as Laméch moved towards the amphitheater, and he grinned at the thought of proving Ruallz wrong, but doubted he would be able to find him in the audience. He had only visited a few times as a child—usually when forced by his father or caretakers to increase his "culture". Attending this performance would also prove that he was open to new things and not "encased in granite".

As he approached, he heard the crowd quiet, indicating that the play was about to begin. He quickly climbed the alternating staircases along with other latecomers and soon emerged at the back edge of the amphitheater, looking down onto the stage far below.

The orchestra began, playing an ethereal shimmering music, which accompanied a bank of artificial fog that was slowly rolling onto the stage. In the orchestral pit there were a variety of stringed instruments, several large brass horns, and a large harp. They provided a solid wall of background sound that changed subtly around a fixed harmonic progression. In front was a bank of etherophones, charged by the energies of the Power House. The performers stood behind their instruments, moving their hands in slow controlled arcs, creating eerie, yet mellifluous, contrapuntal melodies that moved upwards in ever-increasing complexities.

To the right was a small dais where a young soloist was playing a collection of tuned crystal goblets that spun underneath her deft fingertips. The same energies that powered the etherophones also turned a small, silent motor that kept the liquid-filled crystals rotating at a constant speed, allowing the performer to select her high, piercing descant with great accuracy.

Laméch walked towards a portion of the nearest stone tier that was still unoccupied and sat down, realizing with a stab of frustration that, in addition to being illiterate, he also knew practically nothing about music.

A large drum (apparently hidden behind the other musicians) began a low, powerful rumble that crescendoed into a loud roar which thundered and echoed around the amphitheater—assisted by antiphonal drums hidden around the perimeter of the audience. At the same moment, a large collection of miniature green and white noble-globes descended from the top of the stage, piecing holes of light into the fog. As the mesh to which they were attached reached the stage floor, it appeared to Laméch as if the lights were suspended in a scattered, random manner, reminding him of stars.

However, he knew enough to realize that this screen of lights spelled out actual words—forcing him to think once more of his variance with Aenoch.

A powerful blast from the brass was accompanied by several magnesium flare explosions, bathing the audience in flashes of blinding purple and white light.

ELUCIDATION: VARIANCE

The instantaneous silence and darkness that followed riveted everyone's attention to the stage as the audience waited for the opening act.

Had Laméch been able to read, he would have understood the message glowing in the descending lights:

The Creator of Light
Emerged from on high
Restorer of Man
The Divine to draw nigh.

CHAPTER 21
DISCERNMENT

"Centuries before the Family Wars, numerous expeditions were undertaken to try and locate the lost Garden of the First Ones by attempting to determine the correct rivers and head upstream. Although most were never heard from again, those who returned reported mass disorientation, navigational anomalies, and differing accounts of massive magnetic disturbances, great barriers of fire, and even stories of fellow crewmen going mad.

None ever claimed success."

—Amoela the Librarian,
The First Two Thousand Years, Vol. I

Half a planet away, these very same words were being discussed by Keziah and Gaw-Bolwuen, whose distrust of her new captors was slowly beginning to lessen.

Gaw had remained numb for several days following her terrifying flight to this strange island, but after she determined that these people meant her no immediate harm, she began to relax slightly, choosing to wait and see what would transpire next.

She was inexplicably frightened by the large open spaces and the undulating green swells of the ground moving silently along the contours of the ocean beneath them. She had often stared out of the Haermon Mountain windows at the occasional floating island and tried to imagine what it might be like to visit one; but she now found the actual experience unsettling. She desperately longed for a small, granite room into which she could run and hide away from all of the daunting unknowns surrounding her.

The food they offered her was strange and bland, but they seemed genuinely concerned for her contentment and well-being. Her only real discomfort was the clothing they gave her to wear— primarily because it was much coarser than she was used to, and also because she felt it did not adequately cover her. She had no idea what had happened with her white passage gown with its green sash, her green shoes, and her platinum dragon brooch. Fortunately, they had allowed her to keep her memory-ring bracelet. The colorful agate stones were the only remaining evidence of her past.

She had been with the people of Aenoch (whom she had not seen) for several weeks, but only in the last few days had she begun to speak and initiate any conversations.

Gaw was now talking with the lady who was the wife of the man that had taken her away. A few days after Laméch had left, Gaw had moved in with Keziah, and immediately fell in love with Longfang, a large, beautiful golden cat that had taken an immediate liking to her.

Keziah had been kind, speaking softly and carefully, never demanding any response, but was always reassuring. More importantly, Keziah always spoke intelligently and forthrightly, never condescendingly, presenting a confidence in Gaw's innate astuteness and aptitude that could not help but make Gaw feel good about herself. It actually seemed to her that Keziah was often surprised—and pleased—by the excellent education the Semyaz had given her.

Gaw knew that these people truly believed they had rescued her,

and as they cautiously (and gently) explained their views of the Semyaz and their goals, it began to dawn on her barely pubescent mind
what her former caretakers had actually intended for her. As a result,
she found herself with an inexplicable feeling of relief that battled
within her mind against the indisputable fact that she had been kidnapped against her will.

Keziah had just asked her to recite the Creator's Creed for the
third time, and Gaw began, again, with a slight sigh.

"The Creator of Light, Emerged ..."

Keziah interrupted her.

"This appears to be in the genitive or possessive case, correct?"

"Yes, it is," Gaw replied, more tersely than she intended. "The
Creator created light." She finished with a firm nod.

"Could there not be a different meaning?" Keziah asked carefully. "Could there be any way that this line might be ambiguous?"

"No," Gaw responded, this time deliberately curt.

Keziah nodded calmly.

"We will discuss it later," she said. "Please continue."

Gaw emitted another sigh before reciting.

"Emerged from on ..."

"Emerged?" Keziah interrupted again. "In order to 'emerge'
isn't there something required to emerge *from*? The Creator can't be
the creator of all things, if he came from someplace else."

"Emerged from *on high*," Gaw finished her line, insistently.
She was beginning to feel uneasy as she realized that much of what
she was saying was direct quotes from her catechism—quotes she
wasn't fully prepared to defend or analyze.

"I'm not sure what 'on high' means," Keziah said quietly, "but
it must be something or someplace that existed before the Creator.
And it must have been created by someone or something else."

Gaw paused slightly before responding, her irritation growing.

"I believe you are trying to confuse me," she said eventually.
"The Creator, by nature of the word, means that there is nothing the
Creator did *not* create."

Keziah broke into a large smile, surprising Gaw.

ELUCIDATION: DISCERNMENT

"I absolutely agree," she said. "Continue."

The smile faded and Gaw slowly began the third line.

"*Restorer of Man ...*"

This time Keziah interrupted with a laugh.

"So there *was* a previous Creator!"

Gaw shifted in her strange clothes, feeling slightly trapped.

"No," she ventured slowly. "There is one Creator." Her voice grew in forced confidence as she completed her sentence.

Keziah smiled again, almost in apology, and then shook her head as if to change the subject. She pointed to Gaw's bracelet.

"Tell me about the meaning of these pretty stones," she requested.

Gaw relaxed, confident that her memory stones would help clear her mind.

"This first one," she began, "symbolizes light, constant and unchanging."

She looked up at Keziah.

"It has always existed."

Keziah smiled and nodded for her to continue.

Laméch found it difficult not to become drawn into the performance. The music pulled on his emotions, but the story itself struck him as rather juvenile, and he shook his head repeatedly to clear it.

The main character was a young woman in her mid-twenties—and was most definitely Ruallz's daughter. She seemed to suffer from typical youthful insecurities: feelings of uncertainty and undesirability, restricted ambition, and struggles with the pressures of compromising with oneself for acceptance.

An offstage chorus wailed about the emptiness and fatigue of life, as the young woman wandered through a variety of broken friendships, failed relationships, and a few obligatory betrayals.

Her despair eventually brought her to the barracks of a young Semyaz Security Force officer who comforted her—and presented a message of purpose and hope that only the Creator could provide.

It seemed so transparent to Laméch, and he soon found himself growing more and more disgusted.

The young lady soon began to demonstrate her newfound joy with beautiful makeup and brightly colored clothes—which further attracted the young officer. And the young officer began to share a transcendent wisdom that made him appear to be the perfect man, and the audience was now fully conditioned to desire nothing but the inevitable romance and consummation that was sure to follow.

The music grew with great swells as the motifs of love, honor, and purpose played out in front of the audience. It became clear that true unity and peace would surely come as the peoples of the cities embraced the Semyaz and their ways—the ways of love and peace which no one could possibly oppose.

Laméch watched as the audience became enraptured with the message—and he felt like he was watching fish swim into a large net.

The music began to pound in sensual anticipation, leading into the final scene where the woman, now older, emerged from back-stage carrying an adorable young baby who had beautiful hair like his mother's—and was wearing a small black and green Semyaz uniform.

The audience rose to its feet in passionate approval, and La-méch was certain that every woman in the arena now wanted nothing more than her own Semyaz child—and every male wished he had been born a Semyaz.

Laméch turned to look at some of the exits and thought he saw a few Security Force officers smiling to themselves.

"The second ring is black, representing the void and empty universe before the Light entered it," Gaw continued, "and the third is blue and green representing the earth for its water and life."

Gaw paused in her recitation and glanced up at Keziah, who took advantage of the moment to ask a question.

"Did the Creator *create* the Earth, or does this ring celebrate his arrival to Earth?"

Gaw risked a slight glare.

"The Creator created *everything*," she said tersely.

Keziah smiled and nodded.

Longfang took this moment to awaken. He stretched and yawned loudly before sauntering over to Gaw and nuzzling her with his large nose. Gaw wrapped her arms around his neck and gave him a nuzzle in return before turning back to her bracelet.

"This brown ring", she continued, "represents the first people before the Creator gave them wisdom and ambition." It suddenly occurred to her what Keziah's next, obvious question was going to be, and she tensed.

"So there was something on the Earth before the Creator arrived?" Keziah announced, more as an exclamatory statement than a question.

"No," Gaw retorted instinctively, "I mean yes—but..." she paused to collect her thoughts. "But..."

A sudden inspiration struck her.

"Not everything has to be deliberately created," she said quickly. "Once the Creator initiated his creative processes, almost anything could happen." She paused to continue her thought. "Perhaps he was traveling the universe to see what had emerged."

She looked hopefully into Keziah's face, but Keziah was looking thoughtfully into the distance.

"More emerging," she said slowly, to herself. Then she turned to Gaw with a nod of appreciation. "Yes, I can accept that."

Gaw smiled in spite of herself, a sense of relief washing over her.

"So you are saying," Keziah continued, "that the Creator found these docile, dim-witted people and re-made them in his image?"

"Yes," Gaw said, still smiling.

Keziah's face suddenly became very serious, almost stern.

"And how can you be sure that this *re-making* was an improvement?" She moved her face closer to Gaw. "In fact, how can we know that this Creator didn't actually damage or ruin a *superior* creation?"

Gaw backed away, startled.

Keziah leaned in towards Gaw and pointed towards Longfang who was now resting his massive head in Gaw's lap, his eyes closed.

"What if I were to cut off one of Longfang's legs?" Keziah asked suddenly. "Could I then claim to be the creator of a three-legged cat?"

The intensity of her face and her unfeigned seriousness frightened Gaw, who had never seen Keziah speak in this manner. Longfang's eye opened slightly in response to his name, but closed immediately with no recognition of the cruelty being considered.

"Or perhaps," Keziah continued without slowing, her eyes boring into Gaw's, "I should gouge out his eyes and claim to have created a new, blind species of cat?"

A tiny yelp escaped Gaw and she reflexively wrapped her arms around Longfang's head in protection. She knew that Keziah could not be serious, but she was horrified at the thought—and the possibility. She looked down into Longfang's sleeping face and shuddered.

Keziah continued her look of severe determination for a few more seconds before relaxing into the same gentle smile that had encouraged Gaw earlier. The young girl relaxed with a sigh, but still retained the trepidation of her encounter with such a savage thought—and the confusion surrounding Keziah's intentions.

Keziah reached for Longfang and stroked the top of his head.

"We could never do anything that would harm such a beautiful creature," she said, reassuring Gaw with her other hand as she stroked the girl's auburn hair. Keziah then sat back and looked calmly into Gaw's face, saying nothing.

Eventually Gaw spoke.

"Why did you…?" She trailed off, unable to finish.

"Why did I speak about something so horrible?"

The young girl nodded silently.

ELUCIDATION: DISCERNMENT

"Because," Keziah answered, "I want to show how critical the nature and attributes of the Creator are. When people discuss such things, we can't just ignore differences."

She paused to fix a tremendous look of loving kindness on Gaw. Gaw was suddenly reminded of the final look that Rin-Kendril, her counselor, had given her just before she had been taken, and fought a sudden and inexplicable urge to cry. She had been told that her counselor had been complicit in her abduction, but, until this very moment, she had refused to believe it. Somehow, seeing the same loving look from Keziah threatened to remove her remaining doubts. It was almost as if the same caring person were looking through those eyes.

Keziah allowed their eyes to remain connected for a few more moments before speaking again.

"I promised to address how the 'Creator of Light' phrase could be ambiguous," she began. "I agree the case suffix indicates possession, as in *light's creator*, but we must consider another possibility."

Gaw nodded politely with a slight shrug.

"*If*," Keziah paused for emphasis, "some things existed before the Semyaz Creator—and if light *is*, as you say, constant—we must consider that this same suffix is compositional. This would mean that the Semyaz creator is *comprised* of light—and that *that* light pre-existed this creator; and *he* (as you stated) emerged from that light."

She paused again to state her conclusion.

"The Semyaz 'creator' is made of pure energy, and in fact is a very powerful being, but he could never be the true creator of all things."

Gaw began to shake her head, but Keziah continued.

"You have shared the beliefs and views of your former captors," she said, "and now I would like to share *our* beliefs."

Laméch stood in dismay as he watched the crowds press around him at the conclusion of the performance. Many proselytes of the Semyaz religion were available at the front of the arena—and at all of the exits—to speak with people before they left. In some cases, most notably the rear departure gates, it seemed to Laméch to be more of a confrontation or ambush.

Laméch had not dashed out as soon as possible, mainly because he was simply stunned at how gullible those from his own city seemed to be. He watched as scores of people rushed forward to hear more, and (more disturbingly) he witnessed clusters of young women fawning over some of the green and black uniformed Security Force men—who politely rebuffed them.

Suddenly he thought he saw Ruallz at a distant exit near the front, and turned to walk in his direction. It appeared that his friend was talking with a Security Force officer, but Laméch could not be sure if it truly was Ruallz. All he could see was the side of the man's face, but as Laméch pressed through the crowd and neared the exit, the man had disappeared. Laméch looked around frantically, but could no longer spot anyone who resembled his friend.

With a final grunt of disgust, Laméch plowed through the crowd to a side exit and descended the steps to the street below.

He had a more important mission to accomplish, and he was already running late. He could not believe that he had wasted three hours at this pretentious, pro-Semyaz, event.

He had no time to consider the consequences—and failures—that such "Ascension Plays" meant to his mission of revealing the true nature of the Semyaz to the masses.

It was time to bury his thoughts and concerns with a good dose of adrenaline-laced action.

"There truly *is* a Creator, and He created *light*," Keziah began, "Anything that exists or ever existed was made by Him, and…" she paused to peer into Gaw's upturned face, "as you stated, light is constant—and it was His first and foundational act of creation. All else in His creation depends upon it."

Longfang opened his large eyes, giving the illusion of comprehension.

"It was an act of creation onto a canvas of nothingness. By merely speaking, the reality that is our universe came into being using no pre-existing materials. *That* is what separates the *true* Creator from all other man-made concepts."

Gaw was listening patiently, but at this pause, she interrupted as politely as possible with a question.

"How can anyone know which concept or version of the Creator is the correct one?"

Gaw tensed slightly at the possibility of an irate response, but none was forthcoming.

Keziah smiled, almost as if she welcomed the question.

"Aenoch has traveled the world, collecting tablets that were hidden by descendants of the First Ones prior to the devastation of the Family Wars. It is these tablets—some of which were discovered by my husband—that have given us a reliable understanding."

Her face changed to one of concern.

"Without these, we would be as impressionable as anyone else—and be unable to distinguish truth from falsehood. We would be as prone to enslavement as the rest of the world. Any charismatic leader or impressive technology could be used to sway people to believe anything."

Gaw nodded dutifully and smiled slightly in response to Keziah's kind eyes. Keziah started to smile in return, but suddenly her eyes grew wide with a look of shock and the corners of her mouth twisted violently in a grimace of pain.

A groan escaped Keziah's mouth as she quickly wrapped her arms around her swollen, expectant abdomen. Gaw swiftly lifted Longfang's head from her lap and rose to go to her, but before she could reach her, Keziah pitched forward and collapsed on the ground in front of her, emitting more groans of anguish, convulsing as waves of pain flashed through her body.

Gaw stood helpless for a few seconds, and then began screaming loudly for help.

Laméch hurried through the streets, the beginnings of a grin slowly forming on his face.

He had headed straight for his father's house after that depressing "ascension" play and fixed something to eat. After that, he had collected the materials he needed, plus the chemicals from his father's lab (identifying them with the symbols that Aenoch had described). He placed everything in a shoulder bag and grabbed a long coil of rope which he flung loosely around his neck and under his right arm.

It was now almost an hour after midnight, and the streets flickered in the shadows cast by the pulsating energies of the Power House. There was no moon, yet, but it should be up in two hours—in time for the two men to use its light, assuming this prison break was successful.

His life was now pleasantly reduced to two major thoughts. The immediate mission at hand—and the excitement of returning home before his child was born. Once Aenoch was brought to the village—and the awaiting Dragon Team—Laméch would be back with Keziah in less than a week.

With his grin now firmly in place, he approached a tall building where a small seaport trading firm conducted business. This building was immediately south of the city prison and cast a greenish aura-encompassed silhouette from the lights of the Power House that rose further to the south at the far end of the docks.

He reached the building and immediately clambered up the edges of the limestone blocks, scaling the vertical wall of the building in only a few minutes. He had not climbed like this in years, but he found his abilities came back to him immediately.

Once on the roof, he found an abutment that extended from the northwest corner and immediately attached one end of his rope to it. He carefully uncoiled the rest of the rope and attached the other end to his waist.

Standing carefully on the corner ledge, he turned and faced away from the prison and began running south along the western edge of the building. When he decided the timing was right, he jumped from the ledge, diving as far as he could into the darkness below.

The rope had a special elastic quality from its braiding, and this was the kind of antic that he had been famous for in his youth. However, he had never done such a thing in the dark—and he always had peers around to witness his bravado.

This jump was as parallel as possible to the building, and when the rope suddenly grew taut, Laméch was jerked into a slight loop as he began to swing back alongside the building.

He pulled upward quickly, avoiding the coarse building wall as it sped past him, and he soon began to swing upward across the space between the buildings.

There was a moment of apprehension as he saw the prison roof quickly approaching, but his arc barely cleared it, and within a matter of seconds he slowed, hovered, and ultimately dropped about four cubits onto the top of the prison, skidding into a landing in a painful huddle on his right hip.

Ignoring the pain, he immediately collected as much rope as he could, and cut off the remaining, allowing it to fall and dangle from the building he had just left.

Moving to the eastern side of the prison building, he found another abutment to attach his cable and slowly rappelled down until he was suspended directly next to the high window of Aenoch's cell.

Not caring whether or not Aenoch knew he was there, he quickly anchored his rope and began to pull out the materials from his father's lab. There was a thin aluminum rod about half a cubit long, a small ceramic flask with markings that Aenoch said would contain nitric acid, and a pouch of tooth powder that he had stolen from his father's lavatory.

For the next three hours he worked suspended as the rope cut into his buttocks, carefully dipping the rod into the acid, and then cutting—one small scratch at a time—the base of the four brass bars. As Aenoch had instructed, he covered the areas around his cut with the powder—after moistening it with saliva—to keep the acid from spreading. The fumes were overpowering, at times, but Laméch would just blow them away, focusing on nothing but his task.

Eventually, he had cut through the base of all four, and he began to etch away at the far side of the tops of each bar, slowly creating a notch. He began testing the bars by pulling at their bases with his feet against the wall. After several tries—and a few more swipes of acid—the bars finally pulled away, sticking out from the top of the window.

Aenoch had been watching his progress, and when Laméch removed a second smaller rope from his waist and threw it down to him, he was ready.

Aenoch clambered up the rope, squeezed carefully through the small window (scraping and burning himself slightly on one of the exposed brass nubs), and finally attached himself to Laméch.

Laméch lowered them both wordlessly to the ground and discarded his materials. They quickly crossed the dockyard and exited into the northern woods just as the moon was rising.

After traveling around the northern end of the city, they headed southwest, towards the guides who had been promised them, and as they traveled, the powerful purple and green borealis of the Power House slowly gave way to the pinkish-blue light of the rising full moon.

CHAPTER 22
BETRAYAL

"The apparently random attacks by the Semyaz on the numerous Forest People's communities were not understood at first. Even decades after they had ceased culling them for their experimentation subjects, the destruction of villages seemed arbitrary and essentially meaningless.

Only after the realization that the cities had been used as control groups in the Replacement War was the true purpose of these assaults understood. The forest communities were simply unwanted variables—and had to be eliminated."

—Amoela the Librarian,
The First Two Thousand Years, Vol. II

They headed southwest from the city, traveling slowly through the forest until sunrise. As the morning dews and mists began to saturate Laméch's clothing, he looked around, wondering when or how they would meet their guides.

Laméch was somewhat amused at the fear and anxiety city dwellers held for the forests. He had spent so many years traveling in them, he had almost forgotten how sequestered and unaware those in the cities were. Now, after this brief return to the place of his upbringing, he thought of those in Matusalé who would be terrified of his current journey. He also remembered, with repressed embarrassment, how brave and daring he had imagined himself during his youthful excursions into the woods. There was only the fear of the unknown, and he allowed himself a sigh of pleasant relaxation as he strolled with Aenoch through the trees.

Suddenly three men, wearing leather breechcloths similar to the one Aenoch was wearing, emerged from behind the trees in front of them brandishing small but lethal-looking crossbows—fully cocked.

Laméch stepped forward to meet the men, extending his hand.

"Greetings!" he said with a large smile. "I'm glad you found us."

The men continued to glare menacingly at them and did not lower their weapons. The lead man signaled for his two partners to move and flank Laméch and his grandfather, and then moved closer, pressing the point of his arrow directly into Laméch's throat.

Laméch was suddenly—and uncharacteristically—afraid.

"*What guards the garden?*" the man barked suddenly.

Laméch squinted quizzically with his eyes before responding, allowing relief to set in.

"A flaming sword?" Laméch answered questioningly with a slight roll of his eyes. He tried to sound as bored as possible to hide his initial fear.

The man broke into a grin and moved the arrow-point slightly to the left of Laméch's neck—before releasing it with a loud click, sending the metal projectile whizzing past Laméch's ear causing him to jump back with a yelp.

All three men broke into loud roars of laughter—which ended abruptly as Aenoch lifted his hand and began to speak.

"I want to thank you for your rescue," he began, then turned to look in amusement at Laméch, "*and* for following proper security procedures. I understand we are heading to a community about two days from here?"

The three men nodded in unison.

"Then we should start walking," Aenoch stated calmly.

Immediately they pointed the way, indicating that Laméch and Aenoch should follow them. One of the men moved closer to Aenoch and spoke quietly.

"We had to make sure it was you," he said by way of explanation.

Aenoch nodded his approval—and pardon.

Laméch was still upset, and the guide's excuse angered him further. However, as he looked at his own shabby servant's clothing—and at Aenoch's unkempt hair and facial growth from almost three weeks in prison, he became more understanding.

The three men led at a relaxed but steady pace, but it soon became apparent that each of the guides took turns traveling with them while the other two scouted on ahead and were usually nowhere to be seen.

As they walked through the thick woods, the warm sun began to filter through the overhead branches, drying Laméch's clothing. As he watched Aenoch walking resolutely, as if he had no care in the world, it suddenly occurred to Laméch that he had not informed his grandfather of his soon to be arriving child. He felt slightly ashamed that his bitter attitude at the time had driven his excitement from his mind.

"Keziah is with child," he announced abruptly, speaking for the first time since his yelp several hours earlier that morning.

Aenoch turned abruptly and broke into a large grin, startling Laméch. It was an unusual expression for the serious founder, and Laméch paused for a second before grinning back.

"That is so incredible," Aenoch announced, beaming, as both men stopped walking. Aenoch was very aware—and had often expressed concern—about Keziah's inability to bear children. He was careful never to implicate the Semyaz experiments in his comments, but Laméch always knew he shared his apprehensions.

"It is an incredible honor—and responsibility, the ability to create life," Aenoch said as they walked. "I am very happy for you. I know you have waited a long time for this."

A sense of relief—and sudden camaraderie—broke out between the two men, and Laméch suddenly launched into something that was very foreign to him: an apology.

"I'm sorry about my attitude yesterday," he began. "I'm easily frustrated with our apparent lack of success, and," he paused, "I guess it's easy to take it out on you."

He smiled.

"Especially since you don't fight back."

Aenoch nodded his forgiveness, but scowled in disagreement.

"Oh, I fight back," he said firmly. "I simply fight back against the enemy—not my friends."

Aenoch smiled again, causing Laméch, briefly, to feel worse.

They resumed walking, as their single guide had pulled far ahead of them and was looking back in exasperation.

"So explain your frustrations to me," Aenoch asked, clearly indicating that nothing Laméch said would be held against him.

Laméch immediately launched into his experience at the Ascension Play, and its obvious pro-Semyaz sentiments and propaganda. He railed at how everything seemed to be getting worse, in spite of his now decades of service to Aenoch and his cause. Although the Semyaz seemed to have slowed their culling and kidnapping of Forest People considerably (it was suspected that they were now continuing their experiments with the offspring at hand), their involvement in city administrations and society had increased immeasurably.

"When you first met me," he concluded, "I was trying to get people to realize the hidden dangers of Semyaz policies and taxation, but today," his voice rose, "they have troops in every city and representatives dictating to the city owners how to run them. I actually met one of them for the first time, named Danel, and *he* was practically giving my father orders!"

Laméch paused for a breath and he heard Aenoch sigh with him.

"Yes," Aenoch said. "I met Danel."

He turned to Aenoch.

"Very insidious *creature*," he said, emphasizing the fact that he had *not* said "man".

Laméch ignored him and continued.

"How can we justify all that we are doing, when we can see the situation quickly—and clearly—becoming worse?"

Aenoch nodded, mostly to himself, as they continued to walk. Their solitary guide was replaced with one of the other two as they headed towards a downhill ravine.

"The difference between me and you," Aenoch stated, in response, "is that you are focused on results, whereas I am focused on obedience."

Laméch looked sharply at him, somewhat concerned at the direction this conversation was heading.

"There are two things you need to learn," Aenoch continued, and then smiled. "Actually, there are several, but...we'll consider them later."

Laméch began to respond, but grudgingly stopped at Aenoch's upheld hand.

"The first is this," Aenoch said with a firm nod. "There is no limit to what a person can accomplish when he does not care for the credit, the praise, or the reputation."

He paused for another nod.

"The second is that you are severely limited in resources and willpower when you are only serving yourself."

"What do you mean?" Laméch asked, unable to help himself.

"Unless you have a cause that is bigger than you are," Aenoch said, "you will never find the motivation to accomplish all that you need to do."

"I think I've accomplished a great deal," Laméch insisted defensively.

"You see?" Aenoch asked. "You are more concerned with what I and others think about your contributions."

"That is not true," Laméch said, feeling as if he had been caught. But of course, he didn't care what Aenoch thought—or did he?

"I'm sorry," said Aenoch. "I don't mean to provoke. You have, indeed, been a great success, and have many accomplishments both for yourself and for our cause. What I am saying is that you are very comfortable in who you are and in your responses and reactions to life. You know what to do and say in every situation, and your confidence is based on your ability—and your personal history—to solve situations."

He turned and looked into Laméch's face.

"What you have *not* experienced is something that challenges those reactions. A situation that goes beyond your pre-determined responses and forces you to cry out for help from beyond yourself."

His words sent a strange chill through Laméch. They walked in silence for a few minutes until Aenoch spoke again.

"I am not trying to worry you or bring you fear," he said. "My objective through this entire life is to simply do what is right, what I am supposed to do, and leave the results in the Creator's hands. It is not fatalistic. It is a statement of reliance on the One I serve—and the knowledge that my obedience will be used for His desired purpose—which is something I do not know and dare not guess."

Laméch gave a small shrug of understanding just as the two scouting guides returned.

They were carrying shoulder satchels that contained small loaves of bread and assorted nuts, berries, and bark. Laméch had not realized how hungry he was, and was glad when the guides brought them to a halt at the edge of a small brook.

They sat and munched on the offerings, and drank their fill from the stream which was slightly warm—since it most certainly flowed from a spring further back into the woods.

Laméch glanced at one of the guides.

"How much further do we have to travel?" he asked pleasantly.

The guide stared at him briefly.

"We have been traveling for about half a day," he said pointedly.

"I suppose that means we have a day and a half left." He turned and smiled slightly at his partners who returned the grin.

Laméch shrugged and continued his meal.

ELUCIDATION: BETRAYAL

"Thank you for this food," Aenoch said to them. They all nodded and raised their hands in a small gesture, acknowledging their respect for him. Laméch saw this and wondered, *how does someone who does not care for the praise of others somehow always receive it anyway?* He shook his head, wondering if he had answered his own question.

As they rose to resume their journey Aenoch reached out and helped Laméch to his feet. Aenoch's smile was so warm that Laméch suddenly found himself wishing that his own father had, even once, smiled at him like this.

They spent the rest of the day discussing the amazing creation around them. Leaves, birds, small animals—the tracks of much larger animals—and the wonderful sounds of life that surrounded them provided a great reservoir of topics. Laméch had learned to appreciate this during his years among the Forest People, and knew that this enjoyment was something that those who dwelt in the cities never suspected.

That evening, their guides offered up similar foods, with the addition of a wonderful dessert made from dates and figs. Laméch had spent enough time with Aenoch's people—and knew enough of his teachings—to never expect any meals with meat. The shedding of innocent animal blood, he always said, could only be done for clothing, never food or sport. His own leather breechcloth and those of many of his followers—including their guides—clearly demonstrated this point.

After the meal, the lead guide, whose name was Tareef, approached Aenoch with a simple request.

"Can you give us a teaching?"

The other two nodded eagerly and approached, apparently knowing that Aenoch's answer would be positive. Laméch watched with a mixture of bewilderment—and the tiniest hint of disgust. Something was not right about people giving another man that much deference.

Aenoch nodded politely, glanced over at Laméch as if he knew his grandson's thoughts, and began to speak.

"Laméch grew up in Matusalé, and is well acquainted with my subject for tonight."

He looked to Laméch and actually winked before continuing.

"In the early days of the first cities, it became critical that laws be created to maintain order and protect the people. Laws to protect contracts and punish those who harmed others. It was no longer feasible to simply rely on culture and customs, since the populations of the cities grow rapidly in a confined space. However, there is an inherent problem with any law. Human nature despises being told what to do; and, in fact, the mere creation of a law will often prompt us to disobey—and engage in the very prohibited activity that we would *never* have considered before the law was created."

He paused to wait for comprehensive nods, and continued.

"The Lawgivers of today carry ceremonial daggers of truth, but this practice comes from the earliest days of law formation and establishment when Lawgivers were under constant threat of attack and physical harm from those who disapproved of their statutes."

He smiled.

"You can imagine how tempting it would be to kill the Lawgiver who had just ruled against you."

Laméch was horrified to see how readily the guides nodded. He would have never considered harming a Lawgiver.

Aenoch straightened and continued.

"Here we come to the first truth," he said with conviction. "On an interpersonal or societal level, there is truly only one evil. That is the evil of *coercion*. There can be no greater offence than for one human to force another to perform an act or accept a belief. Free will is the creation—and first gift—of the Creator; and *any* action—or word—that attacks or offends this gift must certainly be considered a transgression."

Laméch watched as the faces of each of the guides lit up in the reflection of the firelight at the mention of the word "Creator". However, it didn't irritate Laméch as it had during previous lectures of Aenoch. Somehow, for the first time since he had known Aenoch, there was a clarity in his mind regarding the different views of the Creator.

Again, Aenoch caught his eye.

"Unfortunately, there are occasions where coercion *must* occur." Aenoch closed his eyes briefly. "It occurs during child-rearing when we force children to avoid danger, and also in the punishment of those who are guilty of coercion."

He lifted his hand for emphasis.

"Here we come to our second truth." He lowered his hand. "Enforcement of the law *is* coercion—and we are faced with the apparent dilemma of employing evil to combat evil."

He paused as if waiting for comments or observations, yet it was also clear to Laméch that Aenoch knew there would be none.

The fire was gradually dying as the occasional pop and cinder rose from the embers. It suddenly occurred to Laméch that since all three guides were present, apparently scouting was unnecessary when they were not traveling.

Aenoch took a breath and resumed.

"We must then regard laws, for the present, as a necessary evil, although the idea of laws made by people that force—or coerce—others to obey them is repugnant. And this is why we must always strive to have as few laws as possible—and limit the damage that this inevitable conflict will always bring to a society."

Suddenly, he smiled broadly.

"However, I believe that someday the Creator will reveal *His* laws. No longer will we be subject to the whim of arbitrary demands from City owners and their Lawgivers—or of community chiefs and their councils."

His smile grew as he slowly rose to his feet.

"And when the true Seed arrives, we will see creation restored, and I believe this restoration will re-create in all people the knowledge of His laws. There will be no need for human lawgivers—or any form of coercion—ever again!"

Laméch watched the upturned faces of the guides slowly lower as Aenoch reseated himself on the ground. But Laméch had also been very moved by Aenoch's teaching, and had to admit that the Seed that Aenoch spoke of would certainly solve many issues that faced humanity.

Imagine, he thought, if all those employed by the Semyaz were to suddenly renounce coercion simply because they had been—in some mystical fashion—restored.

The teaching was clearly completed, and the conversation turned to details of preparing for the night.

Laméch felt an unexpected bond with Aenoch, and he suddenly felt compelled to share with Aenoch (as he had on other occasions) the story in the stars that Kendrach had told to him many years ago. Somehow the account of the Seed and Infant King in the night sky was comforting, and although the tree branches blotted out much of the starry expanse above them, Laméch now knew enough to be able to point in the correct directions while telling the story.

He also had to admit that he was partially motivated by a desire to show the guides that he, too, had knowledge, and he found himself checking to see if any of them were paying attention.

And he found it troubling to realize, yet again, that Aenoch had been correct when he had accused Laméch of caring what others thought of him.

Of course, his knowledge had came from Kendrach, and *his* knowledge had come from Aenoch; but Aenoch was content to simply smile and nod as Laméch completed the prophesies found in the heavens.

His grandfather had a solitary comment when Laméch had finished.

"Someday, you will actually believe what these stars truly tell us."

They rose early the next morning and resumed their travels, eating from the collection of roots and berries that their guides had collected for them.

As they began a gradual descent into a small valley, Laméch noticed that Aenoch seemed preoccupied—almost as if he were concerned or worried about something.

As they crossed a warm, shallow river, and stepped out on the other side, Laméch finally decided to inquire.

"Is something troubling you?" he asked as they shook the water from their bodies.

Aenoch gave him a weak smile which was somehow more frightening than reassuring.

"Do you recall," Aenoch said eventually, "when I told you that you needed a 'situation that goes beyond your pre-determined responses and forces you to cry out for help from beyond yourself?'"

Laméch nodded, confused.

"Well," Aenoch said slowly. "I fear that such a situation may be upon you much sooner than either of us expected."

A chill much stronger than the one from the previous day surged through Laméch.

"What do you mean?" he asked.

"I'm not sure," Aenoch replied. "However, I feel the need to make you an offer."

He raised his eyebrows and looked into Laméch's face.

Laméch nodded for him to continue.

"If something should happen, and I do not return with you to the island, I would like…"

"What do you mean," Laméch interrupted loudly, "not return to the island? I didn't come all this way and go through all of this," he spread out his arms indicating their journey through the forest, "to rescue *you*, and then to have you not return with me!"

He stared at Aenoch, who remained impassive.

Eventually a slight smile spread on his grandfather's face.

"As I stated earlier," Aenoch said with obvious enjoyment. "More concerned with results than obedience."

Laméch shook his head in annoyance.

"Please say what you wish to say."

Aenoch nodded but said nothing until they had reached the top of the rise in front of them. Laméch noticed as their lead guide changed position again.

"I need to know," Aenoch said eventually, "that you will be available to take over for me, in the event I do not make it back."

He turned to look squarely into Laméch's face.

"I want you to take over as leader in my place."

Laméch was stunned, but managed to ask, "What does 'not make it back' mean?"

Aenoch was blunt.

"In the event I am re-captured or killed."

Laméch stared with his thoughts completely frozen.

"I don't know how to respond," he finally stammered. "I need some time to consider…"

"We may not have much time," Aenoch interrupted. "I have made no preparation for anyone to replace me, and I feel…"

This time Laméch interrupted.

"What do you feel?" he demanded. "What do you know—and how do you suddenly know it now?"

Aenoch shrugged.

"I simply need to know you are available," he said.

Laméch shook his head.

"You know that I don't even share your beliefs," he said, hoping to dissuade Aenoch from this madness.

"I am aware," Aenoch smiled with a nod, "but that is not my concern." He paused. "That *may* be a concern that you need to discuss with Keziah, however."

Laméch glared at him. Even after many years of marriage, he had never openly discussed his pretense with his wife. There was an unspoken awareness, but nothing was ever said.

They walked in silence for a few minutes until Laméch responded.

"I suppose," he said guardedly, "if you truly want me to take over for you, I will do it. However, you must know that I will do things my own way."

Aenoch smiled.

"I wouldn't want anything else," he said. "I will count on it."

Aenoch shouted for the three guides to come, and somehow all three were suddenly surrounding them.

"I need witnesses," he said quietly to Laméch.

He then addressed the guides.

"I want to make a public declaration that Laméch, my grandson, is to be in charge of all of my affairs, in the event that I am no longer available."

He was met with stunned stares.

"If I am re-captured or killed, Laméch will take over my duties and I will ask all those who claim allegiance to me to give it to my grandson, if they so choose."

"Is something going to happen to you?" Tareef asked as the other guides shared in his look of alarm.

"Nothing is going to happen to him," Laméch stated with a mixture of fatigue and bluster.

Aenoch smiled.

"I am making this declaration so that you can send or carry the message if needed. I am asking you to be my witnesses."

The three men nodded quickly and solemnly.

"As Laméch says," continued Aenoch, "I'm sure nothing is going to happen."

He nodded to them and they resumed their guide and scouting duties.

They walked in silence for the next few hours, Laméch's mind churning. He was sure Keziah would be pleased. However, what did this mean for his autonomous lifestyle? What would this mean for his child? Why him?

His thought suddenly turned into a spoken question.

"Why me?" he asked abruptly.

"Because you're the only one available," was Aenoch's quick answer, followed by a full laugh.

"No, that is not true," he said. "I'm sorry."

His face became serious.

"It is because you are my grandson and I trust you. I have watched you for many years, and you are always true to yourself, and regardless of our differences, you are a man with great integrity."

His face changed again and dropped suddenly, a look a severe sadness covering it.

"And also because my own son is complicit with the enemy."

"We have been making good time," Tareef reported to Aenoch later that afternoon. "We should arrive soon, shortly before nightfall."

Aenoch smiled and looked at Laméch.

"I have you to thank," he said with sincere appreciation.

Suddenly there was a noisy rustling in the trees in front of them, and the three men tensed as one of the scouts came rushing out of the foliage towards them.

He was gasping for air, desperately repeating the word "smoke".

Tareef calmed him, and eventually he explained.

"I see smoke rising from the place where our village lies in the distance," he said, hunkering slightly to regain the remainder of his breath. "It is as if everything is burning."

Tareef acted immediately.

"Stay with them," he ordered. "I will run on ahead to see what this means." He gave Aenoch a quick nod, and dashed off through the trees.

The second scout arrived and listened to the first one's report. Although he had not seen the smoke, he immediately took control.

"We will travel as swiftly as possible," he said, "but we will pause before the village's edge and wait for Tareef's report."

They pressed quickly through the forest, and soon it became obvious that some darkness was spreading up into the western sky.

After traveling almost an hour, they came over a hill—and immediately all four could now see a thick column of black smoke rising against the sky.

"This is what I saw from the treetops," the first scout confirmed. "Tareef should already be there."

They continued their quick pace for half an hour until the second scout (who was now guiding them) instructed them to stop. They were now close enough to smell the smoke.

"We will move slowly until that rise," he ordered, indicating a small hill to their right. "We can look down into the village from there. It is also the place where Tareef will meet us."

They followed for a few more minutes until he ordered them to drop to the ground and crawl the rest of the way.

He led them into a bank of thick underbrush—and when they emerged, they were overlooking the village center.

The smoke was thick, stinging their throats and eyes, but the desolation beneath them was overwhelming. The remains of huts and other structures were now piles of blackened rubble, smoldering as the final embers of what was once a thriving forest village faded.

But far worse than the smoldering structures were the dead bodies. Laméch counted at least fifty who were either burned to death or had arrows protruding—mostly from their backs.

The two scouts shuddered as they recognized family and friends, and Laméch tried his best to sympathize with them. However, he acknowledged this attack as the work of the Semyaz, and he found himself more overcome with anger and rage towards them.

He rose up to rush down the hillside.

Both scouts grabbed him and pinned him down.

"We wait for Tareef," they commanded together.

Laméch turned to Aenoch.

"Do you think they have left?" he asked. "They usually just burn and kill, and then take whoever they want. They are probably long gone."

Aenoch shook his head slowly.

"No, they have not left," he said. "They do not have who they have come for. They are waiting in ambush for us to enter the city."

"Who have they come for?" Laméch asked, fearing the answer.

Suddenly a loud shriek sounded from the sky far above them, and they turned to look up as a dragon team approached the village—a small cabin suspended between them. The two large creatures were obviously upset at approaching the smoke.

"It's our men!" Laméch exclaimed in a course whisper. "They can rescue us!"

Suddenly, several dozen men appeared in the village center below, emerging from the surrounding trees. They wore the green and black uniforms of the Semyaz troops, and were fully armed with swords and longbows.

"*That*," said Aenoch, pointing, "is who was waiting for us."

Laméch was stunned to see the men below. *Were they here waiting for him and his grandfather? How had they known? Had someone betrayed their mission?*

Laméch was also surprised to see the uniforms. This was the first time that Laméch had ever seen the Semyaz attack a village with men wearing the uniforms of the Semyaz Security Forces. In other village attacks he had witnessed, the Semyaz were identified only by the fact they were not dressed in the simple clothing of the Forest People.

Instantly, the longbows were lifted, and after a silent moment while the archers tracked their target, a volley of arrows arched towards the swiftly approaching dragon team.

Most of the arrows met their mark, embedding themselves deep into the neck of just one of the creatures. It immediately convulsed, jerking the cabin violently up and down. The second creature screamed in panic and pulled away with such force that the cables between the two beasts gave way with a loud snap. The cabin, now dangling from the fleeing dragon, twisted and spun as it lifted rapidly into the air—before breaking free from its restraints and spinning crazily for a few moments. After seeming to hover for a few seconds, it spiraled swiftly into the ground far below—causing certain death to everyone inside.

The panicked creature flew off at top speed into the northern sky, while the one that had been shot careened madly in circles, spewing blood, until it fell like a projectile, landing with an earthshaking thud only a few hundred cubits from where the four, now despondent men, watched from the underbrush.

They turned their eyes back to the village center below.

Although these men were wearing the same uniforms as those who patrolled the cities, there was something very different about them. As much as Laméch despised the Security Forces, they were always polite and deferential, serving the cities with courtesy and professionalism. He had often remarked that he would almost prefer them to behave badly so that he would have a reason to confront them.

Even from a distance, he could see that these men below were sadistic—and were obviously pleased with the carnage they had created. They carried an air of complete disdain, and Laméch was now sure, more than ever, that this contempt for anything non-Semyaz was beneath the surface of every Semyaz.

Another green and black uniformed officer appeared below, holding a villager around the neck—and brandishing a large black knife.

The man was Tareef.

The officer moved to the center of the group of Semyaz and began walking in a small circle, always facing out from the village.

"We have your man," he shouted, not knowing where to look, "and we know that you are out there!"

He continued his walk facing the perimeter.

"You have no hope of escaping us, and we have destroyed your one chance for rescue!"

The other men scanned around the village, looking for any signs of movement.

"We offer you—and your friend here—," he indicated Tareef while pressing the knife against their guide's throat, "a *new* chance of escape."

The man waited a few seconds before continuing.

"We seek only the man named Aenoch," he shouted as he maintained his circular walk. "Should Aenoch come down into the village within the next two minutes, we will release this one, and no longer pursue the rest of you. You will all be free to fend for yourselves as soon as we have Aenoch in custody and he is on his way back with us to Matusalé to answer for his crimes."

Another pause as the circular walk continued.

"We assume that there are those among you who facilitated his escape," the man said eventually. "We have orders from Matusalé himself to allow you your freedom as soon as we have Aenoch. You now have one minute and forty seconds."

The knife blade pressed harder into Tareef's neck. Even at their distance, the men could see a tiny trickle of blood began to emerge along its edge.

Aenoch stirred beside Laméch and began to rise.

"You can't go," said Laméch, grabbing his arm and glaring at him. "I went through all of this to rescue you. You can't just walk down there."

Aenoch glared back at Laméch, startling him.

"This is *not* about you," he said through tight teeth. "Do you truly think I wish to go down there?"

He pulled himself free from Laméch's grasp.

"Sometimes we fight to save lives," he said, "and sometimes we die to save them. True meekness is in knowing which to do at the right time."

He looked directly into Laméch's eyes.

"Remember your promise to me. It is *that* fear that saddens you most about my re-capture."

He shook his head.

"It is never a failure to do what is right."

With that, Aenoch pulled away and began crawling quickly through the underbrush. He attempted to move as far away from them before rising and going down into the village.

"You have thirty seconds," the man called out.

Laméch could no longer see Aenoch, and he was surprised when he saw his grandfather suddenly stand up along a ridge almost one hundred cubits south of them.

"I am here!" he announced loudly, before making the descent into the village.

Laméch and the two guides watched as Aenoch walked slowly—and purposefully—down to the waiting Semyaz. When he arrived, he was quickly seized and bound.

"You have made a wise decision," the officer called out, now facing the ridge Aenoch had descended. He raised his knife in a mock salute—before swinging it down and plunging it deeply into Tareef's throat.

"This is the end for all who oppose their rightful masters!"

He withdrew the knife and Tareef sagged quickly onto the ground.

Without wasting any time, the troops collected their equipment and began marching out of the village with Aenoch, heading north-west towards Matusalé—and past the three remaining men hiding in the underbrush.

Laméch and the two guides watched in dismay and revulsion as the troops passed them and began what was sure to be an all night march to the city.

Laméch was afraid to meet the eyes of his guides who now had no family, friends, or village left. The only thing for them to do was to follow the troops discreetly—and carefully—at a distance and make their way back to the city.

Hopefully they would be able to learn Aenoch's fate. However, none of them could ever enter the city again—and he could think of no way to return to Aenoch's Island or communicate with Aenoch's people. Or would they become *his* people?

His final thought as he and his guides began trudging after the troops:

Now he was certain to miss the birth of his child.

CHAPTER 23
ASCENSION

"The governing structure of a typical city rested on the premise that the one who founded it also owned it. Although a Founder did not own the people within, it was often very difficult to separate the laws of the Founder from the free choices of the city's residents. Generally a city's wealth and productivity were directly proportional to the contentment and well-being of its citizens, but some Founders discovered this only after decades of failed management. Naturally, the citizen was always free to leave, but the suggestion to 'go and found your own city' was never as feasible as it was inviting."

—Amoela the Librarian,
The First Two Thousand Years, Vol. II

L améch and his two guides were seated in the northern forests along the banks overlooking the docks of Matusalé City, where large crowds were already gathering. He was certain that Aenoch would, eventually, be brought back to his prison, and *almost* certain (on account of his return to prison) that he would be brought out for execution in the immersion chamber as quickly as the city's justice system would allow. For a second offence, Laméch knew that the system was swift indeed.

They had actually taken three days to return to the city, choosing *not* to follow the Semyaz, but rather deciding to return as safely—and assuredly—as possible.

He could not get the image of Tareef's murder out of his mind. He had always believed that the Semyaz were arrogant and treacherous, but it had always been carefully hidden and disguised. To view it so openly—even though it was in a remote area with only a few witnesses—was very traumatic.

His guides had been as determined as he was to pursue Aenoch, and Laméch was again overwhelmed with the amount of reverence they had for him. He had also become acutely aware during their return trip that they were now quite ready to transfer this same deference onto him—if the worst were to happen.

Laméch's mind churned over two distinct troubling concerns for which he could find no solution. First, he agonized that there was now no way for him to be present at the birth of his child—and no matter how hard he tried, he could not conjure up any possible solution.

The second was the more immediate concern that had troubled him ever since he had seen the Semyaz uniforms step out into the smoldering remains of the village center.

How had the Semyaz known they were coming and prepared an ambush? If they had immediately discovered the prison break and pursued them, they would have been captured long before they arrived at the village.

Laméch had only spoken to one person regarding the details of this rescue—and *that* conclusion was inconceivable. His mind flickered back to the day when the Enforcer ships had been waiting for him after his flying leap from the Power House in his youth. It had been their appearance that forced him into his discovery—and the life he now led.

He quickly forced any suspicions of Ruallz out of his mind—

just as he had done that morning so many decades ago. There had to be some other explanation.

One of the guides nudged him and pointed to the docks across from their vantage point, bringing Laméch back to the present.

A large group of Enforcers were already in place, fanned out along the docks to provide a barrier between the onlookers and the small procession that was just emerging from the city gates. Low tide had just occurred, and Laméch knew that any daytime execution would be scheduled soon after this to allow the drama—and suspense—to last as long as possible until the height of high tide when death would actually occur.

The procession was led by a small group of Librarians, clad in their formal hooded white robes, who were recording everything, followed by four local Enforcers wearing their official dark-blue headpieces. Walking between the Enforcers was a prisoner who could be none other than Aenoch. He was wrapped head to foot in large swaths of white cloth, the traditional burial garb of the dead, and there was no way to see his face. He was forced to carry a banner above his head, and Laméch knew enough to recognize the characters for Aenoch's name, and also knew that the remaining lettering declared the crimes that justified his death.

Behind them were seven Lawgivers with their ceremonial daggers and additional Librarians to observe from behind. An additional number of Enforcers then followed to support the first group.

Large groups of people were now forming atop the city walls, and some nearby vessels filled with excited spectators—many from other cities—pulled in close to the docks in anticipation of this rare event.

Laméch turned back to the city gate and saw his father, dressed in the finest gold robes, emerge and wave at the crowds, and then turn around and look up to acknowledge those on the wall. Laméch was surprised at the excitement an impending execution was creating. He had only witnessed a few, and they had always been somber events, filled with dread and warning. This was more like a celebration.

ELUCIDATION: ASCENSION

A man appeared immediately behind Matusalé, and Laméch's chest went cold. It was Danel! He was smiling and nodding slightly, but doing nothing to bring attention to himself. Although he emerged after the Founder, his pace gradually increased until he was walking beside Matusalé, and it was clear that he was presenting himself as an esteemed ambassador, advisor, and confidant.

An additional number of Enforcers followed, and Laméch was initially pleased *not* to see any green and black uniforms among the procession. However, his approval quickly disappeared as two columns of Semyaz Security brought up the rear in a manner that suggested they had provided a formal passage guard for the entire procession as it had entered the gate from the other side.

Laméch glowered at the two rows of Semyaz, and was suddenly horrified to realize that many of them were the same men who had met them in the village—and killed Tareef! However, these men were now politely nodding in deference to the local Enforcers and seemed genuinely pleased to serve the needs of the procession and be subservient to Matusalé City and its citizens.

An inner rage swept through Laméch as he realized the depth of the Semyaz deception and subversion. He now felt more than ever that the cities of humankind were being set up for some kind of major assault—but he could not imagine in what manner. Nothing among the Semyaz intelligence suggested they were engaged in any large-scale military preparation. As despicable as their activities were, they were primarily engaged in medical experimentation and the occasional attack on Forest People communities.

Laméch tried to imagine what must have occurred between the time that he had left the city with Aenoch five days ago and the imminent execution that was before him now. Certainly, there must have been an immediate announcement proclaiming Aenoch's escape and obvious guilt, along with exaggerated accusations regarding the danger he presented and numerous spurious attacks on his mental state and social viability.

There must also have been a great proclamation at his recapture and return. A swift mock-trial—and the understanding that any repeat offence was a capital one—and the stage was set for an almost joyous execution that could only be the result of expert public manipulation. Laméch couldn't help but conclude that Danel deserved a great deal of the credit. Laméch also couldn't help but wonder if part of the purpose of this event was to set a precedent—something to ensure that the desired executions of future dissidents would be easily facilitated with great public approval.

Aenoch had now arrived at the immersion chamber, and his Enforcer guards lifted the banner of crimes from his hands. It was turned towards the crowds as Matusalé raised his hand for quiet. When the noise died down, the Founder simply recited the words of the banner in a loud voice.

"For crimes of sedition and incitement against the City, for incurable social and mental aberrations, and for egregious slander and other public and private verbal attacks against our friends and allies, the Semyaz, we have found the man Aenoch, of Qênan City, unable to safely reside within the civilized cities of the world and therefore, sentenced to death."

There was a pause that (to Laméch's dismay) elicited a large round of cheers before Matusalé resumed. Laméch wondered how much Danel had to do with this indictment—especially the subtle snub at Qênan. He also wondered what it would take to twist a man so much that he would actually stand in celebration over the execution of his own father.

His thoughts turned suddenly and unintentionally to his own child who was yet to be born. Was it possible that someday, something could drive his own offspring to behave similarly?

Matusalé lowered his arms.

"That sentence is to be carried out immediately," he decreed.

Cheers erupted from the surrounding crowds as flowers and confetti were tossed from the city walls. Loud blasts of navigational horns sounded from various ships in the harbor, and several of the Enforcers thrust their fists into the air. Laméch was sickened by the display, and was further troubled as he watched several satisfied smiles flicker across the faces of the Semyaz Security men.

Laméch did not doubt the occasional need for an execution, but something in his years with Aenoch caused him to revolt at the celebration of anyone's death—even an enemy's death. And he was also saddened and angered at the manipulation that was soon to bring about the death of a man who most certainly did *not* deserve it— and whom Laméch, although sometimes reluctantly, considered a friend.

The bonds were removed from Aenoch, and the side grate of the chamber was removed so that the Enforcers could place Aenoch inside.

One of the guides grabbed Laméch's arm and pulled.

"Look!" he hissed, pointing into the air away from the docks.

Laméch twisted away and looked out over the bay.

Far overhead, two bright lights were traveling swiftly through the air, coming in from the East. As they grew closer—and larger— they became glowing white spheres that looked to Laméch like pulsating fire-balls, except that their "fire" was incendiary white-hot filaments that flickered in and out from their centers where a piercing white light radiated with fierce intensity, but amazingly was not blinding.

The crowds on the city wall noticed them first and began pointing as a collective gasp resounded across the docks. The people below turned to follow their arms, and soon there was a cacophony of exclamation and disarray as they watched the extraordinary lights head for the dockyards.

Laméch noticed that the shapes were actually amorphous, shifting into a large oval as they drew near. As they descended, heading directly for Aenoch, they seemed to be about nine to ten cubits in length, and by the time they reached Aenoch, they were dropping vertically.

They made no sound, and did not seem to be displacing any air as they moved, but when they landed on either side of Aenoch, the Enforcers that were around him were flung to the ground as if struck by a violent wind.

The deafening noise of the crowd turned suddenly into silence as they watched the two lights press on either side of Aenoch's form, fully enveloping him in their glowing filaments. Aenoch stiffened as the two lights pressed into him, and as his body began to shine with the intensity of molten metal, Laméch thought he could see his grandfather's body glowing through the layers of burial cloth that shrouded him.

No one could see what happened next, but to Laméch it appeared that the two balls of lightning collapsed around Aenoch, and then shot up into the sky heading back in the direction from which they had come, traveling at a much faster rate than when they had arrived.

The door to the immersion cage was still open, but Aenoch was nowhere to be found. The Enforcers who had been thrown to the ground got up slowly and looked around, confused, frightened, and desperate for someone to blame.

Laméch looked to his guides in total shock and confusion. He had never seen or heard of anything like this.

The guides, also, had a look of astonishment in their faces, but Laméch saw an additional sense of awe and admiration in their eyes—almost as if they knew what they had just witnessed.

"What was that?" he stammered, not used to being uncertain about anything. "Do you know what those things were?"

His guides nodded slowly before one of them collected his breath and answered.

"Aenoch spoke of them, but we have never seen them until today," he said as the two men looked at each other. Their eyes were wide.

"They are the *Un-fallen*."

CHAPTER 24
SOLITUDES

"Prior to the Replacement War, the world was clearly divided into two distinct and separate societies. There was the network of forest communities whose daily lives were one of survival from the onslaught of the Semyaz attempt to eradicate them for no apparent reason. Then there were the cities that grew and prospered under the tutelage—and apparent protection—of the Semyaz. The city inhabitants were completely unaware of the existence of the forest communities; disbelieving any rumors to the contrary. The forest communities, however, were fully aware of the affluence of the cities, and it was difficult for them to not resent what could easily be construed as collusion."

—Amoela the Librarian,
The First Two Thousand Years, Vol. II

The lady in the red robe hurried through the lower corridors with a mixture of excitement and anxiety as she approached Tûrell's study. She had been surprised at his summons, so soon after her last visit only a few months earlier, but she knew that great breakthroughs were imminent—although the memory of the abduction of one of her candidates reminded her that the forces of the resistance were growing.

Even before she arrived at his doorway, Tûrell's head emerged with obvious excitement, and he smiled when he saw her.

"We are ready," he said as he escorted her in without any greeting. He pushed her into a nearby chair. She looked up somewhat startled, unused to this level of enthusiasm from him.

"I know you have been wondering what to do with the remaining eleven candidates from your first class," he began, "and I'm happy to say that, due to some recent breakthroughs, we may not have to discard them."

She looked up sharply at this. She was aware that this had been a possibility, but she had never fully acknowledged it to herself.

"In fact," he continued, ignoring her, "if all goes well, we may not even need your younger classes."

His smile grew—and then faded as he saw the consternation in her eyes.

"They *are* ready?" he asked expectantly, as if searching for a reason for her discomfort. "They have adjusted to their loss?" he insisted with a nod.

"Oh yes," she answered quickly. "They were told she fell from the cliffs in an accident, and the room was sealed immediately for repairs."

She drew a deep breath.

"What has been more difficult for them is the replacement of their mentor. There is quite a bonding that takes place when the person who was their guardian and councilor has been with them since their arrival."

She paused and thought angrily of the painful interrogation she had presided over with the class's mentor, Rin-Kendril. That traitor had almost destroyed an entire class! It was only providential that the Semyaz had requested a lone candidate that day. A warm, almost contented feeling rose up in the midst of her rage as she contemplated how that woman had received everything she had deserved—

ultimately begging for her own death long before she had finally received it. Rin-Kendril had possessed intense blue eyes, and no matter what agonies she received, those eyes had continued to shine with determined, rebellious life. Sadly, nothing had been learned from the session. The lady in the red robe felt a flush of grief as she contemplated the waste.

"I'm sure they will be fine," Tûrell said quickly, interrupting her thoughts and pulling her back into the present.

She nodded, focusing on the mission at hand.

"I have some more good news," he said, almost in a teasing way, his smile returning. She had never seen him this animated.

"Yes," she prompted. "What is it?"

He clasped his fists and closed his eyes briefly in anticipation.

"The leader of the resistance," he said eventually, "is no more. Aenoch is gone!"

A sense of triumph surged through her system, almost causing her to stand.

"The one who floods us with spies and undermines our research?" she said excitedly. "The leader of those who create havoc with our outreaches and recruitment? That is indeed good news!"

"Yes," Tûrell said, nodding vigorously. "And without his head-ship, his resistance will surely collapse." He lowered his voice con-spiratorially. "And I understand that most of his followers weren't nearly as drastic in their views as he was."

She nodded, matching his enthusiasm.

"When did this happen?" she asked.

"Only a few days ago," he answered. "In Matusalé City. He was executed for treason."

She nodded again, more contemplatively this time.

"This would signal a major shift of public opinion in our favor, correct?"

He nodded back.

A sudden thought occurred to her.

"How can you know of this if it has only been a few days?"

Tûrell stepped back slightly.

"The Semyaz have many advanced methods of communication," he answered guardedly. "One of them was there and witnessed the event."

He became silent for a moment, suddenly reverting to the reserved composure that she was used to seeing from him. It was as if he suddenly remembered that he had special access to the Semyaz, and as such, he should not be speaking with her as an equal.

"Please have your candidates ready as soon as possible," he said, resuming his role as her superior. "They have been groomed for a very sacred honor."

"I understand," she said, rising.

He gripped her arm suddenly, startling her.

"No, I'm not sure that you do," he said, all signs of his earlier jubilance gone. His face was far sterner and more serious than she had ever seen before.

"They are to be the mothers of a new *race*."

Laméch spent the night in a stupor, sleeping fitfully on a pile of leaves that were totally soaked with morning dew long before sunrise. His mind swirled with unresolved questions—and the realization that the situation that Aenoch had predicted had now, uncannily, come to pass.

He had no quick answers or instinctive responses left.

How was he going to get home? *Was* Aenoch's Island his home? How was Keziah – and had his child arrived?

Was he now the leader of Aenoch's resistance? Would anyone else believe it—or accept it?

Did he want it?

However, the most pressing question was: What happened to Aenoch?

He had heard of amazing and unexpected phenomena occurring in the vicinity of the Power House. The constant energies created strange ball lightning, magnetic mirages, and a host of spectacular light shows that could occur unpredictably at any time. People also often observed large orbs of glowing light circling the pyramid—but only at night.

But this had occurred in bright daylight—and the lights had moved with such apparent purpose and direction.

And he had never seen such light incinerate a man with a flash of incandescence that left no trace or residue behind. It was almost as if the lights had enveloped Aenoch and taken him with them.

Laméch's guides had been little help. They had insisted that the evil, incorporeal Semyaz (those original Semyaz whom Aenoch considered inhuman) had beneficent, non-evil (hence, *Un-fallen*) counterparts that appeared on very rare occasions. It was surely these entities that had rescued—and removed—their leader. It all sounded like children's stories or bad fiction. Beings of pure energy simply did not exist.

Whatever the case, his companions were convinced they would never see Aenoch again and were already looking to Laméch for leadership and guidance.

He shook off the wet leaves and rose from the ground, brushing mud and bugs from his legs. He felt disgusted and irritated—mostly at his own consternation—and finally made a decision.

He was going to take a bath.

He stood and strode purposely through the trees in an easterly direction, not caring if his guides followed him. Of course, they could not be considered guides anymore since he knew these woods intimately. They could certainly help him survive off the land, but they knew nothing of these regions.

He was heading towards a special hot spring—the one past the underground bunker that he had discovered, which had permanently changed the direction of his life. He pushed through the underbrush, ignoring the hunger that had suddenly sprung up in his stomach, and concentrated on one thing: to sink into some warm water and some- how wash away all of his concerns.

His companions followed quickly, almost as if they were re- lieved their new leader had finally chosen a course of action.

* * *

Two Semyaz Security officers met Ruallz as he was entering his place of work, startling him. It was unusual to see them this far from the docks. Usually only local Enforcers patrolled the inner city.

"How may I assist you?" he asked cautiously.

"We have a simple request," one of the officers responded. Ruallz could identify the man's higher rank armband.

"I have already done as you requested," Ruallz responded with a bit more antipathy than he intended. He felt something cold blossom in his stomach.

"And we thank you," the officer continued. "You were asked to let us know the moment Laméch returned after your absence so many years ago, and since that time you have prospered in peace." The officer nodded towards the textile and garment facility where Ruallz worked, somehow managing to imply that any success he enjoyed— or might lack in the future—was under the officer's control.

"I was promised that I would be left alone once I informed the authorities of his return," Ruallz stated. He was feeling sickly now, wishing the two men would leave.

Both officers nodded briefly.

"And you shall be left alone," the officer responded, "but we do have one final request for you."

Ruallz stared blankly at them, suddenly understanding that this game of betrayal had no end.

The lower-ranked officer spoke.

"I understand that you are no stranger to helping the local Enforcers," he said pointedly.

Ruallz nodded dumbly. Although he had never wanted to harm anyone—and certainly, as a youth, had been a strong supporter of The Path—he had always felt a strong civic duty when he thought a situation was getting out of control.

A situation like his friend Laméch deciding to jump from the Power House as a youth, he thought glumly. He had hoped Laméch's arrest might scare some sense into him.

Ruallz took a deep breath.

"What do you want?" he said with resignation.

"Oh, nothing that will interrupt your life," the first officer promised. "We only need you to be watchful for certain information, should you encounter it."

"What information is that?" he asked, feeling somewhat relieved. They would have no idea if he came across anything—nor would they know if he even tried.

The officer explained exactly what they were looking for, and even suggested to Ruallz various methods he could use to accomplish their request.

"We are in no hurry," the officer concluded. "This is an ongoing search, and we simply want as much assistance as you can offer. However, the sooner you can supply this, the better it will be for everyone."

Ruallz nodded quickly, wanting nothing more than for them to leave.

As the Semyaz officers turned to leave, the lower-ranked officer spoke.

"Your daughter was particularly lovely in the Ascension Play the other evening," he said carefully. "I'm certain that you would love to see her career blossom." He nodded, prompting Ruallz to nod with him.

"And it would be a shame to see that career—and all of that talent and beauty—struck down so that no one would ever enjoy it," he continued, nodding, even as Ruallz tried desperately to mask his look of revulsion and anger at the not-so-subtle threat.

The two officers walked away quickly, not allowing Ruallz to respond. As he watched the backs of their green and black uniforms, he suddenly had many questions—and he was surprised to discover that he wished Laméch was available to answer them.

What if everything that Laméch had said about the Semyaz was true? Was there something else going on—far beyond the normal human experience—that Aenoch and his people understood?

He had refused to observe the execution (he could not endure seeing the results of his betrayal) but he had heard the official story. Somehow, nature itself had sent fiery balls of lightning to strike Aenoch down as an example to those who spread such hate and slander against the Semyaz. Such people who stood in the way of progress would ultimately be removed—and if society didn't do it, providence itself would.

But he had also heard a very different story from dozens of those who had attended. Apparently, it had seemed to many, as if the lights had engaged in a rescue rather than an execution.

Laméch surged downward into the depths of the hot spring, his ears and lungs protesting from the mounting pressure. He used the pain to wash all other concerns from his mind, imagining that when he finally resurfaced, all of his cares would be gone.

At this level, the clear waters of the spring were laced with silt from the subterranean mudflow which fed it, and Laméch remembered with a slight grin how he and Ruallz had escaped from that very mudflow decades earlier.

He continued down, mentally calculating the halfway point of his air reserves—and deliberately pushing past them. One of the philosophies of his youth came back to him.

Death-defying activities are the only way to truly know that one was alive.

He made two final kicks downward, and then turned abruptly and headed for the surface. His grin widened, threatening to allow the pressurized water to seep through his clenched lips.

Would he make it?

His head throbbed with the pounding of his heart and it took all of his willpower to not give in to his instincts that were commanding him to inhale.

The bright light from the morning sun grew closer as it refracted through the clear surface waters, and he deliberately exhaled his remaining air as a mental diversion.

He felt his head swelling, and his eyes began to go dim as he listened to the roar of blood rushing behind his ears.

This is what separates men from animals, he thought ecstatically as he shot up through the final cubits of water.

Man can override his instincts.

He relaxed his lungs in their exhaled state as his mind faded. His feet continued to propel him upward, purely by reflex, as his consciousness faded away.

Splashes of water from his head breaking the surface revived him, and he spun his head vigorously from side to side, gulping in large quantities of air. As his breathing stabilized and his heart rate returned to normal, he awarded himself with one of the largest grins he had ever fashioned.

I'll try anything twice, he reminded himself.

He swam lazily to the edge of the pool, enjoying its warmth, and watching the late morning sun rise over the ocean behind him. Eventually he pulled himself onto the surrounding rocky ledge, shaking out his hair and wringing out the servant's clothes that he was still wearing.

As he sauntered up the embankment, he noticed his two companions were facing away from him, standing with their crossbows armed and aimed at a lone figure draped in a gray cloak and dark hood.

Laméch's companions turned slightly at his approach, and one of them pointed to the figure.

"This person gave the correct passphrase," he said, "but we were waiting for you."

Laméch looked at the figure and watched as the hood was thrown back.

"Lyn-Golnan!" Laméch exclaimed in recognition. He waved at his companions to stand down and ran towards the Librarian.

Lyn smiled at his approach and accepted his outstretched hand, but held him at arm's length to keep his wet clothing from spoiling her attire.

"It is good to see you," Laméch exclaimed, pulling on her arm a little too vigorously.

"And you, also," she said, smiling as she extracted her hand.

Laméch's companions relaxed, enjoying the reunion.

"How did you find us?" he asked, daring to hope that he might find a way back to his family.

She nodded her thanks to his two companions for lowering their weapons, and began to explain.

"After you left the island, we developed a backup plan for your escape, should you fail in your rescue. We had no way of contacting you, but once you succeeded in liberating Aenoch, we dismissed our plan."

Laméch nodded, slightly insulted that they thought he might fail, but still grateful.

"However, after Aenoch was recaptured," she continued, "we were not sure what had happened to you or your party. We heard no word from the village where you were heading, and we have heard nothing from the dragon team that was sent to retrieve you."

Laméch raised his hand and told her of the village's destruction at the hands of Semyaz officers and also of the retrieval team's deadly fall and the shooting of one of the dragons.

Lyn-Golnan looked sharply at Laméch's companions as he spoke, and addressed them as soon as Laméch had finished.

"I am deeply saddened at the loss of your loved ones and your village," she said, sincerely overwhelmed with sadness. It was very un-Librarian of her. "Such a tragedy was never meant to happen."

They nodded their acceptance as Laméch suddenly realized with a pang of guilt that he had never truly acknowledged their loss. He nodded to his companions to add his regret to hers.

He turned back to Lyn-Golnan, feeling defensive.

"I spoke to no one in the city," Laméch lied. There was no way Ruallz was responsible. "I don't know how anyone could have known we were coming."

Lyn-Golnan shook her head.

"I don't know," she said. "However, after the events surrounding

Aenoch at his 'execution', and since there was no news of you or any accomplices, we thought you might be hiding in the forests and wanted to try and locate you—or anyone else who might have news for us."

She smiled.

"I hoped you might return to this pool where we first met," she said, pointing to the hot spring behind him. "Well, actually, our first meeting *outside* of the city."

She smiled.

"I asked some friends..."she paused and raised her hand in some sort of signal. Immediately a small group of forest people emerged from the trees behind her.

"I asked them," she continued, "to watch for you here and in the surrounding areas."

She turned and nodded to her 'friends'.

"I received word that you had been spotted last night, and they followed you to *our* hot spring." She grinned in an almost suggestive manner. "I came here as quickly as I could, and—I am pleased to see you after all these years."

Lamèch nodded his appreciation.

"What is our plan now?" he asked.

"We have secured a..." before she could finish, one of Lamèch's companions moved closer and interrupted her.

"Please excuse me," he began, courteously but forcefully. "We have something of great importance to share with you that Lamèch failed to tell you."

He looked at Lamèch with deference, and continued.

"Founder Aenoch told Lamèch, in our presence, that he wished Lamèch to continue on in his stead as leader of our resistance. Aenoch asked us to be official witnesses in this matter."

Lyn-Golnan raised her eyebrows with surprise.

"This should prove interesting," she said, almost in reflex. She looked to Lamèch's other companion for confirmation.

"This is what Aenoch instructed," he said with a decisive nod.

She looked back at Lamèch.

"I will be sure to send this news on ahead," she said with an air of dispassionate formality that reminded everyone that she was still a Librarian.

"On ahead?" Laméch asked, impatient to hear more of her plan.

"Yes," she nodded. "While you were traveling here, a dolphin team was dispatched from Qênan to facilitate your return if needed."

She paused and placed a small metal tube to her lips, blowing gently. No sound emerged, but immediately a chorus of chirping could be heard from beyond the cove on the far side of the hot spring. Soon a small skiff appeared in the inlet followed by several dolphins that were nosing it to shore.

"I rode this up the bay to meet you and my friends this morning," she said. "You will take this back to Aenoch's Island. Unfortunately, we do not have a navigator to spare, but the team knows how to get there."

She pointed, indicating that Laméch was to go immediately to the skiff.

"You want me to leave now?" he asked, surprised by the suddenness of her plan.

"Yes," she said firmly. "You are needed back at the island. Great undertakings are in motion—on all sides of this conflict."

She smiled slightly.

"And now that you are our new leader, you are needed more than ever."

Laméch looked at her, at the forest people behind her, and finally at his two companions whom he had never really bothered to befriend. He felt quite alone.

"What about my guides?" he asked, "will they be coming with me?"

"No," she said, shaking her head. She turned to her friends.

"Will you allow these men to join you in your community?" she asked, already knowing the answer.

Her friends responded with smiles and waving hands.

"Please join us," they insisted, expressing extra warmth in response to the tragedy the two men had endured.

Laméch's companions turned and approached him. They embraced him in turn, ignoring his damp clothing.

"Thank you for bringing Aenoch to us," one said. The other was silent for a moment, but eventually said, "You will become a great leader one day."

Laméch wasn't sure what to make of either of these comments, so he waved his farewell and watched them join the other forest people who welcomed them excitedly.

He turned back to Lyn-Golnan.

"I will be traveling alone?" he asked, voicing his suspicions.

"Yes," she answered. "We have no idea where the island is currently located, since that information is never contained in our communications, but the team is certain to take you there. We have placed three weeks of rations on board—one week longer than your trip here. Be sure you use them sparingly, though, in the event the island has drifted much farther away. Your trip could be much longer."

Laméch nodded slowly and began to walk down to the shoreline, but was surprised when Lyn-Golnan did not join him. He had assumed she would be taking the skiff back to the city before he left.

"You are not riding back to the city?" he asked.

"No, you must leave at once," she said quickly. "Your family needs you."

She smiled to dismiss him, but at the mention of his family it seemed to Laméch that she was hiding something.

She motioned for him to leave.

"I am walking back to the city," she said quickly, and then added, "I will be safe," as if countering any objections he might have.

Laméch tensed immediately with alarm.

"Is there something you are not telling me?" he asked. "How is my family? Has my child been born?"

Laméch was suddenly filled with anxiety.

"I'm sorry," Lyn-Golnan said slowly. "I did not want you to be concerned during your trip."

"Tell me," Laméch insisted.

Lyn-Golnan sighed in defeat.

"Your wife was taken gravely ill," she began as a cold shudder shot through Laméch's stomach.

"How is she," Laméch demanded. "Is my child well?"

"I'm sorry," she said again. "I don't know anything else. I simply know that she is under care—and that you need to begin your trip as soon as possible."

Laméch nodded.

"Very well," he said. He turned to dash down to the shore, but remembered to thank her.

"I am glad to see you again," he said, "and I am truly grateful that you found me and provided this way home."

He smiled at her and then waved at the forest people behind her. Then he turned and ran down to the shore and into the water, sloshing his way to the skiff. He clambered aboard, and as he turned back to wave farewell, he saw Lyn-Golnan pull her hood back over her head and raise her whistle to her lips.

Immediately there was more chirping followed by a tug from the dolphins' harnesses.

He was on his way.

Laméch stared out over the bow of his skiff, watching as the dolphins skimmed swiftly along in a southeasterly direction. It seemed that he had traveled due west on his trip to Matusalé, but he couldn't be sure. He was certain that the dolphins knew where they were going, but he hoped the island had not moved too far away.

His mind churned with anxiety over the news of Keziah—and the lack of news regarding his child. Was Keziah well? Was he a father?

What *truly* had happened to Aenoch?

As the stars came out he lay on his back peering into the heavens. The stars were so brilliant that he thought he could discern individual sizes and colors, and the dazzling swath of stars bisecting the heavens reminded him of a sparkling stream of fiery milk.

Once again he recounted the story of the Infant King using the constellations that Kendrach had shown him, but this time he considered the hunter who was crushing the serpents head. The traditional narrative always mentioned that the serpent was attacking the hunter's heel—but none seemed to consider whether or not the hunter actually survived. It was always about the glory of the hunter crushing evil, but he had never heard anyone—not even Aenoch—consider the fact that even a dying serpent can still kill a man with its poisonous bite.

What if one had to die to destroy evil?

The thought came unbidden to his mind. If the lesson of the legend was one of overcoming evil—or as Aenoch liked to compare, of overcoming the Semyaz—did this mean that all efforts to combat evil were doomed? Or did it mean that there was a secret plan behind the scenes where death was only a feint—a ploy that would reveal a greater success for those who came after.

Was there a master plan—one that he could never get more than a glimpse of?

A churning in his stomach brought him back to his anxieties about Keziah and his coming child. There was no way he could get to them quickly enough, and his frantic impatience—while being forced to wait during this long, solitary voyage—was enough to drive him insane.

He found himself sleeping during the day under the expandable awning so that he could lie awake and stare into the stars at night. At times he would imagine that he was the only person on the planet. Perhaps the rest of humanity had disappeared. Was this what it had been like to be a First One?

He imagined all of those on Aenoch's Island coming to welcome him when he finally returned. Would they expect him to fully take on Aenoch's role of leader and advisor? Would they follow him even though he was bound to have very different ideas from his grandfather?

Would they accept him at all? Would they test his beliefs to determine if they were acceptable?

What *were* his beliefs?

His usual staid confidence was slowly being eroded; replaced by a desperate sense of inadequacy and even helplessness. Unknown demands of family, leadership, and responsibility loomed as he neared the island, and in desperation he looked angrily into the heavens demanding help and explanations—yet feeling foolish as he did so. Cycles of rage, tears, screaming, and fear swept over him, and he loudly expressed all of them as men only do when they are totally alone. More than once, to his shame, he found himself hoping he would not survive the journey so as to escape the inevitable, but his desire to see Keziah and their child forced such wishes from his mind.

He became used to the rhythm of the dolphins as they regularly signaled their rest periods when they would come alongside requesting attention, and although he welcomed their company, sometimes it served as a harsh reminder just how alone he was—drifting in total solitude in a world filled with nothing but water.

At some point during the eighteenth night he noticed the dolphins had begun traveling almost due south. His return journey was already four days longer than his trip to Matusalé had been, and if the team was only now making a course correction, he hated to consider how much farther he had to go.

He had been eating very sparingly, and figured he had enough food for five or six more days—after which he would have to resort to gorging on the stale water in an effort to trick his stomach into feeling full.

On the twenty-second day—the day after the three-week mark—he began to panic, wondering if this dolphin team was lost or somehow being misled. Could they have missed their signal? Would he simply coast behind them until he starved to death?

Certainly *this* could not be anyone's master plan.

ELUCIDATION: SOLITUDE

His sleepless nights turned into sleepless days, and he lost count of how many times the sun and stars rose and passed over him. He was unaware of the dolphins' request for attention when they rested, ignoring them and everything else around him.

Dazed and faint he lay prone on his lone skiff as it skimmed along the surface of the water toward his indefinite destiny.

CHAPTER 25
SURRENDER

"Aenoch's second and final disappearance created a powerful but short-lived backlash against the Semyaz, who discovered the unexpected surge of resolve that a martyr can bring to a movement. Powerful, in that large numbers of people throughout the cities who had never seriously considered Aenoch's warnings before, now began to heed them and work towards spreading his message and admonitions. Short-lived, because soon after, arrests and eventually executions of those who spoke out against the Semyaz became commonplace.

If a cultural icon and Founder like Aenoch could be removed for sedition, what hope did the average citizen have?"

—Amoela the Librarian,
The First Two Thousand Years, Vol. II

G aw stared silently at Keziah's still form resting on a cot in the island's infirmary—a large thatched roof with curtained walls and two open doorways. She knew that she was witnessing something that few people had ever seen—a person struck down by sickness.

Throughout the commotion of the past several weeks Gaw had overheard a great deal as attendants rushed around her, expressing dismay at Keziah's situation and also some complaints that this facility was meant to handle wounds and injuries, not unusual illnesses.

Only a few minutes earlier, Gaw had finally been allowed in to see Keziah for the first time in four days. Keziah's beautiful dark skin was now pale and ashen and Gaw searched intently for any sign of consciousness. The only proof that Keziah still lived was the very slight rise and fall of her breasts under the thin sheet that covered her. Also, noticeably absent from four days earlier, was the swollen abdomen where a child had once resided.

Gaw had become increasingly fond of this strong yet caring woman, and she continually allowed herself to draw favorable comparisons between Keziah and her old counselor Rin-Kendril.

A weak groan emerged from Keziah's mouth and Gaw quickly looked back to her face just in time to see her eyelids slowly pry themselves open.

"Keziah!" Gaw said breathlessly, peering directly into Keziah's newly opened eyes and watching as they struggled to focus.

Keziah smiled weakly.

"Little Gaw," she whispered before closing her eyes again.

Gaw noticed an attendant walk past the enclosure and called out.

"She opened her eyes and spoke!" she shouted, causing the young man to stop and enter the room. He hurried to the cot, accepting Gaw's proffered hand that pulled him firmly to Keziah's side.

"That *is* good news," the attendant said, after looking into Keziah's face. He turned and smiled at Gaw.

"She will be fine," he said. "She must rest until her blood supply has been renewed."

At the sound of his voice, Keziah's eyes suddenly snapped open, and Gaw was startled to see a look of fear and panic in them.

"My baby!" Keziah gasped, her unused vocal cords rasping together. "What has happened to my baby?"

The attendant opened his mouth to speak, but as he was searching for words, a female attendant rushed into the room.

"Laméch has arrived!" she said with great excitement. "He is on his way here."

She looked down suddenly, realizing she was interrupting, but Keziah's eyes were closed again, although her face was still contorted with the remains of her anguished question.

"On his way here?" the first attendant asked, apparently relieved at avoiding Keziah's question.

"Yes," she said. "He is very malnourished and dehydrated, but he will be fine. He is long overdue, but you know how those dolphin trips can be."

The attendant looked down at Gaw as if seeing her for the first time.

"You must be especially excited about seeing the man that rescued you," she said, stooping down slightly.

Without waiting for an answer, she rose and grabbed the other attendant's hand.

"Let's go," she said, pulling on him. "Laméch will be staying a few rooms from here. We have to be prepared."

Gaw watched as the two attendants rushed from the room and looked back at Keziah who was now sleeping peacefully, her face relaxed again.

Not really, she thought as she mentally responded to the departing lady's comment.

Gaw also wanted to know what had become of Keziah's baby.

Laméch regained consciousness briefly as his skiff was suspended from the struts and winch that were lifting him in to the island. He felt the sun's heat beating down on him and was vaguely aware of loud cheering sounds before returning to his stupor.

ELUCIDATION: SURRENDER

He awoke much later on a small cot with dozens of people standing around him in a room that he recognized as part of the infirmary. People often returned from trips hungry and exhausted since it was never possible to accurately predict the length of such voyages, and these rooms were where they were often nursed back to health.

Gasps of excitement and a smattering of applause accompanied the opening of his eyes, and he recognized Mendos, Aenoch's security and communications officer, standing in front of the group of people.

His onlookers surged towards him, but Mendos held them back, eventually waving them out of the room.

He approached Laméch with an unexpected scowl, speaking before Laméch could form any words about Keziah.

"I understand that you are our new leader," Mendos said, foregoing any pleasantries or any expression of welcome or relief.

Laméch was dazed and weak, and was unsure of how to respond.

"I see that you heard," he said eventually, his mind unable to focus. His voice cracked from disuse.

"Yes," said Mendos. "The news arrived long before you did."

His strong square face peered down into Laméch's.

"Aenoch was a very dear friend of mine," he said earnestly, "and a fellow soldier. He will be greatly missed."

Laméch was surprised to see moisture forming in the security officer's eyes. He was also becoming increasingly unsure of himself and his current status here. He desperately wanted to interrupt and inquire about his wife and child, but felt very constrained by the current conversation.

Mendos stood erect and sniffed.

"We will be honoring his instructions," he said with an exhale that almost sounded like resignation.

"All that was Aenoch's is now yours."

Mendos reached over and grasped Laméch's arm and smiled slightly, his eyes suddenly and unexpectedly warm.

"That includes my friendship and loyalty," he said as all signs of reservation immediately vanished.

Laméch relaxed and hurriedly voiced his most pressing concern.

"Keziah," he stated with a slight cough. "Is she all right?"

Mendos smiled broadly, his grip on Laméch's forearm increasing.

"She is well," he said enthusiastically. "She is weak but recovering."

His grip on Laméch became almost painful as he continued, preventing Laméch from asking his next question.

"And you are a father!" he proclaimed. "You have a baby boy!"

Waves of joy and relief flooded over Laméch as he allowed years of concern—and weeks of anxiety—to wash away. Keziah must be overjoyed.

"The child was born weak," Mendos continued, "but he is being cared for by midwives until your wife recovers."

"When can I see Keziah?" Laméch asked, pulling away slightly from Mendos' grip.

"We need to get some water and broth into you first," Medos said. "When you can walk, you can see her. She is in an enclosure near this one."

Laméch shook his head.

"Can't you at least let me lie in the same room as her?" he asked, slightly irritated.

"Soon," Mendos responded, his smile fading. "She is healing."

He shook his head.

"We had to remove your son surgically." His voice softened. "We still have no idea what manner of illness threatened her—or where it originated—but it was very difficult to save both lives."

His smile returned.

"Thankfully, we now have all three of you here, safe and soon-to-be healthy."

He released his hand completely.

"And you are now alert enough for liquids."

As if on cue, several attendants entered carrying a flask of water and cups of various warm liquids.

ELUCIDATION: SURRENDER

Laméch smiled as he allowed himself to be propped up. He thrust all concerns from his mind as the liquids entered his system and permitted himself a few moments of ecstatic anticipatory joy as he contemplated his imminent reunion with Keziah.

Gaw arrived early in the morning to visit Keziah, and was pleased to find her friend awake and alert.

Keziah smiled warmly at her.

"Good morning, little Gaw," she said, lifting her head from her cot. "I am very glad to see you."

Gaw smiled back and placed her hand on Keziah's arm.

"I heard them say that your baby was going to be fine," she said warmly, thinking of Keziah's cry from the previous day.

"Yes," Keziah's smile broadened. "I was informed earlier this morning." Her eyes closed with joy. "I have a son."

She turned abruptly to Gaw and when she reopened her eyes they were overflowing with happiness and anticipation.

"And I was also told that Laméch has returned! Isn't that wonderful?"

Gaw smiled and nodded, masking a brief moment of jealousy. She had started to enjoy her time with Keziah and was not looking forward to sharing it with anyone else. Both Laméch and the new baby would interfere with her newfound friendship. Disgusted with herself, she quickly suppressed such thoughts, and somehow found it within herself to focus on Keziah's joy and accept it as her own.

She reached across Keziah's body and gave her a careful hug.

"I am very happy for you," she said sincerely.

Keziah rested her head back on the cot and closed her eyes, exhausted from her brief bout of excitement.

"Yes, the Creator has blessed me greatly today."

A thought occurred to Gaw.

"I'm glad your creator has worked things out for you," she said, "but if he is as powerful as you claim, could he not have kept you from the pain and sickness? I mean, I'm glad he provides solutions—but wouldn't it be better if he prevented the problems in the first place?"

Keziah's head turned on the cot to face Gaw, her eyes intense and almost angry.

"Never blame the Creator for our adversities," she said sternly. "The First Ones brought those upon us."

Her eyes softened.

"Instead we must always be thankful when He *does* provide solutions and comfort." She smiled as if remembering she was addressing a child.

"Remember, any situation can be a blessing when it turns our thoughts towards Him."

Gaw's response was interrupted by a commotion at the doorway.

There, standing pale and thin, was Laméch, his dimpled chin somehow more pronounced from his loss of weight. He looked weak, but he pushed quickly into the room, his unkempt hair flapping about his unshaven face.

"Keziah!" he called out just as her head was rising to greet him.

As he moved past Gaw, she was suddenly shocked and somewhat dismayed when the words, *He's cute,* passed unbidden through her mind. She shook her head to clear it, but admitted that Laméch *did* have a nice chin.

Laméch bent over Keziah.

"I have missed you terribly," he said, shaking his head. "I heard you were ill, but I had no way to return home any faster."

She reached her arms up to encircle his neck.

"I was worried sick," she said. "I knew when you left, but I had no way of knowing how long your trip would be—or if you would have enough food."

Gaw watched, intrigued. She had never seen anything resembling a family before—and again she chose to accept their joy as her own. She stared as both adults began to cry.

They kissed briefly, and then more passionately, until Gaw

wondered if they would run out of air. When they released, Laméch cradled Keziah's head in his hands as Keziah stared lovingly into his eyes.

She turned suddenly, looked at Gaw, and held out her hand.

"Come here," she said quietly.

Gaw accepted her hand, and Keziah pulled her in and immediately included her in their hug.

"Gaw has become a wonderful companion for me these past weeks," she said with great appreciation. Laméch turned to smile his thanks at her, and Gaw suddenly wondered if *he* could get jealous. However, she reasoned that adults probably overcame such childishness as they matured.

Gaw basked in the happiness that filled the room, enjoying a peace and togetherness that she had never before experienced in her life. She could not imagine feeling better than this.

Another commotion at the doorway produced an attendant carrying a tiny baby.

"Here is your son," the attendant said as she smiled.

She brought the baby to Laméch and Keziah, and Gaw instantly saw Laméch's dimpled chin at the bottom of its tiny round face.

Now that is cute, she thought as an uncontrollable desire to hold the child came over her. She realized she had never seen a baby before. Her entire life in the Haermon complex had been classes, training, teachers, and classmates. No parents, no babies, no family. She experienced a brief flush of anger as she considered the life that had been stolen from her.

The attendant placed the child in the arms of Laméch, who awkwardly cradled its head in his right hand before placing the baby carefully between Keziah's breasts.

Keziah grasped the baby's head with her left hand and broke into more tears. She stroked its head vigorously but tenderly, her fingers maintaining contact with Laméch's right hand.

She reached for Gaw with her right hand, grasping the girls fingers and bringing them to the baby. Gaw carefully touched the baby's tiny eyebrow with her finger, amazed at the softness of the skin. She traced the tiny dimple, but she was startled when she ran her finger across his lips because they immediately puckered up and tried to suck on it.

Gaw resonated with the powerful ecstatic emotions that filled the enclosure, and was surprised to find that she was crying uncontrollably in sympathy with it. Her senses were overpowered by the peace and relief that surrounded them and her whole body shook as she surrendered to it.

Eventually the three dried their tears and Keziah was the first to speak.

"What shall we name him?" she asked, her voice shaking.

Laméch shook his head to blink away his tears and thought for a moment.

"I had considered many names during my trip," he said eventually, "but somehow, for this moment, I feel we have arrived at a place of rest and peace, so I believe we should name him accordingly."

Keziah smiled and nodded.

"Quickly, before the moment changes," she grinned.

Gaw was unable to take her eyes from the beautiful infant, as the powerful emotions surrounding this experience were being permanently etched into her mind.

Laméch drew himself up for his formal announcement.

"His name shall be called Noach."

He had created a life!

Laméch was still reeling from his time with his newborn son as he and Mendos walked slowly towards Aenoch's home and study— the large one-story house of leaves and branches where he had been escorted during his first visit to this island.

He had created a life!

Objectively he knew he couldn't take full credit, but he kept hearing Aenoch's words to him from their walk to the village.

It is an incredible honor—and responsibility, the ability to create life.

He recalled that Aenoch had often said that the source of much of the Semyaz hatred for humanity was mankind's ability *to* procreate. It was part of Aenoch's insistence that the original Semyaz were not a race, but rather a "host" of rebellious energy beings fallen to Earth to subvert the Creator's plan of restoration.

He shook his head with a smile.

He had created a life!

Nothing could dampen his joy right now, as he followed Mendos into the room where he had first met Aenoch so many years ago. He felt a sense of proud, almost smug satisfaction that was almost euphoric. Nothing would ever be the same.

This second room had not changed much over the years, but Laméch could see that his grandfather's collection of clay tablets had grown.

"This is all yours," Mendos said as he gestured around the room. "It is from here that you will take on your duties as leader of our resistance."

Laméch choked slightly at the word "duties". He could sense that his moment of peace and rest would soon be coming to an end.

"Through here," Mendos motioned towards the far doorway. "You have never passed beyond this room," he said, "but all that Aenoch had—his work, his equipment, and his writings—are now yours."

He smiled and lowered his head slightly as Laméch passed him and headed through the doorway.

Laméch was stunned by what he saw. This room was much larger that he could have expected from the house's exterior, and it looked more like a wide hall or personal auditorium. It was filled with small tables, each covered with a wide variety of objects that were illuminated by thin beams of light emitted from beveled openings in the ceiling.

He stared in amazement as he slowly identified the nearest items to the best of his ability. There were numerous flasks of diverse colored liquids, large metallic and ceramic constructs of unknown purpose, and, on every remaining free space, stacks of clay tablets filled with writing.

At the far end of the room, something was emitting a tiny shower of white sparks, and Laméch suddenly realized that Mendos' right hand was on his shoulder.

"This is where Aenoch worked when he was home," Mendos said. "His sleeping quarters are at the far end of this lab. Of course, his main lab, nearer the Island's main generator station, is much larger."

Laméch nodded as he sensed feelings of helplessness and panic begin to envelope him. He knew where the main lab was, but had never entered it. He had never been interested, since he had always been off on practical adventures with Keziah.

Was he expected to learn and understand everything is this room? If he was expected to take Aenoch's place, would those in the resistance assume that, because Aenoch had named him successor, he had the same knowledge and understanding of his grandfather? He stared with great anxiety at the stacks of tablets. Only Aenoch and Keziah knew of his inability to read.

Mendos' hand lifted and then patted him on the shoulder.

"I'll leave you to your work," he said. "I'm sure you have a great deal to catch up on."

Mendos gave a smile of both excitement and admiration. It was the same smile that Aenoch usually received, and Laméch's panic grew.

Mendos turned to leave.

"I recommend you begin by reading Aenoch's latest reports," he said. "You need to learn what he was working on and be ready for our next assembly."

With that, Mendos left—and Laméch's defenses against the attack of helplessness and panic completely collapsed.

How could he possibly be expected to continue what Aenoch had been doing?

He walked slowly and aimlessly among the different tables, each stack of tablets creating new terror within him.

He new nothing of technology—and nothing of leadership.

Leadership.

ELUCIDATION: SURRENDER

That word suddenly generated great fear—an emotion with which he had very little experience, and very little ability to cope. He suddenly felt weak as he thought of others in the resistance depending on him.

A month earlier he had been brazenly bluffing his way through the streets of Matusalé, feigning wealth and power. Now, he was cowering inside of an unknown lab, adrift on an unknown island—and he realized that soon, feigning would no longer be an option.

He had never been burdened by caring for others. Now he would be expected to care for hundreds or more—while concerning himself with the possible fate of humanity.

His spinning mind turned towards his new son, who would also expect guidance, protection, and care.

Laméch sat suddenly in the middle of the floor, the various streams of light pointing at the tables surrounding him. He realized, honestly, that he could not even handle the demand of caring for one son and a wife. How could he possibly accept—and endure—the responsibilities over many.

Aenoch's words appeared in his mind, frightening him even further:

What you have not experienced is something that challenges those reactions. A situation that goes beyond your pre-determined responses and forces you to cry out for help from beyond yourself.

This certainly seems to qualify, Laméch thought as he tried to assess his situation. He knew he would gladly welcome any help, but could not imagine where such help might come from.

Aenoch had presented one other idea, and at the time it had seemed to Laméch to be nothing but an evasion—a cop out. But he was now open to anything.

As he sat overwhelmed in his terrified stupor, that one idea gave him a hope for escape. All of his fears would disappear, but his ability to embrace this strange idea seemed all but impossible.

What if I cared only for obedience and not results?

THE DAYS OF LAMÉCH

* * *

Four days later, when Keziah was well enough to return to their hut, Laméch and his wife carefully reunited, with the joy of knowing that a new chapter was looming in their life.

They had much to be thankful for. Keziah's scars were healing, Laméch's weight was returning, and their beautiful baby Noach was now nestled between them in their bed.

Still, Laméch's thoughts would not let him rest. This new and unprecedented feeling of insufficiency haunted him—and it seemed like his only recourse was to take Aenoch's advice.

But first, a confession was in order.

"Keziah," he said softly.

She turned to him, her lovely jade eyes fixing on his with such overpowering love that it distracted him for a moment. Suddenly he felt very unworthy. Her eyebrows rose slightly as she smiled, forcing him to continue.

"Now that I have been placed in charge…" he began, and then decided to try another approach.

"You are aware that I never really got along with my grandfather," he said.

Keziah nodded politely, still saying nothing.

"I mean," he continued awkwardly, "I've always respected him, but, well, his manner and—zeal—often conflicted with my—ways—and…" he paused.

Keziah placed her index finger on his nose and pressed lightly.

"Now you are their leader," she said helpfully, "but you know you are very different from him?"

"Well, that's true," Laméch nodded, "but what I really need to tell you is…"

He paused again and Keziah lifted her finger, waiting.

"I have never believed as he did," he finished.

It came out more sudden than he had intended, and he followed it quickly with an attempted explanation.

"I mean, his views on the Creator and faith in a larger purpose

~ 348 ~

were things I never fully accepted," he paused again, taking a breath.

"And in all of our years of marriage, I've never been fully honest with you about this. I'm sure this is no great surprise to you, but I feel this has been an unspoken understanding that now needs to be spoken."

Laméch stopped and waited for her reaction, suddenly aware that he had no idea what to expect from his wife. Shock? Anger? Sadness? Somehow he began to feel ashamed for expecting the worst.

Amazingly, Keziah opened her mouth with one of the sweetest smiles he had ever seen, followed by a gentle laugh.

"You are right," she said, her jade eyes sparkling with apparent joy. "It is no big surprise. However, I am overjoyed that you have finally shared this with me."

"You are not upset?" Laméch asked, slightly confused.

She laughed fully this time.

"Of course not," she said.

Laméch smiled in relief. Her love for him was intact.

"But," he countered, new concerns entering his mind, "does this not make me unqualified to take over in Aenoch's role? Won't others question me?"

Before she could respond, he asked a final question.

"Shouldn't I question myself?"

Keziah placed her finger back onto his nose and smiled.

"I never thought I'd hear that kind of admission from you," she grinned. "However, all I can say is that Aenoch chose the brightest, most honest and most dedicated and resourceful man I have ever met, and if Aenoch made that choice, who am I—and who are you—to doubt it."

She finished her sentence with a firm, almost painful tap on his nose to emphasize her point.

Laméch smiled back at her before proceeding.

"Well," he said slowly, "I have another question for you that you certainly never expected to hear. It is a request for help."

Keziah sat up suddenly, her eyes wide open.

"This *is* a time of miracles," she smiled at him before grasping his face between her hands.

"What can I do for you?"

Laméch took one more breath before making his request.

"Will you teach me to read?"

PART IV
EXCHANGE

The important thing is this: to be able, at any moment,
to sacrifice what we are for what we could become.

Maharishi Mahesh

CHAPTER 26
LEGACY

"Common to all family cosmogonies was the view that things were created at a point in time, prior to which, nothing existed. They all credited a 'Creator' with this act, but few could agree on the nature of this unknown—and perhaps un-knowable—entity. Rarely did one contend that no creator existed, as this either required the emergence of existence of its own accord from nothing, or demanded that the universe had an unchanging and eternal past. Since holding either position rendered the disciplined study of origins futile and absurd, none would do so publicly and thereby demonstrate one's intellectual laziness."

—Amoela the Librarian,
Comparative Family Cosmogonies, Vol. VII

N oach sat on the ground with the thin crystalline sheet held carefully in his hands, studying the ugly small brown mounds that were attached to it. There were three of them and they looked like lumps of dirt or perhaps tightly rolled leaves that were long since dead.

He had been raised on Aenoch's Island and—except for the occasional visits to the fixed land for supplies or research—he had spent all of his twenty-three years living with the island's constantly growing community.

The island's inhabitants now numbered more than three thousand. Most of this was from the normal growth of families and children, but sadly, many of the recent newcomers were refugees from the escalated Semyaz attacks on the numerous Forest People communities.

From his earliest childhood, Noach had demonstrated a great affinity for nature, spending hours studying insects, making numerous pets of even the most unusual animals, and (as he grew older) breeding animals to observe the amazing variety of hereditary characteristics contained within each kind.

As with the rest of the inhabitants, he had been raised with the teachings of the island's founder, Aenoch, and Noach devoutly accepted these beliefs as his own. He also had become increasingly aware that this island was a sanctuary from the encroaching oppression and control that the Semyaz were spreading throughout the cities—and Noach knew that it was only their inability to discover their island's constantly changing location that had kept them safe thus far.

As he turned the crystal pane over in his hands, a shadow—and a beautiful scent—passed over him and he looked up into the lovely face of his fiancé, Gaw-Bolwuen.

Her lovely auburn hair draped down, creating a curtain that framed a mischievous smile and her glistening emerald eyes.

"Am I to be honored," she began, "that you prepare for our upcoming marriage by studying bugs?"

Noach rose hurriedly, yet careful to protect his sheet of crystal. They had grown up together, and although she was almost thirteen years his senior, they had always shared a close friendship and bond. It was only in the last few years that Noach had even considered a more romantic relationship, and as he had clumsily pursued this, he discovered that she had been patiently waiting. Her most common statement to him on the subject was, *I swore that I was going to marry you, and I've been waiting until you were old enough.* Supposedly, it was something about his eyes that she liked.

He kissed her quickly on the cheek.

"You should look at these," he said, fixing those same eyes on hers. He lifted the crystal pane up to her, and he watched with a small amount of pleasure as she wrenched her eyes from his and focused them on the sheet.

"These are chrysalises," he said simply. "I managed to coax these three caterpillars to form their cocoons onto this crystal sheet at different times."

He pointed.

"This one attached two days ago," he said, "and the second one has been here for a week."

He moved his finger as his voice became more excited.

"*This* one attached two weeks ago."

Gaw circled an arm around his chest.

"They all look the same to me," she said, knowing that there was more to come.

"We should move to the shade," he said, pulling her with him as he walked to the covering of a nearby tree.

As she pressed close to him he flipped the crystal sheet over, revealing the cocoons through the transparency—fastened against the far side of the crystal.

"You can look inside of each cocoon from this side," he said eagerly. "I managed to spread them open as they formed against the pane. I've tried several times, and I had to keep it dark, but this time they joined fully."

As Gaw peered into the first one, Noach explained.

"As you can see, this one contains what appears to be a decaying caterpillar. No different than if it was dead on the ground."

He pointed to the second one.

"This one is now a week old, and looks fully decayed, like a pool of putrid mush."

He turned to Gaw and grinned, expecting her to make a face. Instead, she simply raised her eyebrows.

He turned back and pointed to the third chrysalis.

"Somehow," he said, his voice betraying his excitement, "after one more week, it has transformed to this!"

He motioned her closer, and she peered through the crystal into the third cocoon.

Inside was the shimmering beginnings of a beautiful butterfly wing, and the strong black center of its soon-to-emerge body could be seen through its translucent covering.

Gaw stepped back in surprise.

"That *is* amazing," she said sincerely, her eyes wide with wonder. "How is it possible that a puddle of rotting decay can transform itself into a living butterfly?"

Noach smiled, pleased with her reaction. He placed the crystal pane carefully on the ground against a tree, then wrapped his arms around her waist, facing her.

"Do you want to know what is *really* amazing?"

She responded by wrapping her arms about his neck and smiling, fully expecting a romantic shift in the conversation.

"What is *really* amazing," Noach continued, "is that adult butterflies have baby *caterpillars*."

Gaw pulled away with an offended shriek, somehow managing to give him a punch in the stomach.

"No," she retorted, "what is amazing is that I waited all these years for you, and now in two days I will be marrying a strange, introverted, bug-loving man…"

Her arms returned to encircle Noach.

"Whom I love more than life itself," she finished.

Noach returned her embrace and peered into her dark emerald eyes.

"I love you, too," he said simply. "I do not know what the Creator has in store for us, but I know it will be monumental."

He kissed her and she relaxed in his arms.

"Yes," she said as the kiss released. "We have been brought together for a purpose."

Noach thought of what he knew of her early years as an

experimental subject in the Haermon Mountain complex, and was impressed—as always—at her faith in providence. It was easy for him.

They kissed again, passionately, and slowly sank to the ground. Somehow they managed to carefully avoid the crystal pane as they held each other, the ground of their floating island rising and falling beneath them.

The disc was approximately five cubits in diameter and rested on a three-legged platform made of wood in a large clearing behind Aenoch's (now Laméch's) labs. At the edge of the disc was a thin metal ring that was currently spinning around the circumference, energized by the island's small Power House.

In the center of the disc was a small hammock-chair where Laméch was seated. He had conducted trial experiments with much smaller models, but there had been no way to control the results, so now there was no choice but for him to personally test out his theories—regardless of the personal risk.

Laméch had been amazed at the worlds of history, technology, and thought which had opened up to him once he had mastered—with Keziah's tutelage—the art of reading. The accumulated knowledge and information that he had discovered in Aenoch's library was overwhelming at first, and then simply astounding. Accounts of long lost history including the first explorers, city founders, and inventors. Transcripts of trials from before the Family Wars where people were banished—or executed—for exhibiting attributes that were decreed mutations. Speculations and research into the nature of the universe and the rules that governed it. And most importantly, the tablets that Aenoch had recovered containing the account of the Creator and the failures and struggles of the First Ones—although Laméch still had never, personally, been able to accept all that Aenoch had taught.

Perhaps reading and inscribing were simply additional tools for servants, but Laméch had almost come to feel sorry for his father, who depended on Librarians who made house calls and relied on their knowledge for his research—and to publish his "writings".

Although Laméch had actually learned to read very quickly, it had taken him many years to decipher much of Aenoch's own writings on math, energy, and science. A great deal of Aenoch's knowledge had not been inscribed, since he had meant his writings for his own personal use, and what he *had* written often used special symbols and codes that made comprehension even more difficult. At the moment, however, he was trying desperately to bring to fruition one of the theories that he had found in Aenoch's writings on technology.

His grandfather had written extensively on his speculations about how Semyaz platforms moved and operated, but he had never demonstrated any viable explanations or even formulated repeatable tests.

Perhaps today Laméch would succeed where his grandfather had not.

Seated in the center, Laméch looked out at the spinning outer rim.

This rim was the heaviest part of the craft, and he had spent years casting and molding it into perfect balance. The remainder of the disc had been constructed from the lightest possible wood or cast aluminum.

The rim was propelled by magnetic energies, and each half rotation brought about a reverse in polarity that created a constant series of repulsions that flung the ring into faster and faster revolutions. The same magnetic field kept the ring away from the inner disc, allowing for frictionless movement, and only three containment clamps prevented the ring from separating from the rest of the disc.

This ring had been the easy part—and the critical solution to the issue of stabilizing a floating object such as the Semyaz platforms. The difficult part had been to harness the energies of a Power House to create a separate, powerful magnetic field which would (according to Aenoch's theories) actually repel the craft against the Earth's own magnetic field creating the illusion of levitation.

Of course, the strength of the magnetic field on the craft could not be controlled since it was at the mercy of whatever Power House was nearby—so Laméch had devised a shielding mechanism much like the cones that extinguished noble-globes.

Instead of a cone, a metal sphere fully encompassed the magnets at the center of the disk. A sliding panel that slid back into the curvature of the sphere allowed the Power House energies to enter and spin the magnets creating the field. A simple foot pedal controlled this panel so that (in theory) ascent and descent could be controlled.

There were three hurdles to be overcome: lift, stability, and maneuverability. The first of these had required the solution to the second—and his tests with much smaller objects had shown he was close to solving the first.

However, he had no idea on how to control direction, but Laméch was certain he would eventually solve this. Perhaps he could design a third generator that would oppose—to varying degrees—the natural pull to the north—or south. All of his test discs had suddenly veered and shot off in one of these directions with no apparent reason why they had chosen one over the other.

Or perhaps he would design something as simple as a sail or rudder contraption—although he had never heard of anyone observing this in any of the Semyaz platform sightings.

Laméch lifted his foot slightly, pulling the panel back on the central sphere and exposing the generators within to the powers without. He held his breath as he braced himself for the unknown.

He felt flickers of electrical energy and ionized air tug at his skin and hair, and he was reminded of his youthful encounter at the peak of the Matusalé Power House.

For a brief moment he imagined that he was rising, when it suddenly occurred to him that the platform beneath him was on the surface of an island that rose and fell with the swells of the waves underneath.

He lifted his foot some more, and was ecstatic to feel a definite lift away from the platform. A small whine began to increase from the sphere beneath his feet, and he lifted his leg to slide the sphere's panel open to the halfway position.

There was a sudden jolt upward as the disc lifted swiftly—but smoothly—away from the platform. An excited yell from Laméch sounded over the growing whine from the sphere, and the unexpected speed of his ascent caused him to slam down his foot, dropping the disc back down onto the platform with a shudder.

He grinned and lifted his foot more carefully this time, and the disc rose gradually until it hovered, fully stabilized, about twenty cubits from the ground.

Laméch's grin widened as he looked over the clearing, excited about his success, as his skin tingled with magnetic energies. He turned his head, wishing now that he had not been doing this in secret. Admiring spectators would be most welcome right now.

His thoughts turned next to the question of how to make this new craft move—in any direction. Somehow, he would have to find a way to steer and propel it if it was to have any real value.

Suddenly, the disk tipped (impossibly) to one side and began to move with ever-increasing speed over the clearing and away from his labs. Laméch pressed his foot down to close the panel, but the disk continued on its own inertia until it crashed into the trees at the edge of the clearing, ripping Laméch from his seat and snapping the central disc in two. The spinning rim tore from its clamps and continued to cut a swath of destruction along the treetops until it finally tipped and slammed into the ground, resting at an angle in the small ditch it had dug.

Laméch tumbled down the tree, branches slapping him as he finally fell in a heap in the foliage below. He stood carefully, checked to see that nothing was broken, and then broke into a huge grin.

He had done it!

He glanced back towards his labs which were, according to the island's current orientation, directly north. For some unknown reason his disc had hovered for a few moments and then suddenly gone south. Somehow, he reasoned, it picked up some form of charge that quickly flung the craft along the earth's magnetic lines.

He walked carefully back to his labs, now glad that there had been no witnesses. As he brushed the remaining leaves from his body, he saw Mendos in the distance, running from the doorway.

"Did you see that?" Laméch called out as he approached.

"Yes, I did," Mendos nodded with admiration. "But you had better be glad that Keziah did not."

Laméch nodded and grinned as they met.

"Yes," he agreed. "Keziah is always upset when I hurt myself. You know what she would say." He paused as both men knew what Laméch would say next.

"Nothing and no one has the right to hurt me but her."

They laughed together as they walked towards the doorway.

"If I can only find a way to steer and control that thing, we would be much closer to solving how the Semyaz platforms operate," Laméch said, shaking his head.

"Not really," said Mendos, his dark brows scowling slightly.

Laméch scowled back, awaiting his friend's inevitable practicality.

"At most," Mendos said, "you have shown that you can achieve some degree of levitation near a Power House or some other energy source—nothing that can explain Semyaz platform travel between cities."

Laméch nodded, his grin fading. He was suddenly aware of soreness in his shoulders and lower back from his fall. It was not a feeling he was accustomed to.

"And furthermore," Mendos continued, "to the best of our knowledge, the Semyaz do not use Power Houses or anything similar for their energy. We still have no idea how they light and power their complex—and you are one of the few people who has actually been there."

"Yes, I know," Laméch said, sounding more frustrated than he intended. He dismissed Mendos' comments with a wave of his hand and the two entered the doorway.

As they sat at the main table, Laméch gave a small groan of pain.

"Are you sure you are uninjured?" Mendos asked.

"Yes, I'm fine," Laméch said. He flashed Mendos a forced grin.

"You had better not be hurt," Mendos said, his scowl growing. "You have a marriage to officiate in two days. No one would forgive you if you were unable to fulfill that obligation."

Laméch smiled and nodded, thinking of his quiet, introspective son who had only in recent years noticed Gaw's almost obsessive interest in him.

"Actually," Mendos interrupted his thoughts, "I was looking for you to bring you some more bad news."

Laméch looked up sharply, not wanting anything to disturb his recent success.

"Yes," he said slowly. "What is it?"

"We've lost another community," Mendos said solemnly.

Laméch shook his head, a knot of dread forming quickly in his stomach.

In the many years since Aenoch's passing, Laméch and his people had continued the work of mapping and identifying all of the Forest People communities, creating a network of information and protection.

The Semyaz had always attacked the communities, initially culling them for research subjects. However, for the past twenty or thirty years, these enslaving activities had all but ceased, and instead it seemed that the Semyaz were more interested in simply wiping them out, one village at a time.

In the last several months these attacks had escalated, and news of a newly destroyed community had now increased to almost one per week.

"The same manner?" Laméch asked.

Mendos nodded.

"Yes," he said. "Supposedly a single mountain fell from the sky. No explosions or fires, but the few survivors who were far from the village when it happened say they felt the ground shake and heard the loudest rumble they had ever experienced. Several lost their eardrums. When they made it back to their homes there was nothing there but a smoking crater where the village had once been."

Laméch nodded. It was the same as the others.

Mendos took a deep breath.

"The good news…" he began.

"*Good news*?!" Laméch exploded. "How can there be any good news as these attacks keep happening." He felt quite ill and, as always, hated his position of leadership. He still felt responsible for things that he truly had no control over.

Mendos held his ground.

"Yes," he answered. "We have enough eyewitnesses who saw the 'mountains' or whatever the projectiles were, and they have been able to collaborate and confirm a common point of origin."

"Which means?"

"We now know where these attacks are coming from. Somehow these attacks are being launched from a single location."

"Where?" Laméch demanded.

Mendos produced a map that he had brought with him and rolled it out in front of Laméch.

"Here," he pointed. "Someplace to the south of the Haermon Mountains, but at the equator and far inland." He looked up at Laméch. "We think the equator would be an optimum location for reaching as far north or south as possible."

Both men thought silently for a moment.

"We need to send a team," Laméch finally announced. "We have to see what kind of mechanism can launch these attacks—and destroy it if possible."

"I agree," Mendos nodded. "I've already assembled…"

"I'm going," Laméch interrupted, "and I'll decide who goes with me."

Mendos shook his head.

"No, we need you here," he stated.

"And I need to see firsthand what is happening," Laméch insisted. "We have too many unanswered questions. Why are the

Semyaz targeting the Forest People? What form of technology are they using?"

He paused to fix his gaze on Mendos' eyes.

"More importantly, we need to discover how they know the locations of the Forest People communities. We have always assumed that we were the only ones with the knowledge of their locations—but these attacks are very precise—and somehow they know even better than we do where these villages are."

Mendos nodded his agreement, but before he could reaffirm his protest, Laméch continued.

"I'm going," he repeated.

Mendos nodded again, but it was now a nod of defeat.

"You will have to wait until after your son's marriage," he reminded Laméch.

Laméch nodded.

"Where is our island currently?" he asked.

"Right now we are north of Irad and Jaebal, but far out to sea."

Laméch nodded again.

"We'll use the next two days to prepare. As soon as the marriage is complete, I leave with my team."

"Let me know what you need," Mendos said, now fully committed to Laméch's plan. "However, we have one more question that may be more important than all of them."

"And that is?"

"Why is it so important to the Semyaz to exterminate the Forest People?"

"You are leaving me behind?"

Keziah's eyes flashed with her peculiar mixture of feigned anger and teasing resentment. She had risen up on one arm in their bed to turn and look down at Laméch—who had just announced his upcoming mission.

Laméch twisted on his side to explain.

"This is not a normal expedition to discover new Forest People communities or to exchange in trade or information. These attacks have escalated and we truly have no idea what we will find—or if we will even make it to the source of these attacks."

He reached out and held her right cheek in his hand to demonstrate his sincerity.

"My grandfather began the initial work of finding, mapping, and connecting these communities; and implicit in his outreach was the understanding that we would do everything in our power to defend them."

Laméch paused as Keziah slowly nodded.

"You know how much I hate leadership," he continued as Keziah added a slight smile to her nod, "but I can't help but feel responsible for these attacks—at least for *not* being able to defend their villages. I know it is not my fault, but I can't rest until I have discovered with my own eyes what is happening."

Keziah's nodding stopped, and she raised her eyebrow, insisting that he respond to her original question.

"This is too dangerous," he said, knowing that this would be insufficient for Keziah. He continued quickly before she could interrupt.

"As I said, we have no idea what we are facing—no idea what new technologies or horrors the Semyaz have developed."

He paused, a new thought emerging.

"We will only be gone a short while," he said, "since this trip is only to gather information. We will simply spy out the region to see what is happening."

Keziah's face broke into a sudden smile.

"So you are saying it *won't* be dangerous."

"No, I'm saying..." Laméch stuttered, "It's a different danger, something that we haven't..."

Keziah reached over and placed her hand over his mouth, silencing him.

"How many years have we been married?" she asked quietly.

Laméch thought fast and tried to answer, but her hand remained firmly over his lips.

"Yes," she continued. "Many, many decades. And it is because of you that I am alive today. It is because of you that I have had, and will continue to have, the best possible life—better than I could have ever imagined. And it is because of you that our child is marrying someone else whom you rescued."

She removed her hand, but Laméch had nothing to say.

"You will take Endrath and Klaven, correct?" she asked, shifting the topic back to his mission.

Laméch nodded, a warmth and love for Keziah spreading through him, causing him to miss her already.

"I love you, Keziah," he said, simply.

"And you know I love you," she answered. "But remember what Aenoch taught you."

Laméch scowled in confusion.

"Most women," she continued, refusing to explain, "demand that their men demonstrate their love by giving in to their demands. I, on the other hand…"

She paused to give Laméch a chance for concern.

"Aenoch taught you that striving for obedience is more important than striving for results. Of course, he was speaking of obedience to the Creator. What this means to you is that you should always do what is right, regardless of the potential consequences."

Laméch's scowl increased.

Keziah laughed suddenly as her hand reached forward again and slapped him lightly on his nose. Her finger drew down his face and eventually nestled in the dimple of his chin.

"*You* demonstrate your love for me when you do what is right. Nothing can prove your love more, or make me happier—and that is something that you have always done ever since I met you in that yellow compound at the Semyaz Complex."

Laméch's scowl instantly turned into a look of revulsion as he contemplated the conditions where he had met her.

She leaned over to kiss him.

"And I know that doing what is right is what you will continue to do."

EXCHANGE: LEGACY

* * *

The *Emergence* was just one of the many parts of a traditional marriage ceremony that Laméch understood far more, now that he had read the tablets of Aenoch. Naturally the ceremonies he had seen in Matusalé City were far more lavish than the simple one that he was about to officiate, but he was certain that none had been more beautiful.

He had seen couples emerge from trapdoors under a stage, walk from behind silk screens, step through curtains of strung sand, and even appear through an actual waterfall situated in the center of an arena. No matter how a couple chose to emerge, the idea was to make a spectacular—and if possible—miraculous entrance as the two who were to be wed suddenly appeared in front of the audience. When the Officiator called, the couple materialized—wearing the traditional garments.

Almost all of the island's inhabitants were in attendance for today's ceremony as they all were excited to witness the marriage between Laméch's son and the woman who had, so many years ago, been rescued by Laméch.

The stage was a simple platform that was covered with traditional sand, but today it resembled a beach. Thick beautiful foliage provided a backdrop, and at the front of the stage stood a small red awning supported by four wooden posts.

"Come Forth!"

Laméch's voice echoed across the audience, who stared in expectation at the stage.

For a moment nothing happened, and then, suddenly, some of the trees in the backdrop began to move.

Noach and Gaw emerged, fully covered in hooded robes made entirely of leaves and ferns! They had been standing there in plain sight the entire time, but were completely blended with the foliage until they had stepped forward at Laméch's command.

As they stepped out onto the sand, they dropped their robes, revealing the traditional marriage outfits made of sewn fig leaves. They stopped mid-stage and waited.

"Come Forth!"

Laméch's voice sounded again, and Noach stepped forward and stood under the red awning, his strong jade eyes peering out over the audience. His youthful beard was neatly trimmed, and he waited patiently for the next directive.

Although the Officiator was never supposed to be seen, the audience soon caught a glimpse of Laméch as he stood just inside the stage's left wing. The Officiator was meant to symbolize a disembodied voice coming from all directions.

"You have been brought forth from the earth and are now called to choose." Laméch's voice addressed Noach.

"Do you accept the gift of Gaw-Bolwuen from the Creator as your sole partner, confidant, and mate, and to seek and accept none other for the duration of this life?"

Noach stood silent for a moment, and then slowly lowered himself until he was kneeling in submission.

"I accept," he announced loudly—although there was a slight crack in his voice, and the sound of suppressed amusement went through the crowd.

All eyes turned to Gaw, who was wearing—in addition to the fig leaf loincloth worn by Noach—a lovely blouse and a wreath headpiece also made from fig leaves.

"Come Forth!"

Gaw strode gracefully towards the awning, and Laméch marveled—as he always did—at her eyes. Although both she and Noach had green eyes, hers were shiny and transparent, while Noach's were strong and sincere, and somehow more opaque.

She stepped under the awning and stood beside the kneeling Noach, awaiting her directive. Her eyes danced with joy and anticipation.

"You have been brought forth from his side, and are now called to choose."

Although she was not supposed to turn toward Laméch, she briefly looked in his direction before catching herself.

"Do you accept the gift of Noach from the Creator and choose to return to his side as your sole partner, confidant, and mate, and to seek and accept none other for the duration of this life?"

Gaw quickly dropped to her knees with a smile on her face.

"I accept!" she announced, almost shouting, as her smile broadened. She looked over at Noach who was also smiling, obviously flattered at her excitement.

"You have both chosen and both accepted," Laméch continued the ceremonial lines, "*but*—the Creator must still decide to accept your choice."

A huge gasp came from the crowd, who had witnessed the identical ceremony many times, but played along with enthusiasm.

"The awning above you represents your separation from the Creator, and he is unable to look upon your union until this separation is removed."

Laméch paused for dramatic effect and waited until the audience would no longer tolerate his silence.

"*Who will remove this separation?*" he called out.

Instantly the crowd yelled back, "The Seed, the Seed!" chanting it over and over again, some of them standing to their feet and stomping the ground.

"And where will the Seed come from?" Laméch shouted over the crowd.

"The woman, the woman!" the crowd shouted back, as every eye suddenly turned to look at Gaw and hundreds of fingers pointed at her.

The yells of the crowd grew louder in expectation until Gaw very slowly lifted her right hand. At the sight of her hand, the audience instantly grew silent and waited for what was to come next.

Gaw bent forward and began to dig in the sand. Eventually she found what she was looking for and extracted a large sword.

In one swift movement she stood and sliced the awning from front to back, separating it into two pieces, but as the two poles on either side of them fell, something that had been resting on the awning dropped onto the ground between them.

The crowd gasped in mock fear. The object was a large snake that was now writhing slowly on the ground. Although the crowd knew it was drugged—and de-fanged—they still screamed out warnings to the couple.

"Kill the serpent, kill the serpent!"

This was the part of the ceremonial tradition that had most confused Laméch until he had read the tablets of the First Ones.

Noach remained kneeling and motionless in response to the serpent twisting next to him, while Gaw stood up fully and lifted her right foot, poised directly over the serpent's head.

"Kill the serpent, kill the serpent!" the crowd continued to shout, and Gaw kept her foot in the air encouraging the audience. At the last possible moment she brought her foot down on the serpent's head, grinding it into the sand with her heal.

The crowd rose to its feet, cheering loudly.

Gaw dug into the sand and pulled out the serpent, now supposedly dead, and flung it over her head back into the foliage behind them.

Immediately, Noach rose next to her and kissed her cheek, symbolizing his thanks for her defeat of the serpent.

The crowd quieted, and Laméch was allowed to continue his lines.

"The Creator now sees your union and accepts it. You are now man and wife and are now free to go as one. This night, as you remove your fig leaves, remember how your union represents His union with all those who have accepted His Seed."

The crowd resumed its cheering, and Noach and Gaw now began waving and smiling at them. They stepped down from the stage and began to mingle and thank everyone for being there.

A special orchestra of chimes, timbales, and tuned conch shells played long into the evening. Laméch quietly watched all of the guests and considered his own life, the path that had led him here to this island—and wondered where his path would lead next.

That night, Laméch watched with many of the other islanders as his son and new daughter-in-law left the island with a dolphin team. The sun had just set beneath the ocean's horizon, and the pink and blue light from the rising moon scattered playfully across the waves from the east.

Noach and Gaw were heading south and would spend the next several weeks on the fixed land near Irad enjoying each other's company and living alone in the forests. For some reason, this time alone after a wedding was traditionally called 'planting a new garden'.

They turned and waved one final farewell as Laméch stood with Keziah holding her hand. His ever-strong wife was weeping quietly, and Laméch knew better than to ask her why. And although he knew it was inappropriate, Laméch's thoughts immediately turned to his upcoming mission.

Early the next morning, as Laméch prepared for his trip, Mendos approached him, holding a note.

"I have some information concerning your friend, Ruallz," he said quietly.

"What is it?" asked Laméch. He thought often of his friend, and wondered how Ruallz—and his daughter—were faring under the increased Semyaz occupation. Perhaps Ruallz was not as enthralled with them as he had once been.

"He is in prison," Mendos said simply, with care. "Lyn-Golnan risked a great deal to encode this information, and we have nothing else. We don't know if he was arrested recently, or if he has already been imprisoned for some time—perhaps even years."

Laméch winced. Lately the Semyaz had been holding suspects—and accused dissidents—indefinitely. There had also been reports of interrogation and even torture. Mendos saw Laméch's face and responded.

"I'm sorry," he said kindly. "I thought you would want to know."

Laméch nodded.

"Thank you," he said, his mind rebelling against the news.

He truly hated leadership. It always meant sacrificing personal priorities in favor of the movement's. If he had his way, he would be organizing an assault on the Matusalé prisons right now instead of investigating a possible threat to the Forest Communities.

He shook his head.

It was strange how leadership often *reduced* one's options and freedoms instead of expanding them.

He pushed the thought from his mind and replaced them with more immediate concerns.

What *would* he find south of the Haermon Mountains?

CHAPTER 27
SABOTAGE

"In the decades after Aenoch's final disappearance, there was a shift in the purpose and function for prisons in the cities. Previously, prisons had been final holding cells for repeat offenders awaiting their imminent executions. Now, in response to anti-Semyaz protests, they had greatly increased in number and were used to detain political dissidents—often for many years—for interrogation and deterrence. Soon, all protests ceased as the residents were encouraged to forget about those who were hidden away—and justifications for imprisonment continued to expand unchecked."

—Amoela the Librarian,
The First Two Thousand Years, Vol. II

Tûrell was startled and more than a little apprehensive at his latest directive. He had spent more than eight decades in the service of the Semyaz at their Haermon Mountain Complex, and during that time the translucent doors that led to the chambers where his Semyaz masters resided had always been totally forbidden.

Now he had been summoned to descend to these very same doors—and walk through them.

He turned the corner and started his approach, his heart racing. Somehow this was more exhilarating than anything he had experienced in many years—although his amazing successes in translating and implementing the language of life, and his breakthrough achievement of raising up the first generation of improved humans, had made him quite famous among his peers within the complex.

He paused in front of the doors and slowly raised his hand to push forward. As he hesitated in fear and indecision, the left door suddenly slid to the side of its own accord and Tûrell was astonished to find a man standing on the other side of the doorway, his hand raised in greeting.

"Thank you for coming," the man said. "I am called Danel."

Tûrell bowed slightly, unsure of the proper way to respond.

"All praise to the Creator," he said awkwardly.

Tûrell was surprised at Danel's simple demeanor. He had not known what he *should* expect, but it certainly was not this pale, smiling, blond man in a simple white robe.

"Come with me," Danel beckoned, and as Tûrell moved past the doorway, Danel waited briefly so they could walk side by side.

The walls and ceiling were white, unlike the granite corridors of the complex. They seemed to pulse with a subtle light of their own, as if they were constructed entirely of a single *tsohar*. In fact, he could not see the usual lighting strip along the ceiling.

They moved quickly along the bright corridor and then turned left to a stone spiral staircase that led downward.

"You have become quite a celebrity," Danel remarked as they began their descent.

Again, Tûrell was unsure of what to say, but this time he simply nodded as humbly as he could.

Danel ushered him into a small white room with the same glow as the corridor. Although the lighting was unusual, Tûrell was slightly disappointed. Somehow he had envisioned the facilities in these lowest levels would be more extravagant.

A simple table and three chairs were the only items in the room, in addition to a small wooden box that rested on the table. Tûrell waited until Danel indicated he should sit, and soon the two were facing each other across the table.

Danel lifted the lid on the wooden box and produced a black bottle that bore the insignia indicating that it contained the finest Jaerad wine from the famous vineyards between the cities of Irad and Jaebal.

Tûrell relaxed some, thinking that this must certainly be a celebration and perhaps a reward and congratulations for his decades of hard work.

Danel did not disappoint.

He lifted two crystal goblets from the box, carefully opened and poured the wine into both of them, and offered one to Tûrell.

Tûrell took a sip of the Jaerad wine as Danel spoke.

"I have summoned you here to personally reward you for your amazing successes and breakthroughs."

Tûrell was immediately overwhelmed by the praise—and simultaneously by the beauty and intensity of the wine. He had only tasted Jaerad wine once before, and it had been many years ago. The exquisite taste and sublime fragrance went to his head as quickly as the praise.

Tûrell nodded in appreciation as he set his goblet down.

"I thank you for the opportunity to serve," he said, "and also for your recognition. It means a great deal."

Danel nodded with the assurance of a man for whom everything is going according to plan. He sat silently, staring unfocused for several minutes, and Tûrell wondered for a moment if Danel had somehow fallen asleep with his eyes still open.

Suddenly Danel's eyes flickered, as if an internal light had been restored, and he turned and fixed his gaze on Tûrell. For a brief moment, it occurred to Tûrell that Danel's eyes were cold and lifeless, but he pushed that thought from his mind as his Semyaz host began to speak.

"We have been promising the people of the world an improved, superior human being for almost two hundred years now, and it is amazing and exciting that we are on the verge of fulfilling that promise."

It was a statement, and Tûrell nodded appropriately.

"However," Danel continued, "*you* know, as a breeder and student of heredity, that for a *new* population group to succeed and flourish, it must completely replace the preceding group."

He paused for Tûrell to fully appreciate his words.

"I am certain that you have considered this," Danel stated.

Tûrell nodded.

"Naturally," Tûrell replied. "However, I have not thought a great deal about it since I assumed you would inform me of your implementation procedures at the right time."

Danel smiled a thin smile.

"That time is now," he said.

Tûrell raised his eyebrows expectantly.

"You are familiar with control groups?" Danel asked rhetorically.

Tûrell nodded.

"The cities of the world have been secured as control groups," Danel said, "and as such, will serve as the staging area for our next phase."

Tûrell nodded, suddenly appreciating the great deal of work that the Semyaz must have been doing around the world while he toiled in his labs here at the complex.

"To prevent contamination and reduce the chance of inferior material re-entering the target group," Danel continued, "those population areas that are *not* in our control group are being eliminated as we speak."

Tûrell nodded again as the enormity of their project began to dawn on him. He had never fully considered all of the ramifications of their objectives.

Danel took a breath and smiled.

"The people of the world have excitedly embraced our goals without fully considering what will ultimately—and soon—be asked of them." His smile widened. "They desire an improved species, and we will deliver. However, the price—as always—is the eradication of the old."

Danel's smile grew into a relaxed grin, and Tûrell was astonished to realize that Danel actually seemed happy. It was quite incongruous accompanying the somber words.

The Semyaz grasped Tûrell's hand, and as Tûrell glanced down, he was surprised to see that Danel's arm was completely hairless.

"The final objective is this," Danel said, quivering with excitement. "Ultimately, every human on the planet must bear the mark of the Semyaz—the mark of all of our work—a mark that will indicate and prove that *we* are an integral part of humanity's future—and are fully included in its destiny!"

Tûrell listened, somewhat confused. Danel's eyes, while still cold, now flashed with fervor. Danel's final word rang out around the small white room as he paused, and eventually took a deep breath.

"What is that destiny?" Tûrell asked before he could catch himself.

Danel shook his head suddenly and refocused his eyes on Tûrell.

"That is not your concern," he said, his smile gone. "However, I have one final task for you."

"Yes?" said Tûrell, eager to please.

"Contingency," was Danel's one word answer.

Tûrell raised his eyebrows in question.

"As you know," Danel said, "when one tries to improve certain traits in breeding, often there are unforeseen weaknesses in other parts of the physiology."

"Yes," Tûrell nodded. "Improving speed may put undue strain on the heart, or increasing metabolism may damage the immune system. But I and my team have fully adjusted and compensated for all such issues."

"Yes, I'm sure you have," Danel nodded. "However, none of us can ever assume that we have not overlooked something."

Tûrell shrugged slightly in agreement—but his flicker of doubt about the superiority of the Semyaz returned.

"My task?" he asked, resignedly.

"We need a kill switch," Danel stated.

"A kill switch?" Tûrell asked. He truly had no idea what Danel was talking about. He took another sip of wine.

Danel nodded.

"In the labs we have panels that release incendiary gasses in the event of escaped pathogens or compromised containers. Technicians are trained to push them in the event of a failure or other emergency—and the resulting combustion incinerates everything and everyone in the compromised lab."

Tûrell nodded, recalling several times when work was lost as a room full of burnt corpses was removed after such an incident.

"We anticipate," Danel continued, "that the replacement phase of our project will ultimately be successful, but…" he paused to get Tûrell's full attention.

"We have no way of knowing what hidden abnormality, mutation, or unknown consequence may suddenly emerge, generations after we have succeeded."

Tûrell nodded for Danel to go on.

"If this should happen, we will have to admit our entire venture has failed."

Tûrell nodded again, now fully confused and concerned. He had never heard talk like this before.

"My task?" he asked again, cautiously.

"We need you to construct an agent—probably biological in nature—that will completely destroy our new breed. It must be capable of wiping out the entire human race." Danel's face remained placid. "This will not involve anyone else on your team. It will be your own project."

Tûrell was stunned and also slightly angered.

"That would wipe out all of my—*our*—work," he protested, startled by his own outburst. He recoiled slightly in anticipation of Danel's reaction.

But Danel simply smiled his thin smile.

"We are nothing if not patient," he said, "and we must be

prepared in the event we have to repeat all of our work again some day. Naturally we will safely preserve remnants of the original population groups safely in the complex."

He looked sternly at Tûrell.

"We simply need to know that this option is complete and available for us," he said. "Can you do this?"

Tûrell nodded.

"Absolutely," he responded, his mind already considering which direction he should take.

"And we must be able to count on you to execute this contingency, should the need arise."

"I exist to serve the Creator," Tûrell answered as adamantly as he could.

Danel's thin smile returned.

"You are so much more than a faithful servant," he said. "We knew we could rely on you."

Tûrell smiled in response.

"Naturally," Danel continued, "we don't foresee any reason to make use of this contingency, and if we ever did, it would be hundreds of years or many generations in the future."

"I understand," said Tûrell.

The meeting was over and Tûrell finished the last of his wine, savoring its exquisite taste and symbol of opulence.

On their way back to the forbidden doors, Tûrell caught a glimpse inside another room whose door was slightly ajar.

Inside he saw another pale man looking out a giant window that was separated into several panes—but each pane appeared to present vastly differing images, creating a blurry collage of colors. He didn't dare to slow his pace, so there was no time to focus or try and make any sense as he passed, but he also thought he noticed a small golden disc that seemed to float just above the white desk next to the man.

He looked away quickly as he kept pace with Danel, and soon they arrived at the translucent doors.

"You have excelled in demonstrating the amazing power of creation," Danel said as Tûrell stepped through the doorway. "However, you will soon understand the greatest power of all—the power to destroy. This is the foundation of *true* supremacy."

Tûrell nodded uncomprehendingly as the door slid shut behind him.

He turned back to the forbidden entrance and stared in silence. Once again he contemplated the enigma of the Semyaz desiring to improve humanity on the one hand, yet callously despising them and preparing for their possible eradication on the other.

Perhaps if Tûrell was successful in this new task, Danel would be pleased—and might be persuaded to enlighten him.

It looked, to Laméch, as if a giant basin had been carved into the earth—but this basin was more than three hundred cubits wide and plunged so deeply in the center that he could not see the bottom from his vantage point.

They had spotted this structure from the air and had landed their team a distance of almost two days walk to avoid being seen or captured. Laméch, Endrath, and Klaven were now resting on a small ridge overlooking their discovery. As yet, they had not seen a single person, but there was a loud hum in the air, not unlike the sounds near a Power House.

The entire basin was covered with shiny yellow stone tiles, and the edges seemed flush with the surrounding landscape—but Laméch noticed that there was a ten to fifteen cubit swath of dead brown foliage along the bowl's rim.

The angle of the bowl's sides changed gradually around its perimeter. At the side nearest them, the bowl sloped downward gradually, but this angle increased as the edge of the bowl became thicker, creating an almost vertical descent at the far side of the bowl.

A sharp drop separated the steep angle from the extremely shallow one to the left, and Laméch found his eyes repeatedly tracing the circumference of the bowl, moving from the shallow incline in front of them, around to the almost vertical slope on the far side, and then dropping to the almost level slant that slowly increased as his eyes continued their circle.

But what dominated the structure were two giant shining metal pipes that emerged from the center and rested against the edge of the basin. They were parallel rods—each about four cubits in diameter—and Laméch could see powerful stone or concrete clamps that held them together at regular intervals as they rose up the left side of the basin and extended a short distance over the rim of the bowl.

"It is a targeting system," Klaven announced quietly.

Endrath looked at him, confused for a moment, but then nodded in comprehension.

Laméch looked at both of them, completely bewildered.

"Would you mind sharing?" he chided as his two companions exchanged a small laugh at his expense.

Endrath responded.

"As you can see, the two metal pipes are currently pointing south and are rising up at about a seventeen-degree angle."

He pointed to the northern edge of the basin.

"If," he continued, "these rods were to be moved around to the right, they would rest against the side of the basin at a fifty or sixty degree angle, and," he pointed to the far side, "over there they would point upwards at almost eighty degrees."

Laméch was still confused.

"How can two metal pipes be used for targeting?" Laméch was becoming annoyed. "Tell me this," he demanded, "is *this* the device that has been destroying the Forest People communities?"

His two companions nodded slowly.

"I would say, yes," answered Klaven. "This looks like a very, *very* large version of a weapon system I once worked on many years ago. However, it was very impractical for defense and impossible to maintain."

"Magnetic propulsion?" Endrath suggested.

"Yes," answered Klaven.

"How does it work?" Laméch asked, frustrated. He was not used to being confused for long.

Before anyone could answer, they were interrupted by a deafening grinding sound, and as they watched, the two metal pipes began to move around the sides of the basin exactly as Endrath had described. The hum suddenly increased in volume to a low piercing whine, and the men were forced to cover their ears with their arms.

Eventually the pipes' movement stopped along the northern side, pointing upward at an angle of about sixty degrees, and Laméch saw Klaven mouth the word "fifty-eight" to Endrath, who nodded.

"They're aiming at their own complex!" Endrath shouted, but Laméch and Klaven could only read his lips. Laméch was still confused, since the Haermon Mountains were a flight of several days to the north, but Klaven nodded in agreement, his face filled with a mixture of dread and comprehension.

"*Watch*," he mouthed back.

A violent rumbling suddenly shook beneath them, and as the ground continued to shudder, they watched as the entire basin slowly began to turn! Soon the two metal pipes had rotated with the basin—still at their fifty-eight degree angle—but now pointing directly at them. The basin's rotation—and rumbling—stopped, but the roaring whine grew louder, causing pain in their ears. They pressed their biceps even tighter against their heads to try and block out some of the noise.

Suddenly, a blinding cloud of light and heat erupted between the two metal pipes, temporarily blinding the men, who looked away, trying to blink the painful mirage from their vision.

A thunderous explosion from far overhead sent concussive shock waves through the three men, compressing them against the ground. Waves of searing hot wind poured down upon them, shaking the surrounding tree branches violently—bending them downward. The entire hillside reverberated as the men lay face down, still covering their heads.

The roaring whine eventually dropped in pitch and intensity until the only sounds were the natural ones of the forest—which the men were unable to hear because of the incessant ringing in their ears.

As their hearing slowly returned, Laméch started to speak, but his two companions were already talking and gesticulating wildly.

"How fast was that?" Endrath asked, his eyes wide.

"I would calculate," Klaven responded, excitedly, "that based on the length of the pipes, and assuming an energy source comparable to that of a Power House, the projectile was probably traveling at nine or ten times the speed of sound by the time it left."

"That is astounding," Endrath said, nodding. "I estimate that, based on the launch angle, it will strike the ground about halfway between here and Matusalé City."

Klaven nodded.

"I would say this device would require almost one week of charging between launches."

"But what amazing control," Endrath added. "By managing the angle, direction, and power charge, this unit can be precise to within a few hundred cubits."

Laméch was becoming increasingly irritated with his companions who seemed more intent on congratulating each other for their insight and calculating abilities than on the real implications of their find.

"What did we just see?" he demanded, angrily. "Did we just witness the destruction of another Forest Community?"

His two companions sobered quickly.

"I believe so," said Klaven. Endrath nodded his agreement.

"What is this thing?" Laméch continued, "and how does it work?"

"It uses magnetic repulsion," Klaven explained, "similar to some of the experiments that you have been conducting."

He smiled slightly, obviously aware of Laméch's recent crash.

"Each metal pillar is charged with a powerful but opposing magnetic field," he continued, "and a projectile that is placed in between them completes the loop and is forced forward. What we just witnessed was the launching of such a projectile—traveling too swiftly to see, but generating great heat and wind in its passage."

"It is held in place," added Endrath, "until the charge has built, and then released much like a normal catapult. But as Klaven stated, it travels so swiftly that the range is virtually limitless."

Klaven pointed to the metal pipes.

"You will see a small groove along the inner beams," he said. "The projectile—or its casing—will have small tabs or fins which align with those grooves. Ideally, the fins never actually touch the grooves because of the incredible heat buildup that would occur, but the guides must be there nonetheless. That casing probably dropped away once the projectile was in flight."

Laméch nodded, still overwhelmed with what they had discovered.

"I understand that we are all properly amazed by this," he said, "but at the moment, there is only one question that needs to be answered."

Endrath and Klaven stared at him, waiting.

"Can we destroy it?"

Both men quelled their misplaced excitement, knowing that Laméch was right.

"There is one major weakness with such a weapon," Klaven responded. He pointed to the metal pipes that were still aimed in their direction.

"The same repulsion that propels the projectile also puts tremendous strain on the two metal pipes. Throughout the entire charging process, they are being repelled away from each other with enormous force, and only those reinforced stone braces *restrain* them and keep them parallel to each other."

Laméch nodded, the next step forming in his mind.

"Would one of your spear-guns take out those braces?" he asked, hopefully.

Klaven shrugged and looked at the pipes.

"I don't know," he said. "Of course, I would have to get much closer, but that stone must be incredibly strong to hold those pipes together."

He looked back at Laméch.

"Of course, we may only need to weaken the braces," he said. "If we can damage even one of them slightly, the next time this device is used, the strain could fracture the brace—and the two pipes would split apart destroying the entire weapon."

Laméch smiled slightly as he envisioned this outcome. Hopefully it would take months to repair—and perhaps a more heavily armored unit could return to finish the job.

He suddenly recalled his promise to Keziah that this would only be an information gathering mission—and just as quickly he dispelled the thought.

"My spear-gun is back at the cabin with the team," Klaven stated, "and I only have two spearheads, but we should be able to get them back here within three days."

Klaven nodded to Endrath, including him in his task. They both knew that Laméch would remain behind to continue surveillance—and perhaps discover what type of security surrounded the structure. There had to be a human presence somewhere—although it was probably all underground in typical Semyaz fashion.

Laméch nodded.

"Hurry back," he said decisively.

Klaven nodded.

"You stay hidden," he said. "There will certainly be people coming out to service the weapon after this launch. Those pipes will have to be polished."

Laméch nodded his agreement.

As the two men dashed off into the forest, Laméch allowed his thoughts to return to Ruallz. He was usually successful at keeping his worries from surfacing into his consciousness, but he now had nothing to do but sit and wait—and the thought of his longtime friend languishing in a cell actually tormented him.

And *that* realization also intrigued him. He had never been one to be tormented by another's plight. Naturally, he cared about the cause and about the people involved with him, but this level of care and even worry for an individual was new for him.

Somehow, he had to learn more—even if it meant abandoning this mission.

Perhaps this is what Aenoch had meant about doing what is right—regardless of the consequences?

Laméch was awakened by his companions returning through the underbrush. It was a few hours after midnight, and they had only been gone three days.

He looked up at them inquisitively from his blanket.

"We moved the team closer," Klaven explained. "We may need to leave quickly."

Laméch grinned and nodded.

"What have you discovered?" Klaven asked.

Laméch shook his head.

"Absolutely nothing," he said. "I still have not seen a single person around this structure. I moved in and searched the perimeter, but I could find no entrances—and nothing to suggest that there is even any security."

He shrugged as he got to his feet.

"There were some water jets that erupted and sprayed the metal pipes soon after you left, and the basin has rotated back to its original position, but anyone associated with controlling or maintaining it must be underground—probably beneath the center."

"They must be very confident that this place would never be discovered," said Endrath.

Laméch nodded.

"Remember," Endrath said, "to the city dwellers, the Forest People don't even exist. It is only our involvement that allowed us to compare information and determine the origin of these attacks."

Laméch looked at Klaven.

"Do you have your spear-gun?" he asked.

Klaven nodded and revealed a large shoulder bag behind his back. He lowered it to the ground.

"I have to assemble it," he said. "We can move in closer at dawn and then fire it at the nearest brace when it gets lighter."

"You don't want to attack in the dark?" Laméch asked.

Klaven shook his head.

"You didn't report any sentries," he said. "I'll be able to make my target better in the morning light. Besides, the flash of the explosion will be more visible at night."

"And the noise?" Laméch asked.

Klaven shrugged.

"It doesn't matter," he said. "Anyone beneath this structure will certainly feel the reverberation."

He smiled.

"Either way, we need to be ready to run as soon as I fire."

The three men nodded in agreement.

"Speaking of leaving," Laméch said, "I've made a slight change in plans."

Endrath and Klaven looked at him with some surprise. As much as they respected their leader, he was not one for unilateral decisions.

"When we leave this place," Laméch continued, "I need to go to Matusalé City."

Endrath responded first.

"We need to get this information to the island as quickly as possible," he said.

"I understand," said Laméch, "and we will. However, I need to see Ruallz, my friend. I'm not sure why, but it is something that I must do."

His companions looked at Laméch carefully, not sure whether to be concerned or impressed. They knew Laméch was given to impulse, but this seemed more contemplative as if it were a personal mission that Laméch had been considering for some time.

"I need you to drop me off outside of Matusalé," Laméch continued. "You will continue from there to the island with your report."

He fixed his gaze on his companions. It was an order.

Both men looked at their leader in the starlight and slowly nodded.

"And you?" Klaven asked.

"I will make my way back to the island somehow," Laméch assured them. He grinned.

"I've done it before."

By sunrise they had positioned themselves to the north where the metal pipes were once again resting. Klaven shouldered his speargun as it finished charging.

He used a chemical charger, just as he had in Gaw's rescue from the Haermon Mountain Complex, but fortunately Klaven's more recent designs were much smaller—and therefore portable. The charger used in that rescue had been the size of a small crate.

They were just outside the perimeter of dead foliage, and the sun was peering over the eastern horizon, creating dazzling reflections from the shiny tiles.

"Coils are ready," Klaven whispered over the hum of the gun. He glanced over at Laméch.

"On your signal."

Laméch looked out over the basin's structure, once again overwhelmed by its size.

He nodded.

Klaven released the catch and they watched as the spearhead slammed into the nearest stone brace supporting the rods.

Immediately a geyser of flame engulfed the brace, followed by a loud blast, but surprisingly there was very little reverberation that they could feel from the ground. There was a second incendiary flash that made the men cover their eyes, and when they looked again, the brace was covered with smoke and soot—but still remained fully intact.

Klaven prepared his second spearhead, waited for thirty seconds to recharge (which seemed like forever), and then fired.

This one struck lower, near where the brace rested on the basin floor. It produced the same detonation and wall of fire, but this time the men could feel the reverberation under their feet.

Again there was a follow-up flash—and when the smoke cleared, they were dismayed to see that, other than extensive charring, the stone brace still seemed unharmed.

Klaven shrugged.

"That's all we can do," he said with a sigh. "We can only hope that we created some stress fractures that will cause it to self-destruct the next time they use it."

Laméch nodded.

"Let's get out of here," he said.

"…and here they come," said Endrath, pointing.

A panel near the ridge where the steep incline and shallow incline met had opened, and they watched several men in Semyaz work uniforms pour out and head across the basin towards the pipes—and towards them—shouting in alarm.

Although Laméch and his men were already concealed among the trees, they began running as quickly as possible, their feet pounding against the ground.

"How far away is the team?" Laméch asked between breaths.

"About six hours away," Klaven responded. "Perhaps five if we keep this pace."

A tree branch almost whipped Laméch in the face, and he caught it to prevent it from striking Endrath. Klaven still carried his fully assembled spear-gun over his shoulder, but Laméch knew that he was fully capable of maintaining his speed even with the added burden.

They had no idea if they had been spotted or not, but they knew their best course of action was to create as much space between them and the structure they had just attacked, so they continued their frenzied charge through the forest.

The two dragons were contentedly stripping leaves from the tops of the trees when the men came bursting through the foliage. They became immediately agitated as they sensed the men's anxiety and exhaustion, but Laméch attempted to calm them as Klaven and Endrath secured the cabin. However, they were well trained, and as soon as Laméch connected the team's harnessing, the three men were ready and Laméch gave the order to fly.

"Do you think we were followed?" Laméch asked as they lurched upward.

"Probably," Klaven answered. "We certainly did not make it difficult for them."

They were all fatigued from their five-hour run, but they could not afford to relax.

"…and there they are," shouted Endrath, pointing out the aft hatch.

There were shouts of men from behind them and movement in the underbrush. The cabin was still close to the ground with the dragon team straining above them.

Laméch could not see any of this from his steersman position, but he had a vivid memory of how the team sent to retrieve his grandfather had been shot down many years ago. He pulled hard on his control cables, trying to maneuver his team into as narrow a target as possible.

"Arrows!" shouted Klaven from behind as a volley leapt from the forest towards them.

Laméch urged his team to increase their speed, but they were already rising as quickly as possible.

Several arrows slammed into the cabin with loud thumps, and one entered the aft hatch and flew through the cabin, striking the wall right next to Laméch's head.

Laméch jumped, but kept his focus.

"We'll be out of range soon!" he yelled back as a grin began to form. They were going to make it!

Klaven and Endrath watched as a second volley of arrows sped towards them—and breathed with relief as they slowed and eventually tipped down to return to earth. They laughed in congratulations and patted each other on their backs.

The cabin floor suddenly tipped to the left, throwing Laméch from his seat and tossing Klaven and Endrath against the port wall.

"What happened?" Endrath shouted.

"I don't know," Laméch shouted back as he returned to his seat. He peered up through his control port and saw the problem.

A lone arrow had somehow traveled beyond the cabin and struck his left dragon just under her wing. It was not a serious wound—just irritating—but the arrow had also severed a cable in the harness—and it was slowly twisting and would soon prevent her from flying.

They could not stay aloft for long—and if they landed they would certainly not be able to take off again for many days. The wounded dragon was valiantly trying to pull her weight—and as the right dragon tried to compensate it only made things worse as it tipped the cabin further and pulled down on her wounded wing.

Laméch could see only one solution, but he would have to act quickly.

He turned to find that Klaven had managed to drag himself to the control chair.

"What is it?" he asked.

"Throw everything out!" he demanded, pointing around the cabin. "Everything! Our left dragon is wounded and we are over-weight."

"One dragon can't carry us," Klaven protested, attempting to discern Laméch's plan.

"We can't just discard her," Endrath shouted from against the wall, also guessing.

"He won't have to—and we won't!" Laméch tried to answer both men simultaneously.

"Throw everything out," he repeated as he pushed open the hatch over his head where the control cables emerged.

As he pushed himself out of the opening, he looked back over his shoulder.

"Go back to the island with your report!" he shouted. "I'm going to Matusalé."

"What do you mean?" Klaven yelled back, now realizing he did *not* know Laméch's plan.

Laméch did not answer, but pulled himself out onto the cabin's tilting roof. He grabbed hold of the control cable leading to the wounded dragon's harness and pulled himself upright against the twisting cabin.

Bracing himself against the wind—and the downflap of the dragons' wings—he slowly began to climb upwards.

A low scream came from the wounded dragon's throat and Laméch called out to her.

"You'll be fine, girl!" he shouted. Her eye twisted in its socket to look down at Laméch who was slowly climbing towards her. She quieted as she pondered this human moving through her airspace.

Laméch looked down and saw all of their loose items being ejected from the cabin. Crates, weapons, maps, food, and supplies were raining down on the ground below.

The right dragon began to rise, now that the cabin was lighter, and as Laméch continued on to the wounded dragon's harness, he watched as the cabin drew closer, laying on its side.

He grabbed hold of her harness, just under her belly, and began to pull himself around. The arrow had nicked the right wing close to the body, and completely severed one of the harness ropes. As a result, the entire harness had twisted, bending her neck back and cramping her left wing. The loose cable was still hanging, rubbing against her wound, and in a few moments, the harness would be so constricting that she would be unable to fly.

She screamed again, this time pleading for help, and Laméch pulled himself along the harness until he was resting on her back. She continued to flap vigorously, but the harness was now preventing any real lift.

He pulled his knife from his waistband and began to cut away the harness, pulling it through the loops that wrapped across her body and under her neck.

The cabin was now slowly rising (on its side) next to him, and he saw Klaven and Endrath staring at him in astonishment through the aft portal.

"You can't ride that thing bareback!" Klaven shouted to him.

"I've done it many times!" Laméch shouted back, lying. "Cut the control cable, or you'll soon be lifting us again!"

Klaven waved and then disappeared inside the ascending cabin.

Laméch continued to hack away at the harness and eventually the entire collection of slipknots, pulley rings, and guide ropes pulled away and fell from her body. At the same time, he saw the control cables from the cabin separate and soon the entire mesh fell away, contorting into a twisted ball before dropping to the earth below.

With her neck and left wing free, she flapped both wings excitedly, almost causing Laméch to slip from her back as she swiftly ascended. She squawked her thanks, now that the harness was no longer irritating her wound.

He pulled himself up to her neck, and clamped his arms against it.

"That's a good girl," he said calmly, "you'll be fine now."

From the corner of his eye he watched the retreating cabin as it dangled precariously from the lone dragon. It was traveling laboriously under her straining wings, but Laméch was certain that they would make it to the island. It would be a very uncomfortable flight, though, with their cabin tipped on its side.

Laméch slowly managed to straddle his dragon's neck and place his arms alongside her crest. As long as he was gentle, he would be able to steer her from this position. She would now be able to fly slowly for a few hours before needing rest, and then he could take a closer look at her wound.

He gently steered her towards the east, continuing to speak comforting words to her, when he suddenly realized that he had eaten nothing all day.

Eventually the sky began to darken, and he was left alone with his thoughts. He was mostly concerned with his newly discovered obsession regarding Ruallz. Why was he so compelled to discover his friend's fate?

The Infant King appeared over the horizon, and his thoughts turned to Aenoch—and others—who had actually claimed to be able to communicate with the Creator. It had always seemed absurd that the Creator would respond to mental requests, but now he found himself asking for help—for the first time in his life—from the Creator. And, just as strangely, he found himself caring for Ruallz more than he had ever cared for anyone.

He had often felt motivated with a personal mission. He had also—much less often—felt totally helpless.

However, he had never entertained both feelings simultaneously as he did this night.

As the air cooled, he looked for an empty space near a spring to land. He would be spending the next two or three nights alone in the forests with his dragon.

CHAPTER 28
SACRIFICE

"Over the years, Replacement Day festivities in the cities grew to become an event that closed businesses, launched lavish parties, and prompted the exchanging of gifts in celebration. The entire city would come to the docks or line the walls to cheer for the transport that brought replacement Semyaz Security Troops. Joyful and thankful crowds applauded their arrival, and although there was often some sadness as relationships with departing troops were severed, the excitement and security that everyone felt was a source of great merriment.

The possibility that the Semyaz ambitions cared nothing for the protection of the city or its inhabitants never occurred to anyone."

—Amoela the Librarian,
The First Two Thousand Years, Vol. II

The lady in the red robe looked out over the new troops, amazed and almost overwhelmed at the honor that was hers.

This was the culmination of over three centuries of toil and research and she had been privileged to serve in the final decades of this great pursuit and witness the fruition of all their labors—and those who had come before them.

Standing with military precision in the embarkation arena beneath her were more than ten thousand *improved* humans—each dressed smartly in his green Semyaz uniform—and each standing almost a full cubit taller than the average man.

Each man had strong blue eyes, straight black hair that fell to just above his shoulders, strong jaws, and light olive skin. Each one was nineteen or twenty years of age and had received very specialized physical *and* philosophical training.

She suppressed the urge to weep as she experienced an emotional response that was identical to that of a proud mother.

She knew from her reports that they were twenty percent stronger, had reflexes that were twelve percent faster, and (by some unexpected fluke) had hearing acuity that was seven percent greater. There were many traits that had *not* needed improvement, and, in fact, certain qualities that were inevitably reduced—such trade-offs were the bane of any breeder—but these were not critical for their current purposes. For example, her techs had informed her that these new troops would probably experience a slightly shorter life expectancy.

It was her singular honor to address these troops before their departure. She had never once witnessed an embarkation, and she was thrilled and quite moved by this opportunity.

She stepped to her podium as twenty thousand eyes swiveled upward, eager to hear their latest instructions.

These are my children, she couldn't help but think as they waited expectantly. She felt a flush of pride and once again choked back her emotions. She took a deep breath and began.

"Each one of you has the unique privilege of being the first—in the history of the world—with a special knowledge and understanding that no human before has ever enjoyed," she began.

She waited for a favorable facial response but there was none. They had heard this all before.

"You have the special gift," she continued, "of knowing exactly what your purpose in life is."

This widened a few eyes. Usually they were praised for their physical prowess.

"You already know your duties once you are deployed," she said, "and there is no need to remind you of them. However, you *do* need to be reminded that you have been created to remake and reform all of humanity into a new and improved creation—and to follow in the character and nature of our creator by spreading your enhanced abilities and *contributing* more than any who have gone before you towards the progress of the human race!"

A few undisciplined smiles flickered briefly before quickly fading.

"*You*," she projected loudly, "are humanity's new representatives to the cosmos, and you will provide the means for establishing once and for all the destiny of all intelligence—Semyaz and human—by ensuring our rightful place in the promise of the Seed!"

She stopped briefly, wondering if she had gone too far, but the smiles were re-emerging and she allowed herself a large smile to encourage them.

"*You*," she shouted, panning her hands over the assembly, "are humanity's new namesakes, and *you* will go forth and transform the world into your image—as your creator has done before you."

She lifted her hands to invite cheers, and she was not disappointed. Loud roars rose from the men and she saw them slapping one another on their backs and clapping each other's hands.

When they had quieted down, she concluded.

"We eagerly await news of your future successes, and we are confident that the centuries of hard work, dreams, and study will soon be rewarded—and you will always know that you were instrumental in these successes and will also be greatly rewarded."

There were nods and solemn murmurings of affirmation. They had been conditioned in every possible way for their upcoming task. Their eyes gleamed with anticipation.

The lady in the red robe waved once more and stepped from the podium. She walked offstage where her faithful techs in their red tunics stood, many also wiping away tears, and she embraced them one by one.

She was proud of all of them, knowing *they* were the ones who had provided the hard work, experimentation, and creative breakthroughs that had led to today's success.

She thought back to the secret meeting she had held with the captains of the troop transports earlier that day, and was fully confident that they would follow their orders on their return trip.

She smiled as she envisioned a future world filled with the strength and beauty she had just witnessed in the new troops—and she smiled even wider as she considered the rewards that awaited her when, someday, the Creator would honor her for her decades of service.

"Are you fully aware of the reasons that you have been allowed to live?"

The Semyaz interrogator leaned forward into the face of his frail, emaciated subject.

Ruallz nodded weakly, as he had done numerous times this session. He was fatigued and would agree to *almost* anything. Anything but *that*.

He had been brought into this expanded prison facility almost twelve years ago—and had been left in total solitary for most of that time. Every few weeks—or months—they would suddenly burst in on him and demand the answer to their one and only question.

He had only assisted the Semyaz twice in his life. Once, in an effort to dissuade Laméch from his increasingly dangerous antics in their youth, he had anonymously reported the jump from the Power House when Ruallz thought his friend's stunts were getting out of hand.

The second time had been decades later when he reported the

possible prison break of Aenoch—and Laméch's planned destination. He had been under surveillance and ordered to report if Laméch ever reappeared in the city. However, he had never imagined that Matusalé would execute his own father, and after that day Ruallz swore never to assist the Semyaz again.

Even when they threatened his business and his family, he had remained resolute—always knowing that someday they would come and demand the one thing that he and only one other person in Matusalé City knew.

Twelve years ago they had come with their demands—and for twelve years he had resisted in this place. His wife, Cam-Gindrel, had been killed during the initial arrest, and his daughter had been stripped of her career and now slaved away in a textile factory making uniforms for Semyaz Security Forces. At least that is what he had been told. He knew nothing of the outside world except that which his captors chose to share, and he had no means to determine the veracity of anything he heard.

His interrogator reached out and lifted Ruallz's chin with his hand.

"Please tell me again," he asked in the kind voice that often preceded a strike to the head, "what is the one question that we have been asking you—the one question that will set you free when answered?"

Ruallz groaned and slowly croaked out the requested response.

"You want me to tell you how to locate Aenoch's Island."

"Very good."

The interrogator's grip on Ruallz's chin intensified, pressing painfully against his decaying, malnourished gums.

"And now, the answer." The interrogator pressed into a nerve just under the chin.

Ruallz yelped in pain, and then managed to force out his words over the interrogator's slowly clenching hand.

"There is *no* way that I can possibly know anything about Aenoch," he said carefully, "or even if his people *were* based on some island—that *you* say is constantly moving."

Ruallz's eyes twitched wildly for a brief moment, trying not to wince, but preparing for a physical response just in case. He had emphasized the word 'were' to try and imply that, since Aenoch was long dead, he probably no longer had any followers.

The interrogator's grip tightened until Ruallz was forced to blurt out an additional defense.

"I only know what Laméch shared with me, and I have not seen him since he rescued Aenoch!"

"You are lying!" The interrogator's voice changed abruptly as his hand pushed Ruallz's face backwards, flinging the prisoner's head against the stone wall behind him.

"We know that in your youth you vanished at the same time as Laméch, and we know that there is no record of you ever being in Jubal at that time. We know that you have collaborated with the resistance since that time—and we know that you can tell us how to locate Aenoch's Island!"

Ruallz cowered under the verbal barrage. He had heard all of this before—but there was an arrogance and glee in the interrogator's voice that suggested that something had changed.

The interrogator lowered himself to Ruallz's face.

"We now have *proof* that you are lying," he said quietly, and then paused to allow his words to sink in.

Ruallz tried desperately to not let any surprise—or fear—register in his face.

"We have discovered a third collaborator," the interrogator continued. "She is a Librarian who accompanied you by the name of Lyn-Golnan. Don't pretend you have never heard of her—she has told us everything."

Ruallz tried to suppress his look of despair—and failed.

"It is quite sad that you have chosen to spend these final twelve years in this place instead of sharing what you knew then." The interrogator's voice was kind once again. "You would have been free to enjoy your daughter's vibrant performing career and..." he paused to lean closer. "Please forgive me—I just remembered that her career never happened."

The interrogator stood upright, a sad smile on his face.

"In addition to losing the last twelve years of your life," he said with mock sorrow, "you have now also forfeited your remaining years."

He smiled.

"You will be pleased to know that we confiscated a dolphin team that she led us to, and have just successfully located Aenoch's Island. As a result, we have no more questions for you."

His voice became exuberant.

"Since you *are* fully aware of the reasons you have been allowed to live, then you are now fully aware that there is no reason you should not die."

He smiled and bent forward once more, looking directly into Ruallz's eyes.

"You are to be set free from this place," he said smiling, his voice even kinder than before.

"…set free in time to participate in this week's executions," he concluded. The interrogator smiled, rose abruptly, and walked briskly to the cell door. He barked out a brief command, and the door opened for him to exit.

Ruallz felt more pain from this than any physical strike the interrogator could have given him. It truly had been futile, he thought. He had never honestly known what it was he was protecting, but he *had* kept his resolution to never assist the Semyaz again.

Small comfort, he thought.

He slowly realized that there was a commotion in the corridor outside of his cell—and noticed that the exiting interrogator had not closed the door behind him.

For the briefest of moments, Ruallz considered rushing to the door and attempting an escape, but before he could move, a second Semyaz officer—with a much higher rank armband than the interrogator—suddenly appeared in the doorway, his back to Ruallz.

"And if you *ever*," the second officer was shouting down the corridor, "question a direct order from a superior, you will find yourself marching with the others this coming Execution Day!"

The new officer turned and entered the room quickly, closing the door behind him.

Ruallz looked up nervously, fearing the worst. A second interrogator often came in to replace the "kind" one.

The new officer rushed over to Ruallz, looked down at him—and grinned.

It was Laméch.

Ruallz was stunned in disbelief as bewilderment washed over him. He even felt a flush of fear as he wondered what his old friend might be planning.

"How did you….?" Ruallz began, pointing to the uniform.

Laméch waved his question away.

"Never mind," he said. "Let's just say there is a chilly Semyaz officer wandering around on the docks trying desperately to prove his identity."

He reached his hands out to embrace Ruallz's frail shoulders—and lifted him from his seat.

"We have to get you out of here," Laméch said.

"Where are we going?" Ruallz asked.

Laméch shrugged.

"I have no idea," he said. "We'll figure that out once we're outside."

Ruallz groaned—but for the first time in many months it was not from physical pain.

Laméch tried to steer him towards the door, but Ruallz resisted.

"What are you doing here?" he asked.

"I came to get you," Laméch replied, pulling at his friend.

"But why?" Ruallz asked. It was not like Laméch to risk his life for an old friend—even if they had been co-conspirators in their youth. "They'll kill you if you get caught!"

Laméch grinned again.

"They might," he agreed.

Ruallz shook his head and allowed Laméch to lead him towards the door, but just as Laméch was getting ready to call out for the guard, Ruallz stopped again.

"What has happened?" he asked.

Laméch looked at his friend.

"What do you mean?"

"Well, to be honest, this is not like you," Ruallz answered with a cough. "I just don't see you risking your life to rescue an insignificant person like me—not without a good reason."

Laméch shook his head.

"I don't have time to explain it now," he said. "All I can tell you is that I have now accepted and believe everything that Aenoch taught about the character and nature of the one true Creator—and somehow this has created within me an amazing care—and even love—for you. A love that I can *not* disobey."

Laméch's gaze locked on to Ruallz's startled, disbelieving eyes. This was the last thing that Ruallz had ever expected to hear from Laméch.

"When did you suddenly come to this conclusion?" he finally asked, his brow still furrowed in confusion.

"About four days ago, flying on the back of a dragon," Laméch answered.

He turned to the door, and then looked back at Ruallz.

"Do you know where your wife is?" he asked.

Ruallz shook his head painfully. The silent message was clear.

"I'm sorry," Laméch said sincerely. "What about your daughter? Do you know where she is? I forget her name."

A look of deep pain combined with irritation flashed through Ruallz's eyes.

"You never *asked* her name," he said, accusingly, before his eyes softened.

"I'm sorry," Ruallz said. "Her name is Lyn-Trienan, and I have been told that she works in a textile factory near the pleasure district."

Laméch winced. The term "pleasure district" was a euphemism for that inevitable area that existed in every city where no laws—or law enforcement—existed. Somehow, such areas always evolved, and amazingly there were always plenty of people who actually *chose* to live in them.

"We go to get her next," Laméch promised confidently.

He watched as Ruallz's eyes began to tear up and his head shook sadly.

"Aenoch once told me to always do what is right," Laméch said, "regardless of what the consequences may seem at the moment." He smiled in such a warm, non-Laméch-like way that Ruallz was forced to avert his eyes.

"That is what I am doing right now," Laméch finished with a grin.

He turned to the barred window at the top of the door and yelled.

"Guard! I'm ready to leave!"

There was a grinding of stone and brass gears and the door slowly opened.

Laméch steered Ruallz in front of him and they left the cell, Laméch gripping his prisoner painfully at the back of his neck.

"Do you have clearance to remove this prisoner?" one of the two corridor guards asked timidly, obviously the recipient of Laméch's earlier outburst.

Laméch moved quickly towards the guard, while at the same time wrapping Ruallz's neck in a headlock and dragging him along.

He sure is putting on a good show, Ruallz thought, choking in the embrace.

Laméch glared pure evil at the guard.

"And what rank do you suggest I need to *have* clearance?" he asked quietly.

Both guards winced and nodded quickly as they looked at Laméch's rank armband. The one who had spoken recoiled slightly.

"Your rank will do fine, sir," he said carefully.

"I thought so," Laméch snapped as he pushed past the wilted guards.

He powered down the corridor confidently until he heard Ruallz choking in his right ear. He released his hold and they began to walk together—more slowly.

"Sorry," Laméch said.

Ruallz nodded dizzily.

"I'm glad you care for me," he rasped, "but I hope you don't have to kill me to prove it."

Laméch smiled again in that strange warm manner, and they moved to a staircase that led to the ground level.

At the landing they were met by a large Semyaz officer—whose rank armband was significantly superior to that of Laméch's.

"Where are you taking this prisoner?" he demanded.

"I was told to transfer him to his new quarters," Laméch answered confidently.

"Not this one," the officer responded. "I have a personal interest in this prisoner. Besides, he is scheduled to die this coming Execution Day."

"Yes, I know," said Laméch, nodding. "That is why he is being moved."

The officer reached out and took Ruallz from Laméch's grasp.

"Not today," he said firmly. "Where did you get your orders from?"

Laméch looked confused and apologetic.

"I'm afraid it was only a junior clerk, sir," he said. "I didn't catch his name."

The officer nodded.

"Get back to your station," he ordered. He grabbed Ruallz roughly by the arm. "I'll take this one back to where he belongs."

Laméch nodded contritely. There were more security troops coming down the corridor, and there was no way he would succeed in any confrontation.

He turned away without glancing at Ruallz and walked slowly down the corridor, passing through more troops who stared curiously at him and at the scene behind him.

As he turned the corner towards the street exit, he heard a man shout out behind him.

"That looks like the guy Landrath described!"

"The man who stole his uniform?" another asked loudly.

Laméch began running for the exit as more voices began to shout behind him. He heard feet running after him as he approached the security guards stationed at the exit.

"Lock this place down!" he shouted to the guards, hoping they would misinterpret the noise behind him. "Nobody leaves this facility!"

Laméch dashed past the guards, who noted his rank armband and saluted their compliance. They immediately prepared to challenge and prevent anyone from pursuing him.

Once on the street Laméch ran west towards the center of the city, pushing past people who quickly—and fearfully jumped out of his way.

He turned left into a small alley where he removed and discarded his Semyaz uniform, and then retraced his steps and headed down the opposite alley, dressed only in his island leather breechcloth. There would be no way to explain this if he was discovered now, and he looked desperately for a place to hide.

He pressed into a small entrance at the back of a garment business that sold incense, crystals, beads and other meditation paraphernalia made popular by devotees of the Semyaz teachings. He hunkered down in the darkness of the establishment's storage area and finally exhaled in relief.

He was angry and disgusted. He had been *certain* that he was *supposed* to rescue Ruallz—and he still felt more obsessed than ever with this mission.

Why had things gone so horribly wrong? Had he misunderstood? Had he been imagining things or was his mind deceiving him?

Was he going mad?

All confidence left him as his thoughts screamed out in despair.

This entire trip had been a colossal waste. He had accomplished nothing and learned nothing on this fool's mission. And although the compulsion to help Ruallz still remained, it only compounded his pain.

As his churning thoughts began to calm, a quiet realization entered his mind.

He *had* learned one thing.

He had learned that Ruallz was scheduled for the immersion tanks on the upcoming Execution Day.

Laméch could not fathom why Ruallz was so important—more important than even his family, his people on Aenoch's Island, and even himself—but he could not bring himself to believe otherwise.

He began to doubt his sanity again as this obsession overwhelmed him. He slumped down in the darkness of the inventory room and finally surrendered to his fatigue. Slowly, a new realization came over him and he shook his head, pondering, and gradually a thin smile spread across his face.

He now *truly* knew what he had to do.

His smile turned to a grin.

Mendos re-read the reports that he had just decoded and wondered what they meant.

Nine large troop transports had launched from the Semyaz Complex, according to an agent stationed on one of the floating islands near the Haermon Mountains. Confirming reports indicated that the fleet had split, with three transports heading north and the other six heading south.

Such transports came and left frequently, but never more than two or three at a time. And these transports, reportedly, were larger than most. He had heard nothing about the Semyaz building larger ships.

What was happening? Was this a prelude to an invasion, instead of the usual troop replacements?

He shook his head, suddenly overwhelmed and sickened with worry. He had served Aenoch—and the Creator—his entire life, yet somehow there never seemed to be any progress. They had hoped to someday organize the Forest Communities in their resistance, but simply protecting them had required all of their resources, and this, too, now seemed futile as their villages were systematically being wiped out.

And he still had heard nothing from Laméch and his team—and they should have returned by now.

What had they discovered? And would they bring back any information that could be used?

What if they never returned at all?

Mendos was not a man who surrendered to anyone or anything—but for the first time he began to wonder if all of his—and Aenoch's—efforts had been for nothing.

What if his entire life had been for nothing?

Execution Day was regularly scheduled once a month, but occasionally special days were announced when large numbers of dissidents were discovered or high profile offenders needed to be dealt with quickly.

Ruallz was sickened as he, along with five other condemned men and one woman, walked with the procession through the streets towards the city gate. It was amazing how a culture could change so quickly, he thought. It had only been a few decades since Aenoch's execution, and at that time such an event was rare and even troubling to the residents.

Execution Day was now a time of great festivities and excitement as crowds gathered on the city wall and in the dockyards, cheering as people marched to their deaths. Somehow it soothed a perverse side of their morality as wrongdoers and dissidents received their just recompense.

He looked at the shouting throngs along the street, realizing that almost eighty percent of them had not even been born at the time of Aenoch's passing. He considered the fact that living space within the city had become very sparse, and wondered if many of the spectators were merely happy that today's execution would make more room for them.

As the Librarians led the procession to the city gate—and to the seven immersion chambers beyond—Ruallz began to weep for his daughter. She was all that he had remaining in this life. Lyn-Trienan had never known her father's whereabouts, and unless she was present and carefully read the crime banners, she would never know that he was gone. Ruallz was carefully holding his crime banner which simply stated "Collaborator" beneath his name.

The crowds were now jeering as they entered the city gate, and Ruallz could hear the noise from the spectators atop the walls on the far side of the tunnel. In the sudden shade of the archway he had difficulty seeing through his burial garb, but he continued to follow closely behind the Enforcers in their dark blue ceremonial uniforms as they headed towards the sunlight on the other side.

Suddenly there was a loud hissing sound and the tunnel began to fill with orange smoke! One of the leading Librarians turned and ran back through the confused and coughing Enforcers, pushing them to the side.

Ruallz's eyes were watering and he began to choke on the acrid chemicals that were filling the tunnel. Through his tears he saw the Librarian swiftly lift off his hooded robe—revealing a man fully wrapped in burial clothing!

The Librarian grabbed the crime banner from Ruallz's hands and draped his empty robe over Ruallz's body.

"Your daughter is waiting for you behind the cargo staging area by dock twelve," the Librarian hissed as he pushed Ruallz through the confusion towards the docks.

Ruallz recognized Laméch's voice.

"What are you doing?" he choked as Laméch pushed him through the fog past the Enforcers.

"You are not ready to die," Laméch whispered loudly into Ruallz's ear as he pulled the hood firmly over his friend's head.

"*I am.*"

With that he pushed Ruallz out into the sunlight, and then dropped to the ground holding his friend's crime banner.

As those in the procession poured from the gate, gasping for air and wiping their eyes, the Enforcers finally succeeded in rounding up all of the prisoners—including the one laying on the ground holding the banner of "Collaborator".

One of the Enforcer's kicked him in the side.

"It will take more than a foolish diversion to keep you from justice," he snarled.

The "collaborator" quickly rose to his feet and meekly joined his fellow prisoners, dutifully lifting his crime banner high, as they proceeded towards the seven emersion chambers.

Laméch almost welcomed the rising water as it cooled him from his long day standing in the Immersion Chamber under the scorching sun. He no longer heard the jeering crowds or felt their recriminations as he stood with the tide now rising around his chest.

A strange sense of joy filled him—as it had all day—and he thought again of Aenoch's words concerning doing what is right without regards to the consequences. He wondered if the warrior, Kendrach, had experienced the same elation when he had shared his final words. He thought of those on Aenoch's Island and how they would fare—yet he was lovingly reminded that he had never been the one who truly protected them.

The waters now passed his neck and he tipped his head to secure his final measure of air. The glisten from the spray mixed with his tears, creating flickering sparkles of light.

And as he had done throughout the day, he wept for Keziah, now finally comprehending the amazing love she had held for him. A vision of her piercing jade eyes and lovely wild black hair formed in front of him and her words from their last night together resonated in his mind as if she were right there with him.

You demonstrate your love for me when you do what is right. Nothing can prove your love more, or make me happier.

"I love you, Keziah," he exhaled softly with his final breath as his neck twisted for the water's surface.

She smiled widely in return, expressing her joy and approval of his recent decision.

In the sky overhead, the dancing lights suddenly seemed to coalesce into shimmering orbs that reminded him of the *Un-fallen* that he had witnessed at this same place decades before. They moved towards him, but as he shook his head, the waters covered his eyes, mingling with his tears, and he closed them for the last time.

One of his favorite adages came to mind:

Death-defying activities are the only way to truly know that one was alive.

As he listened to his slowing heartbeat reverberate in the swirling waters, he suddenly knew, at this moment, how wrong he had been, and that he would soon be more alive than ever before.

He thought of his friend, Ruallz—and the strange obsession that had brought him to this place.

He *loved* his friend! The unusual thought startled Laméch as he marveled at its source.

A statement from his past entered his mind.

"Even one is still worth it all."

He had one final act to perform in this life as his consciousness faded

He grinned.

Ruallz walked up the gang-plank holding Lyn-Trienan by the hand and approached the boat captain timidly.

He was still staggered by what Laméch had done, and Ruallz could find no explanation for his action other than the truth of all that Aenoch taught. Only the true Creator could transform a man in that manner—and Ruallz now fully believed. No *person*—on his own—could ever care for someone in that way.

He had found his daughter where Laméch had said, and the two of them had wandered, hiding in the shipyards for days, trying to find illicit passage from the city. They were both overjoyed at their reunion, and he was pleased to see that, in spite of her impoverished appearance, she had become a beautiful woman!

He had also found twenty gold coins sewn in the hem of the robe that Laméch had placed on him!

This life was totally new for him, but they had actually found better meals in the garbage bins around the docks than he had received in prison.

The captain eyed the two walking up his gang-plank suspiciously: a frail man in a dirty torn robe and a younger olive-skinned woman who was filthy with ratty blond hair.

"We need passage," Ruallz stated carefully, presenting four gold coins.

The captain was a large bearded man who looked as if he had never smiled.

"Not without permits, you won't," he snarled. "Or perhaps more of those," he said pointing to the coins.

"I can work," Ruallz offered.

Somehow the captain managed to laugh without smiling.

"Not likely," he snorted, looking at Ruallz's weak frame.

He turned to look at Lyn-Trienan—and this time he *did* smile, but in a way that made Ruallz's stomach lurch.

"She, on the other hand," the captain sneered, "could *definitely* be put to work. Just need to clean her up a bit."

The captain looked back to Ruallz and pointed to his coins.

"Certainly you must have more than those," he said. "I will take you, but since you can do no work, I must make it worth my while."

Ruallz lowered his head in defeat and reached down to the hem of his robe. He lifted it and opened the pocket seam, collecting the remaining coins in his hand.

He offered them to the captain who snatched them quickly and placed them in a purse inside of his belt.

Without any warning, he pulled out a knife and swiftly drove it deep into Ruallz's throat as Lyn-Trienan screamed.

The captain retrieved his knife, grabbed her quickly, and pulled her into the ship's bridge as he kicked the gurgling Ruallz over-board, sending him to splash, dead, in the waters below.

Limp and stunned, Lyn-Trienan stared open-mouthed and terri-fied at the captain.

"Yes," he said, a broad smile forming, "we will definitely have work for you."

CHAPTER 29
PURGING

"The term 'Replacement War' was, in actuality, a euphemism created by the victors in an attempt to glorify and exaggerate the enormity of the successful fruition of centuries of planning, and also from the desire to feel victorious.

In reality, the term 'war' can hardly be used to describe such a one-sided conflict that barely covered two days."

—Amoela the Librarian,
The First Two Thousand Years, Vol. II

The roaring whine of accumulating energies grew louder as the gleaming twin pillars of the magnetic weapon swiveled northward.

The weapon had been charging for almost a week, powered by a column of thermal differential turbines that bored almost a thousand cubits deep into the earth. All personnel had been removed from the surface, but the engineers and technicians had determined that the attempted sabotage had done nothing but cosmetic damage, and that nothing should interfere with today's projectile launch, only seconds away.

The rotating basin ground to a stop—and the roaring whine crescendoed to deafening levels. The projectile was released from its restraints, and from deep in the center of the basin it was flung out by the opposing magnetic fields and accelerated to many times the speed of sound.

As it soared up into the afternoon sky far faster than the eye could see, small micro-fractures in the final support clamp—from Klaven's explosive spearheads—began to spread from the stress of the launch. The concussion wave from the departing projectile slammed into the landscape and shook the basin with shock tremors that further damaged the pillars' support.

In less than a second, the micro-fractures spread and the entire support clamp exploded into a cloud of stone shards and metal reinforcement fragments.

Without this clamp, the opposing magnetic fields forced the tips of the twin metal columns to separate slightly, creating extreme stress on the remaining support clamps. Within ten seconds, the remaining clamps cracked and blew apart one by one, and by the time the final clamp was destroyed, the giant metal pillars were flying away from each other, spinning horizontally end-over-end through the air with a violent flapping sound until they careened into the earth, carving out a large swath of felled trees and destroyed vegetation on either side of the basin.

The tremors continued within the basin, shaking the entire weapon until it began to break apart and collapse in upon itself. Soon the entire bowl was reduced to a pile of stone rubble, and any entrances to the control bunkers and targeting rooms below—and the people within them—were permanently sealed.

The weapon could never be used again, but the projectile continued on its way, undeterred by the destruction behind it.

In a few hours it would create more destruction of its own.

* * *

Noach and Gaw were enjoying the third day of their return trip from "planting their new garden" and they rested in the stern of their skiff, enjoying each other's embrace and listening to the dolphins chirp happily in front of them.

Immediately after leaving the fixed land, they had watched as a lone dragon—dangling a cabin that was tipped precariously on its side—flew overhead. They had waved to it, and although it was close enough for Klaven and Endrath to wave back through a side portal that should have been on the roof, it was not close enough to exchange words.

They had seen no sign of Laméch.

There was no way to know any details concerning Laméch's mission—or of what they may have discovered—and the two new-lyweds had soon exhausted all speculation, leaving only concerns and worries.

The deep emerald eyes of Gaw peered lovingly into the strong jade eyes that Noach had inherited from his mother.

"Your father will be fine," she said, reading his thoughts.

Noach smiled at her, wondering how he could possibly be so blessed.

"I know," he nodded, his beard no longer trim and neat. "I can sense it." He paused and closed his eyes briefly.

"Wherever he is."

Gaw nodded.

"And we'll see our mother soon," she smiled.

A cacophony of dolphin whistles and chirps erupted from in front, and they braced for the sudden slowing that accompanied the team's rest period.

But the skiff continued to move at full speed.

"We had better see what they are fussing about," Noach said, standing.

He turned back to assist Gaw to her feet, and as she looked over his shoulders, her eyes widened.

"Look," she exclaimed. "We're home!"

Noach turned and saw Aenoch's Island looming in the distance.

"That must be why the dolphins are so noisy," Gaw smiled, pointing to the island. "They are excited to be home, too!"

Noach shook his head.

"No," he said, listening to the team's boisterous calls, which were getting louder. "They sound more agitated, as if they're afraid—or warning us about something."

The skiff began to shudder and lose speed as the dolphins' movements became as chaotic as their chatter. Their vessel tipped forward into the team's frothy wake, forcing Noach and Gaw to hold tightly to the railing.

A loud, low whistle sounded above their heads, and as Noach looked up to see what it was, Gaw grabbed his arm.

"Noach!" she shouted, pointing. "What is that?"

Noach turned to follow her outstretched hand, which was pointing towards the island.

A huge geyser of water was rising from the center of the island, and since they were still several hours away, the column had to be several hundred cubits high and dozens of cubits in diameter. They watched as the entire island convulsed, its skyline rippling like a flag in the breeze.

Giant waves emerged from the island's edge and spread swiftly towards them, carrying a deafening roar that flipped their skiff onto its back, throwing Noach and Gaw into the heaving waters.

Coughing and sputtering, they forced their way to the surface and clambered atop their capsized skiff and pressed their hands over their ears. The panicked dolphins swam back to the skiff where Noach desperately tried to shout words of comfort, but it was impossible to be heard over the din of the violent winds that were now buffeting them.

They turned their eyes back to the island where they watched as the unthinkable happened.

Their home was twisting and breaking apart, and as the waters from the geyser fell and pulverized the ground, the island began to slowly rotate.

The edges of the island flipped up slightly and they could see the thick latticework underside. It began to turn more quickly, and they watched in horror as the middle of the island began to submerge.

Entire sections of the island broke free, but none could escape the giant vortex that was forming beneath it, and soon the entire island—and every living thing on it—was sucked beneath the waves. Not even the strongest swimmer could fight against this maelstrom, and although everything that could float would eventually return to the surface, nothing would be returned alive.

Gaw was crying hysterically, watching the destruction of the only true family she had ever known. Noach held her, numb from shock, and wondered what it could all mean.

The waves from the destroyed island began to subside, and as the winds quieted, the frantic cries of the dolphins were now audible.

But Noach and Gaw did not hear them. They rocked silently, holding each other as their capsized skiff bobbed beneath them.

Where their home, families, and friends had been only a few minutes earlier, there was now only a swirling remnant of leaves and small branches that had snapped free of the sinking landscape.

They remained silent, save for the stifled sobbing of Gaw, until the sky began to darken, and they were soon forced to hold each other for warmth. They waited, with no expectations and no thoughts, as they stared out at the endless sea that spread out in all directions. The dolphins were now quiet, but confused, waiting for instruction and encouragement, but like their human masters, none was forthcoming.

Eventually the stars emerged, reflecting in the waters that were calm again, as if nothing had ever occurred.

For the first time since the Semyaz Security Forces were initially installed, *this* Replacement Day was going to take place simultaneously in all the cities of the world.

There was a global sense of excitement, and the festivities of the preceding evening had included lavish feasts, fireworks, and drunken revelry as the residents celebrated the many decades of safety and security that the Semyaz had provided.

It was the same in every city. Throngs of people lined the city walls and filled the dockyards, hoping to catch the first glimpse of the arriving transport. Scantily clad young women with lavish makeup pushed to the front, hoping to be among the first to catch the eye of a newly arriving officer, and pounding martial music elevated the adrenaline of everyone present and echoed throughout the ports.

A large contingent of troops was lined up at the far side of the receiving dock, away from the view of the crowd. They were surrounded by tearful women who were saying their farewells to the men who would be returning on the same transport vessel. Many of the women were pregnant, but each city had established support decrees for all children fathered by Semyaz troops, and they would want for nothing once they were born.

Cheers and screams erupted at the first glimpse of the arriving transport. Waving banners and clanging bells filled the docks as the approaching ship slowly grew larger.

A muted hush fell over the crowd as the vessel neared its dock and they all realized that this was no ordinary troop transport. This ship was much larger, and it dwarfed the dock as it pulled into its slip. Also, there was no one to be seen on the top decks. Usually, the troops would be standing there, waving back at the crowds.

The response was the same in every city, and the cheering resumed again when the transport was tied down and the gangplank lowered.

When the troops began to emerge from the side of the transport and march down to the deck, the noise from the crowds was deafening. But as they began to study the new arrivals, the noise, again, abated as the people began to notice that the troops *themselves* were no ordinary troops!

A surge of exhilaration and elation swept through the crowds as they all slowly realized that these new troops represented the new improved humanity that the Semyaz had been promising since their first encounters!

These troops were taller, larger, and obviously stronger than average men. Lean muscles bulged from beneath their green and black uniforms as they moved confidently and gracefully into the waiting dockyards.

The cheers resumed, escalating into screams of excitement and even swoons and fainting spells. Many of the women were already imagining the beautiful babies these new Semyaz could provide for them, and, although the surrounding men knew that these troops meant increased competition, they still applauded in appreciation and happiness that the Semyaz had finally delivered on their greatest promise.

The musicians increased their volume, and soon there were twelve hundred new troops standing at attention in front of the charged masses—three times the size of a normal contingent.

Several women tried to break through the barriers to reach them, but local Enforcers kept the line secure, even though many managed to throw flowers and other gifts over their heads to the troops in formation.

At a signal, the music stopped, so that the troops could begin their march through the gates and into the city to their barracks.

But the new troops did *not* begin to march.

Instead, each new Semyaz pulled a sword from a hidden scabbard fastened to his left leg, and raised it high above his head.

For the third time that day, the crowds hushed, but this time it was replaced with a collective gasp of bewilderment. No one had ever seen a Semyaz officer brandishing a sword. In fact, the only swords that anyone had ever witnessed were the small daggers carried by Lawgivers.

As the arrivals stood silently with their swords brandished in the air, the crowd slowly began to feel more comfortable with the sight, assuming that this was a new ceremony—or a symbol of strength designed to assure the residents of their continued security.

Behind the transport, the last of the returning troops had already entered the vessel, and as the crowds in front continued to ponder the silent, armed officers standing motionless before them, the mooring cables were released, and the vessel began to pull back from the slip—without taking on any cargo or supplies.

At some invisible cue, the newly arrived Semyaz troops suddenly broke ranks and moved swiftly into the crowds, their swords waving.

Screams erupted as the people recoiled. Many turned to run from the advancing troops, tripping and falling over each other, and even the most aggressive and seductive young women—those who were determined to have a Semyaz man in their bed by nightfall—pulled away with confusion and fear in their eyes.

The scene was the same in every city. Most of the new Semyaz troops grabbed and restrained the women and began to systematically assault them, while the rest mercilessly killed anyone—man or woman—who tried to intervene.

As the people fled the docks and ran from the walls, trampling each other, the troops followed through the gate and entered the city, spreading a swath of rape and murder, encountering nothing but the most futile of opposition. All screams, cries, and pleas for mercy were ignored as the troops changed roles as needed. By nightfall, thousands of women in each city had been assaulted—or killed. Any woman who was pregnant was systematically slaughtered—including those who were discovered on the far dock weeping for their departing lovers.

The only surviving men were those who had cowered in fear or who had been beaten into submission. Steps would be taken to insure that none would ever procreate again.

The assaults continued for three days throughout the cities.

And from every city, the cries of children—who were untouched—echoed across the port waters, accompanied by the sobs of pain and anguish from women who were not only suffering from their attacks, but from many who had lost their husbands and sons.

And from every city, the lights of the Power Houses illuminated streets filled with bodies—and dwelling places that were now empty and ready to be filled with the new, improved offspring of the Semyaz.

* * *

Each transport captain was single-minded as he contemplated his next course of action.

The New Order requires that the Old Order be removed.

The lady in the red robe had ingrained this concept into their minds, and each captain was proud—if not eager—to perform his final role in this centuries-old endeavor.

Now that the transports were several hours out to sea, each captain excused himself from his bridge, acquired a signal flare from the navigator's station, and carefully walked down to the lower decks.

Upon arrival at the level immediately above the cargo and ballast holds, each captain removed a wooden plate in the flooring that opened to the level below and ignited the flare. The blinding light in the small enclosed place burned into each captain's retinas.

"All praise to the Creator!"

Each captain's shout echoed through each transport as he dropped his flare into the hold beneath his feet.

The phosphorus charges that had been secretly installed in the ballast holds exploded violently, obliterating the hull and instantly igniting the ship's wooden frame as the surrounding sea water surged in from beneath.

Acrid white smoke filled every transport vessel, and within minutes, every man on every vessel was dead—even before the white-hot flames had finished engulfing each ship, which broke into pieces and collapsed into a glowing, incendiary ball that sank into the dark depths below.

PART V
EXTINCTION

The righteous perish, and no one considers that
they have been rescued from the calamity to come.

Isaiah the Prophet

CHAPTER 30
IMMINENCE

"There are some anomalies regarding the technological advances that developed in the centuries following the Replacement War. Electromagnetic transmission of information became commonplace, smaller and more efficient engines were developed for transportation, and simple, but weak, anti-gravity lifts were designed for convenience and construction.

However, in spite of these advancements, the Semyaz never shared their secrets of platform propulsion, nor did they ever knowingly divulge their proprietary process of generating energy."

—Amoela the Librarian,
The First Two Thousand Years, Vol. II

Tûrell shook his head and smiled excitedly with an immense sense of satisfaction—an almost spiritual elation that he had experienced only once before in his life.

The *first* time had been when he and his team designed and

perfected the new strain of humanity that was now repopulating the world's cities. After the short-lived Replacement War, now more than a dozen decades ago, the trauma of that violent—but necessary—step in human progress had been all but forgotten. Only a small percentage of the world's current inhabitants had witnessed that day, and most of the Old Order had all been properly sterilized.

However, there were still thousands of Old Order humans, but most had been brought as slaves to the newly opened gold mines in the foothills of the Haermon Mountains. These closely guarded colonies *were* allowed to breed, but mostly for the intention of maintaining a labor pool—and providing potential subjects for any new experimentation. There was vast and varied speculation as to what the Semyaz could possibly want with such large quantities of the precious metal.

There *were* remnants of the Old Order who had been allowed to maintain their status, mostly because their special knowledge or skills rendered them non-expendable. This included many of the Librarians, engineers, industry leaders, and those few city Founders who had not expired from old age. Most were quarantined in special Old Order zones, and severe restrictions were placed on their privileges to procreate.

Tûrell smiled wryly as he considered that he, also, was included among these few. He was thankful that the Semyaz, in their benevolence, had determined that he would be allowed to complete his natural life span.

But he was getting old. His hair was graying, his face was wrinkling, and his joints pained him as he moved. In fact, there had been times during the past few months when he doubted that he would complete the final task that the Semyaz, Danel, had given him prior to the Replacement War.

For decades Tûrell had meticulously searched through the immense research libraries and the vast repositories of chemical and bacteriological agents that had been collected during the human improvement project. He spent years experimenting with vials of fungi, canisters of chemicals, and sealed trays of compounds, trying to create the perfect humanicide.

EXTINCTION: IMMENENCE

Initially he tested on rats, small pigs, and monkeys in carefully sealed and controlled chambers, but he could never overcome the two major impediments to successfully exterminating an entire control group.

Chemical agents were too localized and could not transfer from subject to subject, and it was impossible to create the needed concentrations necessary to annihilate an entire city.

Bacteriological agents traveled swiftly between subjects, but those that were suitably effective, killed the hosts *too* quickly, and often expired before running their course, thereby leaving survivors.

Fortunately, thirteen years ago, he had received some soil samples from the rocky regions along the eastern seaboard near Enoch, where desperate farmers were frantic about the inexplicable deaths occurring in their livestock.

These samples had contained very unusual spores that quickly became the solution to his dilemma.

They were not particularly virulent, but they had the benefit of growing and multiplying *while* attacking the subject, *and* they were airborne. In his first experiments, a single infected subject would eventually cause, on average, a twelve percent fatality rate within a closed control group.

Infected subjects would exhibit fevers and vomiting within a week, and sometime during the second week, they would begin to suffer respiratory failure and organ shutdown. Subjects that died expired from total paralysis, but Tûrell was never able to determine whether this was due to muscular seizures or the shutdown of the entire autonomic nervous system.

After months of artificially selecting strains that achieved only the highest yields, he soon was generating colonies that raised this fatality rate to over sixty percent.

But this is not what Danel had requested.

Tûrell desperately hoped that he had not been pursuing the wrong avenues, but after additional months of research and searching through the libraries, he finally discovered his answer.

Plasmids!

These simple rings of protein had been extracted from other organisms, and when combined with other cells, they altered that cell's processes in drastic and unpredictable ways. For some years during the improvement project, there had been attempts to manipulate and even modify these tiny circular chains, but eventually their use had been discontinued since the results were too chaotic and unpredictable.

For Tûrell, their beauty was in the fact that they effortlessly merged with the target cell, forever changing its makeup.

After more months of experimentation—and many failures—he eventually discovered *two* plasmids, that when combined with his most potent spores, finally showed promise of fulfilling Danel's request.

Another several months of testing with human subjects (the Semyaz maintained several colonies of Old *and* New Order for just such purposes) Tûrell was ready to announce his success to Danel.

His new strain now delivered a fatality rate of one hundred percent—at least within the small control groups at his disposal—and he was ecstatic at the honor and privilege of being responsible for *two* major breakthroughs in his life!

This was the reason for his current sense of exhilaration and personal accomplishment.

He still had to develop a viable means of mass production, and also a delivery system that could be triggered when ordered, but he eagerly looked forward to his next meeting with Danel.

Although Tûrell could never anticipate the strange Semyaz's reactions, he was certain that *this* time his master would be pleased.

And if Danel was pleased, Tûrell hoped to learn the *true* motives and ambitions of the Semyaz.

"This way!" Gaw hissed frantically as she pulled her husband into a small crevice where the stone steps of the structure beside them had separated from their foundation.

As they hid themselves safely behind the limestone slab that supported the stairs, several large rats rushed past them out into the street, squealing to protest the uninvited intruders. Soon the angry slapping of running feet resounded over their heads as several rogue street youth ran up the steps and poured into the building.

"You know what they'll do to us if they discover we've left our suite," she whispered.

Noach nodded, troubled and confused. This was not the first time they had visited a city, but it *was* the first time they had struck out on their own into the streets unescorted, at night—and now lost.

"He was supposed to meet us there," Noach said with uncharacteristic impatience and anxiety. "He promised to help us find him."

Gaw shook her head in the dark.

"We could not wait there in the open," she said. "There were too many Sensors."

Noach nodded with resignation.

"And we are not exactly dressed as residents," he responded, attempting humor.

Gaw gave a small laugh. They had tried to dress plainly in the manner of the city's poorer residents, but they simply didn't have the wardrobe—or the expertise.

"I suppose wealthy tourists don't frequent this section of Matusalé regularly," she said.

Noach smiled and squeezed her arm lovingly.

They sat silently in the dank aperture for several minutes, catching their breath. There was nothing they could do until the streets cleared. Perhaps then they could try again to make their meeting—if it wasn't already too late.

"I should be home completing work on my barge," he said eventually.

Again, his wife's beautiful, but quiet laugh.

"Is that all you can think about?" she asked, sounding slightly offended. "You have hired workmen for that—and besides, your other two sons can manage everything while we are gone."

Noach shrugged and nodded in agreement. He placed his arm

around his wife, and the two hunkered down in the filthy crevice behind the staircase to wait.

Gaw looked at her husband's face, glowing slightly in the ambient street light emanating from the few suspended noble-lamps that were not broken. She knew he was thinking that they should never have come here, but he had acquiesced to her wishes—and her maternal cries—and they had risked this unsanctioned visit.

She found herself thinking about the wonderful life Noach had given her, and her mind went back to that terrible day when her life and loved ones had sunk into the depths.

With the help of their dolphin team they had finally managed to return to the fixed land where they wandered alone for several months, surviving on the land with no idea of what there future held. Eventually they met up with migrant laborers on their way to find work in the grasslands between Irad and Jaebal.

They arrived—along with refugees from the Replacement War— just as the Semyaz were quarantining the entire region as an Old Order zone, and somehow Noach and Gaw found themselves in the employ of Jaerad Wineries.

The Semyaz never interfered with the internal working of the wine industry, partly because of their determination that nothing should impede the production of this highly favored industry, but mostly because the new troops and those of the flourishing New Order wanted little to do with the "throwbacks" who worked and lived in the zones.

After many years of hard labor that earned nothing but shared quarters and meager sustenance, some of the task masters discovered Noach's knowledge and understanding of husbandry and heredity, and eventually he was promoted to work with those who formulated varieties and fermentation schedules. Within a few years, he was supervising research into cross-breeding hundreds of diverse grape species and hybrids, and soon he and Gaw were moved into a small but luxurious dwelling place, complete with servants and running water.

Several years later, Noach had developed several designer wines that demanded top price, and soon he was sharing in the profits of Jaerad Wineries. As the inventor of the new wines, he was also asked to become their spokesman, and soon he was issued something that those of the Old Order almost never received.

Travel permits.

Noach and Gaw began to travel the world from city to city as ambassadors for Jaerad Wineries. Naturally they were under constant surveillance, and there was never any opportunity to "mingle" with any of the New Order, but they found themselves addressing Founders and leaders of industry. Their status became almost that of celebrities, as the novelty of a wealthy, Old Order, innovator seemed to resonate with the masses.

Throughout all of their success, Gaw was amazed to find that Noach always maintained an attitude of humility and gratefulness to the Creator for His blessings—and from this, she always maintained an attitude of thankfulness for Noach.

During their travels, Noach became more and more dismayed—and repulsed—by perverse demands that the Semyaz religion imposed on people. Initiations now included body mutilations, hallucinogenic chemicals, and multiple-partner orgies. Everything seemed, to Noach, to be devised for the purpose of demeaning, or even embarrassing, the human creation—for no apparent reason other than the voyeuristic glee of the *true* Creator's enemies: the Semyaz and others who knowingly served the serpent found in Aenoch's tablets.

Naturally, those tablets had been committed to memory, and as Noach meditated on them through the years and during their travels, he became convinced that the Creator—the true Creator—had a great mission for him.

Gaw recalled when he had first mentioned the plans for the giant barge. Just as Aenoch had taught that a great judgment was coming, so Noach now claimed a catastrophe that would wipe all life from the planet was soon approaching, and that only those safely within his giant vessel would survive.

She had to suppress a feeling of vengeful delight at the prospect of destroying all those who had treated her so badly throughout her life. They had stolen her from her family, threatened to abuse her in vile genetic experiments, and finally, had murdered the only people and family she had ever known or loved. Part of her could not wait to see them *all* perish.

However, Noach calmly informed her that, just as the Creator freely allowed people to fail, He also would freely allow them to be saved.

He hired the finest craftsmen and architects to begin working on the barge, and Gaw was impressed that, somehow, Noach already had complete plans and procedures for the project. He claimed that the Creator had given them to him, and she could see no reason to doubt it.

This message of coming calamity—and of his under-construction barge that was available to rescue anyone who wished to avail themselves—was now included in his speeches. However, this only added to the novelty of his appearances, and soon the words "eccentric" and even "insane" were added to the long list of adjectives that the public used in their descriptions of him. It quickly became apparent that none of the New Order would ever take his message seriously, so Noach and his wife focused their attention on those in the zones.

After several years of work on the barge, Noach and Gaw had their first son, whom they named Japheth. Two years later, their second son arrived, whom they named Shem, followed several years later by their third, whom they named Ham.

All three had grown into fine young men, and because of the family's special privileges and wealth, they were able to travel and study far more than the average old zone resident. As always, there was the inevitable surveillance, and great care was taken to ensure that they were never able to develop any but the most cursory relationships with those of the New Order.

Japheth was a tall man with dark brown eyes and wavy brown hair who spent a great deal of time in the Libraries of the world. He had met a young Controller named Amoela, who came from a long Old Order line of Librarians in Irad. She no longer had to travel between cities to perform her update duties, now that such synchronizations were done via crystal communication. She was a short woman with sandy hair and light blue eyes that sparkled when she spoke, and she had actually spent many months studying with Matusalé—the only city Founder still living.

Their youngest son, Ham, was a quiet man who had little interest in travel, but had a great aptitude for science. He had light skin, deep hazel eyes, and curly black hair. He was engrossed in his own independent research, working hard to determine the power source that the Semyaz used in the mountain complex. He had recently married a tall woman by the name of Nel-Tamuk who had beautiful black skin and thick reddish-brown hair that she kept pulled back behind her neck. She was the only known person to have escaped from the gold mines, and she had sought refuge in the vineyards. Ham had hidden her without his parent's knowledge, but later announced his betrothal to her, and she had soon become a loved member of the family.

Gaw's thoughts returned to the present as she considered their middle son—who was the reason for their sudden, hurried trip to Matusalé City.

Shem had a strong round face with the same dark, ruddy complexion as his father. He was very emotional with sharp brown eyes, and had married an older woman named Lyn-Trienan whom he had met in the fields. She was a quiet migrant worker, and appeared to have endured a troubled past, but she never discussed it with anyone but her husband. The only thing that Gaw knew of her history was that she claimed a mysterious man had rescued her from a forced labor textile plant, and then reunited her with her father—after this same man had somehow helped him escape from prison. She didn't know his name, but he had claimed to be her father's friend. Her father, whose name was Ruallz, had been killed soon after by slave traders. Gaw had a special love for Lyn-Trienan, who was also a shy but gifted singer—and when coaxed, could fill the household with beautiful song.

Shem had suddenly disappeared from working on the barge and left a message that he was striking out on his own for Matusalé City, where he intended to find surviving members of Lyn's family and return with them to be rescued in his father's vessel.

Gaw's maternal instincts had panicked as she considered her son traveling without permission—or documents—and relying solely on bribes and prowess to accomplish his objective. She quickly pulled Noach from his work and the two had swiftly pursued, not knowing how they were going to find their son or what the ramifications of their unsanctioned travel might be.

Upon their arrival in Matusalé City, they had not been received warmly, and were escorted to one of the suites reserved for Old Order guests. A fellow passenger had promised to search for Shem (for a fee) and they had scheduled a time and place to meet a few days later.

On that evening they had slipped out of their suite and ventured into the dark streets, carrying nothing but a mental map and a desperate determination to discover Shem's whereabouts.

Their contact was nowhere to be seen.

They waited several minutes, nervously scanning the surrounding streets and enduring the curious and often hostile looks of passerbys who noticed how out of place the two well-dressed strangers were.

A group of rogue street-youth began to approach them, and Noach and Gaw began running in the opposite direction. The group pursued them, yelling, until some of the youth noticed Enforcers in the distance and slipped away into a side street.

Unfortunately, Noach and Gaw could not approach the Enforcers for help, since they were illegally outside of their Old Order quarters. Besides, Gaw had noticed a Sensor armband on one of the officers, which meant that he was supposedly trained to discern disloyalty and subterfuge—and authorized to respond accordingly.

They had slipped down a side alley, totally lost, only to realize that the youth were again following.

The structures in this section of the city suffered from major disrepair, and it was at the base of such a foundational crack where Gaw had spotted the gap beneath the staircase and pulled her husband to temporary safety.

The streets had quieted down, and she watched as Noach poked his head out of their hiding place.

"Is it clear?" she asked hopefully.

"It *looks* quiet," he said, giving her a slight tug on her arm. They began to emerge when Noach tensed and pushed her back.

"No, wait!" he whispered.

Gaw looked under his arm and saw a little girl approaching. She was wearing little more than a ragged covering and had beautiful dark skin and short black hair. They pulled back into the crevice, but the girl continued to walk straight towards their hiding place.

She stopped at the entrance and peered in.

She smiled.

"There you are," she said in the cheerful voice of someone no older than nine.

"Who are you?" Noach asked.

She smiled and tipped her head slightly.

"A flaming sword," was her reply.

Noach turned back and looked at Gaw, who raised her eyebrows in surrender to whatever Noach decided.

"You must come with me," the little girl ordered calmly, with a sense of urgency and authority beyond her years. She turned and began to walk away.

Noach shrugged and pulled Gaw from the opening. Soon they were following the little girl through the streets, and Noach was intrigued at how the few pedestrians they encountered seemed to stare and then pull away from them.

The light from the Power House informed them that they were heading towards the docks. At one intersection Gaw glanced back over her left shoulder and gasped.

"What is it?" Noach asked.

"It is Myl-Jondrel," she said, her eyes wide. "My sister when I was a girl back in the complex."

Noach turned quickly to see, noting the shudder that went through her voice as she mentioned the Semyaz stronghold.

Mounted high on the wall of a structure behind them was a large noble-screen with the image of a lovely woman smiling out over the city. It was situated to greet travelers as they entered the city, but neither Noach nor Gaw had noticed it before.

A noble screen was a large tapestry with miniature noble-globes arranged in rows. Each globe had a rotating outer shell with filters that allowed each globe to glow red, green or blue—or remain black when fully covered. Behind the globes was a fine mesh of wiring that controlled these shells, and allowed the artist to depict almost any image imaginable. An advanced operator could even perform simple animations.

Myl-Jondrel's image was almost forty cubits high, and she was welcoming visitors. A message banner underneath claimed she was the "Mother of the New Order" for Matusalé city.

"Please hurry," the little girl called back over her shoulder, and Noach and Gaw were forced to turn away from the image and hurry to catch up.

Gaw shook her head thinking of her childhood friend, now the figurehead for unity. Presumably, she was being celebrated as the progenitor of the troops that had decimated Matusalé during the Replacement War.

The Power House was now looming directly to their right, and the little girl headed straight for a small stone storehouse near the main gate, the kind that was meant to be used for live cargo—but more often was used for smuggling.

Loud laughter and flickering lights could be seen through cracks around the stone doorframe, and the little girl walked up to the door, pushed it in, and motioned for Noach and Gaw to enter.

They stepped into a small room and winced at the uneven light from torches mounted awkwardly into the walls. They were surprised, since fire was never used for lighting in the city, but the biggest surprise was the collection of people standing around the room.

They were the same youth who had tried to accost them earlier.

Ragged clothing, unkempt hair, and savage grins turned to look at the new arrivals.

Noach and Gaw spun around to escape, and Noach looked around for the little girl to express his anger at being betrayed—but she was nowhere to be found.

"Where are you going?" a loud voice carried over the noise in the room.

Gaw recognized the voice immediately.

"Shem!" she shouted and turned back.

Their son was pushing through the group as he waved to his mother. Noach turned in time to be included with his wife in Shem's huge embrace.

Before the Replacement War, Shem would have been considered tall. Now, he was simply stout, surrounded by New Order youths who were mostly a half a cubit taller than him.

"What is happening here?" Noach asked anxiously once they had extracted themselves from Shem's hug.

"Your contact *did* find me," Shem answered, "but he was too nervous to meet you in that part of the city once he realized where it was."

He grinned.

"I offered to pay him even more than you did, and I sent some of my friends, here, to meet you." He swept his arms around the room to indicate the youth they had run from earlier.

"They returned here after you evaded them," he said, sighing. "They couldn't risk tangling with the Enforcers."

He smiled again.

"I'm so glad that somehow you found your way here."

Gaw smiled at her son.

"We simply followed the little girl that you sent," she said, nodding.

Shem scowled.

"What little girl?"

Noach turned back towards the door to point, but thought better of it.

"A little girl found us in the place where we were hiding and brought us here," he said.

Shem shrugged.

"I don't know anything about that," he said. He grinned suddenly. "I guess the *Un-fallen* take many forms."

He laughed loudly and shouted to the young people in the room.

"Everyone!" he yelled. "These are my parents!"

The room filled with loud greetings and foot stomping. Several chose to express the welcome by taking big swigs of an unknown beverage from their oversized mugs.

"And who *are* your friends?" Gaw asked when it had quieted down.

Shem lowered his voice.

"Malcontents, mostly," he answered. "But they enjoy upsetting the local peace and being contrary—especially for the right price." He grinned. "Someday they will grow up to be fine mercenaries."

He gestured towards the flaming torches on the wall.

"They prefer to use primitive fire for lighting."

Gaw shook her head with that special love that only a mother knows.

"Were you able to find what you came here for?" she asked quietly.

Shem's face fell, suddenly contorted with grief, and Gaw feared for a brief moment that he might start to cry. Her son had always been prone to drastic mood shifts.

"No," he sighed. "I could find nothing of Lyn-Trienan's family," he continued. "I tried to solicit some local help—but I ended up getting arrested."

Shem's eyes suddenly glistened with mischief and amusement

Both Gaw and Noach were shocked—not at the arrest, but that he was here, alive, to talk about it.

"How did you get away?" Noach asked.

Shem grinned again.

"I demanded to see the Founder," he said, bragging. "I claimed to be his great-grandson, and eventually they took me to him."

His voice softened.

"They have allowed him to live all these years, although all he does is stay inside while Librarians provide research for him. I tried to convince him to come back with me, but he refused."

Shem's face again twisted into sorrow.

"I can't imagine what he has to live for here," he said, "but I couldn't convince him otherwise."

He grinned again.

"Anyway, he put me up in a room—instead of a cell—so I broke out."

His arms waved to encompass the room again as his voice rose.

"With the help of my friends!"

As he shouted, the youth lifted their voices with him.

Shem lowered his voice again and flashed a sheepish smile.

"It's amazing what money can buy," he said conspiratorially.

Noach nodded, not entirely appreciating his son's sentiments.

"What should we do now?" he asked.

Shem shrugged.

"Well," he said, "unless you *must* return to your Old Order suite, I would suggest you eat with us."

Noach looked at Gaw and they both nodded.

"After that," Shem continued, "you can leave with me the first thing in the morning on a small ship that I have hired."

Shem's parents winced slightly.

"Our travel papers are still in the suite," Gaw said with concern.

Shem grinned.

"You won't be needing them on *this* trip!" he said, his voice lowering again.

"I think we all know that the day is coming when such things will be meaningless."

The event happened when they were still two weeks away from their arrival back at the vineyards.

Noach and Gaw were standing at the railing of the smuggler's sailboat, looking up at the stars when they saw it.

The ship carried no cargo—other than the illegal passengers—and Shem had made it more than worth the while of the captain and small crew.

"Do you notice how people never look at the stars?" Noach had been asking. "They simply don't notice them in the lights of the cities, and navigators hardly ever use them any more."

He was pointing to the planet Nibiru traversing the constellation of the Scorpion's Claw, and discussing the various meanings of judgment, when there was a bright flash—and they watched in amazement as the planet slowly dissolved into several much-smaller points of light.

They felt a sense of wonder, as if they were the only two people on Earth to have witnessed this celestial phenomenon, and they stood in silent awe as the points of light continued to multiply.

Eventually Noach spoke.

"Here ends the Age of Conscience," he said, solemnly.

"What do you mean?" his wife asked quietly.

Noach did not speak for several minutes. When he did, it was almost as if he were answering a different question.

"Aenoch was wrong," he said carefully. "His teachings compel us to do what is right, no matter the situation. He taught this, and, although I have no idea what became of my father, I'm certain *he* believed this also."

Noach suppressed a flush of anger. He knew it was impossible, but he had always had the irrational sense that his father must have revealed the location of Aenoch's Island to the Semyaz, allowing them to launch their attack. Although Laméch could never do such a thing, it was difficult to imagine an alternative explanation. Somehow, Noach had learned to forgive his father (if, in fact, he *was* guilty) if for no other reason than to keep his own sanity.

Gaw nodded, waiting for Noach to complete his thought.

"*Every* person does what he *believes* is right," Noach continued.

"*Every* action is motivated by that person's sense of right and wrong. But how can that person know if *his* sense is the *correct* sense?"

He paused, obviously ordering his words with great care.

"What is missing, is something—or someone—to inform that person of whether or not *his* sense of right and wrong is the *correct* one."

Gaw listened carefully, trying to absorb her husband's deeper meaning.

"*This* era of humanity has demonstrated that we are not capable of making that determination on our own. Humanity has used all of its moral resources, yet look at the decisions it has made—the side it has chosen."

He turned and looked deeply into Gaw's eyes.

"A new era must come," he said. "One that will rely upon the Creator informing us of His sense. *His* criteria."

He pulled Gaw close and held her tight.

"I simply can not imagine that, even if we *knew*, we could follow it faithfully."

They stared out across the expanse of space, watching the flecks of light that had once been a planet.

They had no way of knowing the kind of damage those flecks would cause if they ever reached the earth.

CHAPTER 31
CONSUMMATION

"The agonies and sorrows of losing one's world are only partially—and unsatisfactorily—allayed by the premise that a greater plan or purpose exists. Although it is a commentary on human nature that the loss of one is often more painful than the loss of thousands, it is also a vestigial reflection of the Creator's nature within us that we can agonize over the plight of an individual.

Is it this nature that we crave—and for which we were created? Perhaps it is more needed than arbitrary morality, or more necessary than law, which serves to remind us of our inadequacies, but provides no remedy or resolution.

One can only hope that this nature will be among the innumerable benefits to accompany the promised Seed, for without this hope, I can see no expectation for humanity, creation, or eternity."

—Amoela the Librarian,
Memoirs: The Voyage Between Worlds

EXTINCTION: CONSUMMATION

Tûrell hurried to his meeting with Danel, happy and pleased with his latest solutions. He had developed a large cast metal sphere that was able to contain active agents, and could be triggered with a simple coded electromagnetic pulse. A single sphere, perhaps attached to a tall building or even affixed to the side of a Power House, would be more than sufficient to annihilate an entire city when activated.

His previous meeting, four months ago, had gone extremely well, when Tûrell had presented his spore and plasmid breakthrough. Tûrell had been startled—but pleased—by Danel's overjoyed and almost ecstatic reaction to this solution. In fact, Danel's reaction had been *so* vigorous that Tûrell could not bring himself to risk his master's good mood by asking the one question that still burned within him.

Perhaps today he would get his chance.

Danel met him at the forbidden doorway with a smile so big— and almost loving—that it made Tûrell feel uncomfortable.

"I assume you have come here with the final solution?" Danel asked warmly as they walked together along the corridor.

Tûrell nodded silently and handed a stack of parchments to Danel, who glanced through them as they walked.

Eventually they entered the simple white room where all of their previous meetings had taken place.

Although Tûrell had seen nothing in this place other than his one glimpse into an open doorway on his earlier visit, he had every reason to assume that these regions beyond the forbidden doors, and in the further depths of the complex, must be cavernous. He could only imagine the research that must go on down here. Perhaps the Semyaz even kept additional colonies of people in these levels for further testing—or genetic archiving.

As they took their seats, Tûrell was disappointed that his master did not offer him any wine. He had heard of the wonderful new vintages that the Jaerad Wineries had recently developed, and was hoping that Danel would have access to some of them.

However, Danel was busy studying the papers and diagrams that

Tûrell had given him. He was mumbling and nodding to himself, and Tûrell was relieved that his master was apparently quite pleased.

"Excellent," Danel finally said before looking up from the table. He locked eyes with Tûrell.

"In fact," Danel continued, "this is absolutely perfect." He nodded. "This is the safeguard we need."

An uncontrolled smile broke out on Tûrell's face. Perhaps *this* time he would be able to raise his question.

"Assuming your test yields are correct—" Danel began, and then paused for Tûrell's confirmation.

Tûrell nodded vigorously and Danel finished his sentence.

"We will begin manufacture immediately and make plans for transport and deployment."

"I have already started those arrangements," Tûrell said quickly with a bit more pride than he had intended. "I have five spheres complete and fully loaded."

"Excellent," Danel repeated, a large smile on his face. "You have done well."

"Thank you," Tûrell bowed his head slightly. "All praise to the Creator."

Danel's smile disappeared.

"Yes, of course," he said dismissively as he rose from his chair.

Tûrell stood with him, scowling slightly at Danel's reaction, but said nothing.

"Please send word when everything is in place," Danel instructed as he began to walk towards the doorway.

Tûrell nodded as he followed.

"I will," he said, wondering how he could introduce his question. As Danel exited the doorway, Tûrell stalled behind him and took a deep breath.

"I would like to ask a question," he blurted suddenly, his voice louder than he had expected as it echoed in the corridor beyond.

Danel turned to Tûrell, a bored look on his face.

"Yes," he said without enthusiasm.

A cold chill went through Tûrell.

"I was wondering," he stammered, suddenly unable to place his words in order. "I mean, you improve humanity but dislike…"

He stopped, forcing his thoughts together. Danel continued to stare at him with eyes that were suddenly implacable.

Tûrell reformulated his prepared question and asked it just as he had rehearsed it countless times before.

"Your stated objective has always been to improve humanity in all ways, physically, mentally, and spiritually, yet in much of your statements and conversations you indicate a great dislike or even revulsion for others, and," he paused briefly for a breath, "one of the reasons that I have worked faithfully for you and your cause all of these years is the hope that someday I would be able to learn or understand the reason for this apparent inconsistency."

He paused, watching for any indication of a negative reaction from Danel, but his master's expression was unchanged.

"Can you please explain this to me?" Tûrell asked with a voice as submissive and timid as he could muster.

Danel closed his eyes slowly and left them that way for several seconds as Tûrell broke into a cold sweat. When Danel re-opened his eyes, Tûrell was shocked to see they were filled with disdain.

Danel sighed heavily.

"You are such fools," he said slowly, not focusing on Tûrell, "and it is an outrage that you should exist at all."

His eyes flashed as he peered into Tûrell's face.

"However," Danel's eyes closed again, "it *is* humanity that we are forced to utilize as our only means of salvation."

Danel opened his eyes, but the disdain had now transformed into pure revulsion.

Tûrell's mind swirled in bewilderment, trying to process Danel's last sentence.

"But the Creator," Tûrell began, "the Creator is the bringer of light and once we have achieved Transcendence…"

"*Transcendence?*" Danel interrupted with a snarl. "You are despicable. How can any creature made from the same elements as dirt and rocks know anything of *transcendence?*"

Tûrell was completely taken aback by his master's venom. He was also very aware that he was no closer to his question being answered, and, in fact, was more confused than ever.

"What about the five principles?" Tûrell asked, finding a force in his voice that demanded an explanation. "What about the truth in them?"

"*Truth?*" Danel exclaimed with incredulity. "This has *never* been about truth! This is about a plan, a vision that goes far beyond *anything* you could *possibly* comprehend!"

Danel was now glaring at Tûrell with total hate.

"We are forced to endure your insipid weaknesses to fulfill *our* goal."

"What is that goal?" Tûrell asked before he could catch himself, forcing himself to ignore his master's loathing. If Danel answered this, surely it would bring light to his larger question.

"*Redemption,*" Danel hissed quietly, obviously so agitated he was now speaking without pretense.

"What do you mean?" Tûrell asked cautiously. He knew he was getting close. "The Creator offers us enlightenment. Surely…"

"The Creator *offers* nothing," Danel snapped. "Not to us."

Tûrell could not believe what he had heard.

"The Creator offers everything!" he retorted loudly, reacting in defense of all he had been taught.

A hairless arm swung through the air and struck Tûrell in the chest, lifting him from the floor and flinging him bodily across the room to land painfully in a heap against the far wall. Tûrell felt as if his neck was broken, and he looked up, terrified at Danel's impossible strength—far greater than any man should have.

"There is only one *Creator*," Danel yelled, spitting as he said the word, "and *he* is the enemy!"

Danel's voice echoed out in the corridor while Tûrell watched in disbelief, cowering in agony against the wall.

"We conjured up a sham creator to meet your pathetic frail needs for worship, but only the true Creator—the one taught by Aenoch— is responsible for forming the entire universe from nothing."

Danel turned to bend over the trembling Tûrell.

"The universe that was supposed to be *ours*!"

Tûrell watched as Danel stood above him, shaking in rage. He thought back to the objectives of his life's work—and of the emerging possibility that his work had been built on a lie. The idea that this Semyaz was confirming the perverse teachings of the infamous Aenoch was inconceivable.

"What about the Seed?" Tûrell asked, still trembling on the floor. "What have we been doing all these years?"

Danel said nothing for a few minutes, and then slowly turned away from Tûrell.

"The Creator promised to come in human form someday and, as a result, somehow restore His creation."

Danel's voice was quieter now, speaking almost resignedly.

"This restoration would also include full redemption for any human who chose to accept it—regardless of how unfair or unjust such absolution might be."

He turned back to face Tûrell, his voice rising.

"You can see why He has become the enemy. It is nothing short of pure evil to offer this opportunity to vile, fallen creatures of mud, while denying it to those who served Him faithfully—and who deserve so much more."

Tûrell could not get his brain to encompass all that was coming into his mind—although it *was* finally beginning to dawn on him that the Semyaz *might* be something other than human.

"Is this why we performed all of that biological research?" Tûrell asked timidly, still desperately hoping to come to some conclusion. "Is that why you want to wipe out all of humanity? To prevent this Seed from coming?"

Danel spun around and kicked Tûrell soundly in his side, cracking a rib and sending waves of searing pain coursing through his crumpled body.

"You creatures are pathetic," he snarled, ignoring Tûrell's groans of anguish. "You not only share the elements of dirt, but also the intelligence."

He bent over Tûrell, now shouting.

"I told you the coming seed was a *promise*! There is *nothing* that can be done about that. It will happen no matter what *anyone* does. Even if we *did* try to exterminate humanity, somehow there would still be survivors, and the Seed would *still* arrive. You can't alter what is already written!"

Danel straightened up and began to walk around, shouting to no one in particular.

"We *had* to work within this decree. We could not *stop* the Seed—but we could modify humanity with our *own* nature so that when the Seed *does* arrive, it will contain *our* input—*our* mark. It will contain genetics created by *our* hands! The Seed will then *include* us, *represent* us."

Danel raised his arms in defiance, and then whirled to face Tûrell, bending over him, his eyes gleaming.

"We will *demand* that the Seed offer *us* the same redemption that he offers humanity! Even an *unjust* Creator will have no choice but to keep his promise—and surrender to *our* will!"

Danel stood and tipped his face towards the ceiling, his body shuddering as he pummeled the air with his fists.

The Semyaz's final words were still echoing down the hallway when the first pieces of Nibiru struck.

On the far side of the world, the crewmen of a deep sea fishing trawler watched the meteoric display as hundreds of dazzling streaks from the east shot through the midnight sky.

A combination of amazement and consternation filled their thoughts as they silently exchanged anxious glances with each other. Not even the oldest mariner had ever seen a phenomenon such as this.

A rising moon provided a glowing pink and blue backdrop to the spectacle, and as they watched in wonder, they saw that something was happening to its surface.

EXTINCTION: CONSUMMATION

It was sparkling.

Several men pointed as tiny flickers of bright light flashed and leaped from the moon's surface. Soon the flashes grew larger, and as they watched, bewildered, the patches of light grew and coalesced into shimmering clouds of pink and blue light that slowly began to spread out from the orb in all directions.

At first it appeared as if the moon were breaking into pieces, but after watching for several minutes, they could see this was not the case.

The brilliant glow of the moon, the shining light that had always accompanied it, was leaving. In less than half an hour, the moon was surrounded by a quickly fading ring of glowing dust and gasses, leaving behind a dull grey surface marked with lines and tiny circles—a surface that was somehow now partially covered in a deep shadow that gave this remaining area a crescent shape.

As they stared into the east at the dead moon floating behind the blazing meteor trails, the sailors suddenly felt their vessel rise high into the air, knocking everyone to the decks as their weight suddenly doubled.

A swell from the west had lifted their ship at a terrific rate, and as some of the men clambered to the sides, they saw the trough of the giant swell traveling behind them. The giant wave passed so swiftly beneath them that the ship found itself falling backwards into empty air.

The men screamed and clutched their stomachs at the sudden free fall—and when the vessel struck the base of the next wave, it shattered as easily as a raindrop does when it strikes a stone.

The men were sucked down with the pieces of their ship into the ocean below, and amazingly, all were dead from heart failure long before they had the opportunity to expire from drowning.

Matusalé stood on his balcony, high atop his estate, watching the fiery trails of small meteors leave churning wakes of smoke that sliced through the evening sky.

He was joined by thousands of frightened people in the streets below him who were all gazing in amazement and fear at this unprecedented phenomenon. Shouts of panic and loud crying reached his ears, echoing from all parts of his city, but Matusalé stared silently, mentally recording every detail and wondering what it all meant.

He was the oldest of the Old Order, and he smiled slightly, knowing he was among the very few who would be allowed, someday, to die naturally from old age. He had the beneficence of the Semyaz to thank. Danel, his mentor and friend, had told him often of his special role in transforming humanity.

A large explosion sounded far to the east, and he watched as a large fire erupted from behind the horizon where one of these falling rocks had struck the earth before burning up.

It was a frightening spectacle—but not for Matusalé, who had spent an entire lifetime observing events as an historian, objective and detached. A wrinkled hand stroked his thin white beard while another pushed away strands of translucent white hair from his temples.

No one had ever witnessed such chaos in the heavens. Other than the morning clouds, the skies had always been clear and serene, with nothing but sun, stars, and the pinkish-blue illumination that beamed down from the moon when it traversed the night sky.

Matusalé knew he was watching history in the making, and once this aerial display was over, he would have a full report for his Librarian when she came the following morning.

He thought of that strange visit from the young man named Shem, who claimed to be his great-grandson. Shem had spewed some nonsense about the end of the world, and how only those who came to the wine region would escape—in some large boat. It sounded similar to the crazy, fear-inciting tirades of that traveling wine-seller who used to visit his city.

Matusalé shook his head, smiling.

If there *were* any danger, the Semyaz would have informed him—and they certainly would *not* have established a provision in those backward regions.

EXTINCTION: CONSUMMATION

The number of fiery lines increased, creating glowing paths that crackled and screamed with the passage of each meteor. Matusalé looked towards the west, watching to see if any more would strike the ground.

Unlike the fearful residents beneath him, he actually considered this to be exciting—something different. This was obviously a once-in-a-lifetime event—and *he* had lived long enough to witness it.

Screams from the ground were getting louder, and Matusalé thought he could actually hear cries for the Semyaz to come to their aid. What could possibly stop this onslaught of rocks from the heavens? What if one struck within the city?

A flash of gold caught his attention and he watched as a shiny object moved slowly against the evening sky. What should have been a silhouette against the setting sun was glowing as it grew larger, and as it moved closer, Matusalé realized he was witnessing something only slightly less unusual than the meteor storm raging above him.

A Semyaz Observation Platform was moving swiftly over the landscape towards the city!

A loud cry rose up from the streets as people assumed their calls for help were being answered.

Matusalé had never seen one before—at least not one that he had been certain of. The few times he *thought* he *might* have observed one of their discs, it had probably been a glint or reflection of something in the night sky, or a flicker out of the corner of his eye.

This one was *huge*, gleaming clearly in the fading darkness of the day, and was easily eighty cubits in diameter. Although he could not discern any details and the edges of the craft seemed blurry, he was nevertheless impressed.

Any doubts he had ever had of the Semyaz were now totally gone.

Waves of loud pulsating sound emanated from the platform, growing in volume until many people in the streets were covering their ears.

A resonating voice emerged from the pounding noise, but it was impossible to tell whether it was coming from the craft, or somehow resonating within the listener's head.

"There is nothing to fear. Remain calm. We are here to protect. All praise to the Creator."

Matusalé listened to the message clinically, wondering, as an historian, if this event was similar to the appearance of platforms that ended the Family Wars. He observed the crowds as they calmed down and questioned, as a good reporter, why protection was needed if there was nothing to fear. He also wondered if platforms were also appearing over the other cities.

Meteor trails continued to light up the night sky, but many were now arching much closer to the ground. Matusalé watched as several of them headed straight for the platform, suspended far above.

In disbelief, he watched as they struck the leading edge of the platform, full force—and miraculously emerged unscathed on the far side of the disc! The platform remained intact, unaffected by the violent passage of incandescent rocks.

Was the entire vessel some form of illusion? Matusalé quickly filed this away in his mind, knowing it might prove to be an important insight into their technology.

The meteors that had passed through the platform struck the ground, just outside of the western wall, and everyone in the city felt the ground shudder from their impacts.

He scanned the city beneath him, looking around the horizon to make sure he was not missing any detail of this historic event. The meteor trails continued to splay out over the sky, appearing from the east and constantly increasing in number—and traveling ever closer.

He moved to the far end of his balcony, away from the platform, and looked eastward over the expanse of the ocean—and witnessed a sight that the residents could not see from behind the city walls.

His old eyes widened in utter disbelief as a sense of personal dread and stupefaction emerged from his long-forgotten youth; a realization that at one time he had felt alive—and that this unaccustomed exhilaration was about to disappear as quickly as it had resurfaced.

EXTINCTION: CONSUMMATION

What he saw, moving across the ocean, completely destroyed his resolve to remain a detached observer.

A towering wall of water, easily four times the height of the Pyramid, was rolling swiftly towards the city.

Within seconds it slammed into the Power House, twisting it from its foundation, as it continued to curl high over the city. Matusalé had just enough time to glance down and see his residents horrified faces—as they looked up at the ceiling of water descending upon them—before his balcony was swept away, throwing him down into the streets where he joined them in their watery grave.

What he did *not* have a chance to observe was the sudden disappearance of the Observation Platform from the sky at the same moment the ambassador at the Semyaz embassy perished.

The ruins of Matusalé City now rested on the floor of a new ocean.

As the waters continued to roll inland, there was no indication that any city had ever existed there. Flaming rocks continued to shower the swirling waves, creating rising clouds of steam that filled the entire sky.

Skies that had never seen rain were now suddenly filled with voluminous thunder clouds over the grasslands of the wine regions, and thick torrents of water hammered the ground, pulverizing the vast vineyards that had previously been watered only by the morning dews.

Noach and his family were safely in his barge, listening to the water pound on the roof and blow against the sides.

When he and Gaw had arrived home with Shem, his barge was almost complete. Ham and Japheth were stocking grain and supplies while hired workmen were sealing the giant, three-hundred cubit long vessel with pitch.

They had expected to see the barge looming against the horizon when they returned home. What they had not expected to see was a seemingly endless line of animals stretching from the boat back into the thick forests that bordered the grasslands.

Somehow these creatures knew it was time—and Noach and his sons, along with the hired hands, quickly shepherded the compliant animals into their stalls.

The next several days were spent loading last minute supplies—and when Noach declared that it was time, he and his family moved in.

None of the workmen were interesting in joining them. They had been paid well, and could not bear the thought that their new-found wealth had been for nothing. Noach and his family had spent years trying to convince others in the Old Order zones to join them, but ultimately, none were quite ready to believe this eccentric wine maker.

Once inside, the door was closed and sealed from within, and Noach and his family waited.

His giant barge had three main decks. The lowest level contained food and supplies for his family—and for the more than twenty-thousand pairs of land animals that were housed in pens and cages on the second level.

The top deck was practically barren.

Noach smiled sadly to himself, thinking of how he had once been concerned that this level would not be large enough. Later, he had realized that the space would probably be sufficient for the few hundred Old Order people that would most certainly join them.

Now he saw that only his family would survive—just as he had been told.

Muffled screams seeped through the barge's thick walls as people from the surrounding regions rushed through the thick mud, demanding to be allowed in. Scrambling sounds from the roof echoed down into the ship as people clambered atop the barge, trying to find entry—or simply hoping to ride out the rising waters.

But the vessel's only entrance was sealed from the inside, and Noach was helpless to rescue anyone.

Pounding torrents assailed the giant craft, twisting it down into

EXTINCTION: CONSUMMATION

the freshly made mud beneath them. Noach and his family exchanged glances as each member wondered what was happening to the world they knew—and what type of world they would see once they emerged.

Massive waves, similar to those that were washing over Matusalé City, struck the eastern peninsula and northern coasts, inundating those cities with the same ferocity. Meteor assaults on the oceans of the world seared the surface of the oceans, filling the atmosphere with searing vapors and sending out thick clouds that boiled over with torrential rains, washing away any signs of human existence.

Noach's barge was so far inland, that the leading edge of the waves was only about ten cubits high when it slammed into its side.

The barge tipped violently, sucking up massive quantities of mud as it began to separate from the ground. Additional water threatened to capsize the vessel before it ever began its journey, but at the last moment, it righted itself and became buoyant, joining the flowing mud filled with destroyed foliage, panicked animals, and human bodies—many of whom were still alive, having been thrown from the top of the ship.

As the waters rose, the barge finally stabilized, and was soon careening swiftly over the landscape—now many cubits beneath its hull.

Although most of the remnants of the destroyed planet, Nibiru, sailed harmlessly past the earth in their spiraling trajectory towards the sun, many pieces were captured and began long ellipsoidal orbits that allowed them to precede and follow the earth as it traveled around the sun—amazingly providing future protection from further cosmic damage.

However, many large mountain-sized portions did collide. The largest of these slammed into the earth south of the Haermon Mountains, vaporizing the surrounding regions and smashing through the earth's mantle, creating fissures that spread around the globe. The bedrock of the planet's lithosphere cracked, fracturing into several pieces, allowing superheated magma to seep up into the oceans, filling them from beneath.

The vast planetary network of subterranean rivers and springs exploded, filling the skies with violent geysers that sprayed the landscape with even more water—and fueled the steam clouds that now completely filled the planet's atmosphere.

As the mega-tsunamis continued to encircle the earth, the ocean floors filled and lifted, raising the water levels until every part of the planet was covered with the swirling waters—every part except the rising cliffs of the Haermon Mountains, where those within were frozen in terror at the shaking walls.

A giant rift appeared in the east, separating the Haermon Mountain range from the rest of the continent. The cliffs shuddered and tipped headlong into the sea, creating their own underwater shockwaves.

The entire planet was now a hydrosphere. Other than dead bodies, the only indication that any human life had ever existed on the planet was Noach's floating barge—and five cast-metal spheres that had been resting on the embarkation docks of the Semyaz Complex, but were now bobbing chaotically on the water's surface.

Eventually, these metal spheres would corrode and crumble, allowing the specially engineered spores within to escape. However, this would not happen for several centuries.

Within a few weeks, the surface waters reached a stage of relative calm and the thick clouds and violent precipitation subsided—but the geological activities far beneath them were anything but quiet.

The original crack in the mantle grew, creating a massive longitudinal fracture that almost reached from pole to pole. Centrifugal forces pulled it apart, spewing magma that created, not only the largest and tallest mountain chain on the submerged planet, but also the longest trench.

Beneath the waters, the planet groaned and shifted on its axis. Any future humans would now experience seasons, creating the potential of regular cycles for planting and harvesting.

The fractured lithosphere plates twisted and turned on each other, floating on the escaping pressures of the magnetic fires below as they performed a drunken dance, shifting and colliding. In the months that followed, they managed to form a new super-continent beneath the waves—but it was soon broken apart to begin a new, slower dance.

The earth's powerful magnetic field shuddered and fluctuated, even reversing polarity several times as pressurized core fluids twisted and turned from the shifting assaults above them.

After a few more months, the heat and pressures from within the earth began to subside, and the plates were forced to come grinding to a final—albeit unstable—halt, but not before some major collisions forced massive overlaps that propelled towering mountain ranges to emerge from the waters. These new ranges were more than ten times the height and thousands of times longer than the Haermon Mountains—now forever folded into the bowels of the earth.

In many places the resulting ocean bed was also ten times *deeper* than before, and as the waters drained from the new mountains, they filled these vast new reservoirs that were swiftly covered with descending sediment. Surviving marine life quickly began to adapt to their new environment and immediately started to rebuild.

As the lithosphere settled, the new planet, scarred and jagged, shrank in upon itself, slightly increasing its angular momentum and shortening its rotational period, adding several days to its solar year.

The earth would never recover from this unprecedented devastation, and would forever be plagued with storms, earthquakes, and volcanoes in an endless series of chain reactions from this year-long event.

The moon, now cold and grey, would never regain its own light, since her atmosphere of noble gases had been stripped away. It would forever be relegated to reflecting whatever light it received, displaying the marks of celestial devastation, and it would continue to vibrate slowly like a giant gong for millennia in the aftermath of the pummeling it received.

And for all time, the Solar System would also bear witness to this cosmic event with craters and other signs of destruction, while most of the remaining pieces of Nibiru would continue to circle the sun in the path where she once traveled.

Gaw sat with her husband at the large table where their family had their meals—when the abruptly changing oceans allowed them.

For months they had been twisted and spun, tossed and jostled, and had come close to—but never quite—completely capsizing, as the churning waters beneath the barge had treated it like so much driftwood. Something about the barge's dimensions—and the fact that the upper deck was virtually empty—caused it to right itself just as it was about to roll over.

She was thinking of her sons and their wives, wondering what it would soon be like to become the true mother of all who followed.

Japheth was down in the holds, taking his turn caring for their precious cargo, while his wife, Amoela was in one of the studies talking with Shem, teaching him the lengthy history of a planet now perished.

She could hear Shem's wife, the quiet, strong, but physically frail Lyn-Trienan, singing softly but beautifully in the galley. Lyn was with child and was just beginning to show. If this voyage did not come to an end soon, Gaw would become a grandmother while still on this barge. She secretly believed that, someday, the promised Seed would come from Shem and Lyn-Trienan's lineage.

At the far end of the level, Gaw could hear sounds of exertion from the exercise facility that had been installed in preparation for the unknown amount of time that they would be spending in the barge. Nel-Tamuk loved physical conditioning, and had obviously been a seasoned fighter—perhaps forced to perform for the slaves and taskmasters in the gold mines. She was currently practicing kicks and other forms, driving herself, as always, to exhaustion. Soon she would emerge with her reddish-brown hair dripping over her ebony face, smiling with joy at another good workout.

Her husband, Ham, was somewhere in the rafters, attempting to repair some of the *tsohar* modules that he had installed before the cataclysm. They had provided a constant sheet of light from the recesses of the ceiling, covering the entire first deck for most of the voyage—except for those inexplicable moments when some—or all—of the modules had suddenly gone dark.

Somehow Ham had discerned the Semyaz energy source that powered the *tsohars*, but any of his attempts at explanation had ultimately failed with Gaw. It was partly the resonance of a unique form of tuned crystals, partly a phenomena that relied on the earth's magnetic field, and partly something to do with some form of fusion—which, to Gaw, was simply a word that meant nothing when Ham tried to use it in context.

He was the quiet innovator among her sons, and somewhat of a loner, and she was certain that he and Nel-Tamuk would be the first to head out and make their own way in the new world.

She looked across into Noach's kind eyes, thinking of her early beginnings as a kidnapped student in the Semyaz compound, and a strange thought occurred to her as she contemplated her family:

The preserved Old Order has now become the new order.

Noach looked back into Gaw's emerald eyes, *also* thinking of his sons and their wives, but he was contemplating them in a more clinical way—as any husbandmen or student of heredity would.

He was overwhelmed with the amazing diversity and physical variety that all six of them exhibited, and how they had come from every possible background and region. Somehow, his son's wives had found their way to the barge as if they had been led or carefully selected. And Gaw, the mother of his sons, had been kidnapped from an obscure Forest Community, almost certainly the descendant of Family War refugees.

He smiled wryly at the thought that, probably, all eight of the barge's passengers would have been executed during the Family Wars as *non-opts* or mutants, had they lived back then.

As a student of heredity, he knew that eight people were the bare minimum needed to provide a healthy pool of inheritable characteristics, and he was amazed—and certain—that the Creator had designed all of the events of the past centuries to ensure that the eight passengers on board were the exact ones needed to repopulate the earth with as much variety and adaptability as possible.

What the world viewed as *non-opts*, the Creator viewed as multiplied potential.

Noach reached for his wife's hand as the barge shuddered slightly.

"We are blessed," he said, simply.

Gaw smiled.

"It looks like we are the *new* First Ones," she said, nodding.

Noach nodded back, but remained silent, resuming his contemplation.

Eventually he spoke.

"Do you know what the *real* crime—the *actual* offense—of the First Ones truly was?" he asked, not expecting an immediate answer.

Gaw studied his face for a moment, looking forward to what was certain to be a special and deep thought from her husband.

"I *suppose*," she said eventually, "that the *simple* answer is disobedience."

Noach nodded slightly.

"And you would be correct," he said, "but that was only a symptom."

He released her hand so he could use both of his for gesturing.

"Their fault was a lack of trust," he said, somehow looking into the deep past with his eyes.

"It was their profound *inability* to realize how much the Creator *truly* cared for them—*truly* loved them as His own creation. If they truly *knew* Him, truly *understood* His intimate desire for their well-being, truly *trusted* His friendship, the thought of disobedience would never have occurred—although the possibility would have remained."

Gaw thought for a few moments before responding.

"That means," she said eventually, "that we must always teach our children to never doubt His nature."

Noach nodded.

"Casting aspersions on His character and nature becomes the highest crime—and the greatest temptation. We must always guard against this."

Gaw smiled.

"In order to do this we must learn more about the Creator."

Noach nodded, giving her a shrug that, strangely, seemed to indicate futility.

He reached for her hand.

"Come with me," he said, a slight smile forming.

Gaw scowled in confusion, looking around the dining area.

"Where can we go, in *here*, that we haven't already been?" she exclaimed, laughing.

Noach tugged gently at her arm, encouraging her to rise.

They walked to the front of the deck where a small ladder was built into the hull. Gaw followed Noach up the steps into the rafters and across a small walk towards the barge's only window.

They looked down the length of the barge and saw Ham fussing with some support cabling at the far end. He waved.

They approached the small window together, and as they stood on the narrow platform in front, Noach began to release the wooden bolts and peel back the strips of sealant that surrounded the frame.

Eventually he removed the thick wooden hatch that covered the window, and a fresh breeze poured into the opening.

Gaw took a tentative breath, and then inhaled fully.

The air was still warm, but unlike previous visits, any hints of carbon and sulfur were completely gone.

As they stared up into the thick dark clouds, it was still impossible to tell whether it was day or night. Somehow there was a feeling of being trapped beneath the impenetrable sky, even though there was an endless, free expanse of water in all directions.

It had been almost a year since the light from a star had broken through.

"There!" Noach exclaimed, pointing.

In a small sliver of the sky, the clouds parted, and they gazed in astonishment—and intense relief—as more than a dozen stars blazed through.

It was the constellation of the Infant King!

Great happiness welled up in Noach, and he turned to see Gaw weeping with joy. Neither had realized just how terrified they had been that the thick cloud covering might never part.

They embraced each other with great gladness and gratitude as they watched more patches of clear night sky emerge—and more brilliant beams of starlight began to reflect from the dark ocean, creating sparkling wave caps on a sea that had been dark for far too long.

Noach looked into Gaw's tear-filled eyes, enjoying their deep emerald beauty, now discernable in the fresh starlight.

"We must tell the children," he said, excitedly.

Gaw reached out with her hand and grabbed the back of his head, pulling it towards her own.

She kissed him passionately, her tears of joy now washing down both of their faces. Noach cupped the sides of her head and began to weep with her.

He returned her kiss, accepting Gaw's silent request and empathizing with her need to share this moment with him.

EXTINCTION: CONSUMMATION

He held her tightly as they turned to watch the unfolding sky that was now more than half filled with stars. They stood there silently for several minutes, enjoying the togetherness of solitude as the dark barge rose and fell beneath them.

Eventually he spoke.

"We'll tell them later."

Semjaza's ever-present rage reached a new fervor as he looked down on the two people, silhouetted against the window of their floating barge.

He hated people!

He especially hated when people were happy, enjoying their undeserved favor and unjust benefits that rightfully belonged to him and his kind.

He had heard nothing from those who had taken corporeal form, and had no idea as to their fate. No one had considered the consequences when one so encumbered actually perished.

He hated people!

The rage of their failure drove him further into madness. No one could have imagined the foolish winemaker's boat would be used for that purpose. But no one had imagined the extreme lengths the Unspeakable One would take to thwart their plans.

Destroying His own planet!

Semjaza thought furiously, swearing to conceive of another strategy. All was not lost, but they would have to be even more subtle—and more patient. There was much they could still do, even restricted to their current ethereal form, to confuse, delay, and perhaps conceal the inevitable.

Perhaps this restriction could even be used to their advantage. They had learned much about crowd control and mental manipulation during the last two thousand years. All they needed was a few compliant fools. Even one would do!

He hated people!

Yes, they were still stupid and gullible. It was unconscionable how they were destined to receive the honor due to him.

Destined?

Semjaza pondered this word.

Perhaps this is where the fault in their strategy lay.

EXTINCTION: CONSUMMATION

Throughout his entire existence, he had been conditioned to be-lieve that, if the Betrayer had spoken, it would happen.

Inevitable?

Perhaps if they were to cast off such concepts, they could truly be free to pursue true justice.

His rage subsided slightly.

Their scheme to subvert and contaminate the Seed had failed.

They must now plot to undermine and destroy the message—and mission—of the Seed.

He hated people!

AFTERWORD
FACT VS FICTION

B efore I launch into any discussions concerning events and concepts found in *The Days of Laméch*, I must first inform those
who are readers of classic science fiction that the floating forests
found in the story were *not* inspired by those found in *Perelandra*,
the second book in C.S. Lewis' brilliant and mind-expanding *Space
Trilogy.*

Instead, it was while reading an article[7] by Dr. Kurt Wise[8] where
he discusses Dr. Joachim Scheven's[9] research of fossils found in
coal. Dr. Scheven's observation was that a large majority of these
fossils were of extinct trees and plants that exhibited strange branch-
ing patterns and inexplicable hollowness in their trunks, roots, and
rootlets. Entire coal deposits are filled with such fossils and are
found in perfectly smooth layers in seams throughout the planet.

These inexplicable beds of coal, containing the remnants of entire eco-systems made up of these hollow plants and trees, caused
Dr. Wise to theorize that these enigmatic deposits were the remains

---

[7] *Sinking a Floating Forest*, Answers Magazine, Oct.-Dec. 2008, p.41-43

[8] PhD, Geology, Harvard University

[9] PhD, Zoology/Paleontology, University of Munich. Known for his vast collection of
"living" fossils.

of massive floating forests—made up entirely of flora perfectly designed for such an environment.

Such forests exist today on much smaller scales as bogs and floating vegetation mats, but in order to explain the coal deposits studied by Dr. Scheven, our ancient floating forests would have to have been enormous—perhaps on the order of large islands or even a small continent! A forest-filled mat of this size would never survive the storms and climate cycles of the modern world, and, in fact, would almost certainly be unable to form in the first place—even if the required plants and trees were available and not extinct as they are today. Such islands would have been among the final things to remain afloat during the flood—surfing the waters as log mats until sinking and colliding into the shifting continents before being buried and forming into the seams of coal we find today.

Dr. Wise contends that, since such floating forests did exist in antediluvian times, they must have been part of the original creation, unspoiled until they were destroyed in the massive upheavals of the great deluge.

In attempting to ascertain the technological potentials of antediluvian humanity, I came to the conclusion that the only form of technology that would *not* have been available to the ancients was anything based upon hydrocarbons or petroleum, since such resources had not yet formed at that time, being the byproducts of the global flood. I had to eschew gasoline motors and plastics—thereby denying my characters the massive energies contained therein.

In fact, I actually removed a scene from the book where scientists had created crude petroleum from garbage and compost—and were lamenting the fact that it would require unbelievable devastation to provide enough destroyed plant and animal life to form a reliable supply of this incredible energy source.

Here, now, is a list of concepts that *did* survive, along with brief commentaries. More in-depth discussions of the constellation of the Infant Prince and Catastrophic Plate Tectonics can be found in appendices C and D respectively.

AFTERWORD: FACT VS FICTION

Amoela the Librarian: In letters exchanged between Aaron J. Smith, the leader of the 1950 Oriental Archaeological Research Expedition to find the ark on Mount Ararat, and Dr. Philip W. Gooch, Dr. Gooch claimed to have access to a mysterious diary penned by one Amoela, who claimed to be the daughter-in-law of Noach and the wife of Japheth.

This diary, which was obviously never produced, purportedly contained "fine details of what went on during the flood and after the flood until her death in her 547th year". Supposedly, she was a student of Methuselah, "who taught her all that preceded the flood", and her diary was "filled with things that occurred from Adam to her death".

Dr. Gooch claimed the diary was among ancient records possessed by the Masonic order to which he was a member. His final communication on the diary, before his untimely death shortly thereafter was:

"At her death, dying in the arms of her youngest son, Javan, her diary was placed in her mummified hands in a crystal quartz case, with tempered gold hinges and clasps, and was discovered by a high-ranking mason in the later part of the last century. The original and the translation are now in the possession of the Order."

Dr. Gooch never revealed the name or chapter of the Masonic lodge in question; however, it is very interesting that this correspondence—when revealed to the Turkish authorities—greatly expedited the final arrangements for their expedition.[10]

Tsohar: This word for the light panels utilized by the Semyaz comes from the Hebrew, which, in Genesis 6:16, was translated 'window' by the King James scholars. However, this word does not mean window or opening at all, but rather "a brightness, a brilliance, the light of a midday sun". In Genesis 8:6, the more appropriate word *challon* (window) is used to refer to the opening through which Noah released his birds.

---

[10] See *Secrets of the Lost Races: New Discoveries of Advanced Technology in Ancient Civilizations* by Rene Noorbergen, published by Teach Services, 2001

It is also inconceivable that a large opening would be placed around the top of a vessel, allowing water to pour in from every side every time the ship tipped slightly.

Traditional Jewish scholars claim that the *tsohar* was a "light which has its origins in shining crystal", and various Midrash traditions claims that the *tsohar* of Noah's ark was an enormous gem or pearl that was hung from the rafters and, by using a mysterious self-contained power, illuminated the entire ship throughout the flood.

Was there an ancient technology that utilized crystals (perhaps which do not exist any more) or magnetic energies (also no longer available) to illuminate the ark? Is there any indication that such devices may have survived, and were usable sometime after the flood?

An ancient manuscript entitled *The Queen of Sheba and Her Only Son Menyelek*[11] contains this excerpt: "...the house of Solomon the King was illuminated as by day, for in his wisdom he had made shining pearls (*tsohar*) which were like unto the sun, the moon and the stars in the roof of his house".

Florescent Moon: I must admit that the idea of a moon, glowing with the excited energies of an atmosphere made of argon and helium, is solely a contrivance of my own.

However, the inspiration for this came from an online skeptic who challenged the Genesis record by claiming that the moon was not a "lesser light to rule the night"[12], since it only reflected the radiation that it received from the sun and was not, in fact, a producer of light at all.

The surface of the moon, today, is a virtual vacuum, but it does contain some trace gasses, almost exclusively argon and helium.[13]

---

[11] *The Kabra Nagast: The Queen of Sheba and Her Only Son Menyelek*, translated from the Ethiopian by Sir E. A. Wallis Budge

[12] Genesis 1:16

[13] The moon also exhibits some 'outgassing', the releasing of radon (also a noble gas) and helium from radioactive decay in its crust.

AFTERWORD: FACT VS FICTION

I found it exciting that these gases were noble ones—the ones that glow with their own light when energized.

I sought to rectify this skeptic's contradiction by speculating that the moon's current atmosphere is but a remnant of its original one, and that, in fact, the 'lesser light' was indeed created as an actual light—a giant florescent sphere that radiated her *own* light—powered by the solar wind and other cosmic energies.

This lovely but tenuous atmosphere was ripped away during the meteoric bombardment of the cataclysm, leaving the scarred, lifeless, gray surface we see today.

Zipf's Law: This is the statistical formula that Tûrell discovered in chapter 17. Proposed by George Kingsley Zipf in 1935 for analyzing languages, it basically states, in mathematical terms, that the frequency of any word is inversely proportional to its rank in the frequency table. Today, it is considered an empirical, statistical law.

However, it was soon discovered that this law was universally applicable to all languages, and quickly became celebrated by linguists, statisticians, and cryptologists. Using this formula, it was possible to determine whether or not any sample of text contained meaningful information—even if the text itself was untranslated or its meaning was unknown.

With Zipf's law, it can quickly be determined if an unknown sequence of characters represented a meaningful language with informational content, or if the sequence is simply random information (static) or deliberate gibberish. This can be accomplished without having any clue as to the actual meaning contained therein.

Using this tool, cryptologists can save vast amount of time as they decode, avoiding false leads and prioritizing tasks.

In 1994, Physicist Eugene Stanley of Boston University applied Zipf's law to sequences of yeast DNA—specifically sections categorized, at that time, as "junk" DNA.[14] The findings of Eugene and

---

[14] Results published in Science Magazine, November, 1994 Vol. 266, page 1320 by Faye Flam. The conclusion that "junk" DNA is, indeed, a language, is presented clearly, with no concern for the recent paranoia surrounding "intelligent design".

his team proved conclusively that even "junk" DNA contains meaningful information, even though Stanley himself stated that "There's no rhyme or reason why that should be true."

Although Zipf's law proves that "junk" DNA contains a hidden message, no one knows when, if ever, the information contained in this message will be revealed. It does, however, beg the question:

Where did this message come from in the first place—and *Who* put it there?

Bioluminescent Algae: Bioluminescence is very unique in that no heat is generated during the production of light, as all chemical energy is completely converted to luminescence. From an evolutionary perspective, bioluminescent algae are considered one of the most earliest and primitive life forms, yet they incorporate this amazing technology that still eludes our greatest inventors.

Tiktaalik: Tiktaalik is an extinct fish with "fins" that had fully functioning "wrist" bones and fingers. The bones of the fore fins show large muscle facets, suggesting that the fin was both muscular and had the ability to flex. They also had small air-holes (spiracles) in the tops of their heads, making them perfectly designed for living in and around floating forests. They could climb through the roots and vines submerged in the water, clamber out onto the surface, and also use their "fins" to walk upside-down along the bottom.

Many Tiktaalik fossils have been found in coal deposits similar to those containing "floating forest" tree and plant fossils.[15]

Cryptozoology: Although it is entrenched in the dogma of evolutionary thought that humans did not coexist with dinosaurs, there is

---

[15] Recently (2010) a halt to coal exploration in Ellesmere Island, Canada, was threatened because large numbers of Tiktaalik fossils were *anticipated* to be discovered. The Weststar Resources Corporation was asked to shut down their operation until scientists could complete their investigations in Strathcona Fjord, a region on the island.

a growing number of cryptozoologists who scour the modern world looking for signs of unknown or inexplicable creatures. These endeavors are usually devoted to such things as hunting for Bigfoot or searching for the Loch Ness Monster—and much of their research is based on tribal folklore or unscientific anecdotal evidence. However, there is a growing body of evidence indicating that, not only were large reptiles roaming the earth during human history, but that hidden remnants of such creatures may still exist in obscure locations today.

All ancient cultures speak of dragons as if they were common knowledge, and stories of battles against such creatures are legion. Gilgamesh, Beowulf, and even the countless exploits of medieval dragon slayers tell of encounters with large reptiles—many of which actually make more sense if viewed as historical accounts rather than fairy-tales spun by storytellers with over-active imaginations.

One of the creatures described in Job, the Behemoth, is described as having a tail like a cedar tree—not likely an elephant or a hippopotamus! The other, the Leviathan, has thick impenetrable scales and "raises himself up"—again, not accurately descriptive of a whale or crocodile.

Modern cryptozoological researchers have countless reports of large flying reptiles, giant sea creatures emerging from lakes, and a plethora of unknown creatures that, supposedly, have yet to be officially discovered.[16] Part of the reasoning goes like this: Even in India, where the majority of all tigers are located, almost no one in India has actually seen an actual tiger in the wild. What makes us so sure that the scientific community has discovered every animal? Especially a creature like the Behemoth, which, according to Jewish Midrashim, are shy and reclusive animals.

Finally, numerous recent discoveries of dinosaur bones that contain actual, blood vessels and viable red blood cells—the kind of soft tissue that is known to disintegrate within a few hundred years

---

[16] <http://www.newanimal.org>

of death, if not sooner.[17] This 'fact' has suddenly and mysteriously been updated with the pronouncement that "Well, I guess soft tissue *can* survive millions of years of burial", rather that the more obvious, and scientific evidentiary statement of, "It looks like these bones are a lot younger than we thought."

Rail Gun: The mammoth weapon found in chapter 27 is known as a rail gun, and is the inevitable development of electromagnetic technologies. Since before WWII, attempts have been made to utilize this and similar devices as a weapon of war, but numerous issues and difficulties (as described in the narrative) have made this impractical. Overheating, excessive maintenance, and incredible power requirements have made research difficult. They also require a great deal of space if they are to be comparable to conventional weapons.

However, as an occasional-use weapon of terror—especially when deployed in secret—it can be quite formidable.

The incredible speed of a rail gun payload (modern tests in excess of Mach 15—almost half that needed for escape or orbital velocity) allow the speed of the projectile to cause the intended damage—without the need for explosives—since the kinetic energy is converted upon impact.

The weapon in the narrative is immense—allowing for more acceleration time but requiring less energy. A one week charging cycle and a necessary range of less than half a hemisphere, make a rail gun—in the hands of the Semyaz—eminently feasible.

Anthrax: The only difference between the common garden variety of endospores (not to be confused with fungal spores) and the deadly *bacillus anthracis* that causes anthrax are the addition of two

---

[17] See *Dinosaur Shocker*, < http://www.smithsonianmag.com/science-nature/dinosaur. html > Helen Fields, Smithsonian magazine, May 2006

simple plasmid rings which have somehow become integrated into its structure.

Plasmids are simple, self replicating rings of DNA, capable of autonomous replication within suitable hosts—similar to viruses but even less complex.

When considered in their relationship with anthrax, they give every appearance of having been placed there artificially. There is no apparent natural explanation for how these rings were ever added to simple endospores—or how such spores can exist dormant for centuries.

We must assume that the modern anthrax spore is a weaker, frailer, and less virulent descendant of those designed by Tûrell.

Nibiru: The planet claimed by the ancient Sumerians to have orbited in the path between Mars and Jupiter. Their various records claim that it either was destroyed or somehow disappeared.

Dr. Walt Brown[18], in his book *In the Beginning*, presents much of the same cataclysmic scenarios found in the narrative. However, in his theory, the source of the massive destructive energy needed to change the face of the earth does not come from the bombardment of extraterrestrial material, but rather from the released, explosive pressure of vast reservoirs of subterranean water—known as his "hydroplate" theory. According to Dr. Brown, this pressure cracked through with the force of 10,000 hydrogen bombs—and fractured the plates we know today. In the process, vast portions of the earth's surface were jettisoned into outer space, forming the meteors, comets, and even asteroids we know today.[19]

---

[18] Ph.D. Mechanical Engineering, Massachusetts Institute of Technology. Director, Benét Laboratories. Chief of Science and Technology Studies, Air War College.

[19] Supposedly, "solar pressure", or the force of light and energy from the sun, has slowly pushed the bulk of these remnants away from the Sun, where they currently reside between the orbits of Mars and Jupiter. Although such pressure is real and even feasible (it *does* drive dust and other particles, manifest as solar wind), it simply isn't strong enough to propel objects into larger and larger orbits. Also, independent studies have shown that, even if this *were* the case, there simply has not been enough time for these objects to travel out to the asteroid belt—if one accepts Dr. Brown's timelines.

Although the destructive force of this theory is compelling, I chose to combine this with meteor strikes and catastrophic plate tectonics for three reasons.

First, it is more consistent with ancient mythologies. Secondly, as violent as the hydroplate theory is, I don't see it providing enough power to shatter and shift continents, or to propel enough matter into space to account for the combined mass of all meteors, comets and asteroids—many of which are measured in miles. Also, the fact that the vast majority of lunar craters are on the far side of the moon indicates that the brunt of meteor strikes have come from outside—not from the earth.

Finally, the destruction of Nibiru fits within the narrative of *The Days of Peleg* and was, therefore, best suited to be incorporated into the story.

Scorpion's Claw: The constellation is known today as Libra, the scales or balance, with its implication of justice. However, the ancients considered this an extension of Scorpio and called it the Scorpion's Claw (*MUL Zibanu*), more closely associated with punishment.

It is interesting to consider that, when seen as the extension or offspring of the Virgin, it represents justice, harmony, and peace—but when seen as the extension of the Scorpion, it represents judgment and damnation.

Apollo Asteroids: There are currently more than 250 mapped planetoids, known as the Apollo Asteroids, that either occupy or cross the Earth's orbit. Although most either follow or lead the Earth in their orbits, a few of these, due to strange interactions with Earth's Lagrange points, actual take turns doing both. The most famous of these is Cruithne, sometimes incorrectly called Earth's second moon.

Although Cruithne's orbit takes it from Mercury out to beyond

Mars, it is locked into a 'resonance' with Earth, giving it an orbital period almost identical to Earth.

As a result, it interacts with Earth and Earth's Lagrange points on an annual basis, giving it a kidney-bean shaped orbit that gradually shifts around the sun.

Cruithne's speed will increase or decrease based on its nearness to the Earth, sometimes leading the Earth, and at others, approaching it from behind.

When the Earth causes Cruithne to accelerate, the asteroid is thrown into a larger orbit—which ultimately causes it to be slowed by the sun. When the Earth slows Cruithne, it is dropped into a faster orbit. Amazingly, this extremely complex dynamic is completely stable.

The proximity of these asteroids and other "Near Earth Objects" (NROs) is often cause for alarm, since the impact of any one of these would wipe out large portions of life on the planet. However, there are many who feel that the Apollo Asteroids actually "clear a path" in the Earth's orbit, keeping us safe from all of the other debris that travels with us on our path around the sun.

The Days of Noah: One final thought regarding antediluvian life: In writing a novel of this era, one is confronted with the enormity of the time period—and the complete absence of any facts or writings available for study. Such resources *were* available during the writing of *The Days of Peleg*, but in the creation of *The Days of Laméch*, I was forced to rely less on research and more on idle speculation.

From a more Biblical perspective, the only clue I had was the phrase "as it was in the days of Noah" which is meant to be an indicator of a culture so perverse, violent, and wicked that it can only be compared to some future world that will *also* become so evil that it, too, must be judged.

In immersing myself in this fictional culture, I chose not to dwell on the potential for excessive corruption and mayhem, but I often *did* find myself overwhelmed by the probable, unbridled evil that most certainly occurred during that age. In fact, it often crossed my mind that there probably was a very good reason why the Author of Genesis chose *not* to include any details—even though this period traversed almost two thousand years of human existence.

It is probably safe to say that the depravation and atrocities of that time were far in excess of anything chronicled in *The Days of Laméch*—and it is left up to the reader to ascertain what the phrase "as it was in the days of Noah" might actually mean. Does it refer to mass murder and warfare—similar to what we have witnessed in the last one hundred years? Perhaps it simply refers to unchecked immorality—which is something of a difficult concept to process in an ancient world that existed more than a thousand years before the law was revealed through Moses. As in our secular era, how does one define "immoral" when the definition of "moral" is a constantly changing target?

What if the phrase refers to genetic experimentation and organized eugenic efforts to create a super-race? This was attempted by the Nazi's using simple 'artificial' selection as they systematically weeded out that which, in their opinion, constituted inferior strains of humanity. Is it so inconceivable in our near future that more sophisticated attempts at "improving" humanity might be imposed upon us—perhaps globally—as in the narrative? Perhaps efforts to "assist" us in our evolution? One can easily imagine the raging outbursts against those who might stand in the way of such "progress".

Perhaps the true wickedness of "The Days of Noah" is the affront of playing God. Seeking to become "like the Most High"—while refusing to accept the one Provision that the Most High requires. Or stated differently: The Creator has the right to determine—or restrict—the manner in which his creation approaches Him.

I hope that you have enjoyed this journey into unknown—and unknowable—history with me, and it is my greatest desire that those who encounter these books will be motivated to find the purpose, joy, and enlightenment that has been intended for each of them.

For more information, additional commentaries and continuing updates can be found at DaysOfLamech.com.

And again, my sincerest thanks and unending appreciation for those whose encouragement and patience have afforded me—for a second time—this opportunity to share and serve.

Jon Saboe
June, 2011

APPENDIX A
DANEL'S SOLILOQUY

Darkness and timelessness encompass me.
Nothing external exists to mark the passage of time, and no inter-
nal sensations or sounds are present to confirm my own existence.
Yet my thoughts rage on.
Where is this empty, weightless place?
Have I been here for years—or eons?
Does time even exist in this realm?
I know nothing of my kindred, or of what may be transpiring in
time and space.
Isolation and solitude are my only companions, and I can only
dwell on my former drives and ambitions.
Were we successful?
Will we be grafted into redemption as my masters promised? At
any moment, will a light appear, telling us that all is restored?
Did we truly force His hand?
Or is all of humanity destroyed, perhaps in such a display of spite
and vengeance that only He could perform? Would He truly wipe
out all of his human creation, simply to refuse us our rightful
place?
My tortured consciousness continues—not knowing—unsure of its

ultimate plight.
Perhaps this is all that will be?
Stranded in this floating void, perceiving nothing but my own insatiable thoughts?
My only solace is that I have avoided that other dimension, the one created for me and my kindred at our rebellion.
Such injustice!
Our only crime was in desiring that which was rightfully ours!
Mercy for them? But not for us?
The unfairness is a detestable stain on the One who claims perfection.
My rage continues, yet, as I have no physical capacity for exhaustion, it expands, painfully and unabated.
Wait!
A sudden sensation?
Something new in this ageless region of deprivation!
Is it warmth? Is it light?
Something has entered this realm—
News of our victory? Our forced acceptance?
HIS capitulation?
The light grows, warmer, fiery, then painful.
Fear fills me.
Am I to be transported to that other place, before my time?
The light surrounds me, filling me with pain and joy, misery and mirth.
There is no sound as the radiance buffets me from all sides, yet words pour painfully into my thoughts.
"YOU HAVE FAILED. I HAVE COME. IT IS FINISHED."
The light explodes around me, blinding me with waves of sensory overload—as powerful and debilitating as the preceding emptiness.
My anguished mind reels as the light disappears as quickly as it arrived.
The empty abyss still surrounds me, and the only evidence of the vanished light is a radiant sense of mocking and gloating that only He is capable of.

APPENDIX A

Timelessness returns, and my rage continues.
However, I now know that I will not be forever in this place.
Someday I am certain to enter the place that was specially pre-
pared to provide torture and anguish for me and my kindred.
I am now also betrayed by my masters, who assigned my corporeal
mission, knowing this would be my fate.
I now know rage mixed with terror, and if I am ever released before
I go to my inevitable destiny, I swear I will exact such carnage and
devastation in my vengeance upon Him—and his eternally created
ones.
He will have only Himself to blame—for I have learned this be-
trayal from Him.
My mind implodes into madness, awaiting my opportunity.

APPENDIX B
PRELUDE TO AENOCH'S
THIRD DISAPPEARANCE

The roar of two Israeli F-161 *Sufa* (Storm) fighter jets startled the two men as they emerged from the trees high on a hill just below the HaShablul garden, overlooking predawn Jerusalem to the south. According to the terms of the latest peace accord established by the Global Governance Protectorate, Israel was allowed to fly these older planes—without ordinance—to patrol the borders and monitor communication traffic.

The taller of the two men looked at his companion.

"So *this* is how the earth appeared in your day," he said, scanning the horizon with a look of intrigue—combined with that slight disdain that one has for something that is not what it is supposed to be.

The smaller man shook his head, his eyes filled with unabashed dismay.

"Only the landscape," he said sadly, shaking his head.

The taller man smiled at his companion reassuringly.

"Yes," he agreed, becoming visibly more impressed. "We certainly did not have mountains like these when I was here."

"These are *not* mountains," his companion replied with a quiet laugh, "you must go far to the north—where I last visited—to find a true mountain."

The men were dressed in period clothing—something known as "business casual". In addition, the shorter man also wore a traditional trilby style black hat.

Both men looked out over the city, trying to absorb the view in vastly different ways. A slight layer of morning smog was clearing, and they could see and hear the speeding vehicles on a small freeway exchange below them to the east. It was almost sunrise, and the headlights of the morning commuters flickered like dancing swords as the drivers jostled for better lanes.

The shorter man smiled suddenly, pointing to the traffic.

"The chariots shall rage in the streets, they shall jostle one against another in the broad ways: they shall seem like torches, they shall run like the lightning."

The taller man raised his eyebrows, nodding.

"The chariots shall be with flaming torches in the day of His preparation."

The two men smiled at each other, finding a common frame of reference.

Far in the distance, to the east, were two columns of black smoke ascending into the sky. As they watched, the sun began to rise, its face bisected by the two dark lines.

They both took a deep breath, contemplating the scope of their final mission.

"It is appointed unto man once to die," the shorter man quoted again.

The taller man nodded.

"Yes, Eliyahu," he said. "At *least* once. *You* know that."

He grinned.

"I believe we will soon rectify this oversight."

Both men were unique, in that they had left the earth long ago, without fulfilling this simple requirement.

Eliyahu smiled slightly.

"...and after that, the judgment."

"Not for us," the taller man said abruptly. "We have already received *our* judgment."

Eliyahu's smile grew.

"Truth, Aenoch," he said. "*My righteous servant will justify many, and will bear their iniquities.*"

Eliyahu clasped Aenoch's arm as his tall friend responded.

"*Our* judgment is: *Not* guilty."

Eliyahu nodded, his face becoming serious.

"Are you ready?" he asked.

"Are *you* ready?" Aenoch replied with a laugh. "You are the one with expertise in calling down fire."

Eliyahu responded with a smile of ancient memories.

"Let us go," he said eventually.

The two men headed down the hill towards the Yiga'el Yadin Interchange, just beyond the Golda Me'ir overpass.

After more than six thousand years it was time for regime change—and their mission would clear the path for that promised day when the *City of Peace* would finally receive her Namesake— and truly become the political and spiritual center of creation.

APPENDIX C
CONSTELLATION OF
THE INFANT PRINCE

As anyone who has studied introductory astronomy knows, the constellations were the results of bored, unenlightened herdsmen who created images in the clouds by day and drew pictures at night by playing connect-the-dots with the stars.

This explanation, however, is woefully inadequate to explain the fact that the majority of the sky's constellations are globally universal, and that they have remained virtually unchanged for more than four thousand years.

Everyone knows the dismay at being unable to actually visualize the characters that are supposedly represented by random groupings of stars, and the idea that disparate, unrelated ancient cultures happened upon the same groupings requires vast reserves of credulity.

The Book of Enoch tells of the angel Urial or "Light of God" (as contrasted with Lucifer, "god of light") identifying the figures of the constellations to Enoch.[20] Assuming (for sake of argument) that this entire story is pure myth, we must, somehow, find an alternative explanation for finding the same constellations among the Sumerians, the Mayans, the Indus (*Vedic Jyotisa*), the Persians, the Minoans, and the Egyptians.

Our modern constellations are based almost exclusively on those presented by the Greek astronomer and mathematician, Ptolemy, who lived in Egypt. Around AD 150, he listed forty-eight constellations and gave precise locations for each of the major stars, showing how they fit into the corresponding characters. Forty additional constellations have been added since then to accommodate the portions of the sky not visible to him in Alexandria.

Although his constellations encompass all of the brighter stars in Ptolemy's sky, there is a collection of seven stars near the outstretched arms of Virgo[21], the Virgin, that are not assigned to any constellations.

Around 300 BC, a Greek scholar named Eudoxus brought a celestial sphere to Greece. This globe displayed the stars from a god-like perspective, showing them in a mirror image on the surface of the globe. A Greek poet by the name of Aratus[22] describes each constellation on this globe in detail, giving us most of our knowledge of the Greek characters. Unfortunately, Aratus gives no indication that this group of unnamed stars has any designation or significance.

This assembly of stars remained unnamed until 1687 when Johannes Hevelius decided that Boötes the Herdsman needed a pair of hunting dogs and decreed that this mystery group be named *Canes Venatici* (hunting dogs). The brightest star in this constellation had already been named *Cor Caroli* (Charles' Heart) for King Charles I of England.

But did this small group of stars *ever* have a name? Is there any indication that these stars were once considered an actual constellation?

In Egypt, the Temple of Hathor in Dendera contained a detailed map of the sky, which Napoleon's artists faithfully recorded.[23] Al-

[20] 1 Enoch 74:4-7
[21] The very bright star (Spica) in Virgo represents grain that she holds—or "Seed of a woman".
[22] *The Phaenomena* English translation by G.R. Main, *Aratus*, Cambridge, Harvard U. Press, 1960.
[23] Commision des Sciences et Arts d'Egypt, *Description de l'Egypte* (Paris: Imprimerie

though the temple was constructed approximately 100 years before Christ, once the precession of the equinoxes is factored in, it is clear that the constellations depicted on the map are based on astronomical information from many centuries earlier, perhaps sometime around 1500 to 1600 BC.[24]

In the position of our mystery constellation we find a picture of a young woman holding an infant boy on her outstretched hand. Traditionally, this boy has been identified as "Horus, the one who is coming".

Clearly the original name of this constellation had been appropriated by the ancient Egyptians and given the name of one of their gods.

Our mystery is solved when one studies the works of the Persian astronomer, Albumazar, who created a compendium of Persian astronomical history.[25] Although he lived around AD 850, his work covers thousands of years.

His list of constellations is fundamentally identical to Ptolemy's, but describes an extra constellation, located next to Virgo:

> *"Virgo is a sign of two parts and three forms. There arises in the first decan, as the Persians, Chaldeans, and Egyptians, the two Hermes and Ascalius teach, a young woman, whose Persian name translated into Arabic is Adrenedefa, a pure and immaculate virgin, holding in the hand two ears of corn, sitting on a throne, nourishing an infant, in the act of feeding him, who has a Hebrew name, by some nations named Ihesu, with the signification Ieza, which the Greek call Christ."*

Imperial, 1809-1828)

[24] Tompkins, Peter *Secrets of the Great Pyramid* (New York: Harper & Row, 1971), p. 174

[25] It should be noted that the Judean captive, Daniel, was given the task of re-educating the Babylonian astrologers and wise men (Daniel 2:47), and that this information was certainly transferred to the Medo-Persians—whom Daniel also served. In fact, it would have been descendents of these students who followed the star to Bethlehem.

There have been numerous attempts to reconstitute the figure for this lost constellation, but John P. Pratt[26] has reclaimed the stars from *Canes Venatici* and restored the constellation of the Infant Prince, a name totally appropriate for the babe of a virgin queen. Also, the two Hermes are traditionally considered to be Aenoch and Abraham, respectively. In fact, there are Midrashim claims that Abraham brought Aenoch's original constellations to Egypt when he traveled from Mesopotamia.

I would encourage readers to study more at John P. Pratt's pages at johnpratt.com, where you can find detailed information, along with ancient calendars, more from the Book of Aenoch, and additional, unrelated, astronomical and scientific articles and puzzles.

> *"I blessed the Lord of glory, who had made those great and splendid signs, that they might display the magnificence of his works to angels and to the souls of men; and that these might glorify all his works and operations; might see the effect of his power; might glorify the great labor of his hands; and bless him forever."* — Enoch 35:3

---

[26] Pratt, John P. *The Infant Prince* (Meridian Magazine, July 14, 2004). He suggests renaming this brightest star, *Cor Caroli*, to *Cor Christi*.

APPENDIX D
CATASTROPHIC
PLATE TECTONICS

The theory of traditional plate tectonics is relatively new, being first suggested by a creationist named Antonio Snider in 1859. In this same year, an obscure naturalist published a book entitled *The Origin of Species by Means of Natural Selection or, The Preservation of Favored Races in the Struggle for Life*, sadly overshadowing Snider's speculations.

Plate tectonics were presented more formally by Alfred Wegener in his 1915 book, "The Origin of Continents and Oceans". It was immediately dismissed as pseudoscience, since the suggestion that "the continents rested on plates of low density granite floating like icebergs on a sea of denser basalt" was obviously absurd. However, after decades of impetuous schoolchildren continued to raise their hands, insisting that South America *must* fit next to Africa, the theory of plate tectonics and continental drift became generally accepted in the late 1950s.

By the end of the 1960s, several experiments and measuring expeditions firmly solidified the concept into the mainstream of scientific thought, confirmed via five primary lines of evidence:

1. The topography of the seafloor was mapped with depth sounders.
2. The magnetic field above the seafloor was measured.
3. Confirmation of north-south reversals in the history of the earth's magnetic field.
4. The ability to determine with accuracy the location of earthquakes by networking seismometers.
5. Laboratory measurements showing that mantle rock can deform over periods of time much longer than typical geological shifts.

Recently, however, more fine-tuned measurement and other discoveries have produced minor problems with traditional, slow-moving plate tectonics.

First, multiple magnetic "zebra stripes" are encountered in new ocean seabed while descending into drill holes, indicating that large numbers of north/south switches occurred very rapidly, often taking mere weeks to reverse polarity, rather than the expected millennia.

Secondly, entire chunks of surface tectonic plates have been discovered at the base of the earth's mantle! Somehow, *something* forced pieces of lithosphere down into the 7,000 plus degrees of the earth's mantle so swiftly, that they did not have a chance to fully melt—and are still there today, relatively "cold" and not fully absorbed. They are submerged granite islands, resting near the earth's core, much like ice cubes that have yet to fully melt while resting in warm water.

Although uniformitarianism insists that we analyze historical evidence in light of current conditions, it is unreasonable—and unscientific—to assume that sudden or cataclysmic events have *never* occurred.

In fact, geologists agree that the apparent meteor or asteroid strikes that created the Chicxulub crater in the Yucatan Peninsula and also the Gulf of Mexico would have resulted in mega-tsunamis that rose over a mile high and perhaps encircled the entire planet—two or three times!

In 1994, Dr. John Baumgartner[27] published two papers on large-scale tectonics and runaway subduction, which sought to solve some of the discrepancies and remaining problems with traditional plate tectonics. The model contained in these papers actually *predicted* the cold plates injected into the mantle *before* their discovery. His follow-up paper on the physics of Catastrophic Plate Tectonics (CPT) was published in 2003.

Dr. Baumgartner's model proposes that a severe impact—or multiple impacts—could have actually damaged the planet's mantle, breaking apart the bedrock and perhaps even creating the original plates.

Tests have shown that, under the right amount of stress, silicate rock can weaken by a factor of a billion or more—meaning that plates under the right conditions could actually move a billion times faster than today. What might take a billion years to occur under normal conditions could, in fact, require only one year.

The cracking into the mantle, the subsequent ejections of low-mass magma into the ocean floors, the resulting rising of the ocean floors, the swift underwater ballet of the plates colliding with each other, and the eventual slowing are all a part of the CPT. The collapse and fracturing of the low-mass magma then created large trenches for the ocean water to return to as it drained from the sudden upthrust of numerous mountain ranges from the final plate collisions.

The CPT explains the rapid polarity reversals in addition to solving issues of sedimentation and the lack of compression expected by slower plate tectonics.

When used in conjunction with Dr. Humphrey's model of planetary magnetic fields[28], we can see that the Earth's history has not

---

[27] B.S. Electrical Engineering, Texas Tech University, 1968; M.S. Electrical Engineering, Princeton University, 1970; M.S. Geophysics and Space Physics, UCLA, 1981; Ph.D. Geophysics and Space Physics, UCLA, 1983
[28] In fact, extrapolating backwards at the current rate of magnetic decay, the earth's increasingly powerful magnetic field would have rendered the planet uninhabitable as re-

been a serene, uniform one of gradual change, but rather one with great upheavals that are consistent with the universal stories of a global flood, found in all ancient and indigenous cultures.

---

cently as twenty-thousand years ago!

APPENDIX E
RECOMMENDED READING

This list represents the primary resources used for research and inspiration in the writing of *The Days of Laméch*.

Berlinski, David. The Devil's Delusion. Crown Forum, 2008. Brilliant and often humorous mathematician examines the non-scientific basis for modern atheism.

Brown, Ronald K. The Book of Enoch. Guadalupe Baptist Theological Seminary Press, 2000. Translation of the apocryphal *Book of Enoch*. Exegetical presentation with cross references to related biblical passages.

Bryner, Jeanna. How Huge Flying Reptiles Got Airborne. LiveScience, January 7, 2009. Study of how Pterosaurs may have used the knuckle at the fold in their wings to "pole-vault" into the air.

Childress, David Hatcher. Technology of the Gods: The Incredible Sciences of the Ancients. Adventures Unlimited Press, 2000. Documents many examples of ancient technologies included sophisticated use of optics, magnetism, and electricity. Section of Tesla's research into same.

Chomsky, Noam. Language and Mind. Cambridge University Press, 2006. Essays on linguistics and cognition, proposing that intelligence must exist before language formation, thereby challenging the evolutionary notion that languages formed naturalistically.

Dunn, Christopher. The Giza Power Plant: Technologies of Ancient Egypt. Bear & Company, 1998. A mechanical engineer's study of the Great Pyramid and his conclusion that it was used for power generation.

Flam, Faye. Mathematical Biology: Hints of a Language in Junk DNA. Science, Vol. 266, p. 1320, November 1994. Overview of a study performed by Physicist Eugene Stanly of Boston University and his team. In this study, they applied Zipf's Law (a stochastic and linguistic formula used to determine the existence of meaningful information in unknown data) and concluded that even "junk" DNA exhibits all of the attributes of meaningful syntax.

Gaverluk, Emil. Did Genesis Man Conquer Space? Thomas Nelson, 1974. Observations about the unlimited potential of the antediluvians, considering their longevity, superior intellect, and shared knowledge. Also discussions on pyramid power.

Humphreys, D. Russell. The Creation of Cosmic Magnetic Fields. Proceedings of the Sixth International Conference on Creationism (pp. 213–230), 2008. Update to Dr. Humphrey's model of planetary magnetic field generation, which correctly predicted the fields of Uranus, Neptune, and outer moons before they were measured by the Voyager 2 spacecraft.

Meyer, Stephen C. Signature in the Cell. HarperOne, 2010. Overview of the history of the discovery of DNA, plus thoughts on its origin—whether by chance or design.

Noorbergen, Rene. Secrets of the Lost Races: New Discoveries of Advanced Technology in Ancient Civilizations. Teach Services, 2001. Analysis of ancient writings in light of OOPARTS and other archeological enigmas. Special section on Noah's Ark.

Pember, G. H. Earth's Earliest Ages. Kregel Academic & Professional, Originally published in 1884. In-depth study of Genesis 1 to 6, plus an extended discussion of Eastern religions, Theosophy, and the occult.

Pratt, John P. The Infant Prince. Meridian Magazine, July 14, 2004. Article describing the mystery of the Infant Prince constellation: missing from Ptolemy's star map, but described by the Persian Astronomer, Albumazar and depicted in the planisphere in the temple of Hathor at Dendera in Egypt.

Seiss, Joseph A. Gospel in the Stars. Kregel Classics, 1972. In depth study of ancient constellations and their original meanings. Reprinted from the 1882 version by Claxton.

Sherwood, Jonathan. Early Earth's Magnetic Field Stronger Than Believed. <http://www.unisci.com/stories/20011/0302011. htm>, Daily University Science News, March 2001. Review of research performed by John Tarduno, professor of geophysics and chair of the Department of Earth and Environmental Sciences at the University of Rochester. Using the University's Superconducting Quantum Interference Device (nicknamed "SQUID") to study magnetic rock from the ocean floor, they determined the earth's early magnetic field was much stronger in the past.

St. James, Chris. <www.s8int.com>. Exhaustive website on OOPARTS, ancient civilizations, and cryptozoology, with articles, images, and regular blogs.

Ussher, James. Annals of the World. Master Books, 2003. History of the ancient world, originally published in Latin in 1650.

Wieland, Dr. Carl, Dr. Don Batten and Ken Ham. One Blood: The Biblical Answer to Racism. Master Books, 2003. Explains the genetic origins of "races", while demonstrating the non-viability of the term. Shows how speciation can occur rapidly when given enough initial genetic information. Provides both technical and social overview.

APPENDIX F
GLOSSARY

CONTROLLER: Master Librarian who travels between cities to share and synchronize information among other libraries.

FAMILY WARS: The wars fought among the early cities. As living space became scarce, each city created its own criteria for optimum residents and soon began banishing or exterminating those who did not meet its hereditary standards. Conflicts between cities occurred as each city accused the others of refugee warfare.

FOREST PEOPLE: Denizens rumored to live outside of the cities in the wild. Presumably, either the descendants of refugees from the Family Wars, or malcontents who want nothing to do with civilization.

FOUNDER: Either the owner/establisher of a city, or the person for whom a city was built.

HAERMON MOUNTAINS: Range of mountains along the north-west coast--the highest in the world. Inhabited by the Semyaz and the location of their facilities.

IMMERSION CHAMBER: Preferred method of execution in

the cities. The condemned is place in a cage that is above water in low tide—but beneath the water at high tide.

INFANT KING: The constellation that predominates the story of the Seed, as told by Aenoch.

JAERAD WINES: Expensive wines from the grasslands between Irad and Jaebal.

LAWGIVER: Class of people designated to create laws, usually under the authority of a Founder.

LIBRARIAN: Class of people trained in perfect aural or visual memory to provide archiving for books, music, contracts, and history. Most work within the city's central library, but some are contracted by wealthier people or are developed and commissioned for private use.

NOBLE-GLOBE: Lamp filled with various noble gasses that glow when in the proximity of a Power House

NON-OPT: Epithet. Person deemed "not optimum" by the early cities prior to—and during—the Family Wars.

OBSERVATION PLATFORM: Large craft in the form of a golden disc, rumored to be piloted by Semyaz, but few reliable accounts exist. A single large platform was reportedly observed over each city at the cessation of the Family Wars.

POWER HOUSE: Energy dissemination system enclosed in a large pyramid structure near the city docks. Designed by Aenoch and used in his modern cities. Utilizes tidal forces for energy production and coils for storage.

SEED: As taught and envisioned by the Semyaz, the new, improved human of their own making. As taught by Aenoch, the One who would someday come and remove the curse of guilt and death, and restore creation to its original glory.

SENSORS: Semyaz agents, trained to discern mental dissent or rebellion.

THE PATH: Anti-Semyaz resistance movement of which Laméch is a member.

TSOHAR: Lighting modules or panels of indeterminate design used by the Semyaz. They do not utilize the usual broadcast energies of a Power House.

UN-FALLEN: As taught by Aenoch, entities that are related to non-corporeal Semyaz, but chose not to oppose the Creator's plan of creation and redemption.

CPSIA information can be obtained at www.ICGtesting.com
265405BV00001B/1/P